"THIS IS THE WORLD OF TUKAYYID."

The Primus of ComStar yawned. "Interesting, Precentor Martial. I take it you find this world significant for more than its ability to bore the Clans to death?"

"Indeed I do, Primus." Precentor Martial Focht pressed his hands together carefully. "You are looking at the world that will be the salvation of Terra."

"I do not understand."

"As the Successor States have discovered, we cannot determine in advance where the Clans will strike next. By all analysis of their techniques for selecting targets, they should bypass Tukayyid because it presents no threat to them.

"But I know of a way to make Tukayyid a prime target for the Wolf Clan. That is, quite simply to challenge Khan Ulric to a battle on this world, which will decide the fate of Terra. . . ."

BATTLETECH®

The Blood of Kerensky—Vol. 3

LOST DESTINY

Michael A. Stackpole

A ROC BOOK

ROC
Published by the Penguin Group
Penguin Books USA Inc., 375 Hudson Street,
New York, New York 10014, U.S.A.
Penguin Books Ltd, 27 Wrights Lane,
London W8 5TZ, England
Penguin Books Australia Ltd, Ringwood,
Victoria, Australia
Penguin Books Canada Ltd, 10 Alcorn Avenue,
Toronto, Ontario, Canada M4V 3B2
Penguin Books (N.Z.) Ltd, 182–190 Wairau Road,
Auckland 10, New Zealand

Penguin Books Ltd, Registered Offices:
Harmondsworth, Middlesex, England

Published by Roc, an imprint of Dutton Signet, a division of Penguin Books USA Inc.
Previously published by FASA.

First Roc Printing, December, 1995
10 9 8 7 6 5 4

Series Editor: Donna Ippolito
Cover: Roger Loveless
Maps: Mike Nielsen and the FASA art department

ROC REGISTERED TRADEMARK—MARCA REGISTRADA

Printed in the United States of America

To the men and women of Operations Desert Shield
and Desert Storm.
Sic Semper Tyrannis.
If we ever get to the stars, it will be because people with
your bravery and sense of duty lead us.

The author would like to thank Liz Danforth, Jennifer Roberson, and Dennis L. McKiernan for their help in dissecting and repairing the difficult parts of this book. He also thanks John-Allen Price for the loan of a member of the Cox family for this series, and David W. Jewell for the loan of his name and family. Thanks also to Dr. J. Ward Stackpole for the help with medical technology; errors are those of the author. Ditto military information, which was supplied by Captain Patrick T. Stackpole; again the errors belong to the scribe. As always, the author's utmost thanks to Donna Ippolito for bringing this book into mainstream English, Jordan Weisman and Ross Babcock for giving him the opportunity to do the book, then Jordan again and Sam Lewis for pushing the author to an even greater effort. Lastly, the author thanks the GEnie Network, over which this novel and edits passed through e-mail, from the author's computer, through GEnie, straight to FASA.

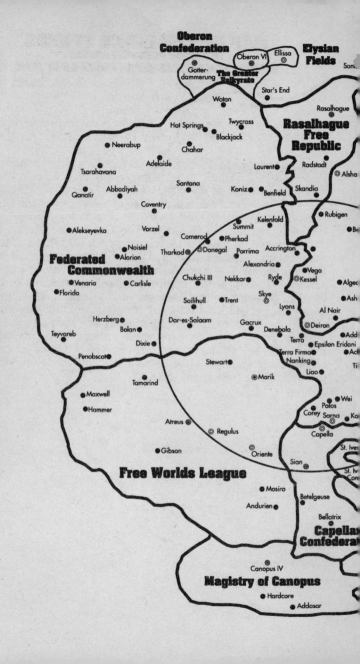

MAP OF THE INNER SPHERE
AND MAJOR PERIPHERY STATES
MILITARY/POLITICAL SUBDIVISION AS OF 3050

er V

Garstedt

Bjarred

Albiero

Qandahar

Pesht ◎

Ningxia

Draconis Combine

Luthien ◉

Kagoshima

New Samarkand

Xinyang

Tabayama

ur

Oshika

Galedon V

Benjamin ◎

Matsuida ●

Kaznejov

Out worlds Alliance

Irurzun ●

Bryceland

Bremond

Milligan ●

Kilbnourne ●

Proserpina ●

Le Blanc

Dahar IV

Woodbine ●

ks

Raman ●

Robinson ●

Mayetta ●

mar

Kentares IV

nov

Marlette ●

Kestrel ●

Tsamma ●

Markesan ●

Anjin Muerto ●

Valexa ●

Leamington ●

Minette ●

New Avalon ◎

Kathil ●

Point Barrow ●

eng

Monongahela ●

Broken Wheel ●

Alcyona ●

Nunivak ●

Federated Commonwealth

Chirikof ●

Islamabad ●

oach

Malagrotta ●

New Sytris ●

Taygeta ●

Ridgebrook ●

Warren ●

ion

Taurus ◎

Taurian Concordat

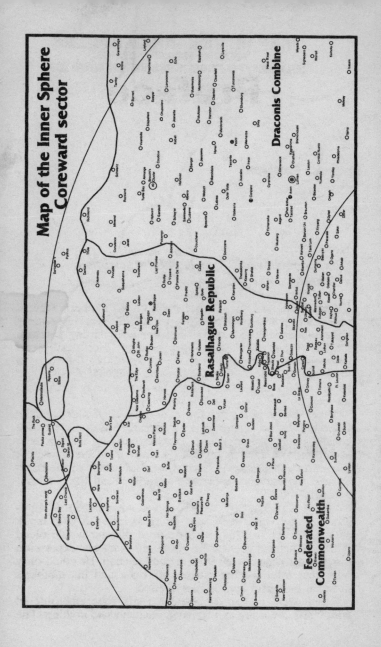

Preface

Sian
Sian Commonality, Capellan Confederation
5 January 3052

When Sun-Tzu Liao saw the smile on his mother's face, it took all the self-control he'd developed over his twenty years to suppress a shudder. His sister Kali, darting past him into the throne room, had no such doubts. Her transfigured expression was the mirror image of Romano's. Glancing at his father, Sun-Tzu felt disgust at the smile Tsen Shang had pasted on his face even though his whole body seemed to cringe.

There she sat in the massive mahogany chair known as the Celestial Throne. The huge disk backing it was carved with constellations and mystical symbols defining the universe according to Capellan mythology. Seated on the throne, it was as though Romano presided over the whole of the Inner Sphere, the universe spreading from her head like a Christian saint's halo.

"What is it, Mother? Why have you summoned us?" Sun-Tzu kept his voice even, not daring to infuse it with mock enthusiasm for fear his anticipation of disaster would bleed into it. Whatever it was, he could tell from her expression that Romano considered it an incredible coup. He could only hope that for once the rational universe and his mother's personal universe were in conjunction.

Resplendent in her rainbow-hued silk robe embroidered with tigers cavorting and striking, Romano said nothing. The diffuse light streaming into the room from the lattice-work galleries around the upper reaches gave substance to thin ribbons of incense smoke drifting from censers hidden behind the throne. The Chancellor opened her hands and indicated that her children should be seated at her feet.

No, not this again. It has been too long. Sun-Tzu held back a bit, though anything short of bodily launching himself at the throne would have made him look stopped dead compared to his sister. Kali immediately draped herself over the steps leading up to the throne and, cat-like, rubbed her face against Romano's leg. As he approached, his sister turned to him, her face momentarily contorted in anger before Romano reached down to stroke Kali's auburn hair.

At the foot of the steps, Sun-Tzu stopped and clasped his hands behind his back like a soldier at ease. Romano's face darkened briefly, then she graced him with a smile. Though accustomed to his mother's quicksilver emotions, Sun-Tzu had felt a true jolt of fear at her look of displeasure, then great relief when she smiled. *More karma burned. I must have been very good in a past life.*

Romano clasped her hands together in her lap. "In the beginning," she intoned solemnly, "Pangu created Heaven and Earth from the egg of his birth, then became the life of his creation. Nüwa created men and women, and from among them chose one family to be exalted above all others."

Kali, anxiously tugging at her mother's robe, was granted leave to speak with an indulgent caress from Romano. "The Liao, recognized for their wisdom and courage, were placed above the rest of mankind, but they did not lord it over their subjects. Mentors rather than dictators, they guided from behind the scenes, except in times of crisis, when only Liao leadership could save mankind."

Romano looked to Tsen Shang, who winced visibly. "So mankind flourished beneath the guidance of the Liao, and mankind prospered. Out and away from his home did mankind go until his settlements were flung as far as the furthest star, and then further yet. And the Liao remained with him, always helping and guiding. The Star League was the Liao instrument and the enlightenment of mankind their goal."

Sun-Tzu took up the story from there. "There rose among the Star League many powers and many people of avarice. Among these were the Amaris, from whom sprang the monster Stefan, an abomination who slew the Star League's rightful ruler, shattered the Liao creation of Star League, and plunged humanity into a dark age."

Romano nodded proudly as her son hit every word perfectly in his recitation. "Once again did the Liao acknowledge their divine charge and accept the mantle of First Lord of the Star League. Alas, for mankind, the Amaris plague had infected the other Great Houses. Davion, Steiner, Marik, and Kurita each believed itself the legitimate claimant to the Star League throne. They engaged in wars, the first, second, and third, that proceeded to strip mankind of the gifts of wisdom the Liao had imparted. With a vengeance, the false Lords of the Great Houses did hunt down and try to destroy the Liao, but they knew no success until . . ."

Kali leaped up and snatched the thread of the story from her mother. "Until a viper came to nest within the Liao bosom. The false Lords knew the Liao weakness was its compassion, so they sent to them a man broken and reviled for his Capellan blood. But this man, this embodiment of evil, was not broken. Rather, he was a vessel of treachery, fashioned and controlled by Hanse Davion. And his name was Justin Xiang."

Sun-Tzu accepted the story from his sister, but stripped away the blood-lust she had woven into the telling. "This Justin Xiang betrayed the kindness the Liao showed him. He seduced the weakest of the Liao and carried Candace off to his Lord's domain, robbing the Liao of their beloved St. Ives." He started to add the line, "And one day this treachery will be avenged," but his mother slammed a fist into the throne's arm to cut him off.

"This treachery has, this day, been avenged! A martyr in the service of the Liao succeeded in exacting retribution for Justin Xiang's foul treason. He and his bitch lie dead on New Avalon, where they foolishly believed themselves safe from my wrath."

Romano's eyes focused distantly as she continued to rant, but Sun-Tzu heard none of her words. *Allard dead? Candace, too?* The frightful look of victory on his mother's face told him she truly believed what she had said, but Sun-Tzu had learned long ago that his mother's beliefs and reality were not always one and the same.

"Father, is this true? Can this be?"

Tsen Shang nodded wearily. "ComStar thought the news of sufficient import to forward it throughout their network.

Speculation is that your Uncle Tormana will be made Regent of the St. Ives Compact, at least temporarily. Kai will be summoned home from the front with the Clans to rule."

Sun-Tzu frowned in concentration as he tried to block out the chortling sounds of his mother's and sister's gloating. "If Kai returns, what are the chances he will lead troops against us? St. Ives soldiers are fighting the Clans right now. What are the chances they will have some of this advanced Clan technology salvaged and in working order by the time they get here?"

His father shrugged. "I do not know."

"Are you not the head of our intelligence service?" Sun-Tzu snapped. "Surely the Maskirovka is keeping track of Candace's troops. Just because we have struck the head from the Davion intelligence serpent does not mean we can relax."

Tsen Shang's head came up and fire sparked in his eyes, but it died quickly. "Yes, *son,* we have reports, but they are highly unreliable. The Clans have chewed up everything else that has been thrown at them, so I expect no better for the St. Ives troops."

"I pray you are correct, Father." Sun-Tzu glanced at his mother. "She may hold her sister's children in contempt, but you and I *cannot* afford that luxury. She believes herself inviolate, but I harbor no such illusions. If we have not yet been hit, it was not because of Candace's inability to strike, but because she withheld her wrath. Her heirs—Kai, Cassandra, or even Kuan Yin or Quintus—may not feel so restrained."

Sun-Tzu chewed his lower lip. "Mark me, Father, they will come. It may wait until after the Clans have been defeated, but one day they will seek to avenge Candace and Justin." He looked at his mother one last time. *And when that time comes, I must be ready to preserve my nation.*

1

Mar Negro, Alyina
Trellshire, Jade Falcon Occupation Zone
5 January 3052

Gray smoke cloaked the dark ocean, hiding Kai Allard as his head broke the surface of the water. The eerie quiet, marred only by his ragged, air-sucking gasps, surprised him. *This is a war zone, but I don't hear anything!* He fought down the irrational fear that his 'Mech's collision with a Clan OmniMech might have deafened as well as knocked him out. *No, if that were true, I wouldn't hear either my breathing or the waves.*

Kai turned in the direction of the cliff from where his 'Mech had plunged into the waters of Mar Negro. In answer to Prince Victor Davion's urgent call, Kai and his lance had rushed to Victor's defense. Equipped with experimental myomer muscles, Kai's modified *Centurion* had swiftly outdistanced his companions. Reaching the battle zone first, he saw Hanse Davion's heir in a damaged BattleMech beset by four of the Clans' finest.

I just went berserk! I got too close and let that one 'Mech drag me off the cliff. Kai looked up at the twenty meters of chalky cliff rising above him at the shoreline and remembered the long drop in the OmniMech's deadly embrace. Hitting the water, he'd blacked out, knowing that the shelf went down a full kilometer here.

When he came to again, he was still in the cockpit of *Yenlo-wang*, his *Centurion*, trapped under the ocean in the arms of a Clan OmniMech. But instead of plunging to the bottom of the sea, the 'Mechs' descent had been interrupted by a ledge only ten meters or so down. Having been under for only half an hour, Kai wriggled free of the cockpit and swam up from that depth without having to worry about decompression.

Reaching the base of the cliff, Kai pulled himself onto a half-submerged rock and took inventory of his gear. The cooling vest from his 'Mech doubled as a bullet-proof vest, but it and the shorts he wore would do little to ward off the cold of the coming night. His heavy, duraplast-armor boots would protect him from the knees down, but they were hardly made for walking. What did count for something was the survival knife sticking up from the sheath in the right boot, and Kai smiled as he fingered the hilt.

"Well, Victor, I get to test your Christmas gift under true battlefield conditions."

Instantly an unfocused dread began to churn in his stomach. *I don't even know if Victor survived! I should have been more careful, I should have been there to make sure. If he died because of me* ... Kai forced himself to his feet and quickly mounted the narrow pathway that zigzagged up the cliff-face. Though his fear urged him to reckless speed, another part of him remained cautious. Slowing his pace as he neared the top of the cliff, Kai noted the bright white gash that marked where the cliff-edge had crumbled beneath the feet of his 'Mech.

White and black smoke spiraled together in a fog that drifted eerily across the plateau's surface. Barely four hours earlier, this had been a verdant jungle, the kind of place Alyina's Ministry of Tourism might have touted as typical of their world. Yet mere minutes of combat had pitted and scarred the landscape. Blackened stumps that once were trees dotted the plain like gravestones strewn across a graveyard. The only remaining scraps of green were scattered clumps of earth that artillery fire had blasted from the ground.

Everywhere lay the shattered bodies and dismembered bits of the war machines that had died to possess what had once been a paradise. When intact, BattleMechs stood five times Kai's height and seemed like invincible, mechanical avatars of man's warlike nature. For as long as he could remember, Kai had dreamed of only one thing: to follow his parents in the path of a MechWarrior. He saw no honor greater than piloting one of these giant martial engines, and no purpose nobler than to do so in defense of family and nation.

But now, battered and smashed beyond recognition, these BattleMechs mocked what Kai realized was the innocence of youth. Lying in broken huddles or staring sightlessly at the sky, they looked useless and even worse. Kai saw that these machines could only destroy. That was their sole purpose, and they had accomplished it beyond even the wildest dreams of their creators.

Kai darted quickly across the quiet battlefield. Kneeling in the shadow of a downed *Hagetaka,* he quickly scanned the killing ground for any sign of the *Daishi* Victor had been piloting. He saw nothing at first, then ran to where he had last seen the Prince's 'Mech. At that spot, he found a foot that had probably belonged to Victor's 'Mech. Glancing at the half-melted armor plates lying just beyond, he saw a track left by a crippled BattleMech limping away.

"Yes, he made it." Kai slapped his open palm against the *Daishi*'s foot. *He made it away from here, but they might still have gotten him,* whispered a cold voice in the back of Kai's mind. *If you had been here, you could have made sure Victor lived.*

The harsh scream of a sea gull brought Kai's head up, startling him from his reverie. The breeze holding the gull aloft parted the smoke and gave Kai a clear view of the dusky sky. Burning brilliantly against the growing dark was a double-diamond pattern of lights moving in unison like a drifting constellation. His spirits lifted instantly as he realized those were the Federated Commonwealth's DropShips burning their way out of Alyina's gravity.

"Victor must have survived. They would never leave so soon if he weren't with them." Glancing around the area, Kai thought it looked like some reinforcements must have arrived to help Victor retreat. From the crests on the uniforms of the dead, he realized they were from the regimental command lance.

The gull screamed again and others joined it as the flock slowly descended. Kai marveled at their effortless flight, grateful for the beauty of their sleek symmetry as a welcome contrast to the nightmare landscape. He smiled as one bird drifted in, then delicately lighted on the shattered shell of a

'Mech cockpit. It was not until another gull tried to land in the same spot and was chased off that Kai understood why the gulls had come to the battlefield.

"No!" Kai sprinted toward the broken 'Mech, waving both birds off. As he reached the cockpit, the stink of blood and burned flesh warned him away, but he did not stop. Peering into the cockpit, he saw what had once been Professor-General Sam Lewis strapped into the command couch. Kai had heard Lewis was attached to the regiment but never thought he'd come out and fight. Things must have gotten really desperate. Half the man's neurohelmet was crushed and half the face beneath it was missing. Kai blanched at the sight and felt his knees turn to water. Turning away, he dropped abruptly to the ground and cradled his head in his hands.

Above him two gulls fought over the eyeball one of them had plucked from the death's head in the cockpit.

Kai's immediate impulse was to pull all the dead pilots—friend and enemy alike—from their 'Mechs and burn them in a huge pyre to keep the birds from feasting on them. No matter his desire, the task was impossible. Not only would it require more strength than he had right now, but the fighting had consumed everything combustible for kilometers in every direction.

He also knew that a pyre would tip off Clan patrols in the area that at least one person had survived the battle. As that warrior would not have reported in to them, they would know he was not Clan, and the chase would be on.

Kai wanted to hate the gulls, but he knew they were simply scavenging to survive. And with those glittering pinpricks in the night sky going away from, rather than coming into Alyina, he was going to have to start doing his own scavenging to survive. The Clans had defeated the Tenth Lyran Guards, trapping Kai so deeply behind enemy lines that escape back to his side was unimaginable. His only salvation would be if a rescue mission were sent back for him. *Twenty years ago Hanse Davion dispatched the Lions of Davion to pull my father off Sian. But then this isn't Sian, and the Clans are not as stupid as Maximilian Liao.*

His spirits sank even further. *And I am not my father. No rescue mission is coming for me. I'm on my own.*

That realization might have driven some to contemplate

suicide, but it fired Kai with the fierce will to survive. *I've already blown my mission, and my 'Mech is trapped on the ocean floor by another 'Mech lying across its chest. At the very least, they probably presume me "missing in action"— and more than likely dead.* Determined not to further dishonor his family and friends by getting captured, he resolved to avoid that possibility with the last ounce of breath in his body.

Like the gulls flying above him and the feral dogs howling off in the night, he searched the battlefield for whatever he might use. He pried open a storage locker in the rear of one *Wolverine* cockpit, and pulled out an olive drab jumpsuit. It had belonged to Dave Jewell, a member of Victor's command lance. The legs were too long because Jewell had been taller than Kai, but that mattered little now. Using his knife, Kai slit the leg seams so he could still wear his 'Mech boots, and he kept on the cooling vest beneath the jumpsuit.

The locker also yielded some survival rations, which Kai slipped into the small rucksack hanging from a hook next to a web belt and gun. The pistol, a Mauser and Gray M-39 needler, felt good in his hand as he checked it out and loaded it with a block of ballistic polymer. As he strapped the belt on, he took in some of the slack to make it fit snugly around his narrow waist.

At the bottom of the locker, Kai found a small packet containing two holodisks, a hologram, and a small verigraphed card. The holograph worked into the fabric of the card showed the smiling faces of two children, a boy and girl who looked several years apart in age. Kai looked at the childlike scrawl in which the message was written and realized that the children had composed a prayer-poem to keep their father safe in combat. It was signed, "Katrina and David, Jr."

The hologram showed a slender, attractive woman holding a baby in her arms. Seeing it, Kai remembered Jewell bragging that his wife, Katherine, had recently given birth to their third child, Kari Lynn. *Not even five months old.* A shiver ran down his spine. "She never even had a chance to meet her father."

Kai looked over at the body hanging half out of the command couch's restraining straps. He slipped the soldier's dog tags from around the man's broken neck and dropped them into the packet, which he tucked into the rucksack. He brushed one hand across the name emblazoned on the breast of the jumpsuit he'd appropriated.

"I promise to get these things back to your children, David Jewell. I will let them know you bought Victor Davion's freedom with your life."

Kai crawled from the cockpit and shouldered the rucksack. Glancing up at the night sky, he could no longer see the DropShips heading out of the system. "Well, I'm about three hundred light years from home and I don't have a good pair of walking boots. The Clans own Alyina and I doubt shooting one of their foot soldiers with this needle pistol would do much more than get him angry." He shook his head. "You've really gone and done it to yourself this time, Kai."

A worse thought followed. On Outreach, they had counted him among the best MechWarriors facing the Clans. If he was in this much trouble now, what hope could there be for the Inner Sphere?

2

Phelan Wolf watched his charge, Ragnar Magnusson, wrestle with the contradictions inherent in the Clan invasion of the Inner Sphere. "Yes, Aleksandr Kerensky left the Inner Sphere more than three hundred years ago to remove his army from the internecine battling that had torn the Star League apart. He wanted to keep them safe from the nationalistic sentiments that were bringing the members of the Star League into conflict with one another. You can see the wisdom of that, Ragnar, *quiaff*?"

The small, blond-haired youth frowned. "But you said his attempt to keep his own people at peace failed. They started fighting among themselves, and it took Kerensky's son Nicholas and a cadre of loyalists to reunite the army. And the Clans stayed away from the Inner Sphere because Nicholas taught them that their job was to protect the Inner Sphere, not mix in its fights and politics. If this is true, why'd they return?"

"Speak properly! No contractions!" Running his fingers back through his brown hair, Phelan ended with a weary scratching at the back of his neck. "Only some of the Clanfolk, the ones called Wardens, still believe in protecting the Inner Sphere." He stretched and stood up, beginning to pace in his narrow cabin. "The others, who call themselves

Crusaders, believe the Inner Sphere is rightfully their home and they are coming back to lay claim to it."

"That's nonsense." Ragnar's blue eyes flashed. "They abandoned the Inner Sphere. What right have they to claim the Inner Sphere as their own?"

Phelan smirked slightly. "The same right your people invoked in claiming Rasalhague a free nation even while under the domination of the Draconis Combine."

Ragnar opened his mouth to reply, but Phelan saw his charge hesitate as he mentally calculated where this argument would take him. Ragnar shook his head, knowing that a dispute over who had what rights to what slice of the Inner Sphere was a fight he would lose. "But you have told me that the ilKhan, Khan Ulric of the Wolf Clan, is a Warden. Why is he pushing this invasion?"

As Ragnar spoke, he tugged at the circlet around his right wrist as if the braided white cord irritated him. Phelan remembered how his own bondcord had annoyed him in his time as a bondsman of the Wolf Clan. He also recalled with pride his adoption ceremony into the Wolf Clan Warrior-Caste, during which the hated cord had been cut off. He let a grin slide across his face at the memory, and Ragnar's expression darkened.

"It is true, Prince of Rasalhague, that the ilKhan is a Warden, yet he pushes this invasion. As you heard him tell the Primus of ComStar, the goal of the invasion has ever been the conquest of Terra, the former seat of the Star League. The Khan whose warriors take Terra will become ilKhan for all time, and his Clan elevated above all others." Phelan raised his head proudly. "When that happens, the ilKhan can order a cessation of all hostilities and begin to rebuild what has been destroyed."

Ragnar's eyes narrowed into a fierce frown. "You obviously love this war of conquest. How is it that you, a cousin of the Davion heir, have come to embrace the Clans and their brutish ways?" He opened his hands in a gesture that took in the spartan cabin to which Phelan had been assigned. "You were once a mercenary, so I assume they bought you, but with what? This opulence? That woman, Ranna? What was your price, Kell-Wolf, or whoever you are?"

Even before Ragnar could finish speaking, the cabin door opened to admit a flame-haired warrior-woman. As ever, she did not hesitate to speak. "His price, Prince Ragnar, is the same one you may be asked to pay. If one has the goal of preventing as much destruction as possible, he must decide how to accomplish it. One may decide, as did you, to fight until defeated, and then to go on fighting, yet accomplish nothing."

Ragnar was not cowed. "Or, Colonel Natasha Kerensky, you could become a quisling like Phelan and lead the enemy against your own people. It was Phelan who gave Gunzburg to the Clans!"

"And did it without a shot being fired. No one died when that world changed hands, Ragnar." Natasha's cerulean eyes sparked with anger. "Not only did he save lives in taking that world by himself, but it sent his stock soaring among Clan Warriors. It makes him a man of great influence, and that influence can be used to slow this juggernaut."

The little prince blanched at the heat of Kerensky's words. He looked down at the floor and blushed. Phelan, aware that it was something more than Ragnar's statements angering her, faced his superior. "Natasha, what is wrong? What has happened?"

The woman known as the Black Widow let her shoulders sag disconsolately. Phelan felt an immediate desire to comfort her, but refrained for fear of disturbing her dignity. "I have news you will welcome, Phelan, and news that, I believe, will sadden you."

A million horrible thoughts ran through Phelan's mind, but he dismissed them immediately. He knew, given the Clans' abrupt break with ComStar, that no word could have come to him regarding his family back in the Inner Sphere. He had already seen reports concerning the Smoke Jaguars and Nova Cats' losses in the battle for Luthien. Both he and Natasha had shared secret smiles concerning the success of their old units—the Kell Hounds and Wolf's Dragoons, respectively—in defending the capital of the Draconis Combine. Neither had seen casualty reports concerning the mercenary units to which they had belonged before the coming of the Clans, but they were confident their friends and kin had survived the fray.

Unable to puzzle out what might be distressing Natasha, Phelan waved her to a chair. "What is it?"

She exhaled slowly. "Cyrilla Ward is dead."

"What?" Cyrilla was the matriarch of the House of Ward, the Bloodname family to which Phelan belonged. The last time he'd seen her, which had been just before the Clans resumed their advance the previous September, she had seemed healthy and hearty despite being in her early seventies. Ever since his adoption into the Warrior Caste, the white-haired woman had instructed and encouraged Phelan in the ways of the Clans. The idea of her death was, for him, inconceivable.

Natasha drew a holodisk in a clear plastic envelope from one of her black jumpsuit pockets. "She recorded this for you. It just arrived in a shipment from Strana Mechty."

Taking the disk from Natasha, Phelan noticed her hand was trembling. "Natasha, I know Cyrilla was your close friend and that the two of you were raised in the same sibko. Though I only knew her for a short time, Cyrilla was my lifeline in the Clans."

The woman nodded solemnly. "She still is, Phelan."

"I do not understand."

Natasha stood and smoothed the breast of her jumpsuit. "The holodisk will explain it all." She glanced at Ragnar. "Come with me, Princeling. Phelan will want to view this disk alone, so let us find you something to do that will annoy Vlad and Conal Ward."

Phelan looked at the disk, then his head came up again. "Wait, Natasha, how did she die?"

The Black Widow shook her head. "We will talk after you have seen the holodisk." She sighed wearily. "Watch it twice or even three times. Remember that she believed in you and in Ulric's vision for the Clans. That thought is just about the only thing that makes any of this even remotely sane."

Phelan waited for the door to close behind Natasha and Ragnar before slipping the disk from its sheath and putting it in the viewer. As he settled down in a chair, he wasn't sure he wanted to watch it. *How strange to receive a holovid from someone who is dead. It is like a letter from a ghost.*

From static, the disk focused the screen into the smiling face of a white-haired woman. She stared straight out at Phelan, and for the barest of moments, he was certain Natasha was mistaken. Cyrilla had to be alive because no one with such vitality could succumb to death. Unbidden, Phelan returned her smile, yet the ache of her loss had already begun in his heart.

"I hardly wish to be melodramatic, Phelan Wolf, but I fear

I must. If you are viewing this, Natasha has informed you of my death. Please, do not mourn or grieve for me because I did not suffer. I did not linger. My death came cleanly and I departed this world with only one regret. Unfortunately, that regret concerns you."

Her expression shifted to one that Phelan knew well from her countless lectures on the rites and customs of the Clans. "You know that the name Ward is one of those accorded the honor of being a Bloodname because Jal Ward fought alongside Nicholas Kerensky during the war of reunification. You also know that, of all those in the Ward bloodlines, only twenty-five warriors may claim the right to call themselves Ward at any one time. Only by defeating all other claimants to a name may a warrior win that right, and with his victory also comes a seat in the Clan Council and eligibility for election as a Khan of the Clan.

"I had great hopes for seeing you win your Bloodname, Phelan. Your service to the ilKhan, your conquest of Gunzburg, and your capture of the heir to the throne of Rasalhague all mark you as a Warrior more than worthy of the honor of a Bloodname. Your actions have guaranteed you a berth among the twenty-four claimants chosen by members of the House of Ward. Another seven will be selected by a committee overseen by the Loremaster. In this case, that is Conal Ward and he is no friend of yours. Even so, you will not have to battle through the preliminary contest to win the thirty-second spot, so your chances in the Trial of Bloodright should be good."

Cyrilla's face knotted with consternation. "At least, that is what I had assumed concerning your chances in the next Bloodname contest. Now I have learned that certain parties, Crusader parties, are dead-set against your ever winning a Bloodname. As Vlad suggested when he tried to kill you in your testing on Strana Mechty, Conal Ward and others would openly welcome your death. Whereas we are not given to assassination, it is entirely possible that, as your fame grows, you might be left to your own devices on a battlefield and die of neglect.

"I have no reservations about your ability to handle yourself in battle, and I am proud of all you have accomplished. I know you can and will accomplish yet more, but if your wisdom is to help guide the Clans, you must be able to give it voice in the Clan Council. That means you must fight to win a Bloodname, and events dictate that you must do so very soon."

Cyrilla sighed and shook her head. "So far this invasion has not resulted in the death of anyone with a Ward Bloodname for which to fight. That reflects well on the Warriors of the House of Ward, but it leaves me with only one choice: the name for which you shall fight will be mine."

A lump rose in Phelan's throat and his stomach seemed to plummet into a bottomless pit. "No!" he cried. "You can't have done this! Not for me!"

Cyrilla's expression became somber. "I would have preferred to die fighting against the Smoke Jaguars, much as Natasha and I had vowed to do so long ago. I would have settled for hunting down bandits, but all available Wolf Clan forces are in the invasion, and no one will give an old woman a 'Mech. Do not worry, though, for I have seen many before me do what I must do, so I shall know how to do it correctly and cleanly."

Cyrilla continued, forcing a smile again. "I have declared, in my will, that you are the designated heir to my Bloodname. That decree has the force of law among us, and even Conal would not dare try to cheat you of your inheritance. I have also arranged that if you and Vlad are to meet in the contest, it will only be in the final battle. This will give you time to study his methods. If there is any justice in the universe, someone from the Inner Sphere might rid you of him even before it comes time to fight him.

"Phelan, none of my gene children have excelled, which has made me feel like a dead end for the House of Ward until you came to us. You are my child, a child of the future. With Ulric and Natasha, you will be one to lead the Clans into a new future where we can recognize our full potential—as warriors and as human beings."

She looked out at him with a satisfied expression. "Do not mourn me, Phelan Wolf. Rather, make me proud of you."

The screen's image dissolved into fragments of white and gray, then went black. Phelan continued to stare at it, hoping and praying for something more, something that would tell him what he had seen was false. He knew that among the Warrior Caste, a Warrior was considered too old at the age of thirty-five. From that point on, his role was to raise and train new generations of Warriors. Many decided to take their own lives when they considered themselves no longer useful.

Not Cyrilla. Involving herself in the politics of the House of Ward, she became its head and skillfully brokered power in the Clan Council. She approved or negotiated exchanges of DNA with other Clans in an attempt to strengthen the House of Ward bloodline. Her life had meaning and use beyond what a member of the Warrior Caste could normally expect. For her to die, for her to kill herself . . .

Phelan's mind rebelled at the frustrating stupidity of it all. Natasha, Jaime Wolf, and even his own father, Morgan Kell, had long ago proved that MechWarriors were not washed up after their mid-thirties. And he knew hundreds of other warriors from the Inner Sphere who didn't consider a Mech-Warrior dry behind the ears until he'd seen ten years in a cockpit, which would certainly put the warrior beyond his prime by Clan standards.

Though Phelan knew the Clan system was madness, the Clan's overwhelming success in invading the Inner Sphere also marked them as the finest warriors. He might have wanted to dismiss their ability as due to the advantage of superior technology, but he also knew their training was far more rigorous and demanding than that undergone by Inner Sphere warriors. Still, his own success in joining the ranks of the Wolf Clan Warriors pointed out that *their* way was not the *only* way.

The door to his cabin opened again, this time admitting a tall, slender woman clad in a gray jumpsuit. "Phelan, I just heard. Vlad was down in the gymnasium preening himself. I had to leave. I am so sorry for your loss." She started to reach out for him, then dropped her arms in a gesture of helplessness.

Phelan managed to muster a brave smile for her, despite the sudden, violent urge to hurl the remote control through the view screen. "Thank you, Ranna." When he held out his hand to her, she came to perch beside him on the arm of his chair.

Ranna nervously brushed a wisp of short white hair back behind her left ear. "What Cyrilla did was for you and the Clans," she said. "You must know that."

He looked again at the blank screen and nodded slowly. "Maybe that is it. Maybe Cyrilla believed her sacrifice was the only way I would be able to prove to the Clans that your system is not the pinnacle of human development. God knows that is a lesson Vlad and Conal Ward could stand to learn." He pointed his remote control at the viewer and started the disk playing again.

Ranna kissed him lightly on the top of his head. "If the result is anything less, my love, her sacrifice will have been wasted."

As Cyrilla's smiling face again came into view, Phelan did his best to shut his heartache away. Settling back to listen to Cyrilla's words once more, he stroked Ranna's back. "All right, Cyrilla," he said, speaking his thoughts aloud. "If what you are bequeathing me is the chance to show the Clans that there is more than one way to live, I will make the most of it. Never again will the Clans need someone to do what you have done."

3

Raising himself up to full height, Precentor Martial Anastasius Focht glared angrily at ComStar's First Circuit. "How dare you even intimate that some incompetence on my part is the cause of this shocking news!" Standing in the center of the wood-paneled First Circuit chamber, he slowly turned, fixing each Precentor with a stare from his single eye. "You are the ones whose arrogance set ComStar on a course of aiding and abetting this invasion of the Inner Sphere."

Gardner Riis, the auburn-haired Precentor from Rasalhague, slammed his fist down on his crystal podium. "I never agreed with this policy!"

"Nor I," shouted Ulthan Everson, the thickly built Precentor from Tharkad. "I have opposed this invasion since the beginning, and I have regretted every act of treason against the Inner Sphere I have been forced to commit."

"Bah! Your empty words mean nothing." The Precentor Martial clamped a brake on his anger. *Control is the key.* As befit his station, he let his slender body slip into an appropriately stiff military stance. "The situation is now painfully clear. The Clans have stated their intention to wrest Terra from us. They say that as Terra was the seat of the old Star League, their invasion was staged for the single purpose of retaking this world."

Huthrin Vandel, Precentor New Avalon, raked fingers back through his salt-and-pepper hair so violently that Focht thought it a mere prelude to the man tearing his hair out. "It seems equally clear that we must sever all relations with the Clans. We should cease administering their captured worlds for them. Our personnel on those worlds should go underground and supply complete intelligence reports that we would pass on to the Draconis Combine and Federated Commonwealth so they can drive these invaders from the Inner Sphere."

"Go *underground*? And how, pray tell, will they hide their hyperpulse generators?" Looking serene and unperturbed in her golden robe, the Primus of ComStar let scorn drip from her words. "We will do no such thing. We will continue to administer the Clan-occupied worlds. As a show of good faith, we will also continue to black-out information coming from the occupied worlds. We will react to this move of the Clans as though the conquest of Terra would mean nothing to us."

Myndo Waterly smiled coldly. "In fact, we will enter into negotiations with the Clans for returning Terra to their control."

Focht spun as Ulthan Everson began to speak in an almost incoherent sputter. "Madness. This is complete and utter madness! They are coming to take our world away from us, and you say you will *help* them do that?" Precentor Tharkad looked at Focht. "Precentor Martial, you must *oppose* this plan."

Focht clasped his hands behind his back. "It is not my place, Precentor Tharkad, to protest anything the Primus chooses to do. I am merely her advisor. We consulted on this course of action during the journey from Satalice to Terra. The constant change of ships and the numerous jumps did make the discussions less than fluid, but the agreement we reached will, we believe, be the means by which the Clans can be stopped."

"But the Primus just said she will negotiate with the Clans to let them have Terra." Everson looked decidedly confused.

The Primus beamed triumphantly. "The offer of negotiations will buy us time to regroup our troops into a force to lead the way in driving the Clans from the Inner Sphere. Our key has ever been ComStar's role as the deliverer of mankind. We have acted as a shield between the populace and the excesses of the Clans on occupied worlds, and we will continue to do so. Already many people believe that our intervention is the only reason the Clans have not committed more atrocities like the destruction of Edo on Turtle Bay. With some careful manipulation of perceptions, we can make our military opposition to the Clans look as if it has come after the Clans pushed too hard, too far."

"But that *is* the truth, isn't it?" Vandel stared down at the Precentor martial. "This plan presumes you can stop the Clans. But can you?"

Focht remained silent for several moments to give the Precentor from New Avalon the impression he was being appropriately cautious in his answer. "The battle for Luthien has proven the Clans are not invincible. All across their front, the Clans have had to adapt their tactics to more closely resemble those of the Inner Sphere forces. With this change and their superior weapons, they are still a formidable force. But the troops we have under arms are not raw recruits, and our equipment is some of the best in the Inner sphere."

The Precentor from the Draconis Combine, a small woman with pronounced Oriental features, pursed her lips. "You have not answered the question, Precentor Martial," Sharilar Mori said.

"True, Precentor Dieron. If a long and somewhat checkered career has taught me anything, it is that absolute predictions of victory are folly. This is never more true than when contemplating a battle with the Clans. The key to fighting them is to choose the grounds and negotiate the goal of the battle. Once the Clans have bracketed themselves concerning the number of troops they will use in the fight and what they are fighting for, it becomes possible to defeat them."

Riis frowned. "The Clans obviously want Terra. If you cannot defeat them, they will have it. If you beat them once, they will only send more troops to deal with you a second time. It is inevitable."

"I beg to differ, Precentor Rasalhague." Focht adjusted the black patch over his right eye. "Wolcott, a world in the Draconis Combine, is located well behind Clan lines. When the invasion force started negotiations with the defenders, the commander agreed that the world would never again be attacked if the Combine's troops could defeat him. The Kuritans did defeat the invaders and Wolcott has not been retaken, even though Combine troops have been using the world to stage strikes at other planets."

Sharilar Mori leaned forward on her podium. "What of Luthien? Will the Clans attack Luthien again?"

Focht shrugged. "No one knows for certain, Precentor Dieron, what they will do. As Luthien is actually on the edge of the invasion cone, and because the Wolves have advanced far closer to Terra than have the Smoke Jaguars and Nova Cats, I do not think Luthien will suffer another assault. The Jaguars and Nova Cats are fierce rivals of the Wolves and will not put themselves in jeopardy of losing the race if they can help it."

Sharilar nodded, but directed her next question to the Primus. "I hear you speak of rivalries among the Clans. I assume your plan for negotiating involves multiple teams of negotiators to set the Clans one against another?"

Myndo crossed her arms, slipping her hands into the voluminous sleeves of her robe. "That was my initial plan, Precentor Dieron, but the Precentor Martial disagrees with it."

Focht heard a strident note beginning in the Primus' voice. He recalled too well the tirades he had endured in opposing her plan to play the Clans off against each other in a game of politics. In the end, the Primus had acquiesced to his point of view, but not willingly, and he dreaded the manner in which she would lay out the argument for the First Circuit.

The Primus gave him a Judas smile. "The Precentor Martial, speaking from the fortress of a military man's phobia for politics, noted quite correctly that the invasion force is made up of military leaders from the Clans' Warrior Caste. Though he conceded that the ilKhan, Ulric Kerensky of the Wolves, is himself adept at politics, Anastasius points out that any political meddling by us would be viewed as a directly hostile act. If we are to keep our people in place on the occupied worlds, we can only negotiate with the ilKhan. Still, the Precentor Martial did concede the point of letting the other Clan leaders know we were negotiating with the ilKhan because, obviously, he was going to win the race."

Myndo's hands reappeared from their hiding places as she pressed them together in an attitude of prayer. "While I think his analysis of the Clans is quite correct, I wish his paranoia about politics had not blinded him to Khan Ulric's obvious motive in this invasion. If he had foreseen it, we would have been better prepared for the defense of Terra."

Damn you, witch! I know enough of politics to know you've just thrown me to the wolves—both here and with the Clans. Focht lifted his white-maned head high and slowly studied the members of the First Circuit. "I would beg to differ with the Primus' characterization of the ilKhan: Ulric has never been obvious. I cannot fathom a way in which I might have learned from him the intended goal of the invasion."

Sharilar Mori's brows knit together in a look of puzzlement. "But I recall from your reports that you enlisted the aid of Phelan Kell to break into the Khan's chambers in an attempt to learn the reasons behind the invasion."

"True, but the death of the previous ilKhan in the battle at Radstadt prevented bringing that plan to fruition. You cannot fault me for that turn of fate."

Percentor Dieron shook her head. "No, Precentor Martial, I do not fault you for that. I note, however, that you seemed to rely heavily on Kell, a Clan outsider, for much of your information. Might not you have found a better source?"

"You are in error there, Precentor Dieron." Focht folded his arms across his chest. "From the moment he was captured, Phelan Kell was considered part of the Wolf Clan. As a bondsman working closely with Khan Ulric, he had access to a vast amount of information as well as virtual free run of the invasion flagship. He was my only window into the Khan's mind, and yet now I believe Ulric was manipulating the both of us."

Vandel clasped his hands at the back of his neck. "Could you not have converted Kell into an information source more quickly, Precentor Martial?"

"I did not have the necessary tools, Precentor New Avalon. As Precentor Tharkad can tell you from looking at Kell's record and the story of his expulsion from the Nagelring, he is possessed of a singularly strong sense of loyalty and an iron will. Ulric earned the youth's respect early on, and getting any concession out of Phelan proved more than difficult."

Focht looked up at the Primus. "I had thought offering communication between Phelan and his parents would be enough to bring him around to our side, but actually transmitting such messages was forbidden by the Primus. This left me with nothing until I could build a rapport with Phelan. By the time I did that, it was too late."

The Primus looked suitably stung by his remark. "What of this rapport now, Precentor Martial?" she fired back. "Might it not have told us what we needed to know before I learned of it from the ilKhan's lips on Satalice?"

"I think not, Primus." Focht drew in a deep breath and let it out in a heavy sigh. "Phelan Kell was adopted into the Warrior Caste, binding him even more tightly to Ulric and the Wolves. Moreover, Natasha Kerensky was assigned as one of his tutors and her love for our Blessed Order is known to be something smaller than a Tau muon. Lastly, I recall the look on Phelan Kell's face when the ilKhan told you the goal of the invasion. He was as shocked as you or I at the announcement."

"Perhaps," she whispered, her tone laden with skepticism. "I hope your read of ilKhan Ulric is more accurate now that he has unveiled his true motives."

Indeed it is, Primus. Focht nodded. "I have watched and studied how Ulric thinks and works. I have gigabytes worth of data on all the Clan assaults, their leaders, their tactics, and their losses. Even now that material is being analyzed at Sandhurst. I am certain that it will deliver me the key to defeating Ulric, and with him, the Clans."

Everson narrowed his eyes. "So while you are considering a way to defeat the Clans, what are the rest of us supposed to do? Do we fiddle while the Successor States burn, or have we a more constructive role to play in this grand drama?"

The Primus bristled at the question, but she delivered her response in a low, calm voice. "Your job, Precentor Tharkad, is to slowly communicate with the leaders of the Inner Sphere. Let them know that ComStar is increasingly alarmed at the nature of the invasion. With the loss of their intelligence chief to Romano Liao's assassin, the Federated Commonwealth *must* want our help in gathering information. Offer it.

"Tell them that we have tried to remain neutral for the sake of the people on the captured worlds, but the Clans are quickly putting us in a position where we must act. With the support of the Successor States, ComStar will lead the way in vanquishing the Clans."

The Precentor Martial quailed slightly at the light gleaming in Myndo Waterly's eyes. He knew that it was her obsession with reforming mankind along the grand design outlined in the teachings of Jerome Blake that had put ComStar in this delicate position. Myndo believed ComStar somehow immune to anything so ignominious as defeat. Worse, she expected the Federated Commonwealth to ignore decades of covert war between ComStar and its intelligence service in order to unite into a force to liberate mankind—in the name of ComStar.

She deludes herself, and in so doing, imperils the very organization she promotes. Focht swallowed hard. "Primus, just remember: the solution to the Clans must be a military one, not a political one. Use politics to get me the troops and time I need, and I will destroy the threat to ComStar and the Word of Blake."

"Of course, Precentor Martial." Myndo smiled with the sincerity of a serpent. "I leave the problem of the Clans to you alone."

4

Teniente, Kagoshima Prefecture
Pesht Military District, Draconis Combine
18 January 3052

Shin Yodama grabbed Hohiro Kurita to prevent him from taking a running dive across the briefing table and strangling *Tai-sa* Alfred Tojiro. "*Iie,* Hohiro-*sama.* We are here as observers."

Hohiro whirled, his brown eyes betraying his surprise at Shin's action. "How can you say that? Even if we're only observers, what we're observing is a disaster." Hohiro pointed to the data-readout hovering holographically over the table. "Tojiro has just ordered the Third Battalion of the Third Pesht Regulars to charge a solid Clan position! The man is fighting in the old style!"

Shin felt his heart sink. "I know that, Hohiro, but the reason we were forced to come here was because Tojiro is such a long-time favorite of your grandfather." He nodded toward the taller of the military leaders in the room. "The same goes for *Tai-sa* Kim Kwi-Nam, the Eleventh Pesht Regulars' commander. We have no authority to depose either one of these madmen."

Hohiro's hand fell to the hilt of the machine pistol he wore. "This is all the authority I need."

Shin's dark gaze flicked from one armed guard to another stationed all around the bunker. "We would be slain in an instant, and our deaths would be accounted to the Clans.

Tojiro demanded observers so he could prove his old ways were enough to destroy the Clans."

Hohiro ground his teeth with frustration. "But they are not! His people are getting picked apart! The Clan leader grossly underbid in his attempt to take this world, and Tojiro is handing him a victory." The flash and fireball of a 'Mech dying on a datascreen bleached all the color from Hohiro's profile. "I cannot simply stand idle and let our people die."

"I know." Shin exhaled slowly. "Be careful."

Hohiro gave Shin a grateful smile. "I will."

The son of the Draconis Combine's Warlord threaded his way through the commtechs and took up a position opposite the small, wizened man commanding Teniente's defenses. Shin drifted in behind Hohiro, but stood far enough back to keep an eye on all the guards in the room. With practiced ease, he shifted his personal assault weapon around, letting the laser rifle with an underslung shotgun-barrel hang by its pistol-grip from his right hand. The yakuza quickly assessed the guards for threat level and determined which, if it came down to it, he would shoot first.

"*Tai-sa* Tojiro, forgive my presumption," Hohiro began slowly, "but you are ordering the destruction of your Third Battalion."

Tojiro's head snapped up as if springloaded, and Shin instantly realized Tojiro would not mince words or abide by the courtesies demanded by polite culture. "Am I? I seem to recall your command was destroyed on Turtle Bay, Hohiro Kurita. But I have never lost a command. How do you presume to lecture me?"

From the hunch of Hohiro's shoulders, Shin knew he was about to explode. "I learned from my error, Tojiro! You have read all the briefing papers, I assume? You are an idiot if you push your Third Battalion forward."

The slender commander of the Eleventh Pesht Regulars pressed his hands together, fingertip to fingertip. "And I would assume his Highness is equally critical of my troop deployment?"

Hohiro stiffened at the man's patronizing tone. "Tojiro is just an idiot, as his strategy indicates. Your folly defines new depths for negligence and malfeasance. If you both continue your conduct of this battle, I will relieve you of your responsibilities!"

"By what authority? I command here." Tojiro jammed his

fists onto his hips. "I care not what rank your father presumes to hold. My authority comes to me by your grandfather. I will command until he relieves me of it."

Hohiro pounded the table with one fist. "Listen to me, you *chimpera*. This whole operation has been run counter to everything we have learned about the Clans. You have let them choose the battlefields. You have not employed your air forces against their 'Mechs. You encourage single combat against a foe that has every advantage against you in that department. About the only thing you've done right is to scatter your supply depots so your troops can resupply themselves on the run, but you're not putting them into a position where they can utilize those supplies or that strategy!"

"I would expect such talk of a man with a yakuza for an aide." Kwi-Nam snarled angrily. "True warriors do not run and hide like bandits. We meet the enemy on the field of honor and kill him or die in the attempt! There is no life without honor. I will not order my troops to dishonor themselves!"

"Then you are surely mad!" At that, one of the guards began to move in, but Hohiro stared him back to his post. Then he returned his steady gaze to Kwi-Nam. "You should be out there in a 'Mech with your troops."

Tojiro began to pale. "I can better direct them from here, away from the confusion of battle."

Hohiro's cry of frustration filled the comcenter. "No, fool, not to fight! Have you read none of the reports about the Clans?" Hohiro's hands opened wide to encompass the whole cylindrical bunker. "Trapping yourself here is suicide. One strike and they wipe out the brains of this operation. In this case, though, it might help."

"Impossible. There's not a Clan 'Mech within fifty kilometers of here."

" 'Mechs, no, but Elementals, yes."

As if summoned by Hohiro's words, a series of clumps sounded from the roof of the bunker. Reacting reflexively, Shin seized Hohiro's right arm and spun him away toward the wall. Hohiro flew out of the way and across a desk, which toppled over on him. A moment later, Shin turned and dove for similar cover, but never made it.

The explosive charge set on the bunker's door blasted it from its hinges and sent it whirling like a blade through the bunker. It passed over Tojiro, missed Kwi-Nam, then sliced through one commtech. Like a giant axe-blade, it bit into a communication's relay, destroying it in a shower of sparks.

The force of the explosion propelled Shin further and faster than he had ever intended. He few into a desk and felt an agonizing jolt accompany the sound of ribs breaking on his left side. He slid to the ground with a bump, which sent another wave of pain washing over him. He grabbed the pain and held onto it to block the blackness nibbling at the edges of his sight. *I must not faint!*

The first Clan Elemental turned sideways to squeeze through the doorway. Over two meters tall, the humanoid figure wore bulky black armor with a blue blaze in the center of the chest. The Nova Cat Elemental raised its left arm—the one that ended in a three-fingered mechanical claw—and raked the room with fire from the machine gun mated to the underside of his forearm. Screaming as the slugs ripped scarlet holes through them, Techs fell thrashing to the bunker floor.

Shin brought his gun up and rested the barrel on the top of his right knee. Aiming more by instinct than design, he hit the firing stud on the laser. The ruby spears traced a flaming line up the front of the Elemental, then punctured the V-shaped viewport. The Elemental jerked back, his shoulders hitting either side of the door, then fell forward as smoke poured from his faceplate.

Another Elemental filled the doorway and Shin jerked the trigger on the shotgun. He barely felt the pain as the automatic cocking mechanism cut parallel lines across the top of his knee. The slug hit the Elemental just beneath the right breast and staggered him. The specially designed ammunition consisted of an extra-long lead bullet on top of a magnum load. *No one expected this stuff to kill an Elemental, just to hurt them.*

One of the guards stepped forward and stabbed the muzzle of his assault rifle into the dent Shin's shell had created in the armor. As the guard burned the clip from his rifle, the Elemental grabbed the man's chest in his claw and cut him in two with the underslung machine gun. A wave of blood washed back over the briefing table, shorting it out in a flash of green flame. The Elemental, dropping the torso of the soldier, fell back into a sitting position, half-blocking the doorway.

A third Elemental stood beyond the doorway, his entrance

into the room prevented by the large missile-launcher assembly mated to the back of his armored suit. He raised his right arm and let the anti-'Mech laser mounted there sweep the room. Everything and everyone the beam touched burst into flame.

Shin dropped onto his right flank, and paid for it with a grinding pain in the left side of his chest. He stabbed the assault rifle forward and jerked the shotgun trigger twice before the recoil twisted the weapon out of his grasp. One of the shots hit the Elemental in his right knee, bringing him down, but also swinging the launch tube on the short-range missile launcher in line with the doorway.

If a missile goes off in here, we're all dead!

Hohiro popped up from behind the desk, machine pistol in hand. Roaring with each shot, the weapon lipped flame more than thirty centimeters long. Hohiro held the trigger down, in two seconds pumping out the full ten shots in the clip. Though Shin knew Hohiro's gun had been loaded with shells similar to those in his shotgun, the lighter-weight pistol cartridges would have less effect than his shots.

Then a nova exploded outside the door.

Seeing the fireball blossom in the launch tube, Shin thought it must be an SRM starting on the path that would obliterate the bunker. Fire streaked out the back of the launch pack as he had always seen it do, but flaming tendrils also curled out the front and sides of the pack. In a second the top corner of the launcher evaporated in a white-gold flash, then a series of thunderous detonations ripped the Elemental apart.

The explosion boosted the bodies of the dead Elementals into the room and drove debris back in a narrow cone starting at the door. One Elemental bounced into a set of data-relay banks, scattering them like ten-pins while the other cartwheeled straight back like a zombie acrobat, hitting the wall beside Hohiro's shelter.

Shin tried to scramble out of the way as the data relay banks fell, but his whole chest felt as though it was collapsing as he clawed at the floor for traction. One cabinet dropped across his legs, pinning him in place in time for a second to slam into his ribcage. Shin screamed as lightning ripped its way through his body, then stopped fighting the darkness and fell unconscious.

* * *

A throbbing sound he couldn't identify greeted Shin's return to awareness. Opening his eyes, he saw himself strapped to a stretcher about to be hoisted into a helicopter. As confusing as that was, seeing Hohiro standing at the foot of the stretcher made even less sense. "*Shosa,* what has happened? Where am I?"

Hohiro smiled at him. "I'm having you medivacced to the DropShip. You're heading back to Luthien."

"You're not coming?"

The Warlord's son shook his head. "I relieved Tojiro and Kwi-Nam of their commands. I've scattered our troops and am sending them to ground. We will fight the sort of war we should have been fighting all along. I want to stretch things out and make the Clans earn their pay."

Shin tried to get up, but the tightness in his chest stopped him. "*Sho-sa,* do not send me away. These broken ribs are nothing. Let me stay here with you. Let me help you."

Hohiro smiled gratefully. "You have to go. I need you to act as my personal envoy." He lifted his end of Shin's stretcher and helped deposit it on the deck of the helicopter. Sitting chained to a bench with scowls on their faces were Tojiro and Kwi-Nam. Both were drenched in blood, but Shin instinctively knew it was not their own.

Hohiro crouched down and shouted into Shin's ear over the competition of the helicopter's rotor. "Those two are under arrest and are in your charge. The DropShip and JumpShip captains are *your* people. These two will not be able to subvert them. I would have shot them here, but they demanded the right to see my grandfather."

"They will make trouble for you, *Sho-sa.*"

"They will try, Shin. You must see to it that they do not." Hohiro rested his right hand on Shin's right shoulder. "It'll take you a month to get back to Luthien. Tell my father I will need another regiment and a half to take this world or to evacuate it in good order. I can hold out for the time it takes for your total round trip, but be quick. Anything much over four months is going to put me in a bad way. As I said before, we will go to ground and just harass the Clans until reinforcements show up."

"I will do as you ask, *Sho-sa.*" Shin forced a smile. "And I will be back with reinforcements as soon as possible." He glanced at the two men Hohiro had deposed. "I will bring you help even if I have to strike a bargain with all the demons in the Christian hell to do so."

Hohiro nodded solemnly. "I know you will, my friend. I am counting on it."

The rotor's pitch increased as Hohiro stepped away from the helicopter. Shin tried to turn his head to watch Hohiro until he vanished in the distance, but his restraints prevented him from doing so. He thought he heard Hohiro shout a final "Sayonara," but he could not be sure.

Somehow, deep down, Shin felt a dread that no matter how swiftly he returned, he would never see Hohiro Kurita alive again.

5

Alyina
Trellshire, Jade Falcon Occupation Zone
19 January 3052

Lean and hungry, Kai Allard crouched beside the roadway. He waited until the truck's taillights vanished around the curve through the forest, then sprinted to the other side. Clutching the ragged swath of camouflage sheeting around him like a cloak, he knew anyone near enough to see him break from cover would probably think him a terrifying ghost.

The fortnight since his stranding on Alyina had not been kind to Kai. He had moved as far as possible from the battlefield where he'd looted Dave Jewell's 'Mech on the first night, pausing only to rest or when he heard people moving. As he headed inland from the peninsula, the amount of destruction decreased. He had not thought himself following any specific course, yet eventually he came to the place where his lance of 'Mechs had waited for the Clans to make landfall.

The tattered piece of camouflage he carried with him had initially hidden *Yen-lo-wang* from infrared and magnetic resolution scans, but now did little more than keep him warm at night. That was no small grace, however, because the monsoon rains soaked him to the bone every afternoon and morning. The camouflage did help keep some of the rain off, but Kai found it too bulky to wear all the time, especially if he wanted to move at all quietly through the rain forest.

Initially he regretted having stressed to his men the necessity for maintaining a tidy camp because now he found little or nothing to salvage beside the 'Mech camo from the Icestorm lance area. Moving a bit north along the line established for the Tenth Lyran Guards, he had more success plundering Frostfire lance's garbage midden, but he was careful in his scavenging to leave no clue of his passing.

From the first, his caution was rewarded. Several Clan patrols swept through the area, picking up stragglers who had not been as lucky as Kai. The Elementals, both in their armor and out, impressed Kai with their size and strength. He breathed a silent vow to avoid tangling with them if at all possible. By taking refuge high up in trees during the day, he frustrated the searchers. After ten days, the patrols dwindled.

His rations lasted for the first week, and then hunger forced him to expand his foraging range. The Clans, he discovered to his dismay, pressed captive warriors into service as clean-up crews. They salvaged their own 'Mechs, but left the enemy machines behind where they fell. They also cleaned up any deposits of material that fugitives might find useful. When small supply caches began to show up in places Kai had never seen them before, he knew they were bait for a trap. No matter how tempting they looked, he avoided them.

Watching one such crew of captives, Kai noticed that the Elementals guarding the crew did not treat them harshly. Each captive wore a braided bit of white cord on his right wrist and seemed to receive a certain amount of respect. He heard the Elementals address the captives as "bondsman," but he attached no real significance to that title. It did strike him that he saw far fewer captive warriors than he would have imagined, given the haste of the FedCom retreat. *There must be more hiding somewhere.*

Watching other captives started Kai thinking about his chances of liberating compatriots and leading them in a revolt. None of those he saw looked mistreated or malnourished, so he imagined them still to be in fighting trim. Yet most of the captives were MechWarriors and hardly schooled in the tactics of an irregular infantry.

Seeing no way to organize a force that could throw the Clans off the planet, Kai decided his real duty was to remain free, and if the chance arose, report back to Hanse Davion and his father about the military situation on the world. He knew that if he could get them credible intelligence, they would send a force to liberate Alyina and to rescue him. Gathering that information would mean traveling around enough to see what the Clans had left on the world, and then reaching a ComStar facility from which he could send his message home.

On the far side of the road, Kai ran down into a small gully and walked along in the chilly stream running through it. Fifty meters downstream, he exited onto a flat bed of rock and went up the far side of the gully into a finger of forest. He waited, listening and watching for any signs of other life, then slowly but surely worked his way forward. Stopping in the shadows of thick pines and carefully avoiding stepping on anything that would make noise, he picked a zigzag path through the woods to the garden he'd harvested two nights before.

Stepping over a low fence made of chicken-wire, Kai dropped to his knees beside a patch of tomatoes. Just as he reached out for one, a light flashed on, accompanied by the sound of a shell being racked into a pump-action shotgun. Kai froze, narrowing his eyes against the harsh glare of the flashlight strapped to the gun's barrel.

"Told the wife raccoons didn't brush away their footprints when they left." The voice came gruff from the big silhouette, but Kai heard no hostility in it. "Your name Jewell?"

Kai started to shake his head, but nodded as he realized the man with the gun was reading the name off the breast of his jumpsuit. "Yeah, Dave Jewell, that's me. Now that you've caught me, what are you going to do with me?"

The light flashed off. "Take you to the house. Clanners can't punish us more for having two Feds under our roof than they can for one, *ja*? C'mon."

Kai stood slowly and stepped back out of the garden. A voice inside him screamed that he should be running away, or at least disarming the man, but he held back. The farmer gave him a fair amount of room, but Kai knew the shotgun was his any time he wanted to take it. Kai nodded and let the farmer lead the way.

The small, two-story wooden house to which his guide led him showed yellowed lights around the edges of drawn shades. Enough of it spilled out across the porch to show Kai which loose, weathered boards to avoid. It also gave him a brief glimpse of his grizzled host, but he could not remember ever having seen the white-haired old man before. Still, by the ease with which the man held the shotgun in one hand, Kai guessed he'd seen military service.

The farmer waved Kai into the building. To the left of the door, a small lamp burned on a dining table surrounded by six chairs. Beyond it, in the far left corner was a kitchen with a wood-burning stove that kicked out wave after wave of welcome warmth. Dominating the center of the room, a staircase led up to the second floor. Off to the right side of the door, a group of chairs had been arranged around a circular carpet to form a comfortable conversation nook. Back in the far right corner, the walls were stacked with shelves containing both old, real-paper books and a host of holovid books along with a reader.

"Welcome to our home, Mr. Jewell." The farmer set the shotgun in a rack beside the door. He turned and pointed to the white-haired woman by the stove. "This is my wife, Hilda. I am Erik Mahler, formerly a MechWarrior in the service of the Archon of the Lyran Commonwealth."

Kai smiled and accepted the man's hand. "David Jewell, Tenth Lyran Guards."

"Tenth Guards?" Hilda smiled and wiped her hands on her apron. "Then you will know out other guest." She walked to the stairs and called softly. "It is safe, my dear. Come down."

Kai loosened the string tying his camo around his neck. Letting the sheeting slip to the floor, he started to remove his backpack, but it hung forgotten as the Mahlers' other refugee descended the stairs. She was tall and slender, with short black hair that barely brushed the collar of her flannel shirt. The yellow discoloration on his brow he put down to the last vestiges of what must have been a nasty bruise. Her blue eyes lit up with surprise when she saw him. "Kai!"

Stunned, Kai dropped his pack. "Deirdre? Didn't you get off with the others?"

She stiffened. "The Clans overran our hospital. I fled with the others." Her right hand rose to touch the bruise above her right eye. "I hit something, I don't remember what. I don't remember anything until I woke up here."

Erik smiled. "This far was the eye in a nasty storm. The battle raged all around, but no one came here. I found Deirdre wandering through the woods and I brought her back here." His right eyebrow arched. "She called you, 'Kay.'"

Kai nodded, "It is a nickname that's stuck since my time at the New Avalon Military Academy. I used to say 'okay' so much that my classmates started calling me 'Kay.' The regiment picked it up. Some folks think my name really is David K. Jewell."

Deirdre's expression of pleasure at seeing Kai began to drain away, but she gave no indication she would betray his deception. Mahler, looking from Kai to Deirdre and back again, either noticed nothing or decided to disregard whatever conclusions he was drawing about the two of them.

Hilda seized the opportunity offered by the momentary silence. "Kay—if you do not mind me using your nickname—you can wash up and I will get you some clean clothes, if you like. Then you can eat something."

"Bitte." Kai smiled.

"Deirdre, why don't you take Kay to the pumphouse out back and show him how to fill the tub." Erik Mahler shrugged with notable stiffness in his left shoulder. "After years of service, I retired and determined to get back to the land and avoid the technological trappings of society. I find it more relaxing. And with the Clans cutting down on the amount of power available to outlying areas, we are less affected than others."

Kai smiled politely. "Having lived off the land for the past two weeks, your home looks to me like a lost Star League depot of stuff." He picked up his cloak and pack, then turned to Deirdre. "If you will lead the way, Doctor, I will become more human."

Kai stripped off his soiled jumpsuit and tossed it onto the pumphouse bench. His almond eyes and bronze flesh bespoke his Eurasian blood, though his dirty face and hands were dark enough to suggest African origins for his family. Catching sight of himself in the door mirror as he pulled off his cooling vest, Kai saw that he'd lost what little fat he'd been carrying. He combed his fingers back through his short black hair, pulling at two snarls, then shuddered.

His fingernails were as black as his hair.

His mirror-image slid away as Deirdre opened the door. "A bit underfed, but you look healthy." She placed the towels and soap she was carrying on a stood next to a huge wooden cask. Her voice grew a bit distant. "Am I allowed to ask why you've appropriated the identity of another member of the Guards, or is that some secret you nobles keep to yourselves?"

The ice in her voice stung Kai, but he reined in his hurt. "Mahler saw the name on the jumpsuit and figured me to be David Jewell. As he had a shotgun on me at the time, I decided going along was easier than explaining the truth."

"Really? Or is it that you think a disguise will make you less valuable as a hostage when the Clans capture you?"

Kai pulled off his own dog tags and tucked them into the small pocket inside the waistband of his shorts. "I don't intend to be captured."

Deirdre gave him a hard stare. "What happened to Jewell?"

He suppressed a shudder as he recalled climbing into the *Wolverine*'s cockpit and looting it. "He was killed in battle. He died protecting Prince Victor."

"Of course." A sour expression sharpened her face and scored lines at the corners of her eyes, but those eyes reflected sadness. "What happened to you?"

Kai crossed to the silver pump beside the tub and began to work the handle up and down. "I was left for dead after it looked like my 'Mech had been destroyed." As water gushed into the tub in frothy pulses, Kai felt his anger getting the better of him. He decided to change the subject to something more neutral. "You said the Clans overran your hospital. What happened?"

Deirdre's face took on a dazed expression and she lowered herself like a zombie to the bench. "It felt like a replay of Twycross. Elementals came into our area and began to shoot up what vehicles we had. Meanwhile, the veterinary hospital we had converted into a clinic offered us no cover. Things just started exploding and there were fires and glass flying everywhere." She covered her face briefly with her hands, as though the memory were too painful. "So much blood. I was working on a boy who'd been hit in the chest and we couldn't stop the bleeding. And then one of my nurses got hit and I realized they were shooting at the hospital."

Tears rolled from her red-rimmed eyes. "I told someone to call for you on the radio because you'd told me you had our sector and that you would protect us." Her hands curled into fists and she stared defiantly at him. "I should have know better."

Kai ground his teeth. "Victor was in trouble. The Clans

had trapped him. I *was* on the way to help you, then his call came through. I knew I was the only one who could reach him in time. I had to go to him."

"Blue blood is thicker than red, isn't it, Leftenant Allard-Liao?" Her lip curled up in a snarl that blasphemed her beauty.

"Come off it, Doctor!" Kai posted off the top of the pump and leaped over the tub. He grabbed her by the shoulders and dragged her to her feet. "It was triage, just the same as you practice in your hospital. Yes, I'll say it, Victor was more important than a whole DropShip full of wounded men. Do you know why?"

"He's an adventuristic noble who leaves broken and bleeding bodies wherever he goes." Her eyes blazed with fury.

"No!" Kai shook her roughly. "No, the reason Victor was more important than your wounded men and women is because he is important to all of them. If Victor died, or was captured, we'd all lose the heart to fight. Every one of those people who died in your hospital had been fighting *with* Victor to oppose something they felt was evil, something destroying their way of life. Saving Victor gave their sacrifice meaning."

"Dead is dead, and there is no meaning in it!" Deirdre pulled away from him. "Damn you and Victor and Hanse Davion and the Clans and everyone. You all see wars as the place where glories can be won. You all brag about courage and bravery and sacrifice as if that ennobles the death of some half-trained schoolboy who's blown apart while carrying a gun. That's obscene, because it fosters the mistaken idea that life is cheap enough to waste if the cause is right or just."

She thrust her right hand toward the Mahler house. "Look at him, look at Erik. He's an old man crisscrossed with scars. He's got a scar on his left shoulder that looks like someone tried to take his arm off with a sword. He's stiff and he moves slowly, but when he decided to wait for you to return to steal food, he was like a commando out there. It was a return to some malignant time that made him feel wonderful, and quite probably would have gotten him killed."

Kai saw her tremble with rage, but he said nothing. He understood that her fury, though vented on him, was not meant for him alone. Her ranting struck chords in him, and brought back memories of the battlefield he'd greeted after escaping his 'Mech.

"You don't know what war really is, Leftenant, you really don't." She slapped her hips in frustration. "I have a boy brought in and I open him up as soon as they can put him under anesthesia. But when I open him up, I find his insides are a jigsaw puzzle. His bowels have been perforated with shrapnel, and feces is mixed with blood and whatever he last ate. I can clean him up and I can resect his small intestine into a colostomy, but I know he's going to be septic and I don't know if I have enough drugs to deal with him. Still, I put him back together.

"Have you any idea what it's like," she demanded, pounding her fists against his chest, "to have a kid ask you to let him die? I had a boy who was looking forward to a professional sports career come into the clinic with the lower half of his right arm hanging on by a tendon. He was out of his mind with pain, but he wouldn't let us put him under until I'd promised that if I couldn't fix it, I'd just let him die. And, dammit, I almost wanted to because I knew, for him, having to adapt would be impossible."

Kai settled his hands gently on her shoulders. "I know. My father lost his forearm."

"Yes, your *father* lost his forearm." Her voice grew cold as she twisted out of his grasp. "Well, let me tell you, not everyone is such a good friend of Hanse Davion that he gets the New Avalon Institute of Science to make him a new arm that functions better than the original. No, you and your father and Victor are all special, and why these people are willing to catch the bullets and missiles meant for you, I will never know."

She picked up the bar of soap from the bench and tossed it into the half-filled tub. "There, Leftenant. Go ahead and clean yourself up. See if you can ever wash all the blood from your hands."

6

Hanse Davion, First Prince of the Federated Commonwealth, lay his half-glasses down on top of the report on his desk. As he did so, one of the massive bronze doors across from his antique desk swung open on well-oiled hinges. Through it the Prince saw a veritable phalanx of security guards and the tall, slender form of his acting intelligence secretary. *Good, Alex, you're right on time.*

Alex Mallory entered the room with a limp that was a remnant of torture suffered on the Liao homeworld of Sian more than twenty years before. Hanse knew the limp only showed up when Alex was tired, and he sympathized with the man. While his gray eyes were still bright, the dark crescents beneath them spoke of too much work and not nearly enough rest.

The Prince smiled wearily, realizing Mallory's face was probably a mirror of his own. "I apologize for sending for you, Alex. I know you did not get to sleep before three this morning."

Alex shrugged, but settled gratefully into a wing-backed brown leather chair facing the desk. "No matter, Highness. I am well used to working on four hours of sleep, or less."

"So I understand. Justin always said you were a workaholic."

Pain shot through his eyes, but Alex forced a gruff chuckle nonetheless. "Coming from him and you, that is high praise, indeed." Alex opened one of the folders he'd brought with him. "This is the latest we have on the front. It looks as though the Clans have momentarily stopped their advance and are consolidating their positions."

Hanse tapped the report on his desk. "They did a lot of world-hopping in their last set of attacks. It makes sense for them to want to consolidate their rear area."

"True." Alex tugged at the cuff of his black woolen jacket. "The Draconis Combine has apparently inserted some forces to their rear. They are staging from Wolcott, but the Clans have so far kept their vow not to attack that world again. Another force went out from Pesht, but did not meet with the stunning success of other Combine operations. Given that two old hardliners were in command of the forces, I am not surprised."

Hanse leaned back in his chair, idly wishing for the days when he could have piloted a 'Mech out against these Clansmen. *Then again, on Outreach, Kai Allard took me down right quickly in his test. And the Clans have taken him. How long would I survive?*

"Alex, have we had any word from Alyina?"

The Intelligence Secretary chewed his lower lip, then shook his head. "Nothing. I think there is little doubt that Kai Allard perished in his attempt to save Victor. I've had people review the battleroms from Victor and Galen Cox's 'Mechs. Even if Kai survived hitting the water, the shelf goes down for a kilometer in that area. If the cockpit had somehow been pressurized to withstand the weight of the water at that depth, Kai might have lived, but there would have been no way for him to ascend to the surface. His 'Mech did not have a modular escape pod like a *Hatchetman* or *Wolfhound.*"

Hanse swallowed hard against the lump in his throat. "So he's dead?"

"He's listed as 'Missing in Action.' Given the other tragedies in the Allard-Liao family, I think it is best we release no information about Kai." Alex grabbed a handful of white hair at the back of his neck. "When the time comes, the battleroms will prove Kai every bit the hero to the Federated Commonwealth that his father was."

Hanse nodded solemnly as little tentacles of pain seemed to wrap around his heart with a squeeze. "Still, you did let

ComStar know that we will pay to have priority transfer of any message from or about Kai."

"I did." The growing smile on Alex's face piqued Hanse's curiosity. "In doing so, I learned something very interesting. I am having a report prepared, but I will give it to you as a thumbnail brief now."

"Please do." *Is there good news possible from ComStar?*

"We have always figured at least benign complicity between ComStar and the invaders."

Hanse grinned slowly, still very much the Fox. "We know that because of the black-out of important data from worlds the Clans have taken. We have also assumed, given the overwhelming successes of the Clans, that ComStar has been feeding them data in preparation for their attacks."

"Right." Alex steepled his fingers in a gesture Hanse found chillingly reminiscent of Justin Allard. "When I got into contact with ComStar, I was instantly transferred to speak with Huthrin Vandel—Precentor New Avalon himself. Vandel assured me that any message by or about Kai would be relayed immediately. He said he was heartsick that this war would cost the lives of so many brave citizens of the Federated Commonwealth. He also let slip some concern within the First Circuit about the Clans and hinted that ComStar might be willing to turn its Com Guards loose on the Clans, given support by the other Successor States."

"What!" Hanse stared blankly at his Intelligence Secretary. "Do you think Vandel is playing some power game against the Primus, or is this official-line material?"

"Too little data to be sure, Highness, hence my wanting an analysis before reporting this. We know that Huthrin Vandel and Ulthan Everson have long opposed the Primus and her activities, but they've never done more than mildly rebuke her. If they are plotting against her, I would ask myself why now? What could she have done that would prompt them to finally make a real move?"

Hanse scratched his head. "Wouldn't aiding and abetting the Clans be enough to make them want to depose her?"

"Surely, Highness, but then we have to assume that ComStar has been doing that all along, so the timing of their move appears questionable. If they had deposed her at the beginning of the invasion, then worked with everyone to defeat the Clans, ComStar would be in a powerful position. Now, having helped the Clans to their series of victories, the

Primus would be quite strong. These two would never dream of openly opposing her, in that case. She could have them expelled from the First Circuit and replace them with one of her favorites, as she did with Sharilar Mori, the successor she handpicked as Precentor Dieron."

"So," Hanse mused, "that means either ComStar sees the Clans as a threat and wants to stop them now, or Vandel is feeling us out for support in some move against the Primus. Why?"

"Again, Highness, I have not enough data to venture more than a guess."

"Guess."

Alex smiled. "I think, Highness, that ComStar finally perceived that the Clans' attack vector takes them on a path that includes Terra. Myndo Waterly must feel the hot breath of the Wolf Clan upon her neck, and she's finally going to call in some support."

Hanse rubbed at his chest. "What are the chances she'll get it?"

"From us? That is up to you, Highness. We could cut some Regimental Combat Teams loose, but that would hurt us on the front with the Jade Falcons. I don't think the Combine has troops to spare, either, but Theodore might be persuaded to throw some of his 'Ghost' regiments to her."

"And Romano Liao would refuse her support. She'd refuse anyone support." Hanse opened a drawer in his desk and pulled out a small roll of anti-acids. "What about Thomas Marik? He was a ComStar Adept before he assumed the Captain-Generalcy of the Free Worlds League. Will he back her? His troops are not pinned down. He could respond."

"He could, but remember how hard he bargained with you and Theodore Kurita on Outreach. All you were asking was for him to start upgrade-kit and 'Mech production for you, not to commit his troops to your defense. He bargained hard and only acquiesced after you offered to bring his son Joshua here for chemotherapy to treat his leukemia. What could the Primus offer him in exchange for defending Terra?"

Hanse swallowed the last of the anti-acid tablet. "A very good question. God alone knows what secrets ComStar has found and hidden on Terra. The Primus would have to offer Thomas something incredible because Thomas knows his troops have no idea how to fight the Clans. He's aware that sending his troops into battle against them at this point would be a sentence of death. That would raise a ruckus at home, which Thomas can ill afford."

Hanse's blue eyes narrowed for a moment, then his vulpine grin grew. "By the way, how is young Joshua Marik doing?"

"Very well. The leukemia is in remission and he seems to be tolerating the drugs we use far better than those his father's doctors were using. The Marik physicians did not take well to the New Avalon Institute of Science staff referring to them as 'witch-doctors,' but we managed to smooth things over. We will keep Joshua here with us for at least another six months to keep an eye on how he is doing."

And time enough to start the field modification kits for our 'Mechs flowing from the Free Worlds League. "Very good, Alex. You have my compliments. I am especially impressed at your ability to slip into Justin's shoes in such an able manner."

Alex shook his head. "I appreciate your praise, Highness, but I do not deserve it. I have a staff of seven helping me do what Justin used to handle by himself before he, ah, went away. Every day seems to turn up another matter he had been holding down that I knew nothing about. His loss is not one from which we will quickly—or possibly ever—recover."

Pain nibbled at Hanse's heart again. "How well I know that, my friend. It's odd. I had envisioned Justin and me handing over our jobs to our respective sons in five or ten years. Now. . . ." Hanse's hands dropped to his desk and lay there like dead things.

"Yes, Highness." Alex opened another folder. "You will be pleased to know that we managed to trace the laser pistol used on Justin and Candace. It has identifying marks consistent with those found in a cache of weapons we located in the Sarna March. It is unlikely the assassin carried it with him from there, so we have been searching for the ship that might have delivered it. We have the suspects narrowed down to three independent trading DropShips and are currently going over the passenger, crew, and cargo lists for each trip those ships made to New Avalon in the last ten years."

Hanse's right hand closed into a fist. "Good. I want every

single one of the individuals in that chain. I want them all to stand trial for murder, then I will be pleased to witness their executions for high treason and regicide." Hanse's anger flooded a tightness into his chest. "I only wish the head of the serpent could be brought here for trial. It infuriates me to think Romano Liao and Tsen Shang are beyond my reach."

Alex nodded sympathetically. "On that, Highness, I have no news, but that is to be interpreted as good news. Romano may be out of your reach, but not out of the grasp of justice. I take some comfort in that knowledge."

"Some comfort, but not the same I'd get from having my hands wrapped 'round her throat, I fear."

Both Alex and Hanse shared a laugh. "Alex, has my son learned of his new orders yet?"

"No, the *Barbarossa* will not reach Biota until the end of this week. Morgan Hasek-Davion has already left in a DropShip to meet the *Barbarossa* when it makes the jump into the system. Morgan will brief him, then the whole of the Tenth Lyran Guards will make their way to Port Moseby for rest and refit. Morgan does not think Victor will like being sent back behind the lines. He assumes Victor will demand a transfer to the First Kathil Uhlans or another line unit. If his request is denied, he will assume he is being punished by being sent back."

Only my son would think that. Hanse sighed heavily, wishing the anti-acid would take effect. "Morgan and I have discussed this likelihood. Morgan can handle him, being far more persuasive than I."

"But you will expect a strongly worded message from your son protesting your pulling him back to protect him."

"Of course." Hanse glanced down at his desk and felt the weight of all his years press down on him like the giant foot of a 'Mech. "Fortunately, I will only have to record a holovid to answer him, so I can edit it until I sound sincere. Yes, the Tenth is badly in need of rest and refit, and we will have them built into a better force than they were before, but they got mauled on Alyina. I almost lost Victor on the same day I lost Justin and his son. My wife is certain Victor will end up dying as did Ian."

Hanse looked at the picture of his family on the corner of his desk. "I am afraid I do not look forward to that eventuality, for more reasons even than the deep dread of losing my son. I was not directly in line for the throne, so I was not expecting to have to assume the role and the power, but I was able to handle the transition. I am not so confident in my other children, mainly because of their youth. Katherine is only twenty years old and not experienced enough to assume the responsibilities of ruling the Federated Commonwealth. And Peter, at seventeen, already sees himself as a Warrior-Prince, which is not what we need right now."

"Have confidence, Highness. They are your offspring. They will do well." Alex rose from his chair and stretched. "I think I will check the latest dispatches, then try to get a little more sleep. I might remind you that the doctors have suggested you should also be getting more rest."

Hanse waved Alex's concern away. "As soon as I know Victor is safely headed toward the rear, I will be able to sleep again. Right now, I feel fine."

"Highness, forgive my directness, but you are still wearing the same uniform from yesterday. Catching a cat-nap in your chair is not getting rest."

"You've been talking with my wife, haven't you?" Hanse smiled easily. "Very well, you've badgered me into it. I will get some sleep."

Alex nodded. "Very good. One more thing before I leave, Highness."

"Yes?"

"If Precentor New Avalon and I speak again, what do I suggest concerning his overtures for aid?"

Hanse let his breath hiss out between his teeth. "Suggest we will support them with everything, but make no promises." Hanse rubbed his left hand along his unshaven chin. "For twenty years, ComStar has done everything it can to hurt us, and now they have aided the enemy in this invasion. They've been playing with fire, and it will be my very great pleasure to watch ComStar get roasted alive!"

7

ComStar Military Headquarters, Sandhurst
British Isles, Terra
5 February 3052

Within the world presented to him by the Interactive Construct Reality helmet, the Precentor Martial strode like a giant across the battlefield. The computer drew the landscape in exquisite detail, providing Anastasius Focht a full-color map of Tukayyid, with a scale of two and a half centimeters real being equivalent to 10 meters subjective. At that scale, the BattleMechs arrayed across the landscape looked like toy soldiers, and a careless misstep by the Precentor Martial could destroy a legion of them.

Focht brought his hands up, cocking his wrists as though preparing to type on a computer keyboard. The data-gloves encasing his hands passed this information to the computer, which obliged him by creating a keyboard template to give him a visual guide for his hands as he typed in a request to adjust the scale of the world. He noted with grim satisfaction that the computer had provided him the same keyboard he would have found in a BattleMech.

Like a time-lapse film of mushrooms growing, the BattleMechs sprouted up until they reached the Precentor Martial's waist. He squatted down until sighting over the torso of one Wolf Clan *Hagetaka,* then smiled as he realized he could see nothing. He reached out his right hand, as he would have from the command couch of a BattleMech, and switched from vislight to infrared to magscan and back to vislight again. In none of the various scanner settings did he see anything.

He stood again and smiled. "Computer, note that because of the landscape's rolling nature, at 150 meters on the Przeno Plain on Tukayyid, the Wolf Clan approached our entrenched forces without being able to detect them."

"Noted," the computer commented emotionlessly. "A call has come in from the Primus. Will you leave the simulation or would you like the call woven into the world?"

Focht sighed heavily. "Project it, per the last time." He knew it would annoy her, but he did not want to leave the simulation of Tukayyid. He had cracked one small portion of the Clans' invincibility and he did not want to lose it. *I know the key to defeating them is here, somewhere. Now I just have to find it.*

The computer shaped a billowing white cumulus cloud in the sky. The Primus' face appeared on the cloud, and her expression gave the Precentor Martial an inkling of how Adam must have felt after eating of the apple. "You know how I hate to speak with you when you are *there*."

"Forgive me, Primus, but I have much work to do, and being able to study the battlefield in the detail provided by the ICR equipment is vital to my purpose." He bowed his head, then glanced at his own image as projected in the sky behind her cloud to assure smooth animation. He knew her greatest objection to working with him while in ICR equipment was the expressionless computer-projected image of him that she saw on her visiphone screen. From the projection, she could read nothing of his facial expressions or body language. That left her at a disadvantage and she did not like it.

"Very well, Precentor Martial. I would not wish to obstruct your defense of Terra. What have you to report?"

He opened his hands wide. "This is the world of Tukayyid. A relatively mild and somewhat arid planet in the Skandia Province of the Free Rasalhague Republic. It is primarily an agricultural world, with most of its land masses comprised of grassy plains controlled by agrocombines. During the era of Kurita rule, several minority religions came to this world and set up monastic communities in the mountains, and in one case, under the Crucible Sea. As a result, the population of the world is relatively small. The government is decentralized, with each corporation running its holdings like a fiefdom, except where theocracies have carved out their little domains."

The Primus yawned. "Interesting, Precentor Martial. I take it you find this world significant for more than its ability to bore the Clans to death?"

"Indeed I do, Primus." Focht pressed his hands together carefully. "You are looking at the world that will be the salvation of Terra."

"I do not understand."

The Precentor Martial took pleasure in the computer construct's hiding of his expression of disdain. "As the Successor States have discovered, we cannot determine in advance where the Clans will strike next. By all analysis of their techniques for selecting targets, they should bypass Tukayyid because it presents no threat to them. It has no native militia and any able-bodied individuals who could be spared from their jobs have long since left for the crumbling Rasalhague front.

"But I know of a way to make Tukayyid a prime target for the Wolf Clan. That is, quite simply, to challenge Khan Ulric to a battle on this world, which will decide the fate of Terra."

The Primus nodded, anxiety flashing across her face like heat lightning. "I had assumed we would have to fight the Clans, and I do not want the battle to take place on Terra, for obvious reasons. I assume you have chosen Tukayyid for more than its lack of potential civilian casualties."

The way she spoke, the Precentor Martial got the distinct impression that the possibility of civilian casualties did not necessarily mean vetoing the plan.

"Primus, Tukayyid has a number of things to recommend it. The world has many open areas for direct confrontations. The mountains are suitable for hit-and-run operations. The weather tends to be superior most of the time, which bodes well for aerospace and atmospheric fighter-craft. Moreover, Tukayyid has countless storage facilities, which, at this time of year, are empty and waiting for the fruits of the coming harvest. We can use them for munitions and supplies for our troops. Best of all, the low population is concentrated in easily defensible positions, which does not allow the Clans to use civilians against us."

The Primus let a predatory grin spread across her face. "So, victory is assured against the Clans?"

Focht stiffened, but the image sent to the Primus did not. "Primus, selecting a suitable battlefield on which to engage the Clans is but the first step in deciding a strategy to oppose them. I think Tukayyid will give us an advantage, but we still have to deal with certain facts. The first and foremost of these is that the Free Rasalhague Republic has not given us permission to land troops on their world or to use it as a battleground."

"They will." The Primus waved away his concern. "Prince Haakon Magnusson is so desperate for anything approaching a victory in his pitiful nation that he will jump at the chance at having us defend that world for him. I will see that all the agrocombines get a message in the morning indemnifying them against any damage we cause. Furthermore, we will expedite all their communications so they will not notice any difficulties if they decide to evacuate their people, which we will recommend highly." She smiled like a mother indulging a child. "If this is the world you require for your victory, you shall have it. One way or another, Tukayyid is yours."

I wonder if she believes she can decree victory this easily as well. "Thank you, Primus. I appreciate your adding the suggestion to evacuate the world. It would lessen my potential problems." The Precentor Martial folded his arms. "I have already begun to issue orders to consolidate the Com Guards and prepare for their reassignment to Tukayyid. I have delivered preliminary requests for equipment and supplies that my Quartermaster has determined we have available. I have planned for a campaign that will take upwards of a month to complete."

"A month?" Myndo Waterly frowned. "I have seen your requests, and with that number of troops, I would think you could defeat the Clans in a matter of hours!"

"No, Primus." Focht pointed to the forest of Clan 'Mechs surrounding him. "The Clans are specialists in quick victories. If the fighting ends in an hour, it is ComStar that will taste defeat. In this battle, we have to assume that the Clans will bid everything they have to oppose us. In fact, I expect Khan Ulric to bring troops from all seven of the attacking Clans to Tukayyid to oppose us. They will pull no punches, so we must become adept at avoiding their punches."

"But a month's worth of supplies? Is that not excessive?"

Focht shrugged. "As I have long told leaders when requesting resources, I can return leftover supplies after I win.

If I run out of munitions, there can be no victory. Moreover, diverse supply points and the ability to move has proved successful for both the Federated Commonwealth and the Draconis Combine. In fact, breaking the Third and Eleventh Pesht Regulars into more mobile forces is all that has allowed Hohiro Kurita's force to survive this long on Teniente."

"I will concede that point to you." The Primus slipped her hands into the opposite sleeves of her golden robe. "You have your battlefield, your troops, and your supplies. What else do you need?"

"My advisors and I are working up different scenarios, based on past Clan performance so we can model their strategies in the computers. We will run repeated tests of our troops against theirs, with everyone from lance leaders on up working with computer simulations so they come to know the enemy. In running through these strategies, we will discard what fails and look at crafting a tactical and strategic guide that should enable us to handle the Clans."

"You do not sound confident in your ability to defeat them, Precentor Martial. I would have expected more from a MechWarrior with your illustrious career."

Focht brought his head up with deliberate motion so the projection would ape it. "Primus, it has been nearly twenty-three years since I last fought in a battle that was not a simulation. Before that, I fought whenever the Archon called upon me to do so. I led the best troops the Lyran Commonwealth had to offer, and I can tell you that our Com Guards are even better.

"I did not always know victory, but I learned to respect my enemies, and the Clans are deserving of every gram of respect I can muster. I cannot imagine the Tenth Lyran Guards performing better under my leadership than they have under Prince Victor Ian Davion, but the Jade Falcons tore them to pieces on Alyina."

While his left hand made a broad, sweeping gesture to distract her, Focht used his right to increase the ICR scale to 1=1, making the Clan 'Mechs rise up and dwarf him. "As we have known from the beginning, the Clans are the greatest threat the Inner Sphere has ever faced, and now their path leads directly to Terra. I will stop them, but I must have your full support in gathering my troops and forming my plans."

"And you *will* have my complete support." The Primus' shoulders slumped slightly. "I will see to it that nothing stands between you and victory."

"Good." *Now to make the final request.* "Then you will grant me permission to travel out to meet with Khan Ulric to bargain this fight in the Clan manner."

Though Focht had kept his voice low and matter-of-fact, the Primus' eyes grew wide and her face flushed. "What? Are you mad?" Within the ICR world, the Precentor Martial expected the lightning in her eyes to shoot out and destroy him. "I cannot allow my Warlord to travel to the camp of the enemy. What if they capture and torture you? I have seen the report on how they broke Phelan Kell. You might last longer than he, but you would divulge all our secrets in the end. That I cannot chance."

"Primus, I *must* go." Focht signaled the computer to increase the time rate so that the world sank into nighttime shadows. "Khan Ulric will know this is a trap. He will know that we are lying in wait for him. The only way I can get him to agree to put the Clans' head into the mouth of the ComStar lion is to beard him in his own den. He will welcome my show of bravery, and he will respect it. Furthermore, my act will challenge the other Clans, so when Ulric calls for them to participate, they will comply. A formal bargaining session with the ilKhan is as vital to this operation as supplies and troops."

He saw her face close over, and he knew he had lost. "No, Precentor Martial. I cannot allow it. I will not allow it."

"Think about it, Primus. Consult the First Circuit before making your decision final." He folded his arms and met her electric stare evenly. "If you do not allow me to meet with Ulric face to face, to set this battle, you should begin practicing."

She looked puzzled. "Don't speak in riddles, Precentor Martial. I know who and what you really are, and such mystical nonsense ill become you. I should start practicing what?"

"Practicing what you'll tell Ulric when he bargains with you for the defense of Terra."

In a flash the cloud went blank, leaving a void amid a star-filled night sky. The Precentor Martial shook his head. "The one thing politicians will never understand is the warrior's need to know the opponent he faces is a true warrior.

It doesn't surprise me, for politicians consider compromise complete victory. In this war, no compromise is possible because anything short of total victory over the Clans will mean the death of ComStar."

Focht drew in a deep breath and sighed heavily. "Computer, Boreal continent, Cokoladu Mountains. Run the approach of the Nova Cat Lancers again. . . ."

8

Victor Ian Davion tugged at the hem of his waistcoat, then knocked on the bulkhead beside the Captain's cabin hatchway. Under normal circumstances, he would have foregone any formality in meeting with his cousin, Marshal Morgan Hasek-Davion, but the message requesting his presence had asked for *Kommandant* Davion, which meant the visit was business, not pleasure. "Kommandant Victor Davion reporting as ordered, sir."

"Come in, Victor." Seated behind the small, spindly-legged desk, Morgan Hasek-Davion looked like a titan trapped in a dwarven hall. His long red hair hung down to obscure the golden epaulets capping the shoulders of his black uniform. With one huge hand, Morgan waved Victor to a chair, but took no offense when Victor remained standing. "I am glad to see you are well. I understand you had a rough time of it on Alyina."

A rough time? My best friend dies saving my life and my command is crushed? And now you're here to take my command away. "I was unhurt, Marshal. The same cannot be said of my people. I don't know what happened. They overwhelmed us."

Morgan stopped Victor by holding up a hand. "Analysis of the battleroms indicates no culpability or negligence on your part. You and your people did all you could. The Clans shifted tactics and came at you harder than they have before. What happened on Alyina was not your fault."

Victor raised his eyes to meet Morgan's green gaze. "If that is so, why have you come here to strip me of my command?"

The question clearly surprised Morgan. "What are you talking about?"

"I know what's going on, Marshal." The diminutive Prince clasped his hands at the small of his back. "The grapevine has already let it be known that the Tenth Lyran Guards are bound on a command circuit for Port Moseby. We're going there for rest and refit, or so it goes, but I know the truth. We're being sent to the rear because we got pounded on Alyina. Other line units are coming up to take our place. You're mothballing the Tenth Lyran and ruining General Andrea Kaulkas' career because of the perception that *I've* screwed up."

"Nonsense. As I said before, Alyina was not your fault."

Victor's gray eyes flicked up. "If that is so, transfer me to another combat command."

"I cannot do that, Victor."

"Not in your Kathil Uhlans. I would be honored to serve there, but too many people would figure I had been given a command there because of who I am, not what I am. I won't have that." Victor closed his eyes and concentrated. "Let me serve in the Eleventh Donegal Guards or the Second Crucis Lancers."

Morgan shook his head slowly. "I cannot do that, Victor. I cannot just give you a command in another military unit. I would not do that for another officer of your rank, so if you want to avoid charges of favoritism, I suggest you refrain from asking for favors."

The remark stung Victor and he gritted his teeth to bite back the pain. "Marshal, there can be only two reasons why I am being sent for R&R with the Tenth Lyran. The first is that my performance in the field is considered disastrous. Perhaps that appears to be the case, as I've had two commands blown out from under me. I do not think it is a fair charge, however, because we faced the Clans for the first time on Trellwan, when we still did not know how to deal with them. On Alyina they shifted tactics, and we saw this too late to adapt to their new approach. Even so, we made them pay for their victory."

Victor pointed toward a porthole with his open right hand. "You cannot forget that we won on Twycross." His hand curled into a fist. "We gave the Clans their first drubbing on a Federated Commonwealth world, and the plan we used was developed by me and Kai and the other young officers . . ."

"And if not for Kai's damnable luck, you would have lost the Tenth Lyran Guards on Twycross, not Alyina," Morgan snapped. His fist pounded down on the flimsy desk, scattering pens and making the computer keyboard bounce. "It appears Kai used up all his luck on Twycross, because it surely ran out on Alyina. Yes, you beat the Clans on Twycross, but only because Kai put himself in extreme danger to destroy the Falcon Guards."

"No, Marshal, with all due respect, Kai's action was not the *only* reason we won on Twycross." Both Victor's hands curled into fists with frustration. "Our plan was solid. We had already begun to react to the threat to our rear before we knew Kai had stopped the Falcon Guards. By the time the Guards could have reached us, we had rotated our position 130 degrees so the Guard would have to fight through their own allies to get at us. We might not have defeated them, but we would have been able to withdraw in good order. Our strategy was strong, Morgan, and you knew that before you approved the plan."

Victor's eyes blazed with anger. "And if I'm not incompetent to lead, the only other reason I'm being pulled back is because someone on New Avalon does not want me in the line of fire. They'd not pull another soldier from the front just because his mother or father wanted him pulled back, so why do they do it with me? As long as we're asking other people to put their sons and daughters at risk, I should be there leading them."

"Go ahead, Morgan, deny these orders transferring me to the rear came from New Avalon." *And my father.*

"Victor, I could tell you that the orders went out over your father's signature, but you know that is true of all orders I receive. That would tell you nothing and is meaningless." Morgan leaned forward, resting his palms flat against the aluminum desk top. "If your mother or father wants you out of danger or to take you out of the line of fire, they have chosen a particularly poor world to which to assign you. Port Moseby may be well behind the line between the Jade

Falcons and our forces, but it is directly in the path of the Wolf Clan's advance. With the Free Rasalhague Republic demoralized and collapsing ever since the loss of Prince Ragnar to the Wolves on Satalice, you are going from the frying pan into the fire."

"I'd rather the frying pan now than the fire later."

A grin cracked Morgan's serious expression. "Of that I have to doubt. I think, however, your reasoning is flawed. You have overlooked a third reason for your reassignment."

Victor frowned, doubt entering his mind. "Which is?"

"Victor, you're only human. You've been involved in some of the heaviest fighting we've seen against the Clans. You've lost a close companion recently and your command has been badly hammered. Out of the forty 'Mechs in your command, thirteen are operational, and that's only in *your* very generous report of your unit's readiness. Another ten 'Mechs are salvageable, but they more closely resemble modern art than they do war machines. You lost fifteen of your pilots to death or injury and another eight will need time to heal up before they can step into a cockpit again. In short, your battalion is really just a reinforced company, and that's only your company. The rest of the Tenth Lyran Guards is in equally dismal shape."

"What are you saying?"

"I'm saying you need a rest. You need the time to rebuild your unit." Morgan put as sympathetic an expression on his face as possible. "You need to go with your unit to Port Moseby."

"No, dammit, Morgan, I can't." Victor poked himself in the chest with his thumb. "All my life everyone has looked at me in one of two ways: either I'm the 'little Prince' who is to be humored, or I'm the Fox's heir and therefore to be feared. Everyone has supposed, because I'm so small, that I have a Napoleon complex and am a hideous warmonger. Every time I tried to do the sort of thing my father or you would do, they say I'm a tyrant throwing a tantrum. I hate that!

"The other side of it is that everyone compares me with my father. If I show any weakness at all, if I do not do everything my father has done, I am to be pitied because I cannot possibly live up to his legendary exploits. Any failure is taken as a disaster because I'm the one who is supposed to lead after my father. Yes, he's a hard act to follow, but I know I can do it. I will do it, and do it very well, but I have to be given the chance. Sure, I expect people to look at me and say, 'That's Hanse Davion's son,' but just for once I'd like to hear them say, 'The First Prince is Victor Davion's father.' "

"Which is precisely why you have to go to Port Moseby with your troops." Morgan opened his hands. "If you don't, you seem callous and indifferent to the fate of your troops. The Tenth Lyran Guards, which is a unit that has long been commanded by individuals destined to be the Archon of the Lyran Commonwealth, is very important in the Lyran psyche. The last Steiner to lead them used that unit to destroy a Kurita offensive during the Fourth Succession War. He and his people knew it was a suicide mission and it's said the commander turned himself over to Theodore Kurita in return for the safe repatriation of the Tenth Lyran Guard survivors.

"Katrina Steiner, your grandmother, rebuilt the Tenth Lyran Guards around that core of survivors, and once again they became a force to be feared. Your command of a battalion in the Guards is taken as a positive sign of stability within the Federated Commonwealth, and the victory at Twycross was doubly special because the heir to the Lyran throne helped lead the Tenth in their defeat of the Clans."

Morgan fixed Victor with a chilling stare. "If you abandon your command, the Tenth Lyran Guards will feel they've been dishonored. They'll know you consider them a failure and their morale will never recover. If you stay with them, if you show them your determination, that unit will bounce back stronger than before. If not, the only thing that will be said of the Tenth is that they were never the same after a *true* Steiner led them on their last mission."

The logic of Morgan's argument hammered at Victor. As much as he wanted back into the fight against the Clans, he felt a bond with the Tenth Lyran Guards that he could not easily sunder. *They did everything for me, gave everything in the fight on Alyina. I do owe them my support.* His hands knotted and unknotted, then he slowly brought them together at his back.

"As much as I hate it, you have shown me the error in my thoughts. I thank you." Victor leaned forward, gripping the back of the chair in front of him. "Dammit, Morgan, you have to remember what it was like knowing you could contribute to the war, yet having to wait for what seems like an eternity to do it."

The Marshal sat back in his chair and nodded. "I do remember, Victor, which is why I know you will survive it. During the Fourth Succession War, I wanted a command so bad I felt like I was on fire. Your father was adamant about not allowing me into combat because, until you came along, I was his heir. While I took great pride in that fact, I wanted to prove to him I could be a capable leader."

The older man smiled with satisfaction. "When he finally called me to him, he said it was a mission he could entrust to no one else. No matter what it was or how many men and 'Mechs I'd have to accomplish it, I would have said yes."

Victor shared Morgan's smile. "That was the Liao raid on Kathil and your raid on the Capellan homeworld to pull Justin Allard and Candace Liao out, right?"

"Right." Morgan shook his head slowly as he remembered the battles. "I was as eager as you were, Victor, and I took hideous chances. I was lucky because the Capellan forces were not the Clans, or else I might have ended up in your position. But my point is this: you have to wait with your troops and prepare them for whatever mission you will be given. I don't know if you'll be brought back to the front, or if you'll be the only unit in the path of the Wolves. You are not being punished or safeguarded. Most other commanders would look upon a break as a reward for having accomplished so much."

Victor wearily hung his head. "I suppose you're right." *I wonder how far I can push this?* "I'm willing to acquiesce to your orders, but on one condition."

Morgan raised an eyebrow. "Conditions on orders? I thought you hated personal favors."

"This isn't for me, Morgan, it's for my troops." His eyes took on a devilish glint. "I want my battalion to be the first one refitted. I want to be able to start my people training immediately. I also want my battalion brought up to an operational strength of fifty BattleMechs."

Morgan steepled his fingers. "What is it you have in mind, Victor?"

"The reason we keep getting pounded by the Clans has to do more with our doctrine of war than it does with their superior weaponry. The most trouble they have had in the past is when they come up against irregular forces. We have tried to face them straight up in battle, and though we can win, as the Kuritans proved on Luthien, the cost of such victories is too great.

"I want to modify a reinforced battalion and train it specifically in tactics that will give us an edge against the Clans. I want my unit to become fast and adept at hit-and-run. We can wear them down, hitting them when and where they are not grouped in enough strength to damage us. We want to harass them.

"We'll be just like the Delta Company Andrew Redburn commanded during the Fourth Succession War." The Prince smiled sheepishly. "I was thinking of calling us the Revenants because we'd have returned from the dead to haunt the Clans."

"And you'd want to go back in at Alyina, right?"

Victor stiffened, then nodded slowly. "Am I that transparent?"

Morgan stood. Coming around from behind the desk, he clapped Victor on both shoulders. "Not transparent, just very much a missile with a hard lock onto its target. General Kaulkas warned me about your obsession."

"You'll give me the unit?"

The Marshal of the Federated Commonwealth nodded. "I will, but it is incumbent upon you, Victor Davion, to make sure your troops, your Revenants, are trained well enough so they do not become known as 'the Remnants.'"

"I will." Victor looked up. "And will you give us Alyina?"

"Perhaps." Morgan's eyes grew distant. "I think, though, you will find this war has more than one Alyina and you may be called upon to avenge more than just the death of Kai Allard."

9

Alyina
Trellshire, Jade Falcon Occupation Zone
8 February 3052

Kai Allard's axe swung down in a bright arc, snapping the log in two. Letting the axe remain in the scarred block, he bent down and tossed the two pieces on the cord stacked at the back of the Mahler home. "No, Erik, you can't persuade me to remain here."

The white-haired man shook his head. "You've been no trouble." He rubbed at his left shoulder, the one Kai knew bore a deep scar. "And I've been very grateful for the help you've been around here."

Kai recognized the undercurrent of concern in the man's voice, but he remained resolute. "You'll never know how much you've helped me over the past three weeks. Shelter and warm food have brought me back up to full strength, and this hard work seems to have put a bit more meat on my bones. That aside, however, both Dr. Lear and I agree that our presence is a direct threat to you and your wife. If the Clans catch us here . . ."

Mahler shook his head to deny the truth in Kai's words, but Kai saw the man's eyes grow distant. "The Clans have all but stopped their activity in this sector. The world has been pacified. You could stay here."

Kai wrenched the axe free of the block and set another half-log on the wooden stump. "You know as well as I that Dr. Lear and I have responsibilities to our commands."

Crack. Wood cartwheeled off the block as the axe clove through it. "You also already know far more about us than the Clans will think coincidental. For one thing," Kai said, wiping sweat from his brow with the back of his left forearm, "you know I'm not Dave Jewell."

Mahler crossed his arms defensively across his chest. "And even if I knew who you truly are, why would I not help you?" His fingers undid the buttons on his red-and-black checked flannel shirt. He pulled it back to reveal the white slash of scar across his left shoulder. "The Dragons did this at Styx when they were trying to take Melissa Steiner from the *Silver Eagle.* The Kell Hounds saved us, and your uncle was one of them. I don't forget debts easily."

A knot formed in the pit of Kai's stomach. For the last month, despite being light years away from home, trapped on a hostile planet with no resources, Kai had felt very much alive. Dave Jewell's identity had suited him well because it freed him of his responsibility as an Allard and as a Liao. It had also relieved him of the painful feeling that he had let his family down, along with the vast pressure he always felt to succeed. That old weight came crashing down again with a vengeance, however, as Erik Mahler reminded Kai of the heroic legacy his family had bequeathed him.

"That is not a debt you owe me, Erik Mahler. Your defense of Melissa Steiner a quarter-century ago is an act that I must reward by removing the danger of the Clans discovering that you have sheltered the enemy." Again Kai set up and split a log. "Having pierced the secret of my identity, you know I have a duty to communicate back to Prince Davion, and you know I cannot and will not let anything prevent me from acquitting that duty."

Mahler hesitated for a moment, then nodded slowly. "You are correct. I knew that all along. I would not have asked you to stay, knowing what you had to do, but I felt I had to make the offer, and my wife already worries about you and Dr. Lear." He tugged his shirt back into place and rebuttoned it. "Are you sure it is wise to take her with you?"

"I would prefer to travel alone, for speed and to minimize risk, but she will not stay here to jeopardize you." Kai placed the quarter-logs on the pile. "Besides, having someone along who is well-versed in medicine might help get me through any trouble we run into."

"That's not what I meant." Mahler snorted a bit of a laugh

and shook his head. "After the first night here, you two have barely exchanged more than formal greetings. Your relationship doesn't seem up to the difficulties you will face if you follow through with your plan."

"Perhaps you are correct." Kai heaved his shoulders and sighed. "But I do not believe Dr. Lear will hamper my efforts. She is smart and competent, and I could not ask for more in a traveling companion."

"Indeed? Then you are a rare man, Dave Jewell." Mahler's gray eyes narrowed. "I, for one, would want a companion who did not hate me."

Despite their protestations to the contrary, Erik Mahler insisted upon driving Kai and Deirdre to the nearby city of Dove Costoso in his hovertruck. Hilda packed them a picnic lunch and filled Kai's knapsack with some civilian clothing she'd tailored to fit the two of them. When Kai refused to take anything that he'd not brought to them, Hilda assured him she had removed any tags that might let the Clans trace their benefactors. Kai knew instantly that she would brook no argument, so he acquiesced.

Secretly he was very pleased with everything the Mahlers had done for him and Deirdre. Hilda had stripped the chemical lines out of his cooling vest, leaving it a warm, bulletproof garment Kai could wear unnoticed under one of Erik's cast-off woolen shirts. She also let out the seams on some trousers so Kai could wear his 'Mech boots beneath them without attracting too much attention. She'd even removed all traces of his and Dave Jewell's name tags from the clothes he had carried with him.

Erik and Kai labored to fill the bed of the hovertruck with a blocky table Erik had made and some firewood Kai had chopped. With Erik, Deirdre, and Kai crammed into the front seat, they would look like a family from the outlying area heading into Dove Costoso to do some selling in the farmers' market there. That was their cover story, so Kai hid his needle pistol under the bench seat in the unlikely event a patrol became suspicious.

Hilda, her eyes glistening with tears, nodded approval. "You can always come back here, you know, if you must."

"I know," Deirdre said, putting her arms around the older woman and hugging her tightly, "I cannot thank you enough for all your help."

"Just be safe, Deirdre. That's all I ask."

Kai also hugged Hilda and gave her a kiss on the cheek. "Thank you very much, *Frau* Mahler. We will be fine."

"Send word, if you can."

"We will," Kai told her, but both of them knew it was a lie.

Erik's route to Dove Costoso took them straight across the Bolliti swamp. "For the two of you to have traveled this way on foot would have been disastrous. If the alligators and quicksand missed you, the *brutto vapore* would surely have ended your little trek."

Deirdre frowned and squirmed between the two men. "Ugly vapor?"

"Clouds of insects that live in the swamp. If you've not got a thick hide or fur, they hit you with a narcotic sting, then implant eggs. The victim generally remains unconscious for the two days it takes for hatching, then the pupae leave for the swamp to continue their breeding cycle."

Kai felt decidedly queasy at the thought of bugs chewing their way free of his body. "Not a high survival rate on hosts, I take it?"

"Nope." Erik shook his head. "Of course, they tell me one of the Clan Elementals survived a hatching, but that's just a rumor."

Free of the swamp, the hovertruck started up the gradually sloping plains that led to the Riscaldamento Mountains, where Dove Costoso nestled in the foothills. In the predawn, its lights were the only signs of human habitation until the sun completed its slow climb over the mountains. With the coming of dawn, Kai could make out occasional homesteads similar to that of the Mahlers. The city itself, for that matter, seemed small by any true civilized standard.

"I have a question." Deirdre chewed her lower lip. "We're going to Dove Costoso to use its ComStar facility to send a message to New Avalon. That would be very expensive, but we don't have the money to send such a message. What do you plan to do about that?"

Kai shifted in his seat. "The message will be expensive, but there are ways to get one sent without money."

She cut him off. "Oh, forgive me, I had forgotten your word should be considered golden to ComStar."

The oblique attack on his nobility set Kai back for a moment. "Actually, Doctor, I'm surprised you don't realize I am in no hurry to use my family's resources when the Federated Commonwealth itself has provided us with a means for sending a message." He frowned. "Besides, I would just as soon avoid broadcasting who I am, for the time being."

"You do well to ward your family's reputation of infallibility, Leftenant."

"It's not that." Kai felt a shiver run down his spine. "Something is wrong. The Clans knew Victor was on Alyina and they went directly after him. I don't want to put myself in a position to be used against my father or Hanse Davion."

Mahler steered the hovertruck around a flock of sheep crossing the roadway. "So you will continue to be Dave Jewell?"

Kai shook his head. "Under the circumstances, I don't think identifying myself with the Federated Commonwealth troops is a good idea, either." Kai caught his reflection in the hovertruck's side mirror. "With my black hair and oriental eyes, I should pass easily for a Combine expatriate living here. How does Kevin Abunai sound?"

"It works, but I still don't understand how or why ComStar will send a message from this Kevin Abunai to Hanse Davion."

Kai smiled. "The Federated Commonwealth has set up a number of blind accounts with ComStar, as have corporations and other organizations. By knowing the account number, we may send a message to New Avalon and the Prince pays for it. Depending on how the account was set up, the message will be considered priority or some level of routine below that."

"What? I never heard of that." Deirdre frowned angrily. "Why wasn't I informed of this secret number system—or is it reserved for blue bloods?"

Mahler raised an eyebrow. "It is reserved for officers of your rank and above, so you *were* informed, Doctor, unless you were not trained in survival and evasion techniques."

Deirdre blushed. "I was at a medical conference when I was supposed to take that course. That's not what my records reveal, but . . ."

"Doctors are seldom asked to perform some of the sillier training the rest of us endure." Kai smiled reassuringly at her. "It's no problem. Do you know your unit designator?"

"1024."

"And your rank code and Commonwealth identification number?"

"G15a and 4432-44323-19826."

Mahler smiled. "Then you know what number to give ComStar for sending a message back home. As a G15a, your message would head out at a near-priority level, if I remember correctly. Isn't that right, Leftenant?"

"Huh? Right." Kai blinked twice. "Yes, it would be a quick message."

Deirdre looked over at him. "What?"

"Nothing." Kai looked down, refusing to meet her gaze. What she'd just told him was as revealing as it was puzzling. Her personnel file had said she was from Odell, a world in the Crucis March of the Federated Commonwealth. Her identification number, however, began with a 4, which Kai knew meant she'd been born in the Capellan March of the Federated Commonwealth, well before the war that sliced the Capellan Confederation in half.

Does her hatred of me have something to do with the war? Hanse Davion sent my father to spy on Maximilian Liao, but his cover eventually had him directing much of the Capellan war effort against the Federated Suns. Did she lose a relative in that war? Is that why she loathes me?

Erik slowed the hovertruck as it joined other outland traffic heading into the city. "I will take you into Dove Costoso and drop you within four blocks of the ComStar station. It's still located in temporary headquarters because the city refused to rezone unless ComStar gave them preferential rates on communication. Still, all their equipment works, or so I have been told."

"Thank God for small wonders." Nearing the end of the journey, Kai felt reluctant to leave Erik Mahler on his own. "Look, Erik, after you drop us, just get the hell out of the city. I've got a bad feeling about things."

"Don't worry, Mr. Abunai. I picked you and your wife up here on the road and brought you into town. I don't speak Japanese and your German stinks." He scratched at his left shoulder. "Don't like you Dracos anyway, y'know. Maybe I'll report you myself."

Kai nodded solemnly. *"Domo arigato."* Reaching under the bench, he slid his pistol into the pack at his feet. "All set."

"Here you are."

Kai opened the truck door as the vehicle slowed to a halt. He helped Deirdre out, then closed the door with a thump. "What can I say?"

Erik shook his head and smiled. "Once a MechWarrior, always a MechWarrior. God be with you."

Kai slung the pack on his back, then he and Deirdre headed down the road, finding the ComStar facility easily enough. ComStar was currently ensconced in a long, narrow building in the middle of a street bounded by debris-strewn alleyways on both sides. A wrought iron fence topped with razorwire warded the front yard, but the gate stood open. Only a camera mounted on the wall of the building watched it.

To Kai the building looked bigger and more ostentatious than other ComStar satellite facilities he'd seen in the past. "Why would ComStar take this building? A storefront is more their style in a tiny city like this."

Deirdre shrugged. "I don't know." She stared up at the edifice and shivered. "I'm not sure I like it."

"Me neither," said Kai, "but we've got no choice but to go in."

Deirdre trailed Kai as he crossed the street and mounted the steps to the building. Before he could push the buzzer, the door opened and a yellow-robed Acolyte greeted them with a smile. "Welcome to the House of Blake. How may we be of service?"

The Acolyte then waved them into a round foyer whose floor was a checkerboard pattern of black and white marble. A corridor led deeper into the building, cutting beneath the sweeping, curved stairway along the far wall. To the right and left, large double doors opened onto beautifully appointed rooms furnished with antiques. Overhead, hanging down from the second-story ceiling, a crystal chandelier provided light for the foyer.

"I am Kevin Abunai and this is Denise Stratford. We would like to speak with the Precentor for this station. We wish to send a message out through a receiver account."

The Acolyte bowed, his smile frozen in place. "Please, wait here."

He withdrew down the corridor, shutting a door behind him. The second the latch clicked shut, Deirdre turned on him. "Denise Stratford?" she hissed in an angry whisper. "How did you dream that up? Some spy trick?"

"Denise is close to your own name, promoting recognition. That's why I'm Kevin." Kai smiled sheepishly. "Stratford came from Stratford-upon-Avon, the home of . . ."

"Will Shakespeare, the author of King Lear." Her blue eyes sparkled, the anger slowly draining out of them. "Pretty quick, Kevin. Almost easy to remember."

"That's the idea." Kai looked around the foyer again. "ComStar's put a fair amount of money into refurbishing this place—if the condition of the neighborhood is any indication of how it must have looked before. Why waste the money if this is just temporary?"

"I don't know." Deirdre knelt and flaked a droplet of dried paint from the black marble wall edging. "This gold paint is recent and I don't remember a ComStar station in Dove Costoso *before* the invasion."

"Nor do I." Kai frowned. "I get the feeling this place is more of an embassy or government hall than any message-drop for ComStar."

The Acolyte's return cut off further speculation. "Demi-Precentor Khalsa will see you now." He pointed to a chair beside the front door. "You can leave your pack there. I will see to it that it is not disturbed."

Kai wanted to keep the pack with him, as it contained both the gun and the knife Victor had given him, but he could not risk attracting undue attention. "Thank you, Acolyte." He set it down and followed the man down the hall and into a large, walnut-paneled office.

Rising up from behind his desk, a scarlet-swathed, rotund man extended his hand toward his visitors. "Welcome, welcome. The Peace of Blake be with you." He shook Deirdre's hand, whispering, "Be seated, my dear." Then he enfolded Kai's hand in both of his and gave the MechWarrior a smile that Kai found uncomfortably familiar.

Kai sat down next to Deirdre and felt pleased when she slipped her left hand into his right. Khalsa lowered his bulk into a huge chair, then leaned back until the light from above glowed off his shaved pate. "How can I help you, Mr. Abunai and Ms. Stratford?"

"As I told the Acolyte, we need to send a message."

"Well, that's what we're here for." Khalsa swung the monitor for his data station around so Kai could see nothing of the screen. He drew a keyboard toward him. "To whom is this message addressed?"

"Consolidated Manufacturing NA." Kai smiled as he gave the demi-Precentor a military-intelligence dummy corporation name. "It needs to go to the central office."

Khalsa arched a black eyebrow. "That's on New Avalon. This will be a costly message to send."

"I have a number." Kai closed his eyes. "1024-G15a-4432-44323-19826." He opened his eyes again as Khalsa punched the numbers into the computer. "I think that should be enough to get the message off."

Khalsa nodded. "That is a Davion military code."

Kai felt a microtremor pass through Deirdre's hand. "Is it?"

"I am afraid it is. And, of course, Consolidated is a FedCom Milint cut-out." Khalsa frowned as the light reflected in his eyes told Kai screens of data were scrolling by. Like a teacher disappointed with a student's improbable excuse, the demi-Precentor shook his head. "Really now, you shouldn't have tried to fool us. We know who you are."

Kai raised an eyebrow. "What difference does it make? I have given you an account number. You should accept my message and send it."

The ComStar official shook his head. His jowls jiggled, making him look more like a basset hound than a man. "I'm afraid you don't understand. The Clans own this world now, and ComStar is administering it for them." The door behind Khalsa opened and two men with automatic rifles entered the room. "We will have to detain you until an escort arrives to take you to our holding facility."

Deirdre glanced at Kai. "I thought the account code wasn't supposed to betray us."

Khalsa smiled coyly. "It didn't, Doctor Lear. You did. You were betrayed by your beauty: I recall seeing you at a concert here in Dove Costoso a week before Christmas. I had hoped for a chance to meet you and have kept an eye out for your name on the lists of detainees we have gathered. I could never let someone like you be billeted with mere warriors. That would never do."

Kai looked over at her. "Glad to see the Alyina branch of your fan club in such good hands."

Deirdre's eyes asked forgiveness, and Kai gave her hand what he hoped was a reassuring squeeze.

The demi-Precentor stood and bid the two ROM agents forward with a flick of his fat hand. "Please forgive the shoddy nature of our accommodations, but I cannot afford to take any chances with Dr. Lear just yet." Khalsa tapped the screen of his monitor. "Your file was one of those we recovered from some damaged Davion computer equipment. Says here, Doctor, that you scored two points shy of perfect on your survival and evasion course. I'm afraid it's the dungeon for you until more suitable arrangements can be made."

Kai let her hand drop. "Surely you don't have to put me away with her. I'm harmless."

Again the demi-Precentor looked at his screen, but ruefully shook his head. "Do not try to play innocent with me. Despite your diligent attempts to erase all traces of your identity, we know who you are. We are too smart for you. You cannot fool ComStar."

"I suppose not."

Khalsa nodded sincerely as a ROM guard prodded Kai with a rifle. "You suppose correctly. Tracing you through the contents of your rucksack was simple. The holodisks were sent through ComStar, after all." The demi-Precentor sighed wearily. "ComStar does not appreciate deception. I suggest that be something you consider long and hard while awaiting transport to the reeducation camp, Mr. Jewell."

10

JumpShip **Dire Wolf,** *Pre-assault Orbit*
Hyperion, Free Rasalhague Republic
8 February 3052

Phelan Wolf looked across the room, drawing in a deep breath, then trying to expand his chest and look more massive as he exhaled. Dressed in a gray jumpsuit with a red dagger-star on its right shoulder and the red and black patch of the Thirteenth Wolf Guards on its left, he knew the uniform, at least, was impressive. In the three weeks since learning of Cyrilla's death, he'd trained hard and honed himself to a fine edge, but it might all be for naught in this first round of the Bloodname battling.

His first opponent, a huge Elemental, nodded slowly. With his clothing peeled to the waist, the man's bronzed flesh looked as if it had been spray-painted over veins and bulging muscles. His right hand twitched and Phelan caught the flash of a silver medallion. As the Elemental's hand closed over it, the MechWarrior had no doubt the man could have bent the coin in half without raising a sweat.

Phelan turned his own coin over in his right hand. On the head it displayed the Wolf Clan crest: a wolf's-head with narrowed eyes and high, alert ears. On the reverse, as he turned it over, Phelan saw the name "Ward" emblazoned on a scroll. Beneath that, this name, "Phelan Wolf," was inscribed with the date.

Phelan looked up at the Elemental again and took no comfort in the man's evil smile.

Natasha slapped Phelan lightly on the back. "Can't let him get to you. He's just posturing, because if you win the decision, you'll pound him flat."

The younger MechWarrior frowned. "I am not yet clear on this. If I win the decision, I choose the nature of our battle, but he chooses where it will occur, correct?"

Natasha nodded. "If you win, you choose to fight in your 'Mech. He'll don his armor and unless he's very good *and* very lucky, you'll smear him all over the battlefield."

"Hardly fair."

The Black Widow's eyes narrowed. "Fair has nothing to do with Bloodname battles. You are fighting for an honor that knows no equal in the Successor States or beyond them! Defeat him, defeat the rest of those you face, and you prove yourself one of the ultimate warriors in House Ward."

Her fierce expression shifted down into a wry grin. "Besides, if he wins the decision, you know he'll choose to fight you bare-handed. You're no slouch in unarmed combat, but . . ."

Looking at his opponent, Phelan saw a pec heave like a tectonic plate in an earthquake. "Yeah, I don't want to get near him outside my 'Mech, either." He shuddered slightly. "I surrender three decimeters in height and at least thirty-five kilos to that clown."

Natasha winced. "Best not call him a clown until you beat him."

"Good point."

Back beyond Natasha, Phelan saw the small visitor's gallery slowly fill with his friends. Evantha Fetladral, the Elemental with a long red queue hanging from her nearly shaved pate, sat next to Ragnar and appeared to be explaining the whole procedure to him. Next to Ragnar sat a small man with an oversized head topped by a shock of blond hair. Carew, like Phelan, was unblooded, so he listened intently to Evantha's explanation of the ceremonies. In the same way that Evantha and others had been bred for the massive size Elementals would need, Carew's smaller size had been deemed desirable for aerospace fighter-pilots.

Last into the box walked a tall, slender woman whose white hair was cut boyishly short. Ranna smiled at Phelan, her blue eyes flashing encouragement. Phelan returned her smile and felt his spirits buoy. Ranna sat down next to Carew.

Natasha passed a hand in front of Phelan's face, breaking off his stare. "Think about her later."

Phelan smiled mischievously. "Sorry, but you and your granddaughter are mesmerizingly beautiful."

The Black Widow shook her head. "Fine, dream if you want to, but when I was in your shoes, I was trying to figure out how to even the odds in a straight-up fight with an Elemental."

That sobered Phelan. "What did you do?"

Natasha shrugged. "I won the decision."

The MechWarrior turned the warm coin over in his hand, then stopped playing with it as ilKhan Ulric Kerensky stepped into the room and took up a position in the center. Natasha gave Phelan a pat on the back, then retreated. The Elemental's friends and supporters also withdrew, leaving the combatants alone with the ilKhan.

As Ulric drew himself up to full height, his white hair and goatee seemed to glow beneath the harsh lights overhead. "I am the Oathmaster and accept responsibility for representing House Ward here. Do you concur in this?"

"Seyla," Phelan breathed solemnly.

"Seyla," echoed the Elemental.

"Then what transpires here will bind us all until we all shall fall." The ilKhan nodded respectfully. "You represent the best the House of Ward has to offer the Wolf Clan. Yet it is not for the Wolf Clan that you fight today, it is for the right and honor of bearing the name Ward. This name is exalted, as were the names of all who remained loyal to the dream Aleksandr Kerensky had for his people. Do you understand this?"

"Seyla."

"And in accepting your part in this battle, do you understand that you sanctify, with your blood, Nicholas Kerensky's determination to forge the Clans into the pinnacle of human development? That you have been chosen to participate already marks you as elite, but victory here will rightly place you among the few who exist at the zenith of all the Clans hold sacred."

Phelan nodded solemnly. "Seyla."

Ulric looked at the Elemental. "You are Dean and you have seen twenty-seven years. Why are you worthy?"

Muscles rippled like molten steel as the Elemental stood taller and answered in a deep bass. "I have been nominated to this Bloodname by my elders because of my bravery in the conquest of Rasalhague and the taking of Satalice. I have consistently tested out at the top of my sibko and have never known defeat in single combat."

Ulric nodded stiffly, clearly pleased with the accomplishments of a Wolf, but reluctant to show any sign that could be interpreted as favoritism. "And you, Phelan Wolf, have seen twenty years. Why are you worthy?"

Phelan, as he had been coached by Natasha, raised his head and spoke in a clear voice. "I was chosen by Cyrilla Ward to be heir to this Bloodname. Captured and made a bondsman, I was adopted into the Warrior Caste after proving my worthiness for that honor. I trained and tested out as a Warrior. Single handedly I conquered Gunzburg, and on Satalice I captured Prince Ragnar of Rasalhague. For these things I have been chosen."

Again Ulric nodded formally. "The heroism and courage displayed by both Warriors have been established and verified. Your claims are not without substance. No matter what fate you meet in this battle, the brightness of your light will not be diminished." The ilKhan took a step forward and beckoned both men toward him. "Present the tokens of your legitimate right to participate here."

The two combatants solemnly lifted their coins like holy relics and approached him. As they did so, a small panel slid back in the floor and a conical stand mounted on a slender post rose up through it. Where the cone joined the post, it had been fitted with a section of clear plastic pipe that could be slid free. On opposite sides of the cone, Phelan saw a slot wide enough to accept his coin. On the part nearest to the ilKhan, he noticed a small button, but could not puzzle out its purpose. The shape of the whole device reminded Phelan of a Nagelring demonstration of how gravity wells operate.

Ulric accepted their coins and set each one in a slot. "Though we train to be able to cope with the myriad situations of combat, we cannot control everything. A warrior worthy of a Bloodname must be able to rise above adversity to defeat the superior foe, even when at a gross disadvantage. The horrible chaos of war is reflected in this Trial of Bloodright.

"When one coin has successfully stalked the other and they complete their transit through this cone, the hunting coin will be superior. The Warrior will win the choice of style for the fight. The owner of the inferior coin will then decide the venue for the fight. In this way, each will fight on a battlefield not wholly of his choosing. Do you understand this?"

"Seyla."

As the last echoes of that word reverberated off the walls, the ilKhan pressed the button, releasing both coins. They slid down independent tracks and started rolling down the inside of the cone. Faster and faster they went, picking up speed as they sank lower and lower into the narrowing cone.

Phelan watched in both fear and excitement. *Just like the gravity-well demo at the Nagelring! I'd levitate my coin higher if I could, but gravity is like death and taxes.* Somehow he was sure his coin was winning the race, thereby ceding the decision to Dean. Then, as the coins started their descent into the post, they slammed into one another in a ringing collision and dropped from sight.

The two coins clunked down into the plastic pipe. Ulric carefully slid the clear section free, holding it out so all could see no sleight of hand had changed the outcome of the choice. His slender fingers plucked the top coin from the vessel and flipped it over to read the name. "Dean, you are the hunter."

Dean cracked his knuckles and grinned confidently. "The hunter sees no reason for an augmented fight. This pup has boasted beating an Elemental in a fist fight. Let us see how he does against a Ward."

Ulric looked at Phelan. "The style has been decided. Where will you be hunted?"

Phelan swallowed hard and saw his chances for victory getting sucked down into a gravity well. He started to open his mouth, then snapped it shut. He gave Dean a savage stare and smiled slowly.

Ulric watched him closely. "Phelan, where will you be hunted?"

Without breaking eye contact with Dean, Phelan raised his right hand and pointed upward. "Out there."

The DropShip's hold had been stripped of every last bit of equipment, leaving it a tall, empty arena for his fight with Dean. Aside from the exterior bulkhead, which gently curved inward to where the ship narrowed at the upper decks, the walls were normal and the angles all 90 degrees.

Only scuffed-paint markings on the deck and oddly shaped stains from 'Mech-coolant spills hinted at this area's original function in the DropShip.

Never seen a 'Mech bay this empty. Standing there, clad only in a pair of the shorts he'd normally use in a 'Mech cockpit, Phelan had also never felt so naked. His choice of fighting in the zero gravity of space certainly helped neutralize the Elemental's strength, but it brought a whole array of other variables into play. All things being equal, he still wished they'd have let him wear the pistol he usually did when in a 'Mech cockpit.

Have to remember, equal and opposite reactions. As a child traveling with a mercenary military unit, Phelan had spent much of his youth bouncing around in the holds of DropShips in zero gravity. He couldn't remember ever fighting for his life in zero-G, though he did recall a couple of fierce wrestling matches that gamboled otterlike through the air of a hold. *Not quite the same, I fear.*

Phelan felt the ship tremble as the pilot fired the forward retrorockets. Grabbing a nearby stanchion, Phelan fought the tendency to float up off the deck. A second blast of retros brought the ship to a standstill in space.

The droplet of sweat that had collected at the tip of his nose jumped off and floated ball-like toward the upper deck.

It still amazed Phelan that the Clans would go to the incredible expense necessary to create this battleground for Dean and him. Here they were in a combat zone, preparing to invade Hyperion, and they cleared the 'Mechs from a deck of an assault DropShip. They detached the ship from the *Dire Wolf* and let it burn tons of fuel just to accommodate a one-on-one brawl by two men scrapping for a title.

But it's more than a title, he reminded himself. He knew the Bloodname held enormous power for the Clan Warriors. Winning one would assure the use of the Warrior's DNA in the Clan breeding program. It also gave the victorious Warrior a seat on the Clan Council and made him eligible for election as one of the two Khans of the Wolf clan. And, as in Cyrilla's case, a Bloodname could even provide a way to be useful to the Clans when one's military career was long over.

The Captain's voice crackled through the loudspeakers mounted in the interior bulkhead. "The ship is at zero acceleration. You have your battlefield. Skill, Warriors."

"Phelan Wolf, I will make this fast for you." Dean floated gently above the deck, drifting toward him like a ghost. The Elemental balled his fists, tensing every muscle up and down his arms into hard knots. "A freebirth like you is a disgrace to House Ward. Cyrilla must have lost her sense long ago."

Phelan bristled at the derision in Dean's voice, but forced himself to smile. "Is that so, Dean?" The MechWarrior opened his arms wide. "If you want me, come down and get me."

It took Dean about three seconds to fully comprehend his situation. He looked impressive floating there, but without propulsion gear, he could do little to affect his course of travel or speed. In a frantic effort to do anything at all, Dean began to flail about, but that only started him in a slow roll up and away from Phelan.

Pushing down on the stanchion, Phelan squatted with his legs coiled beneath him. With the swiftness of a striking snake, he kicked off and drove both his fists into the thick muscles over Dean's kidneys. The Elemental groaned with the impact, but was too intent on twisting his body around to pay much attention.

Using his opponent like a vaulting horse, Phelan spun around at an angle and drifted back down toward the deck. Most of his momentum had passed into Dean, sending the Elemental careening, but he maintained enough of it to get near the deck and bulkhead. Bending his legs to cushion his landing, Phelan prepared himself for whatever strategy Dean decided to employ in counterattack.

The Elemental smacked into the upper deck on his right side, but Phelan thought it probably made Dean mad more than it hurt. The Elemental grabbed on to a ribbed girder with a vise-grip, then snarled at his foe. "That is the sole attack you will launch on me."

Sidling over to another bulkhead support, Phelan shrugged again. "I am all yours, Dean."

The Elemental launched himself at Phelan, his powerful legs accelerating him smoothly. Fists cocked, he came in like a rocket. His grin grew as he sailed in, then faded when Phelan sprang up and away from the floor. With no target to cushion his charge, Dean crashed into the deck.

Phelan retained his grip on the reinforcement girder and his leap took him up and to the right. He let himself swing all the way around so his feet his the bulkhead on the other side of the girder. Clinging to the wall, he pushed off again and reversed his swing, snapping his heels down into Dean's shoulder blades. He jammed the larger man into the deck, then kicked off from the Elemental's broad back and twisted into the air.

Dean pounded a fist into the deck, but grabbed the reinforcement bar as he started to drift up. He spun quickly, spraying blood globules from his nose and mashed lips through the air. "Damn you, Phelan. Stand still and fight like a Warrior."

Reaching his hands above his head to soften the impact with the upper deck, Phelan laughed aloud. "Stop thinking of me as a freebirth, Dean. I am a Warrior and a member of House Ward. Think any less of me than you would think of Vlad, and you don't stand a chance."

"I will crush you!"

Phelan pointed at him. "Put it this way, Dean: I outbid you and now you have to fight at a disadvantage."

Part of that taunt got through to Dean. He slowly began to ascend, keeping one hand on the reinforcement girder. He reached out with his free hand and clawed menacingly at the air as he worked his way upward. "When I get my hands on you, it will be all over." Dean's derisive snort blew a spray of blood down his chest.

Phelan's mouth went sour. His early attacks had taken advantage of Dean's ignorance of the battlefield and his lack of respect for Phelan's fighting skills. Evantha had put Phelan through his paces in unarmed combat training, but most other MechWarriors disdained fistfighting. Though he had hoped, especially with Dean's dive, that the Elemental might knock himself out on the deck, he knew that was unlikely.

Phelan knew that zero gravity destroyed the hideous hitting power in Dean's muscles. At the same time, it also made any attack Phelan might choose less effective. Dean was not going to let Phelan trick him again, nor would he give him another missile-like attack.

The only way to beat Dean was to do what he wanted: get in close. Though Phelan's rational mind acknowledged the wisdom of that strategy, something in his soul recoiled at the idea of grappling with that monster. Blood and sweat glistened on Dean's body, and muscles moved smoothly beneath taut flesh.

He's a python waiting to crush me!

As Dean gathered his legs beneath him to spring, Phelan gently pushed off the upper deck and started to float down. Dean released his grip on the reinforcement girder and shifted around to push himself straight at Phelan. He launched cautiously and kept his arms outstretched expectantly.

Phelan whipped his legs up and tucked his torso down into a ball. The movement started him spinning in a backward somersault, but he kicked out just as Dean came in range. His feet clipped Dean's left ear with a glancing blow, killing Dean's downward momentum and starting him into a flat spin. At the same time, Phelan tossed his head back and arched his spin so he came out of his tumble with Dean's legs in easy reach.

Phelan grabbed Dean's ankle and pulled himself up. Twisting the larger man, and starting them both to spin, Phelan used the Elemental's waistband to haul himself higher up, then settled on Dean's back like a leech. He wrapped his legs around the man's middle, then snaked his left arm around the man's bull neck.

The blow to his head had dazed Dean, but he came out of it full of fight. Immediately he tried to jam an elbow back at Phelan, but his own broad frame made the blow miss wide. Still, it imparted a twist to the two of them, setting them spinning crazily through the hold. Dean's left hand tore at Phelan's arm, but the MechWarrior held on tightly.

As soon as he realized Phelan was not trying to break his neck, and had failed to crush his windpipe, the Elemental shifted the focus of his attack. He kicked his legs to increase the spin and bring them closer to a bulkhead. His nostrils flared with exertion and blood splashed down on Phelan's arm. He smashed his fists into Phelan's legs, punishing the MechWarrior for his audacity.

Phelan pulled his legs free and twisted up and away from Dean's torso. He tightened his grip, determined not to lose it. Dean reached up and grabbed at Phelan's head. Phelan ducked it down closer to Dean's head, then tensed his stomach muscles and brought his right knee down into Dean's spine.

"Arrgghhh!" Breath hissed sharply from Dean's mouth. "Idiot, you can't even choke me right!"

Before Phelan could reply, the rotation caused by his knee in Dean's back brought the Elemental's legs within striking distance of the upper deck. Dean kicked off hard, shooting them both down at the deck. They hit solidly, Dean's bulk crushing Phelan against the floor. They drifted up again, but Dean kicked off and sent them at another bulkhead.

Again they hit, with Dean's shoulder battering its way into Phelan's ribs. The MechWarrior groaned aloud and the Elemental managed a harsh laugh. "Weakling! Kill me, break my neck or I crush you!"

"Not here to kill you, Dean. Just here for the ride."

"Then you get your wish."

Dean managed to grab a girder and whipped his back against the bulkhead, hammering Phelan into it. He reared back to do the same thing again, but Phelan planted his right leg firmly against the wall. Dean pulled his own body back into Phelan's knee, which tore a cough from the big man.

Instantly the giant tried to shift in Phelan's grip, then twisted forward, trying to smack Phelan's head against the girder. Phelan hunkered in close, keeping his head down. He tightened his grip one more time and braced himself against being driven back into the bulkhead, but Dean let go of the girder.

He knows! Dean clawed weakly at Phelan's arm. His fingers dug into the MechWarrior's muscles, leaving deep bruises, but Phelan never let go. It felt as if Dean were trying to strip his arm clean, layer by layer, of flesh and muscle, but Phelan clung to him like a tattoo. *It's too late, it has to be too late.*

Dean's struggles faltered, then ceased altogether. Phelan hung on for another ten seconds, then pushed the Elemental away from him. The man drifted up and away while Phelan grabbed the support girder. Phelan looked over toward the hatchway, then kicked off and floated over to it. He hit a button on the intercom. "It is over. Dean is defeated."

The hatchway slid open to reveal Natasha standing there. She smiled broadly. "I watched on the monitors. I was impressed, though you could have ended it sooner by breaking his neck."

"No need." A shudder rippled through the ship as the Captain applied some thrust. With the return of apparent gravity, Phelan suddenly felt the weakness in his legs and the weariness in his body. "There is no reason to kill when it's not necessary. My job was to defeat him, not kill him."

Phelan pointed to where Dean drifted down toward the

deck. "He kept trying to figure what I would do, based on what he would do. He thought I was choking him or trying to break his neck. But I was using the naked-strangle technique Evantha taught me, and I cut off his carotid artery. All I had to do was hang on while his brain shut down from lack of oxygen."

Natasha nodded approvingly. "You do know, don't you, that the other fifteen first-round fights in this Bloodname fight ended with eight fatalities."

Phelan frowned. "Vlad?"

"Won the decision and killed his Elemental opponent in twenty seconds." The Black Widow smiled slyly. "They'll say you don't have the heart to kill, and therefore, you'll lose."

"Good," Phelan growled as he scraped Dean's blood from his arm. "I hope everyone I face keeps chanting that like a mantra." He jerked a thumb at Dean's unconscious form. "It will only make my job that much easier."

"Seyla," Natasha breathed, and then followed Phelan out of the hold.

11

Dove Costoso, Alyina
Trellshire, Jade Falcon Occupation Zone
8 February 3052

Kai Allard-Liao, sandwiched between two ROM agents bearing automatic rifles, followed Demi-Precentor Khalsa down the creaking stairs to the basement. Pulling an old key from his pocket, the rotund ComStar official made a great show of unlocking a wooden door and swinging it open on squeaking, rusty hinges. The ROM agent behind Kai gave him a shove, sending the slender MechWarrior sprawling into a pile of clutter.

After crossing the threshold stiffly, but under her own power, Deirdre knelt beside Kai in the rectangle of light from the doorway.

Khalsa eclipsed the light. "I apologize for such messy surroundings, but we have not completed our renovations on this building." He flicked on the lights from a switch outside the room, then pointed to a waterpipe and spigot. "You can refresh yourselves there, and something in this midden should serve as a chamber pot if you need such. The Com Guards have already dispatched a squad to take custody of you, so your wait should be no more than twenty-four hours. Again, my apologies for your lodgings, but I cannot trust you otherwise."

Kai rolled to his knees. "Just wait until you get our return invitation to pay back your hospitality."

Khalsa smiled painfully. "Keep your wits about you, Mr.

Jewell. You'll need it." The demi-Precentor stepped back out of the doorway, and a ROM guard swung the door shut. With a grating creak and heavy thunk, the key turned in the lock.

Kai shook his head. "You have a score for survival and evasion exercises forged into your records and you just *had* to make it near perfect, eh?"

Deirdre shrugged. "The guy in administration and I were dating at the time. What can I say?"

" 'I'm sorry' would help." Kai stood slowly and raised a finger to his lips. He pointed to the floor above and tapped his ear. Deirdre's puzzled look faded quickly as she understood his warning about possible listening devices being present.

"I'm sorry."

"You're forgiven." Kai nodded. The single, bare bulb hanging down from the ceiling did little but cast a web of shadows radiating out from the center of the room. The basement walls were made of fitted stones of odd sizes, shapes, and colors. Four thick, wooden, support pillars split the room into nine areas, with the one in front of the door and the one in the middle the most clear. The rest were choked with trash piled up to two meters high—all of which Kai quickly characterized as broken.

"As long as we're going to be here for a while, we might as well make ourselves comfortable. Let's sort through this junk and see if we can find anything useful. We need a chamber pot, and anything passing for a mattress or cushions would help."

"Yes, sir." The mock seriousness in Deirdre's reply lacked the venom she usually directed at him. She held up a battered tin stewpot. "Personal hygiene objective obtained, sir."

Kai turned and raised an eyebrow. "You outrank me, remember, Doctor?"

She thought for a second, then shook her head. "Military situation, let the military handle it. Military and civilian don't mix well."

Sorting through a pile of miscellaneous tangles of wires, electric switches, and old paint cans, Kai disagreed. "As much as you hate war, Doctor, even you would have to admit military technology has positive benefits in the civilian sector."

The sarcastic tone in her voice lowered the temperature in the room by several degrees. "Is that so, Mr. Jewell?"

Kai coiled a frayed extension cord around his left forearm, then tossed the looped wire into the center of the floor. "Without a doubt. In your own field, you know that surgical procedures developed to deal with medical tragedies carry over into the civilian sector. Reconstructive surgery on military casualties has created techniques used to help people born with genetic defects. Even something as primitive as radar was developed for military use first, but it allows civilian air traffic and weather-detection."

"I'll concede you the latter point, Mr. Jewell, but not the first. It is well that the means for relieving the suffering and tragedy of a war victim can be put to good use, but I'd rather not have that suffering in the first place." She stopped and clawed away at a heavy piece of canvas. "Yeeeaaagh! What's this?"

At her yelp of horror, Kai leaped over a half-buried water heater and crossed to her side. She reached out for him and he felt her trembling. Though the thing was still partially concealed by the canvas, she hung back from a large, slug-like mass of tissue sagging at the base of the rough-stone wall. The exposed end looked hard and white and rectangular, but had nothing to indicate whether it was the head or tail.

"Is it alive or dead?" she asked in a whisper.

Kai yanked the rest of the canvas away. "Neither, I think." When the thing was more fully exposed to the light, Kai saw where long strings of tissue had been stripped away from the back. "This is myomer. Looks like a finger actuator from a 'Mech."

"That is myomer? I've never . . . I mean, the myomer I've used in surgery was different."

Kai nodded. "Yeah, it probably was. This is one of the artificial muscles used to move a 'Mech's finger, all right." He pointed at the serial number on the underside of the white insertion cap. "Came from a *Valkyrie*. This is the industrial-strength stuff. The myomer you use in surgery is manufactured differently and has to be layered in with real muscle tissue to be useful. In surgery the stuff is used more like rubber bands."

Folding her arms across her chest, Deirdre looked down at him. "When did you get a medical degree?"

"My . . . ," Kai hesitated, "friend's mother had breast cancer. She'd had some myomer replacements in her shoulder from an old war wound, and when they discovered the cancer they did a radical mastectomy. They rebuilt her pectoralis major with myomers. The doctors explained it to him and I was there." From the distant look in her eyes, Kai knew Deirdre realized he was speaking about his own mother.

"So what's this actuator doing here?"

The MechWarrior ran his hand across the area from which long strips of myomer fiber had been peeled away. "Offhand, I'd say whoever lived in this house before ran a little repair business on the side." He picked up a slender strand of wire with a bead on one end. "He may even have been a musician using myomers to replace broken guitar strings."

"What?"

Kai handed her the broken string he had found. "Myomers contract when an electric current is run through them. The contraction is instantaneous, but by varying the power level, you can control the amount of contraction and how quickly the fiber will lose its tension. It's a very exacting task, but with a computer chip and electric power, it's fairly easy. Some folks started experimenting with this variable-tension idea in things like tennis racquets, but it really only caught on with musicians. But with the need to rearm after the war, myomers have been hard to come by for this sort of application. Somehow the person who owned this house got an actuator and was making some money from it."

Deirdre's face solidified into a pitiless mask. "Don't tell me—another civilian benefit of military atrocities."

"Hey, I don't commit atrocities!"

Deirdre turned from him. "You kill people for a living."

Kai spun her around. "Listen to me, really *listen*! I do what I am called upon to do. If that results in the death of another human being, I regret it more deeply than you know."

"Yet you keep on doing it." She tried to wrench herself free of his grasp, but his hold on her upper arms was too tight. "You keep on killing like it feeds a hunger in you."

"When I was very young, my father told me, 'Killing a man is not easy, and never should be.' He wasn't talking about tactics, he was talking about the toll it takes on your spirit. Killing is not something I revel in. It is something I hate."

At the mention of his father, Kai felt her go stiff, then felt the fight drain out of her. *My God, it is my father! What could he have done to her?* He released her and she crossed her arms over her chest, shivering as in a cold draft. She drifted off to stand near the light bulb and Kai squatted in her shadow. *Now is not the time to ask her about my father. I've got to get us out of here.*

He reached down and snaked a length of garden hose from beneath a rat's-nest of heavy nylon cable and mangled bed springs. He glanced over at the water heater, then down at the hose. *I have all the things I need . . . Might just work, if she's willing to cooperate.*

Demi-Precentor Khalsa keyed up Deirdre Lear's file and sighed as the computer layered colors onto her picture. There was something about her that *infected* him, just as it had the first time he saw her. The way she moved and the light, polite laughter that rolled musically from her slender throat. From the first, she had appeared in his dreams—and then to find her *here* in his office.

Fate, he thought, was compensating him for having dumped him on such a backwater world.

And you are spurning its gift! It struck him like a physical blow that the object of desires ComStar should long since have trained out of him was in his hands, and he had stuck her in a dark, dank hole with a young, virile man to comfort and chase away her fears. *How could I be so foolish?*

As his fantasy world started to implode, the demi-Precentor mentally chastened himself and moved to remedy the situation. "I can segregate her from Jewell and make sure she is not taken off to the Reeducation Center." The memory of an earlier visit to that facility made him shudder. "No, she should not be wasted there."

Khalsa heaved himself up out of his chair and quit his office. At the door heading down into the basement, he waggled a finger, causing two ROM guards to follow him down the wooden stairs. He crossed to the door and flicked open the little viewport, but saw nothing.

With a frown, he stepped over to the light switch. "The light is out, but the switch is on." The ROM guards stepped closer to look through the viewport, and Khalsa flicked the switch up and down several times. "They've broken the bulb!"

As Jewell usurped the demi-Precentor's place in his erotic fantasies about Deirdre Lear, the ComStar bureaucrat quivered with rage. Giving the light switch a last flip, he pointed at the door. "Open it! Open it!"

In the 1.27 seconds it took from Kai's activation of the cut-out switch connected to the light, to the power drain knocking that whole city sector from the power grid, the damaged myomer actuator contracted. It went from a gelatinous consistency to one of spun steel as it snapped taut, cracking both the pillars to which it had been bound with nylon cables. When the power died, the myomer relaxed, too soon for it to bring down the house, but not soon enough to prevent it from accomplishing the task for which it had been prepared.

The water heater, filled up to the crack in its side with water, launched forward like a stone from a slingshot. As it left the myomer, it began a slow rotation, with the lower, heavier section lagging slightly behind the upper part. Kai saw the cylinder slam into the door, blasting the half-rotted wood into a cloud of splinters. He heard one man's muffled scream of pain, then another snapping sound.

The projectile continued its flight, skipping off bodies and the cellar corridor until it hit the far wall and crumpled. Water gushed from the crack and slowly spread back along the floor. In the glare of battery-powered emergency lights, it looked like an oversized beer can that had been mashed underfoot.

Squinting against the harsh illumination from the emergency black-out lights, Kai shot forward and leaped from the room. With a snap-kick to the chest, he sent the demi-Precentor spinning into the far wall. As the corpulent man collapsed in a moaning heap, Kai plucked the autorifle from the first ROM guard's dead hands, then stripped off his ammo belt. He looped it over a shoulder, then looked toward Deirdre. "C'mon, do it!"

Motion above him caused him to backpedal and bring the autorifle up. A ROM guard at the head of the stairs jerked his trigger at the same moment Kai tightened down on his. Both guns filled the cellar with smoke and strobing muzzle-flashes. The ROM guard's throat exploded in a spray of blood, then his nearly severed head lolled to the side as his body toppled back into the hallway above.

Kai felt the impact of three bullets as they hit his chest.

Knocked off his feet, he crashed back against the wall. His head hit hard and sizzling rainbow lights exploded before his eyes. As darkness began to close in around him, he tried to fight it off, but blacked out nonetheless.

When his eyes snapped open again, Kai knew from the smoke still drifting upward and the single, bloody rivulet dripping down step by step that he'd only been out for a second or two. The pain in his chest that came with each breath reminded him of the ROM guard's marksmanship.

Deirdre dropped to her knees beside him. "Oh God, I've got to get you to some place where I can operate."

Kai rested his left hand on her shoulder. "Just help me up."

"You can't. You have to lie still. Massive chest trauma." She bent over him and peered into his eyes. "Pupils are slightly dilated. You must be in shock."

"I'm just in pain." He patted his chest with his right hand. "I've got my cooling vest on, remember? Ballistic cloth. It stopped the bullets, but I think ribs got bruised."

"Or broken. Be careful." She helped him to his feet and pulled the ammo belt from the second ROM guard without his asking. "How do you feel?"

"Rocky. I blacked out for a second." He shook his head to clear it, but was less than satisfied with the result. "We have to get out of here."

She looked down at the ComStar staffers. "The first guard's dead. His neck is broken. The other two are just out cold. Are you going to finish them?"

He looked at her as if she were mad and mounted the stairs. "They're no threat. Let's move." Hugging his left arm to his ribs, he worked his way up the stairs with the autorifle's muzzle leading the way. At the first-floor landing, Kai crouched near the body of the man he'd shot, but saw no one. He signaled Deirdre to follow him and cut down the hallway to the demi-Precentor's office.

They ducked inside and Deirdre shut the door behind them. "Why are we here? Let's just go!"

Kai walked over to Khalsa's desk. "Can't. I made a promise." He scooped Dave Jewell's holographs into the small pack he'd brought to the ComStar center. He checked it and smiled when he saw his pistol and the survival knife still in their place.

"Besides, I want to see what the demi-Precentor can offer

us to help our escape." He wrenched open the central desk drawer and nodded. He scooped out a series of magnetic cards and tucked them into a pocket. "Trip-cards. All we have to do is get to the garage in this place and his hovercar will provide us a way out."

Deirdre nodded. "Let's go. Hurry."

Kai dropped a new clip into the autorifle and shook his head. "One more thing. We pay this clown back for betraying us." He tracked a burst of fire across the desk, then along the wood-paneled walls. The computer console exploded and a few splintered paintings dropped to the floor.

Deirdre clapped her hands over her ears. "It's a good thing you're a warrior," she shouted.

"Why?" Kai asked as he put another clip into the gun.

"You make a lousy decorator."

Khalsa's harsh stare sent his subordinate scurrying from the ravaged office, but had no effect on the Clan Elemental standing before him. The plaster on his left-arm cast had not yet dried, and it felt cold and clammy pressed over the dressings binding his ribs and shattered collarbone. The painkillers even made him feel a bit loopy, but his sense of duty to ComStar cut through the narcotic haze.

"I was quite reluctant to summon you, Star Captain, but I had no choice. You see what he did, don't you?"

The Elemental nodded solemnly. Even without his armor, Khalsa thought the man improbably large. His close-cropped blond hair and military bearing contrasted with the brightness of his blue eyes, at least to the demi-Precentor's way of thinking. *Not the eyes of a killer.*

"I saw his handiwork throughout your station here, demi-Precentor. Pity about the chandelier in the foyer." The Elemental kept his hands clasped at the small of his back. "Had you informed us about your capture of a FedCom, we would have taken him off your hands with less inconvenience for you."

Khalsa bristled at the derision in the man's voice. "Yes, Star Captain, I am certain you would have, but my authority here allows me to determine the disposition of those people we capture, as you have control of those people you capture. This Dave Jewell is obviously very dangerous, so I have called you in.

"He kidnapped Dr. Lear, perhaps with some hideous motive, and stole my Migliore hovercar." Khalsa picked up a sheet of paper from his war-ravaged desk. "This is a list of the destinations and routes for the trip-cards he stole." He extended it to the Elemental, but the man did not take it.

"From everything I have seen, he will use your vehicle as a decoy. It does not matter where it ends up, he will not be there." The Elemental studied the line of bullet holes tracking along the wall. "I can also tell you the woman is traveling with him of her own accord."

Khalsa's eyes narrowed. He did not care in the least for the condescension in the man's voice. "And how, pray do tell me, do you know all this?"

The Elemental continued studying the damage until it brought him to the desk and Khalsa again. "Shooting this place up took time, during which she could have escaped him. Furthermore, they looted your first-aid center, taking things that she, as a doctor, knew would be useful on the run. Their partnership has allowed them to live behind enemy lines since we took this planet. If they were not working together, we would have had them before this."

Khalsa could not believe the admiration he heard in the Elemental's voice. He slammed the paper and his fist down on the table. "You think this is amusing! Well, I do not! I want Dave Jewell's head on a stick. Do you hear me? On a stick!"

The Elemental stared hard at Khalsa and the demi-Precentor felt a chill run up his spine. "Let them run, Khalsa. We will get them eventually. Where can they go?"

"I don't care where they can go, Taman Malthus, and I do not want them 'eventually.' They are a disruptive influence on this world, and in my capacity as planetary administrator, I *order* you to make their capture your first priority!"

The Elemental swallowed hard. "As you wish, demi-Precentor. Your will is now mine."

12

Imperial City, Luthien
Pesht Military District, Draconis Combine
19 February 3052

Shin Yodama, sore from travel and the multi-G journey into Luthien, tried to hold himself as tall as possible in the briefing room. He struggled to keep the disgust and fury from his face as *Tai-sa* Alfred Tojiro and *Tai-sa* Kim Kwi-Nam made their case to Takashi Kurita. *They twist words and facts to justify slaughtering their own men.*

Alfred Tojiro's wrinkled face wore a pained expression of regret. "We would have defeated them, driven them from Teniente, had our strategy been allowed to unfold. Our men were valiant and refused to succumb to baseless stories about the Clans and their invincibility. We were prepared to add the name Teniente to the names Luthien and Wolcott as places where the Clans knew defeat."

"It is as *Tai-sa* Tojiro says," nodded *Tai-sa* Kwi-Nam. "We had the Clans where we wanted them, but how could we issue orders while arguing with Hohiro? His distraction jeopardized not only our operation, but it tore Techs away from the radar screens that would have told us the Clan Elementals were nearby. Your grandson and him"—Kwi-Nam thrust a finger at Shin—"have cost our troops their general staff."

"We would not have evacuated the world except that your grandson arrested us and left us in the charge of this bandit."

Tojiro spat at Shin. "We ordered, we demanded to be returned to our command, but we were brought here."

Takashi Kurita, looking serene and lethal, leaned back in his chair. Clad in a green and black silk kimono, he rested his elbows on the arms of the chair. He interlaced his fingers and peered over them at Shin Yodama. "*Sho-sa* Yodama, these are grave charges against you. Did you and my grandson interfere with the conduct of these officers as they sought to prosecute their war?"

Shin growled in a low voice. "We tolerated incompetence until we could no longer stand seeing faithful soldiers being slain by their own leaders. These men have studied none of the tactical planning reports. They fought in the old style, and fought badly in it at that."

"Quiet, fool!" hissed Tojiro. "Do not imagine you can elevate yourself beyond your station. The Coordinator knows better. He knows the sort of filth you are."

A door slid open behind Takashi's chair. A tall, slender man entered the room with a fluid gait Shin recognized instantly. As the dim light bled color into his features and blue rob, Theodore Kurita regarded Tojiro like a curiosity. "And if I claim Shin Yodama is vital to our war effort, to the new way of defeating the Clans, what would you say, *Tai-sa* Tojiro?"

"I would say you are a fool." The small officer turned to the Coordinator. "We know better than to imagine the old way has been swept aside, Lord Takashi. We appeal to you, to your justice. We have been wronged and we demand your judgement." Tojiro glanced at Shin. "We need an example to show the reality of the Combine."

Takashi Kurita looked toward his son. "He is a warrior in your command."

"But we all serve the Dragon." Theodore bowed to his father and Shin followed his example.

"Very well." Takashi nodded slowly at the two officers. "You are correct. The old ways have not been totally swept away. We still demand respect for authority. You know this?"

"*Hai,* Kurita Takashi-*sama*."

"Then you know what must be done." Takashi waved them away. "You may use the garden."

Tojiro blinked twice. "*Sumimasen,* Kurita-*sama*. Forgive me. We may use the garden for what?"

"For slitting your bellies, you treacherous dogs!" Takashi stood abruptly and both men cringed. "You claim to be my servants. You claim to follow me, yet you ignore everything the man I have placed in charge of my armies has told you to do! You place your honor above the life of the Combine!"

"No, my Lord, you have been deceived." Kwi-Nam dropped to his knees and bowed deeply. "Your son and his yakuza compatriots insulate you from reality!"

"*lie!*" Takashi roared as he kicked Kwi-Nam aside. "Do not whimper, do not whine. You have certainly cost the Combine the world of Teniente, and you quite possibly have cost me the life of my grandson. Be glad I allow you to take your own lives. Be gone from my sight so I can try to remember when you were still men."

The two officers scurried from the briefing room, leaving Takashi, Theodore, and Shin alone around the holographic projection table in the center of the room. The Coordinator caught the yakuza's eye. "I admire the restraint it must have taken to endure a month aboard a DropShip with those traitors."

"I was sedated for the first part of the trip." Shin unconsciously rubbed his ribs with his right hand. "And when I was not, I made certain they were."

Theodore leaned forward heavily on the table. "The latest from Teniente is that Hohiro is alive. He has combined the Third Pesht Regulars and the Eleventh Pesht Regulars into one unit. They have supplies, but have gone to ground. They are gathering intelligence for a possible strike later, but the prognosis for their survival is poor."

Shin swallowed hard, his premonition of never seeing Hohiro again working its way in icy steps up his spine. "Hohiro asked for a regiment and a half to help relieve his position. With those troops, he thinks he can drive the Nova Cats from Teniente."

The Warlord of the Draconis Combine shook his head. "He might have thought he could defeat them at the time you left, but it is no longer possible at this point. The units took too much damage while Hohiro consolidated his command."

"But that sort of force should be sufficient to get him off the planet." Shin took a deep breath. "My ribs are healed. Assign me to a relief unit and we will get Hohiro out of there. We may lose Teniente, but we can pull the troops out."

Again Theodore shook his head. "There can be no relief for Teniente."

The Coordinator stiffened. "What do you mean? It is your son we're talking about."

"I know that."

"You must save him."

"How, Father?" Theodore dropped into a chair at his side of the table and punched out a request for data on the keyboard located below the rim. A map of the Combine and the Free Rasalhague Republic flashed to life, though fully a quarter of the worlds it displayed lay in Clan occupation zones. "I have the Smoke Jaguars and Nova Cats in position to hit fifteen different worlds. The Ghost Bears are ripping their way back down through the Rasalhague holdings, which exposes more of our flank to possible attacks. Just because they have not crossed the line between their apparent advance zone and that of the Smoke Jaguars does not mean they will not do so."

"You posit hypotheticals, Theodore, when it is your son who is in jeopardy." Takashi swiped a hand through the holographic map. "Hohiro is your heir. Ragnar Magnusson has already been lost to the Wolves. I would not have my grandson a captive of the Clans."

"He has been their captive before."

"And because of Yodama here, he was freed." The Coordinator hammered the table with his fist. "Give Yodama troops and let him go."

"What troops?" Theodore stood abruptly, his teeth clenched to hold back his anger. "Who, Father, who do I send? Can I send your Dragon's Claws? You and they fought valiantly in the defense of Luthien, but you were as shattered as every other unit that protected our homeworld. Wolf's Dragoons and the Kell Hounds have left to lick their wounds, but it will be two or three more months before they'll be back to operational strength."

"There are other units."

Theodore sighed heavily. "Yes, Father, there are other units, but they are protecting other worlds. Were Hohiro not on Teniente, we would not be having this conversation."

"But he is, so we are." The Coordinator sat down in his

chair and stared broodingly at the map. "There must be a way."

"If there is, Father, it is beyond my ken to find it."

Omi Kurita's light, feminine cough spun Shin around to see her enter through the doorway behind him. The slender woman shuffled forward, keeping her gait politely modest. Her white silk robe rustled as she moved, and Shin smelled jasmine as she drew to his side. "Father, Grandfather, I must ask: if it were possible for a friend of mine who had a brother trapped by the Clans to obtain the troops necessary to rescue him, would they be used for that purpose?"

The Coordinator nodded sharply. *"Hai!"*

Theodore watched his daughter with hooded eyes. "Perhaps."

Omi's face remained an impassive mask. "You would not allow her to save her own brother?"

The Kanrei sat down slowly, resting his elbows on the briefing table. He steepled his fingers and watched Omi with restless blue eyes. "Omiko, I have already devoted more time to your question than I would allow anyone else asking such things. Still, I am on the horns of a dilemma. If I give your friend this leeway, what do I do if these troops she has obtained later become needed to defend a more important target?"

"Keep your word to her, Father."

Theodore shook his head gravely. "This is not some coy game to play, Omi. This is not the same as you asking to move a pawn for me while I play chess against your brother. You must know that if your friend were able to raise those troops, they would be vital to the defense of the Combine. We could not spare them."

Omi's eyes became sapphire slits. "Then, Father, what if she obtained them from outside the Combine?"

Shin felt his stomach tighten as Theodore recoiled from her question. In an instant, Shin knew her source for military support. As much as he wanted Hohiro safe, her suggestion struck him as treasonous. That Theodore had covered himself as well as he had surprised Shin.

The Warlord leaned back in his chair. "Your friend has grown up, hasn't she, Omiko? She plays at adult games."

"As her father often reminds her, this is not a game. If she were able to get a regiment of troops, would she be allowed to send them to rescue Hohiro?" Omi's composure began to crack and Shin saw a nervous tremor of her lower lip.

Her father watched her face, then nodded. As she reined in a blossoming smile, Theodore raised a hand. "However, daughter, your friend must understand that adult games do not always allow for total victories. Yes, if she musters troops, they may be sent to rescue Hohiro. I will even assign *Sho-sa* Yodama as her liaison officer. My offer is not without conditions, though, and she will have to agree to my terms before I allow her to proceed."

Omi glanced down at the floor. "As you would have it, Father."

"My condition is this, and it is one she may choose not to accept: From this point forward, she will no longer communicate with Victor Davion."

Except for the way Omi caught her breath, Shin would not have been sure she had even heard Theodore's words. She continued to look down and delicately wet her lips with the tip of her tongue. "She will, out of love for her brother and the Combine, accept your condition as long as your ban only goes into effect after one last message."

"Hai, Omiko, *hai!"* Theodore nodded solemnly. "Go. Let her compose her final message. *Sho-sa* Yodama will act as her messenger."

Bowing to her father and grandfather, Omi retreated from the chamber, leaving all three men to consider her courage and sacrifice. Inwardly, Shin was jubilant, for the first time daring to hope that Hohiro might be saved. He knew what Omi had done required courage, both in making the offer, then agreeing to abide by her father's terms. *When his sister becomes the Keeper of the Family Honor, Hohiro may wish he had stayed on Teniente.*

Theodore looked at his father and saw the smile half-hidden behind the older man's hands. "You have something to say, Father?"

The Coordinator shook his head. "She is very much your daughter, Theodore." His grin broadened, but he respectfully refrained from laughing aloud as he added, "Now you will discover, as I have, that in fighting with your children, you win only the battles, never the war."

═══ 13 ═══

DropShip Dire Wolf, *On-station, Alurial Continent Hyperion, Wolf Clan Occupation Zone* 25 February 3052

Phelan Wolf clasped his hands behind his back as the door to the ilKhan's ready room slid shut behind him. "Reporting as ordered, sir."

The ilKhan looked up from his desk and gave the Mech-Warrior a smile. "Punctual as always." He tapped the screen of the monitor on his desk. "Natasha was rather specific about your timing in her report. She says that if your unit had not moved so quickly, Simmons Dam would have been blown and the resulting flood would have wiped out the Guards."

"I think Natasha overstates matters a bit. Carew and his wingman pretty much had the Rasalhague commandos pinned down. We finished them, then engaged that lost militia lance. Though they might have been able to trigger the explosives already planted, they all live in the area and would have wiped out their own homes. I have spent more time chasing stragglers through the Teeganito Astako breaks."

Smiling only with his eyes, the ilKhan leaned back and watched Phelan. "How apt it is that you are battling for that particular Ward Bloodname. You suit its pedigree quite well."

Phelan frowned. "I do not understand." The fact that Cy-

rilla had taken her own life to give him a slot in a Bloodname contest still made his heart ache.

Ulric rose from his chair and waved Phelan to a campaign
chair in a conversation alcove to the right of his desk. "As
well you know, Bloodnames are limited to the surnames of
the loyal warriors who fought with Nicholas Kerensky to
end the barbarism that tore our people apart. When Nicholas
reformed our society into the Clans, he outlawed all surnames with the exception of Bloodnames. He decreed that
only twenty-five individuals would be given the honor of
possessing any one Bloodname. From the first, the competition for Bloodnames was fierce."

"I have seen that." Phelan shook his head. "Warriors have
been killed in this contest already."

"And more will die for the honor." Ulric's face hardened.
"Each of the twenty-five Bloodnames for each House has its
own pedigree. A particular name is known for the deeds of
those who have worn it before. It is not unlike 'Mechs being
handed down from father to son within the Successor
States."

The ilKhan leaned forward. "Take, for example, the
Kerensky name I am honored to wear. Bloodnames have existed among the Clans for just under 300 years, yet only
twelve individuals have ever worn this name."

Phelan half-shut his eyes as he mentally did some quick
math. "That means each of them averaged twenty-five years
with that name, and Cyrilla said you have had it for the last
fifteen years."

Ulric nodded. "And you know that Natasha won her
Bloodname at age twenty-two—the youngest person ever to
win a Bloodname. I won mine at the age of thirty. You see
the significance, *quiaff*?"

"Aff. Within the Clans a warrior is considered old by the
age at which you won your Bloodname. Even if I assume
you were late in winning your Bloodname and that the others who had this one managed to win it at twenty-five years,
the average puts them over fifty years, which is remarkable."

The ilKhan nodded. "In truth—and I mention this not as
a boast—I could have participated in Bloodname contests
when I was younger, but I declined until this specific name
became available. I wanted it because of those who had
worn it and the deeds they had performed."

"I don't understand. You turned down the honor of the Bloodname just to wait for a particular one?"

"Of course." Ulric chuckled mildly. "Why would I want a Bloodname that dozens of Warriors had worn? Yes, it is still a Bloodname, but its pedigree is less than desirable."

The younger MechWarrior nodded. "If the best Warriors hold themselves back for the better names, less fit Warriors will battle for the poorer ones. They perpetuate the cycle." He smiled slowly. "I can also see a case where someone with a poor Bloodname might attempt risky things to bring prestige to his Bloodname, but thereby put himself at risk."

"Again, you are well suited to your Bloodname. Like Cyrilla and the others who have borne it, you are capable of insight and remain realistic about your own abilities and accomplishments. This Bloodname for which you battle is one of the most valued within the Clans."

"I imagine the invasion is improving the pedigrees of a number of Bloodnames." Phelan smiled as he tried to imagine what the pedigree of Natasha's Bloodname would be.

The ilKhan shrugged. "It has enhanced some and destroyed others. One of House Malthus' Bloodnames was disgraced on Twycross. The leader of the Falcon Guards led his troops into an ambush and they were destroyed. While we were on Strana Mechty, they conducted a contest for the name, but no MechWarriors would touch it, so it went to an Elemental."

The disgust in Ulric's voice made it clear that he considered the commander's stupidity second only to that of someone actually entering a contest for that Bloodname. "I do not imagine you brought me here to discuss Bloodnames. How may I be of service?"

"I want you to help solve the ComStar enigma."

"ComStar enigma?" Phelan frowned as Ulric rose from his chair and began to pace. "Last I heard, ComStar was negotiating the return of Terra to us. We know it is a delaying tactic, but to what end?"

"Exactly." Ulric stopped and looked out the porthole at the Wolf Clan armada. "We have participated in the negotiations and we have allowed ComStar to continue to administer our worlds to make them believe we are lulled into complacency."

"But ComStar must know you do not fully trust them, *quiaff?*"

"Aff."

Phelan frowned. "Then is it wise to let them continue administering our captured worlds?"

The ilKhan nodded almost absentmindedly. "Quite. If nothing else, it creates a drain on their resources. Were they to rise up in revolt, what would it get them? We can return to any world they attempt to take, and if they manage to defeat our garrison troops, we put them down again."

Ulric turned and narrowed his eyes. "No, we have to assume they are delaying until they can organize a military response to the threat we pose. What are ComStar's chances of forging an alliance between the various Houses of the Successor States?"

Phelan fought to choke off a laugh. "Ah, I think they are very slim."

Ulric let a low chuckle rumble from his chest. "That answer is the same given by Natasha and her archivist. In this, all three of my advisors who know the Inner Sphere agree. This means, then, that ComStar will attempt to oppose us themselves. What do you know of their military?"

Phelan looked down at his boots and concentrated. He remembered bits and pieces of conversations overheard as a child, but could dredge up nothing definitive. "ComStar has its Com Guards. I think I have seen estimates that put their strength at somewhere between forty and fifty 'Mech regiments, but those estimates are highly unreliable. Most of their troops are stationed in lance- or company-sized units protecting various facilities. ComStar has, in the past, used mercenaries heavily to protect their centers, adopting them and fixing up their 'Mechs for them. Of course, the Com Guards have infantry, aerospace, and vehicular support."

The ilKhan rubbed his left hand over his goatee. "Their military strength is actually not so great a concern of mine. We will, after all, learn what they are using to defend or attack during the bidding process, *quiaff*? No, I should have stated my question more clearly. Assuming they are going to seek a military solution to our invasion of Terra, I want you to tell me what you know of the Precentor Martial."

Phelan's heart leaped in his chest. *Does Ulric know that I once agreed to help the Precentor Martial discover the true goal of the Invasion?* "I don't believe I know that much about him."

"Oh?" The ilKhan arched a snowy eyebrow. "You spent a great deal of time with him, at my request, so you must have gained some impressions of the man. Tell me what you know."

Phelan concentrated, trying to remember every detail possible about the leader of ComStar's military. "He comes from the Lyran Commonwealth—his name and his German are enough to tell me that. He also mentioned having stayed at the Lestrade estate on Summer at one point. That would suggest to me he was a noble or was assigned to a military unit stationed on Summer." Phelan frowned. "He also went to the Nagelring, which pegs him solidly as being from the Commonwealth."

"I see." A predatory smile spread across Ulric's face. "Would it surprise you if I said no one named Anastasius Focht ever attended, much less graduated from, the Nagelring?"

Phelan thought for a moment, then shook his head. "Neg. It has only been in the last ten years or so that ComStar has even had a Precentor Martial. You think Anastasius Focht is an alias, *quiaff*?"

"I have no doubt of it at all. You see, Phelan, the name Anastasius means 'one who will rise again,' or resurrection. Focht is an old German name meaning 'one who fights.' " The ilKhan smiled grimly. "I can see the man who is the Precentor Martial adopting that name in triumph at his return, or as a constant reminder to avoid that which caused his downfall before. A man who is capable of choosing that name is most dangerous."

"Then I take it you want me to work on discovering who he is?"

The ilKhan nodded. "Natasha's archivist has lain the groundwork for the study, but I have reassigned him to another investigation. I need you to crack Focht's identity, but I also need you to provide me the insights I will need to outbargain and defeat him."

"I will do this, my Khan."

"Understand, Phelan, that your mission is more important than anything else you have been asked to do as a member of the Wolf Clan. If we are not the ones to take Terra, if another Clan does it, there will be no way to stop them."

Phelan looked up, confused. "Stop them?"

"The Clan that takes Terra will appoint a new ilKhan. If a Crusader is chosen, the war will not end at Terra. It will continue until every world acknowledges the Clans their masters, or has been burnt to a cinder."

Phelan let the shower's hot water drum numbness into his brain. Hours and hours of sitting in front of a computer console reviewing thousands of files had made his eyes burn and his shoulders ache. When he realized he'd placed a cup of soup in a microwave, then forgot to turn it on, he decided to call it a day. As Ranna was working to reconfigure her *Lupus* before their next assault, he decided to relax by taking a shower.

The gymnasium shower room was empty when he arrived, but the hiss of a second shower spray brought Phelan around. He smiled until he could clear the water from his eyes, then he spat at the floor. "Taking a shower, Vlad? I thought you had to be *degreased*."

The other naked MechWarrior returned Phelan's venomous stare. Though Vlad was not a bad-looking man, the scar that ran down the left side of his face from eyebrow to jaw was neither exotic nor attractive. Phelan felt that was because it mirrored the man's cruel streak. "Degreased? I think not. I spend no time with you, therefore I remain unsoiled."

Vlad looked at Phelan and his lip curled up in a sneer. "It appears the bruises Dean inflicted on you have healed. How fortunate. Seldom are those who tangle with Elementals allowed to learn from their mistakes."

"At least I met my foe on equal footing."

"Such is the defense of those who are hunted." Vlad stepped into the stream of water, then smoothed down the hair from his black widow's-peak. "I obtained my kill in near record time. Your fight looked like those staged combats we have seen broadcast from Solaris. It was a joke."

"Tell that to Dean. At least he is still alive." Phelan's hands itched to close around Vlad's throat.

"You are too delicate to win the Bloodname, Phelan. Cyrilla made a poor choice in you." Vlad shook his head contemptuously. "Not killing your foes is a weakness you must overcome, freebirth."

"You can bet I will, Vlad." Phelan laughed. "Just in time for our battle in the finals."

14

Primus Myndo Waterly reveled in the Precentor Martial's obvious discomfort at having been summoned to her presence. "It is so good to have you back here on Hilton Head, Anastasius." *No more of your little "virtual-reality" games when we speak.*

"As always, Primus, I am pleased to be in your presence." The taut lines around his mouth betrayed his true feelings to her, but Myndo was absolutely certain he had no clue he had given himself away. "You said you had reached a decision on my plan concerning the Clans and battling with them."

She left him standing in the center of her circular chamber while she moved toward the demi-lune window overlooking the courtyard below. She knew that the sunlight streaming through the window would wreath her in a fiery nimbus. She sought that effect, pleased as the light glancing off her golden silk robe hurt even her eyes. Her ploy forced the Precentor Martial to avert his eye and denied him the ability to see more than a silhouette of her face.

"I have reviewed your plans and I believe you have chosen correctly in selecting Tukayyid. Your plans for safeguarding the population were well-conceived, but I believe we will have to evacuate the world."

The Precentor Martial reacted visibly to that suggestion. "Evacuate the world?"

"Of course. That is the only way to truly minimize the possible civilian casualties, is it not? We want to present the correct image in arranging this battle."

"I doubt very sincerely the Clans will care one way or another what we do with the civilians, Primus."

Who cares about the Clans? Myndo folded her arms into the sleeves of her robe. "Anastasius, I am concerned about how the public views our action. By evacuating the world, we will show ourselves more concerned with the people than any government."

Focht adjusted the black patch over his right eye. "And the government of Rasalhague has agreed to this?"

"They will if they wish their ragged intelligence network to continue to function." Myndo scowled as the Precentor Martial frowned. *Yes, Focht, it is politics dictating to the military what will happen. That is the way it has always been, and will always be.* "Precentor Martial, do not think ill of me. You know it is best to evacuate those people, and I will do what I must to care for them."

"I thank you for this unexpected boon. This means I no longer have to commit troops to protect civilian targets." Focht brought his head up. "And my troop requests?"

Myndo opened her arms. "Aside from small infantry garrisons on the worlds we are administering for the Clans, the Com Guards are yours. Before you protest, let me say that we need troops to protect our facilities after you defeat the Clans. I am just being cautious."

The Precentor Martial nodded slowly and turned away. "Concerning the BattleMechs stored here beneath Hilton Head. They will be made available to us?"

"Of course." The Primus moved away from the window and descended to the floor of the chamber. "How can you wonder if I would deny you anything in this battle to save Terra? The Clans are poised like a dagger over our heart and you are the only person who can prevent them from killing ComStar."

Focht turned to face her again. "Forgive me, Primus, but I have witnessed enough debates in the First Circuit to know that you are quite capable of manipulating individuals, myself included. You will forgive me for speaking frankly, but I would have expected more opposition to my plans."

Myndo forced herself to laugh lightly. "Anastasius, you have not fooled me. I know your demands for supplies and troops were padded because you expected me to slice away at them. And I intended to do just that, but as I studied your plans, I saw how important it was to support you fully. If you planned to defend us with only a portion of the things you requested, I could empower your plans more fully by giving you all you requested.

"Make no mistake about it, Precentor Martial, I understand very, very well the historical nature of the battle you are going to undertake. You will have nearly fifty regiments of BattleMechs. You will have armor and artillery and aerospace and infantry at your disposal. You will have under your command the largest armed force ever gathered since General Aleksandr Kerensky left with the Star League army."

The Precentor Martial watched her intently while she managed to keep her expression innocent. Her dark eyes met his stare but without challenge. "I hear what you are saying, Primus, but I find myself unable to fully believe it."

Myndo concealed her irritation with a soft, gentle voice. "But you can trust me, Precentor. We have the same goal. If I betray you, we both die."

The tall man nodded. "I am reminded of a story in which a scorpion and a blind dog have to cross a stream. The scorpion says, 'Let me climb on your back. I will direct you across the stream.' The blind dog tells the scorpion that he cannot trust him because the scorpion can sting him to death. The scorpion counters that if he stings the dog in midstream, they both will die. The dog agrees, but when they are in the middle of the stream, the scorpion does sting the dog. As they slowly sink, the dog asks, 'Why did you sting me? Now we will both die.' The scorpion replies, 'I stung you because I am a scorpion. It is my nature.' "

"I am not a scorpion, Anastasius."

"But you are a politician!" Focht touched his eye patch. "Politics has forever been my bane. It cost me my eye, my command, and my old life. Even my being here, being your Precentor Martial, was because taking me into your service consummated an alliance between you and Theodore Kurita."

This is not an argument I wish to pursue. "Your points are well taken, Anastasius, but even I know when politics must be subsumed by reality. No speech ever stopped a particle beam. No secret deal ever defeated a 'Mech regiment, and no political deals will ever slow the Clans. Even I can see that."

"Can you? Do you really have a grasp on what it means for us to be forthright and honest in dealing with the Clans?" The Precentor Martial reached out to grab her arms, but stopped short. "The battle for Tukayyid is not to be taken lightly."

This time Myndo did not hide her anger. "You have reminded me of this at every turn, Precentor Martial. You have made your case well. Why do you doubt that I have finally seen the wisdom of what you have been suggesting all along?"

Focht started to reply, then closed his mouth and bowed his head. "Forgive me, Primus. As I am a half-blind dog, perhaps I see scorpions everywhere."

Myndo nodded sagely and brushed her left hand down his right arm. "You are my Precentor Martial because you look for scorpions. I would not want the leader of armies to be ignorant of political realities, but I do not want him consumed by them either. You are ComStar's hope and our future is in your hands."

"Your faith in the Com Guards is well founded, Primus. I take it I am given leave to find ilKhan Ulric and bargain for the battle of Tukayyid?"

"Go with the blessing of Blake."

"His Word will be done."

Myndo suppressed her smile until the door slid shut behind Focht's back. "Go, Precentor Martial. Focus their intent upon you. Win or lose on Tukayyid, while you prepare for battle, I will ensure the ultimate victory of ComStar over the Clans."

15

Fort Ian Training Center, Port Moseby
Virginia Shire, Federated Commonwealth
28 February 3052

Victor Davion looked up as a blond man flipped a holodisk onto his desk. "New test results, Galen?"

Galen Cox, Victor's aide, nodded. "We've screened all the people who came in on the last DropShip. Granted that simulators are not 'Mechs, but most of these folks are pretty damned good. Only one or two seemed to go nuts with the added power the refitted 'Mechs provided. Most played it conservative and were always running well low on heat. Out of the fifty we tested, only eleven pushed the 'Mechs to their logical maximum."

Victor leaned back in his chair and pressed his hands together, fingertip to fingertip. "Any standouts?"

Galen shrugged nonchalantly. "A few. There is one guy you're going to want to talk with. He was at the Nagelring with you."

"Who?"

"Renny Sanderlin."

The way Galen said the name told Victor the news was not the best it could possibly be. "Renny was my roommate. What's wrong?"

Galen dropped into a chair and leaned forward. Only his eyes were visible over a stack of reports on Victor's desk. "He was marginal, Victor. Because of his rank, I gave him a lance to command. He played everything by the book—but the book is four years old. He and his people survived, but he was very cautious. His file says that he was treated for combat fatigue after his first engagement with the Clans. His tentativeness is probably because of that."

Galen glanced down at the floor, then met Victor's eyes again. "Given his rank, we'd have to bump one of our own lance commanders to find a place for him."

Victor chewed his lower lip. "Renny pulled me through the last two years at the Nagelring. I owe him. How would you rate his personal performance?"

Hauptmann Cox's expression eased. "He's game, no doubt about that. I had the feeling he was afraid his people would think he would fail them. He hesitated, but then fought hard and shot pretty well when we had his lance jumped."

"Hesitation can get someone killed out there." The Prince scratched his head. "I guess I'll have a talk with him. I'll offer him a position, but it will be at the cost of rank, provided General Kaulkas approves. Murphy's lance is still shy some people, right?"

Galen nodded. "If we take the eleven I mentioned, and Sanderlin, that will bring us up to 90 percent of our authorized strength. Two more DropShips of volunteers are inbound, so I think we can find the rest of our pilots in that lot."

"Good."

Cox rose to leave, then hesitated. "Kommandant, do I file my report on Sanderlin, or do I leave it out of his dossier?"

Victor swallowed past the knot in his throat. "What have you been doing with the others?"

"I file the test evaluation."

If Renny has a negative evaluation in his file, it could hurt his career later on. Victor drew a deep breath, then let it out in a sigh. "You really think he would endanger the other warriors in a lance he commanded?"

"Some people are not cut out for field commands, especially commands in an irregular unit like this one."

Victor nodded. "File it. If you believe what you just said, you might add that to your evaluation."

"Yes, Kommandant." Galen smiled. "Do you want me to send Sanderlin in? He's waiting outside."

The Prince stood. "By all means."

Galen crossed to the door and opened it. "Leftenant Sanderlin, the Kommandant will see you now."

Renny Sanderlin turned sideways to squeeze past Galen, then drew himself up to attention and snapped a salute at Victor. "Leftenant Renard Sanderlin reporting for duty, sir."

Pride swelling in his chest, Victor returned the salute, then grabbed his friend's hand to shake it heartily. "Damn, Renny, it's been far too long."

"Not since Sudaten and planning for the assault on Twycross." The tall blond man smiled broadly. "I heard you were recruiting, so I decided to volunteer."

Galen started out the door, pulling it shut behind him, but Victor stopped him. "Galen, can you get me the figures on how our refitting is going?"

Cox nodded. "How fast?"

"Fifteen minutes. Include projections to end of this week."

"Done."

As Galen closed the door, Victor steered Renny to a chair, then returned to his desk. As he seated himself, he saw Renny was still standing. "What is it, Renny?"

"Sir, I want to be frank with you. Permission to speak freely?"

Victor nodded slowly. "Granted."

"Kommandant, I ran into some trouble in my fight with the Uhlans." Renny blushed. "I'm better now. I won't let you down."

"Thank you, Leftenant." Victor pointed him to the chair. "Because we're friends, I'll give it to you straight. Galen liked what he saw of your fighting ability. He said you were really willing to get in there and mix it up, which is good. We need people who are game and are willing to push the 'Mechs to their maximums."

"Thank you, sir."

Victor met Renny's blue-eyed gaze. "Unfortunately, your leadership skills are not suited to this type of unit. That means that, if you choose to stay with us, you'll not command a lance."

Renny looked down. "I'll lose my rank?"

"As it is right now, I've got some excellent lance commanders. I can't bump one of them just because you're an old friend." The Prince opened his hands. "And Galen thinks it will take some time for you to be at ease working within our system. I cannot give you a lance until you are ready to lead."

Renny shook his head. "You haven't changed at all, have you, sir? You hated favoritism when it was show to you at the Academy and it's the same thing here."

Victor's gray eyes narrowed. "Does that surprise you?"

The MechWarrior smiled. "No, it's just what I expected, so it's kind of a relief. If you are willing to have me in the trenches, I'll take the step down to do it. You know me and you know how to use me. More than fearing death or failure, I fear never getting the chance to try."

The Prince smiled. "Well, if General Kaulkas approves your selection, the Revenants will be glad to have you aboard."

"And I will be honored to serve in the Revenants."

Victor smiled. "Now let's drop this formal 'sir' stuff. Tell me, are you still seeing Rebecca Waldeck?"

The large man nodded and held up his left hand. "We got married last year while I was . . . away from the Uhlans." He blushed and spun a gold band around his finger with his thumb. "She's already expecting. Due some time in May."

"That's fantastic, Renny." For a moment, Victor envied his friend's ability to meet and marry a woman without having it become an issue of national security. *The only woman I would consider marrying is light years away and as inaccessible as the Clans' homeworld, wherever that is.*

A red light on top of Victor's visiphone burned to life. The Prince hit the answer button and a very nervous commtech appeared on the screen. "Highness, forgive the intrusion, but General Kaulkas wants to see you immediately in her office."

"On my way." He glanced over at Renny. "I'm afraid that's it for now, Renny. Do me a favor and find Galen. Tell him to meet me at the General's office, please."

"Yes, sir."

Victor returned Renny's salute, then bolted from his office. Around the corner, he took the stairs two at a time, then slowed just before he entered the General's outer office. There he saw the commtech who served as Kaulkas' aide and was waved straight through into the General's office. Victor passed through the interior door without a moment's notice, and saw the reason for the nervousness in the commtech's voice.

General Kaulkas stood behind her desk watching the monitor mounted in the far wall. On it Victor saw a graphic representation of the Port Moseby system. In space he saw the symbol representing a JumpShip, and a smaller icon moving away from it and toward the planet where he now stood.

"Here I am, General." Victor frowned. "Incoming?"

Andrea Kaulkas's head jerked down in a nod, the stark economy of motion characteristic of her personality and command style. "It's a Combine JumpShip. It just appeared in the system. It released a *Leopard* Class DropShip, the *Fukakaina*. Our records show that ship in service to the Royal Family. ETA twelve hours."

"The *Fukakaina*?" Victor took a step closer to the screen. "Why would they be sending it here?"

Kaulkas shrugged. "Don't know, but will find out."

The commtech appeared in the doorway. "General, I have Orbital Defense Command. They want to know what you want to do."

"Scramble an aerospace fighter lance to escort it in."

The commtech looked puzzled. "Escort, sir?"

Kaulkas nodded. "Escort. You don't think the Kuritans are going to attack this planet with the four 'Mechs that *Leopard* could be carrying, do you?"

"No, sir." The commtech pressed a hand to the earpiece in his left ear. "Highness, the ship is requesting a clear, secure channel to communicate with you."

Victor glanced at the wall screen and the General nodded. "Put the message through here." Victor fought to keep his curiosity and surprise from his voice. He locked his attention on the screen as the picture shifted. Instead of the system display, Victor saw a young Oriental man whose face he easily recognized. "*Komban-wa*, Yodama Shin-*san*."

"And greetings to you, Prince Victor Davion." Shin's face remained impassive, but Victor thought he heard some joy in the man's voice. "I have come on a mission of great import to the Combine. I hope you and your commanding officer will see this in whatever inadequate explanation I offer. First, however, I have been asked to play a holodisk for you. May I?"

Victor nodded, his stomach knotting up. "This line is secure."

"Good. Beginning transmission now."

The image on the screen blew apart like a house of straw hit by a tornado. It reformed itself into the picture of beauty and serenity Victor had come to expect in communications from Omi Kurita. Yet neither the robe of white silk embroidered with pink cherry blossoms nor the smile on her face could deceive him with their sweet calm. Victor knew something was very wrong.

"Victor, this message fills me with hope and despair. I know the great burden on you as you rebuild your command, so I had resolved to only present pleasant moments of diversion in my messages. In return, from you, I have received messages I cherish because of your openness in expressing your feelings concerning us, the war, and the loss of your friend. You said in your last that you felt your communications were unworthy of me, but, in truth, the reverse has been true.

"I fear this message will continue this trend, because I must prevail upon you, ask you for help in something that is not your concern. You have your duties and responsibilities to the Federated Commonwealth, and I have mine to the Draconis Combine. These responsibilities are what make our relationship so difficult, yet I know neither of us would truly abandon them. We, you and I and our siblings, are symbols that make our people take heart and believe victory against our enemies is possible. We may have inherited these roles by the accident of birth, but we both hold them sacred, even to the point of honoring them to our own personal discomfiture."

Victor clenched his jaw against the emotions her words stirred in him. Though they had resolved to be just friends when they had parted on Outreach, and knowing they probably would never see each other again, their messages back and forth had deepened their feelings immeasurably. Victor knew, deep down, that he loved the woman on the screen before him, and it frightened him that he might consider never marrying if she could not be his bride.

The camera recording the holovid slowly zoomed in on her angelic face. "On 18 January the Nova Cats overran Teniente. My brother Hohiro and Shin Yodama were both present as observers during that assault. Things went badly for our forces and the command post was hit hard. As a result, my brother assumed command of the forces on the planet, and Shin, who had been wounded, was sent to Luthien to obtain a rescue force. Hohiro assumed he could hold out for two or three months, and has the supplies to do just that. Without a rescue force, he will never be able to safely pull his men out.

"Shin reached Luthien a month after the disaster, but my father pointed out that we had no troops to send to rescue Hohiro. As much as it pained him, my father had to abandon his son to preserve the realm Hohiro will someday guide."

Omi looked away from the camera for a moment and brushed a tear away. "I asked my father to allow me to send troops to rescue Hohiro, if I could find them. He gave me permission to do so. Thus, do I turn to you.

"Victor, I am asking whether you can send your unit to save my brother. Shin Yodama and the other men with him have all our intelligence on the world with them, and reports will arrive as soon as we have more information to send you. Word has been sent to Hohiro for his people to go to ground because we know it will take time to prepare and mount the operation. His salvation is in your hands."

Omi held up one hand. "Before you agree, and I pray you will, you must know one other thing. To win permission to make this request of you, I had to bargain with my father. In return for permission to give my brother this one chance at life, I agreed never to communicate with you again. As much as that hurts me personally, I know Hohiro's death would hurt the Combine more. Like you, I am trapped by who I am. Forgive me."

Victor sat back in his chair, stunned by Omi's words. Part of him instantly evaluated and gloated over the disruption Hohiro's loss would cause the Combine. House Kurita was not likely to let Omi accede to the throne for she was being so carefully groomed to become Keeper of the House Honor. That meant leadership would pass to Minoru, the youngest of Theodore's children. What little Victor knew of Minoru indicated the young man was more a mystic than a warrior, and that did not bode well for the Combine's militaristic future.

The Prince immediately killed any pleasure he got from imagining the Combine's collapse. He acknowledged the Combine had long been a thorn in the Fox's side, but now it formed a buffer between the Clans and half of the Federated Commonwealth. Furthermore, the training and agreements on Outreach had all been directed at creating a united front to oppose the Clans. Though there had been no combined operations with the Kurita forces, the redeployment of forces along their mutual borders bespoke a trust between the two nations unprecedented in the history of the Inner Sphere.

He could not deny Omi's anguished plea for help, but he felt punished by the deal her father had forced upon her. He started to tell himself his father would never have done that, but then he stopped to consider what he truly knew about his father. *Hanse Davion would have struck the same bargain in an instant, and I would have been lucky to get off as lightly as she did.*

As she said, we are trapped by who we are.

Galena knocked once and entered the room. "General, Kommandant, Sanderlin said you wanted me?"

Victor nodded once and saw Shin had reappeared on the screen. "Unless the General objects to it, I believe we need guest billets for some Kurita officers."

Galen raised a blond eyebrow. "Kurita officers?"

The General nodded solemnly. "You better step up training and refitting. You have an assault to plan."

=== 16 ===

Alyina
Trellshire, Jade Falcon Occupation Zone
1 March 3052

Kai remained crouched on one knee, watchful, as Deirdre drank from the stream. He studied the surrounding grassland, his gaze deliberately not lingering on her slender form or lovely face. No matter how much he was growing to like her, they were running for their lives and the least distraction could turn fatal. Once or twice during the insanity that defined their fugitive existence, Kai almost thought tempting fate would be worth it, but he always managed to keep a hold on his heart and his hormones.

Luckily he had an ally in Dr. Lear herself. In the three weeks since their escape from ComStar, her manner toward him had eased, but she could still be distant and restrained. Whenever he tried to steer the conversation around to probing her hatred of his father, she immediately sidestepped the maneuver and pulled back into her shell.

With her usual efficiency, she had tended his broken ribs, insisting on finding a place to hole up until it was easier for Kai to travel. Though he wanted to keep moving, they finally reached a compromise: they would get out of the immediate area before stopping for a bit. A small cave became the camp where they would settle until Kai could persuade her that his ribs hurt much less than they really did.

Having drunk her fill, Deirdre's head came up, water dripping from the ends of her hair, as a dragonfly skittered across the top of the water. She half laughed, then refilled a bottle they'd been using as a canteen. Staying low, she crawled to where Kai crouched hidden in the brush of the treeline. "Your turn."

"Thanks." Kai reached out and brushed away a droplet of water hanging from the tip of her pert nose. "Ever wonder what your medical school buddies would say if they saw you now?"

She smiled. "Well, given how long we've survived, I don't think many would argue with my score on the evasion test."

"True enough."

"Of course, you're a better instructor than any I had in my training."

Kai grinned as he set the autorifle down. "I'll take that in the spirit intended, ignoring the fact that you avoided as much military training as you could manage." He crawled over to the stream, then went flat on his belly at the bank. Ignoring the dragonfly, he plunged his head into the water.

The cold water felt good to him, soaking through his hair and washing away the oppressive heat of the day. It got into his thin beard, tickling the flesh that had, till now, itched with the new growth. Like a magical elixir, the water revitalized him and even the minor aches in his body seemed temporarily dulled.

He pulled his head back out and shook like a dog might, the water spraying everywhere. He wanted to shout aloud, but that would be needlessly foolish. For the first time since realizing his unit had left him on Alyina, Kai actually believed he might succeed in eluding the Clans.

Then he felt the gun barrel poking his back.

"Easy now, fella. Just you turn over slowly so we can get a look at you."

Kai rolled over onto his back even slower than his captor had drawled out the order. The man closest to him, the one who had poked him with the hunting rifle, was fat enough that his belly, from Kai's point of view, eclipsed the lower half of his face. His soiled clothing looked to be of native manufacture, with the only brightly colored bit the Jade Falcon patch newly sewn on his shoulder.

Back beyond him, bracketed by Kai's feet like a target in a sight, another, more muscular man stood with rifle at the ready. He looked meaner and even nastier than his boss, but held himself more aloof as if sensing Kai was not alone.

"Oh, Jocko, we got us a good one here. His black hair's a bit long, and the beard ain't there in the picture, but this is Dave Jewell sure as I'm Harry Truper." Truper jabbed Kai's belly with his rifle. "Don't know what you did, boyo, but the Clans and ComStar want you bad."

Kai stared up into Truper's face. "You're going to turn me over to them?"

"They pay, we play," Jocko growled. " 'Bout time we score a big one."

Truper nodded in agreement. "You're the first contract case we've actually found. This'll take care of our rep and rent for a long time."

"But I'm like you, I'm from the Federated Commonwealth. You should be helping me, not betraying me."

Truper spit into the stream. "You ain't the same as me, boy. I've got a gun on you and you're wanted by ComStar and the Clans. Besides, I can tell from your accent where you're from. Your Hanse Davion ain't done squat for us since he took ole Melissa as his bride, 'cept drain our economy and get us into a war with the Dragons. I come from Tamar originally and he's ignored our claims for Pact worlds in the Free Rasalhague Republic. Given all that, I think you'd best not be pushing this FedCom brotherhood stuff too much."

"Harry, stop jawing and get it over with."

Kai stiffened at the implication of Jocko's statement. He knew Truper's rifle, at that range, would rip through his bulletproof vest in an instant. "Wait, don't shoot. I'll go with you quietly."

"Sorry, sport," Truper drawled as he worked the bolt on his rifle. "Dead prisoners don't escape."

A bullet punched straight through Truper's cruel sneer, blowing most of it out the back of his head. His rifle flew from limp fingers as his body turned head over heels and splashed down into the stream. The explosion echoing over the meadow swallowed all sound of the stream sucking Truper's body down.

Kai clawed for the needle pistol on his right hip. It cleared the holster as Jocko completed his spin toward the thicket from which Deirdre had fired. Kai tightened down on the pistol's trigger as Jocko swung his rifle around on target. His first cloud of needle made a hash of Jocko's left knee. As he let recoil track the pistol upward, the subsequent shots shredded Jocko's hip, flank, and shoulder.

Despite his shots, Jocko still jerked his trigger. A jet of flame shot from the rifle's muzzle, stabbing straight toward Deirdre's hiding place. Then, as Kai pumped round after round into him, Jocko's body whirled in a lazy pirouette. The barrel of his gun scythed through long, golden summer grasses, but never fired again. His body a bloody ruin, Jocko fell from sight.

Kai rolled to his feet and bolted for Deirdre. He tore through the brush and stopped short when he found her slumped over the smoking autorifle. Dropping to his knees, he reached out to gently turn her over, but he met resistance. His mind flashed to images of corpses locked in rigid poses by rigor mortis, but the trembling of her body told him she was not dead.

"Are you hurt, Deirdre? Did he get you?"

She tried weakly to push him away. When she failed at that, she pulled the autorifle from beneath her and cast it aside. "Get away," she breathed in a harsh whisper.

Anger filled Kai. He jerked her roughly around. "Are you hurt?"

She twisted up into a sitting position and showed no sign of having been hit. She thumped his chest with fists. "Get away, dammit." A grimace snapped up all the beauty Kai had ever seen in her face. "I don't take life. I save it. You've tainted me. You've made me over into your image!"

"What are you talking about?" The vehemence of her attack surprised him, but he recognized a thread of pure terror in her voice. "You saved my life!"

"But I killed to do it. The thing I swore never to do. I became what I am so I would never have to do that!" Tears streamed from her blue eyes. "Because of you, I killed a man. I never even looked him in the eye, I struck like a coward, from hiding. I executed him, and it's your fault!"

She slapped Kai hard, snapping his head around to the left. Kai tasted blood in his mouth. She tried to slap him again, but he blocked the blow and pushed her down with a none-too-gentle shove to the shoulder. "No, Doctor, it is not my fault. If you want to blame anyone, blame the man who gave you no choice. Truper forced your hand. You know that. You do!"

Kai slowly stood. "I've not tainted you. Reality has. You made a decision a long time ago to save lives. That was good, no matter who or what your motivation was. The only mistake was believing you might never find yourself in a situation where you had to kill someone. Perhaps being a general practitioner on some backwater world near the Periphery would have granted you that luxury, but life in the military does not."

Deirdre slowly rolled to her side and pulled her legs up toward her chest. Kai refused to give in to his desire to hug her until she gave in and saw reality. "I cannot say I am sorry you had to pull the trigger, Doctor. You saved my life, and for that I am grateful. The culture in which my mother was raised has a tradition: if you save someone's life, you are responsible for it."

"I don't want to be responsible for you. You have inherited other traditions of which I want no part."

"That could well be." Kai swallowed hard. "One thing I do know, however, is that I am heir to a tradition of honesty that allows me to look at and evaluate situations for what they are. Despite what you might like to believe of me, I find killing no easier than you do. I regret being forced to kill Clansmen and I regret having to shoot Jocko."

The bitterness returned in Deirdre's voice. "If you regret killing so much, why are you in the military? Why don't you follow the advice you gave me a moment ago and leave it?"

"Perhaps because, like you, Doctor, I have reasons that demand I remain." Kai looked down, avoiding her angry eyes. "Being willing to accept the responsibility of taking another person's life does not mean I enjoy it. Here, now, killing those two was the only expedient way to continuing to survive."

"You and your kind are animals."

"So aren't we all, Doctor." Kai scooped up the autorifle and slung it over his shoulder. "Some of us just aren't afraid to admit it."

Scouting along the bounty hunters' backtrail, Kai found a beat-up old hovertruck. A quick search of it produced a packet of information sheets issued by ComStar to provide the bounty hunters with targets for their searches. He found the warrant for his own capture and destroyed it. He also discovered two other fugitive warrants that described other things he had done but that had not been linked with Dave Jewell.

More important to him, however, was the discovery of a grid map of the area. Truper and Jocko had been assigned to search a wedge of territory that included the small meadow through which the stream ran. It narrowed to a point that Kai recognized as an old firebase. It had been little more than a compound with some quonset huts and storage facilities, but the map made it look as if ComStar had found a new use for it.

"Definitely worth checking out, I think." It occurred to Kai that if one team of bounty-hunters had been given that slice of territory, others would be working similar search zones. Assuming not all the hunters were as bloodthirsty as Truper and Jocko, it struck Kai as quite possible that other refugees had been rounded up and imprisoned at the firebase.

After a minute or two of fiddling with the ignition panel, he overrode it and punched in a code that started the hoverfans. By the time he brought the truck back to the meadow, he'd hit on a perfect plan for getting into and out of the firebase. Drawing his pistol, he set to work.

Deirdre looked up at him with red-rimmed eyes. "I thought you'd abandoned me."

Kai shook his head. "Nope. Just making sure our cover story holds together when we get where we're going."

"I heard shots . . . two. Was there someone else out there?"

"No." Kai hesitated. "Just something I had to do."

"What?"

"You don't want to know." His tongue played over the split in his lip. "Trust me, you don't want to know."

Deirdre stood slowly and brushed pine needles from her clothes. Hugging her arms around herself, she met his eyes with a steely stare. "Tell me."

"Jocko still had a face." Kai's eyes narrowed as he braced for her reaction. "It's time for Dave Jewell to die, and Jocko's the right size."

Deirdre blinked several times as what he was telling her sank in. She opened her mouth to say something, but Kai cut her off before she could utter a sound.

"Yes, Doctor, not only do I kill, but I'm willing to mutilate an enemy corpse." His hands knotted into fists. "Perhaps, if pressed, I'll even turn cannibal. There, does that fit your image of me?"

Her lower lip trembled, but she got it under control quickly enough. "What I wanted to say, Kai, was that I've been doing a lot of thinking. I still abhor pulling that trigger, and I'll have nightmares over that decision for the rest of my life, but I do not regret saving your life. In the instant I pulled the trigger, I understood my action would cost the fat one his life, but that did not matter to me than. That it does now is part of who I am, and I must deal with that."

She reached out with the hand that had slapped him and stroked the side of his face. "You are right, we all are animals. I would have liked to believe I was further removed from the savage passions I ascribe to you warriors. I want to be different because I *must* be different. I don't expect you to understand that."

"Deirdre, I . . ." Kai reached up to take her hand, but she stiffened at his touch. He saw emotions warring in her eyes and let his words trail off. "We better get going."

Deirdre turned away and squatted down to gather up their packs. "Where to?"

"Nowhere special, really." Kai accepted his pack from her and swung it onto his shoulder. "We're just going to drop these two off at a ComStar base, collect the bounty for them, and get away as quickly as we can."

Teeganito Astako Breaks, Alurial Continent
Hyperion, Wolf Clan Occupation Zone
8 March 3052

Sitting high in the cockpit of his modified *Nova* Omni-
Mech, Phelan felt, for a moment, like king of all he surveyed. The twisted arroyos and canyons of hard-baked red
earth stretched out around him as far as his 'Mech's enhanced senses let him see. Heat shimmered up off the land,
softening the sharp edges on the earth's crust and blurring
away the little dust devils dancing in the distance.

Phelan allowed himself an incautious smile. *Suitable king-
dom for me. It's as desolate as my chances of winning this
Bloodname battle.*

For the second time, Phelan had participated in the decision ritual of a Bloodname contest. Natasha had overseen the
ritual because both Phelan and Glynis served in the Thirteenth Wolf Guards. When asked to express his worthiness,
Phelan had repeated the same litany of successes as before,
then added, "On Hyperion I led the defense of the Simmons
Dam and hunted renegades in the badlands. Prior to the battle today, I defeated an Elemental, Dean, for the right to participate here."

Glynis, a small woman with the oversized head of all Clan
aerospace pilots, stated her accomplishments more coldly. "I
slew my first Smoke Jaguar before even testing out of my
sibko. In the invasion, I have downed ten other fighters, and
have killed five 'Mechs on the ground. On Hyperion I added

two more fighters to my count, then scoured the plains of retreating armor. Prior to battle today, I slew a MechWarrior, Manas, for the right to participate here."

Phelan had heard, in exquisite detail from Vlad, how Glynis had ripped Manas to pieces. Manas had made the mistake, Phelan decided, of configuring an OmniMech for a straight-up battle with an Omnifighter, then he offered to meet Glynis on an open plain that gave him a clear shot at her. *Of course, it also gave her easy access to him, which is why he died.*

Once again Phelan's medallion won the race and made him the hunted one. Glynis immediately chose to fight augmented, which, Phelan knew very well, made them far more than equal on the battlefield. Her aerospace Omnifighter packed much more in the way of weaponry and speed than any 'Mech he could find in a similar weight class.

Being the hunted, the choice of venue again fell to Phelan. Having just hunted down Rasalhague stragglers in the Breaks, he knew how treacherous and tricky the labyrinth of canyons could be. He recalled in particular that Carew and the other pilots assigned to give him air cover had experienced trouble spotting and shooting their enemies in the tight, twisting gauntlets.

If it worked for them against our fighters, it ought to work for me. He had planned to begin down in the maze, but Natasha had advised him that hiding and waiting to ambush his foe was not appropriate for a Bloodname battle. He recalled that the Black Widow had been unimpressed when Phelan scoffed at the idea of a 'Mech being able to ambush an aerospace fighter.

"An ambush is just taking a flyer by surprise," she commented. "That should not be difficult for someone of your inventiveness."

Not on paper, no . . . For the fourth time since being set down on the planet, Phelan checked his weaponry. The *Nova*'s boxy torso rose up above the cockpit and housed his NARC beacon equipment and deployment pods. That space could have been better filled with another weapon, but if he attained a hit with a NARC pod, it would mark Glynis' fighter with a targeting beacon. That would make his long-range missiles far more effective, and that was devoutly to be desired.

The 'Mech's shoulders supported two thick arms. In the

left Phelan had placed an LB10-X autocannon and its ammo. He'd specified a load of ammunition that he hoped would surprise Glynis. The right arm mounted a long-range missile launcher and sufficient missile racks to fight a long battle.

One of the Techs working to modify his *Nova* had commented that Phelan was going out with enough munitions for a siege, not a skirmish. Phelan had laughed off the remark, but deep down, he knew the Tech was right in wondering about Phelan's choices. Phelan realized Glynis' Omnifighter, a *Visigoth,* was capable of blowing chunks out of his 'Mech with each pass, while he was set up to slowly grind her fighter to debris. Phelan's only chance at winning was to survive long enough to use as much of his ammo as possible.

A red warning light flashed urgently on his command console. Phelan brought up a radar map of the area, and the computer highlighted a fast-moving object on a course that would carry it right over him. By manipulating the joysticks on each arm of his command couch, Phelan brought the twin crosshairs to the center of his holographic display. The computer condensed a 360-degree view of the area into 160 degrees, but Phelan only watched the center, his eyes flicking between it and the radar display on his auxiliary monitor.

Coming in at over 450 knots, the aerospace fighter made itself a target for less than three-tenths of a second. Phelan's crosshairs flashed on the screen and his fingers tightened down on all three fire-control triggers. The *Nova* rocked back with the recoil as the left arm autocannon spit chunks of metal at the closing jet. The right arm sent a flight of missiles arrow-straight at the fighter. From above and behind the cockpit, the NARC system also sent out a small missile, trailing in the wake of the more deadly LRMs.

Searing blue light washed away Phelan's cockpit view as the *Visigoth*'s particle projection cannon hit in its first pass. The jagged bolt of artificial lightning ripped an uneven line up the *Nova*'s right side. Steaming hunks of ferro-fibrous armor spilled to the ground as the 'Mech lurched badly to the left.

Phelan fought to regain control of his 'Mech as the fighter's LRMs blasted craters in the ground all around him. They'd not hit, but hadn't missed by much and the shrapnel drummed across the surface of his 'Mech's cockpit like heavy rain. Ruby beams slashed through the cloud of dust and grit, but only one hit, and that was on the fighter's way out.

The *Nova*'s computer painted a grim picture of itself on the secondary monitor. The PPC beam had all but stripped the 'Mech's right side of armor. The laser had melted a huge hole in the rear armor on his left torso. Another hit in either place and Glynis would be into his 'Mech's internal structures. That left his engine and gyro-stabilizers vulnerable, not to mention the whole endo-steel skeleton supporting his BattleMech.

Only two things made him happy. When he shifted over to infrared sensors, the *Visigoth* stood out like a supernova in the night sky. Glynis had used all her weapons in the initial attack, probably hoping to take him out in one fell swoop. Despite the fact that she'd almost succeeded, the heat those weapons had generated would force her to delay another attack run so she could cool down. As the speed of her run had carried her well beyond his weapon ranges, Phelan assumed Glynis would reduce her speed a bit and take her time in coming back.

That would buy him some time, time he badly needed to get off the ridge and down into the canyon. The vulnerability of his right torso made it imperative that he find a defensive position that would force Glynis to be more cautious in her next fly-by. If she dropped 100 knots from her speed, he might get a chance to get off a good shot with his LRM launcher.

Phelan grinned as he saw a blue light pulsing coolly on his command console. His LRMs and his autocannon had missed their target, but the NARC missile had nailed the fighter in its pass. When it hit, it deployed a small homing beacon in the target that would attract the attention of his LRMs. The rhythm slowed as the aerofighter sped away. "You got away with near-murder, this time, Glynis. Now it's gonna be my turn."

Phelan started his 'Mech in a run up over the crest of the ridge, then down and to the east. He knew his 'Mech's image would vanish from her radar screen, as had her fighter from his, but that didn't bother him. Months of training with Carew had taught him what her response to that move would be.

Gingerly, Phelan began picking his way down a long rockfall. The boulders, which ranged in size from that of a hovercar to some that dwarfed his 'Mech, provided him broken cover, for which he felt thankful. Using his 'Mech's nearly vestigial hands to steady himself against some rocks, he descended toward the floor of a narrow canyon.

Suddenly his radar screen reported a high flyover by the *Visigoth* and the NARC indicator light began to quicken its flashing. As he had expected, the trajectory showed that Glynis was coming in on a new vector, just to confuse him, as she searched. The MechWarrior smiled and pointed his right arm skyward. As the fighter cruised over his position, and the NARC light matched his heartbeat's accelerated pace, he let fly with a whole swarm of missiles.

She's good. Got to give her that. It looked as though Glynis had kicked the *Visigoth* onto its right wing and cranked the nose up in an effort to evade the LRMs streaking from the ground. Though her maneuver might have worked under normal circumstances, the NARC beacon pulled the missiles in like a net scooping up fish. The LRMs peppered the fuselage, from nose to engine, but did little more than blast paint and armor from the fighter.

I just may have made her mad, Phelan thought, with a sinking feeling in his belly. The fighter vanished beyond the lip of the canyon, but Phelan knew with certainty that it would be back. He started his 'Mech literally hopping down the slope, wrestling with the controls to keep the behemoth on balance and upright. Glancing at the NARC beacon, he saw by its steady pulse that Glynis was close.

Despite that warning, Glynis' attack came as a surprise. In a daring move, she dropped her speed and popped up over the lip of the canyon in a strafing run. Her ship a silver specter of death, it hung there for a second with fire blossoming from both wings, then slipped away again.

She caught Phelan in a mid-leap with two LRM flights. The first barrage missed, blasting a spray of rock fragments through the air. The second one hit the airborne *Nova* on its left side. The missiles ripped armor from both the torso and left leg, but failed to breech either.

More important, however, the missiles hitting the left leg helped unbalance the *Nova.* As the fifty-five-ton 'Mech came back down, the left leg folded under the body. As much as Phelan fought to keep the 'Mech upright, the huge war machine tipped drunkenly to the left, then began to somersault down the half-kilometer rockfall to the canyon floor.

Warning klaxons and the shriek of metal filled the cockpit. Phelan cried out as the command couch's restraining straps dug into him, then slammed him back into his seat. Knowing he could no more control his fall than he could defy gravity, he brought the 'Mech's arms in across its middle and started praying.

The *Nova* landed with a jolt so hard that Phelan thought Glynis must have managed another run and direct hit with her missiles. More shocks shook the *Nova,* but it took Phelan a second or two to realize they were from boulders loosed by her miss rather than live munitions she was shooting at him. *Bad enough I have to fight an ace pilot, but my choice of battlefield is against me, too!*

The computer readout on his secondary monitor told him just how much the battlefield hated him. The tumble down the hill had scoured armor off his 'Mech's front and back, though no area was fully breached. Folding his arms in had saved them from most of the damage, though the right-arm diagram showed a feed-mechanism failure. *Dammit, that means the one rack of missiles I have in there is it! I've got enough ammo for a siege, but no way to shoot it.*

Worst of all, the *Nova*'s left leg had taken severe damage. Almost all its armor had been chipped off. The endo-steel bones in the shin had been twisted and warped so the 'Mech's left foot toed in. As Phelan brought the 'Mech upright, using its hands to brush off chunks of rock, he discovered the leg could support weight, but all pretense of mobility was gone.

In frustration, he pounded his fist against the command console. "*Stravag* machine! Freebirth! The only thing left for me to do out here is die." He reached for the ejection switch, but stopped as the *Visigoth* cruised by like a shark waiting for a diver to rise from an ocean wreck.

Part of him wanted to signal Glynis that she had won, but he stopped. He was not about to eject because that was no guarantee she wouldn't make another strafing run to kill him anyway. He didn't think she was that bloodthirsty, but in a Bloodname battle all normal conventions went by the wayside.

Yet it was not fear for his life that moved his hand away from the ejection button. That he should lose was no surprise, for he had started the battle grossly outgunned. But the fight was over something as stupid as a title, and he could live without that. Trying to get out of there, to live out that possibility, was logical and sensible.

Logical and sensible, if you're not of the Clans.

Even as those words formed in his mind, Phelan felt a shock of cold recognition that surprised him. Growing up in the Inner Sphere, he had always felt a bit apart from everyone else. Yes, he had loved his family—and still did—but he had always felt as though he belonged somewhere else. It was as though the world was not quite in focus, making him chafe whenever he had to deal with authority figures and rigid structures.

A bondsman like Ragnar when he joined the Clans, he spent too much time trying to puzzle out who the Clans were and what Ulric wanted of him to be concerned with where and how he fit into their society. Oddly enough, he came to realize that the Clans' predatory nature, which made them constantly pit themselves against one another to prove who was the best, suited him well. Because the Clanspeople regarded him as an outsider, he fought to prove he was their equal. In doing so, he also defined who he was.

Not until this very moment did he understand that in shaping himself to face the challenges of the Clans, he had become very much one of them. Though he could still recognize and appreciate the values he had grown up with, the Clans' urgency and drive superseded those fragments of his background. Three years before, he might have been trying to find a way out or a way to sell himself dearly, while now he sought a way to knock Glynis' fighter from the sky and win the battle.

Because that's the only logical and sensible thing for a Warrior of the Wolf Clan to do.

He twisted his gunbelt back down to a comfortable position and quickly assessed his position. His 'Mech stood beneath an overhang in the canyon wall that helped hide him from Glynis' overflights. Looking up he could see a 20-degree arc of the sky, which narrowed her attack vector appreciably. With the rockfall to his right, the only open avenue of attack was for Glynis to come down the canyon from his left and try to strafe him with her PPC and forward lasers.

The NARC beacon indicator started to blink faster, building up speed little bit by little bit. Phelan put the *Nova*'s back to the canyon wall, then swiveled the 'Mech's torso to the left. The little blue light flicked on and off with a faint click that came faster and faster.

Only have one shot with these missiles. Gotta make it good.

The light burned solid on.

The *Visigoth* swooped down the canyon like a hawk spotting a mouse. The PPC in the fighter's nose raked its blue beam along the canyon wall. Shards of stone shot down to rattle off the *Nova*'s cockpit while hot rock-vapor drifted up into the air from the strike. On of the *Visigoth*'s two forward lasers studded the canyon wall with a line of burning holes, while the other blistered armor from the *Nova*'s torso.

Phelan tracked the *Visigoth* as it swept through the canyon. His autocannon fired first as the fighter came into view. The hail of slugs disintegrated the armor on the tip of the right wing, but didn't so much as make the craft shudder. Bringing the torso around to the right, he triggered a second volley, blasting more armor from the aft end of the fuselage, but it, too, had no visible effect on the Omnifighter.

Phelan almost took a stumbling step forward to send the missiles after Glynis, but she gave him no clear shot. She brought the *Visigoth*'s nose up, kicking the ship into a graceful loop that skimmed it over the surface of the rockslide. Breaking immediately, she then executed a perfect barrel roll to the right, vanishing from Phelan's universe.

The NARC beacon slowed. "It's going to take forever to bring her down," he muttered. He glanced at his ammo indicator for the autocannon and triggered two volleys into the empty air. That took him down to his cluster munitions, which were the closest thing to birdshot a 'Mech could pack. "If I fill the air with this stuff, it'll do more overall damage."

As the NARC beacon's light began to quicken its pace, his heart began to sink. "It's still going to take forever, and she only has to get moderately lucky, while I have to survive her runs *and* knock her down. Dammit, she's not sloppy enough to fly into one of these canyon walls, and she flies too fast for me to waste these missiles on a chance shot." He ground his teeth with frustration. "If she'd only consent to become a stationary target!"

Suddenly the solution dawned on him. As the NARC indicator pulsed faster and faster, Phelan reached out and hit the button, disabling it. As he swiveled the *Nova*'s torso around to face the fighter's line of attack, he heard the rumble-roar of Glynis' engines filling the canyon.

At first sight of her, Phelan's autocannon bucked and roared. The clustered shell sprayed hundreds of metal fragments into the air, biting away bits and pieces of armor from the aircraft's wings, fuselage, and cockpit. In response, Glynis again triggered her PPC and twin forward lasers, but all three energy beams missed the *Nova*.

Phelan whipped the *Nova*'s torso around and extended its right arm. *Now or never!* As Glynis started to pull the *Visigoth*'s nose up, he launched his missiles. Without the NARC to guide them, they missed the *Visigoth,* streaking below past its belly.

However, they landed dead on target.

The score of missiles Phelan loosed hit the rockslide 200 meters in front of Glynis' fighter. The fiery explosions heaved huge chunks of stone into the air, directly in the *Visigoth*'s flight path. At the speed her craft was moving, Glynis had less than half a second to react.

Her attempted roll was not enough.

One triangular rock sheared through the left wing as if the fighter was little more than a wood and paper model. That sped up Glynis' desperate roll, inverting the plane. It spiraled down into the rockslide and cartwheeled. When the *Visigoth*'s right wing touched down, it crumpled like brittle bone, armor flaking off into a glittering cloud of useless ceramic. The fuselage split open right behind the cockpit, then the missiles spilling out of it exploded, obliterating any trace of the Omnifighter's existence.

Phelan looked up at the pyre burning on the rockslide. A piece of him wanted to mourn for Glynis, but he shut those feelings away. "This was a battle for a Bloodname," he heard himself say aloud. "She knew the stakes and wouldn't have shed a tear if it was me at the heart of that blaze."

But was a Bloodname reason enough to needlessly spill blood? And was killing for a title any more sensible than this Clan war against the Inner Sphere?

Phelan acknowledged those inner doubts with a nod of his head. "I am of the Clans now. Their concerns are my concerns." He started the *Nova* on the slow climb upward. "But their concerns are not my *only* concerns."

He smiled and headed off to see if, by some miracle, Glynis might have survived.

═══ 18 ═══

Firebase Tango Zephyr, Alyina
Trellshire, Jade Falcon Occupation Zone
9 March 3052

Kai studied the former firebase through the binoculars and felt his stomach tighten. Coil upon coil of razor-wire encircled the collection of quonset huts and low bunkers like a silver thorn thicket. Individuals manned the two watchtowers, though their weapons had been shifted around to cover the interior of the camp, not the killing ground surrounding it. A proudly waving ComStar banner topped the flagpole.

Through the field glasses, he could not recognize any single person, but he saw plenty of hobbled individuals wearing soiled remnants of Federated Commonwealth uniforms. Most appeared skeletally lean and walked with a listless shuffle that transformed them into zombies. Some tended a garden plot near the center of the camp while others worked in chain gangs improving and widening the dirt track leading up to the camp's double gate.

"How bad is it, Kai?"

He lowered the glasses and scratched at his beard. "It's bad, but not as bad as it could be. The camp guards appear to be locals, like Truper and Jocko, but the administrators are ComStar. I didn't see any Clanfolk, but that doesn't mean they aren't there."

Deirdre nodded as she gathered her hair back into a short ponytail. She tied it with a piece of string, then wrapped a dirty length of gauze around her head to obscure her right eye. "You think this will be enough of a disguise?"

Kai turned and smiled. She'd dressed in one of Truper's jumpsuits, which fit her like an elephant's skin would fit a yappy little dog. Along with the dirty rag wrapped around her head, it worked to hide all vestiges of her beauty. "If ComStar had fashion police, you'd be taken out and shot. I don't think anyone would recognize you. What about me?"

She squinted with her good eye, then gave him a grim smile. "The beard and some of your hair gathered into that topknot do make you look like a Kurita renegade. No one is going to connect you with either David Jewell *or* Kai Allard."

"Good." He tossed the binoculars back into the truck, then slid into the driver's seat. "Ready to beard the lion in his own den?"

She shifted the shoulder holster and pistol she wore to a slightly more comfortable position, though she still looked uneasy touching it. "Let's go now before I get some sense and try to talk you out of it."

Kai looked over his shoulder at the two body-bagged lumps in the rear. "Wouldn't matter. You'd be outvoted because they want to go home." He punched the ignition code into the dash-panel and the hovertruck rose on a cushion of air. Turning the wheel, he started it down the dirt track and on into the mouth of the dragon.

The dust cloud the hovertruck raised forced all the prisoners on the side of the road to turn away and cough out the choking haze. As much as Kai hated doing it to them, he knew it seriously reduced the chances of his being recognized. The last thing he needed was to be identified while in the clutches of the enemy.

A tall Com Guard stopped the hovertruck at the gate. "What's you business?"

Kai jerked a thumb toward the bed of the truck. "Deliveries. Two ripe ones."

The man glanced back at the two bodies, then wrinkled his nose with disgust. "Take 'em to Building Three. That's the morgue and disbursement center." He signaled someone to open the first of the double gates.

Kai eased the hovertruck forward. After the gate behind him closed, the one in front opened. He steered the truck through and then toward the rear of the camp. "Remember, you don't say anything, okay?"

Deirdre nodded mutely and Kai smiled approval that she'd passed his test. He pulled the truck around to the small door beneath a huge scarlet number three painted on the front of the Quonset hut. He killed the engines, dropping the truck to the ground, then waited for the curling cloud of dust to settle a tan patina over the windscreen before he opened the door.

Deirdre followed him two steps back. Kai pushed the door open with his foot, then stepped inside to dust himself off. Deirdre slipped in behind him and slumped against the wall.

Three horrified ComStar clerks looked up at him as if he were a ghost. One man, clearly outraged as dust covered his papers, shot to his feet. "Must you?"

Kai looked at him through narrowed eyes, then spat into his wastebasket.

Another man, older and wiser, pulled his compatriot back and forced him down into his chair. He looked up at Kai with a wan smile. "May I help you?" he asked in strained tones.

"Got two fer ya, see?" Kai sucked at his teeth as if trying to remove a bit of food stuck between two of them. "Bit messy and flyblown, but good ones."

The man's expression soured a bit. "You have two renegades?"

Kai nodded.

The man motioned Kai toward a chair beside his desk. Kai settled into it and slumped down so that the back of his head rested on the top of the seat's backrest, and his butt all but slid off the seat itself. He perched his elbows on the chair arms and his left hand strayed toward playing with a small ComStar flag on the desk.

The clerk moved the flag to the other side of the desk. "Do these renegades have names?"

Kai nodded.

The man waited for a bit, then cleared his throat. "What were their names?"

"Harry Truper and Dave Jewell."

The other two clerks turned to look at Kai.

Kai smiled and spat into the wastebasket again.

They went back to their work while the first clerk nervously punched the names into his computer. "Ah, Mister, ah, Harry Truper is a bounty hunter just like you."

"Not no more."

"Excuse me?"

Kai slowly levered himself up in the chair. "He's dead, see? Him and this Dave Jewell came to a shack me and the woman found after the Fedrats burned down our farm. They was planning to kill me and turn me in as Jewell. They said they'd use the woman and then cut her just like they did someone Jewell was running with before."

He glanced back cautiously at Deirdre, then leaned forward to whisper conspiratorially with the clerk. "They shouldn'ta said that. The woman ain't been right since some Fedrats took their liberty call out on her, without so much as leaving a C-bill behind, *wakarimaska*? She went and did for Truper, see, and I got Jewell after a bit of a gunfight."

They both looked over at Deirdre. Right on cue, she giggled a bit and sucked on her fingers.

The clerk shuddered.

Kai picked at one of his molars with his little finger. "Anyway, we thought they was renegades until we backtracked them and found their hovercar. I figgered we might'es well get some money for them. They are worth money, right?" With the last, Kai let his voice rise and tightened his left hand down into a fist.

The clerk nodded rapidly. "Once we've identified them, you will be paid."

Kai winced and made a "tch" sound by sucking at his cheek, then cracking the corner of his mouth open. "Truper took one round through the face, and Jewell looks pretty gnawed on, *wakarimaska*? I got a bit angry, see, 'cause no one but no one, lays a hand on the woman 'cept me." He lightly punched the clerk's shoulder. "Same way with your missus, eh? Husbandly duties, right?"

"Er, right."

"Right." Kai smiled unevenly. "Look, don't know how much those wankers were worth, but this bounty-hunting stuff seems easy. We got Truper's truck and his gear. You got more assignments fer us?"

The man nodded and pushed an electrotablet toward Kai, then held out the light-pen. "Sign here and you'll get your money. One hundred C-bills is more than you should get, but you were so put out by these people."

Kai forced his eyes wide open. He knew that Dave Jewell, according to the warrant he'd destroyed, was worth ten times that amount, and he had a fair idea who was going to end up with the difference. He turned toward Deirdre and smiled. "Hear that, sweet? Seventy C-bills for those two. Your share is a whole twenty-five!"

She giggled again.

Kai winked at the clerk as he turned around. "Cute thing, but high finance is beyond her, *wakarimaska*?" He gripped the light pen like a dagger and scored an X across the tablet.

The clerk smiled smugly and dug the requisite amount of ComStar scrip from a cash box in his desk drawer. He covertly slid that over to Kai, then handed him two more wanted posters complete with pictures of the individuals being hunted. Kai recognized one name as that of someone who had been with the planetary militia, but his expression remained blank.

"Since you have Truper's truck, you can keep his sector for searches. Good luck on these two." The clerk refrained from offering Kai his hand. "Two of my people have already removed the bodies from your truck, so you are free to go."

"Astral! I'll get these two wankers and we'll be back." Kai smiled and patted the man on his shoulder. "You'll be seeing lots of us in the future."

Back in the hovertruck, Kai started it up and headed out toward the gate. He drove slowly enough to scan the faces of prisoners working within the camp and outside on the road. Once through the twin gates and beyond where chain gangs were working, he increased his speed.

"How did they look to you, Doctor?"

She pulled the gauze from her head. "Malnourished. Some are obviously sick. I didn't see many with bandages, so either they sent the battle-wounded to a hospital . . ."

"Or they've buried them somewhere." Kai frowned. "That's what I was thinking anyway." His gaze flicked to the rear-view mirrors, but the dust curtain let him see nothing of the camp. "I'm happy we've not been captured."

"I second that." She shivered within Truper's outsized clothes. "What do we do next?"

Kai shrugged. "The way I see it, we have two choices. The first is to run as far and as fast as we can."

"That has merit. What is the second?"

"They assigned Truper's old territory to us. Therefore we know of at least one place on this planet where the hunters won't find us."

She nodded, then looked at him sidelong. "Tough choice. I'll have to think on it. By the way, did you mean what you said back in the camp?"

Kai frowned, trying to remember exactly what he'd said. "You mean the part about you being cute?"

Deirdre shook her head. "No, the part about twenty-five of those C-bills being mine."

Kai smiled. "Go you one better, Doc. Nothing but a fifty-fifty split for the two of us. Let's see, I got seventy C-bills . . ."

"Kai . . ."

It amazed the ComStar clerk that Taman Malthus could study the stinking corpse of Dave Jewell without gagging. "That's him, Star Captain. There's your Dave Jewell."

The Elemental's head came up and the clerk regretted having drawn attention to himself. "You are in error, Acolyte." Malthus reached down and brought the body's right hand up into view. "This man has calluses on his right hand, suggesting it is the hand he used most. He was right-handed. Jewell was not."

The clerk swallowed hard. "That is not possible."

Malthus smiled easily and let the hand thump back onto the examining table. "It is. You yourself paid Dave Jewell money for bringing in his own corpse." The Elemental snorted, then shook his head. "This Jewell makes for most interesting prey, *quiaff*?"

The clerk nodded mutely.

Malthus closed the bag and wiped his hands on the clerk's shirt. "I will ignore the fact that you let your own greed blind you to what was going on here. *That* is ComStar business. I see no need to complicate things by notifying Demi-Precentor Khalsa."

"No, sir."

"Good. You said you gave the bounty hunter and his woman more targets?"

"Yes, Star Captain. They are working Truper's old territory."

"Excellent." Malthus steered the clerk toward the door

with a heavy hand on the back of the man's neck. "You will provide me with a map of your search sectors."

The Elemental glanced back at the two bodies stretched out on tables in the morgue. "That is what happens when you pit members of the criminal class against a warrior. Now we will show you freebirths how real Warriors deal with another Warrior. The bidding for this assignment will be fierce, but the hunt will be worth it."

19

Bethel
Capellan March, Federated Commonwealth
20 March 3052

Nicholas Chung fastened the straps of his safety harness across his chest. "I'll be decelerating to only a decimeter per second for docking. Please fasten yourself into the jump seat."

His passenger laughed lightly. "Come now, Chung, you need not sound like such an old woman. I've not lived this long to die from a bump when your DropShip docks with the JumpShip."

Chung hit a warning button on his command console's left side. It caused a series of five tones to sound throughout the ship, warning of an impending jump. "You may have been my commander on Spica, lo, those many eons ago, but I am in command of the *Te Kuaiche*."

"But I am the one who has hired your DropShip to carry me home."

Chung let a smile wash away his nervousness. "True enough, but then is it not my duty to ensure the safety of my patron?"

"You are quite correct in pointing this out."

Chung's smile remained in place as he heard the jump seat snap down into place and the metallic click of the safety straps being fastened together. His hands slid down to the joysticks on the ends of his command couch. On the primary screen in front of him, he had the docking link for the

JumpShip *Kensing Bay.* As he moved the left joystick up a bit, the computer-projected crosshairs centered themselves on the dock link. The crosshairs pulsed and Chung hit the button on top of the joystick to lock the DropShip on course.

"Not unlike lining up a target for a 'Mech's weapons, eh, Chung?"

"True." With the right joystick, he cut his velocity so the DropShip drifted very slowly to the appointed link-up. "Fortunately, JumpShips do not shoot back."

His passenger did not answer immediately and Chung sensed deep and dark thought emanating from that corner of the pilot's station. He knew that when his ship hooked up with the JumpShip *Kensing Bay,* the JumpShip's Captain would trigger the jump to Daniels. In the blink of an eye, the very fabric of space would warp around both ships and they would reappear in another star system over thirty light years distant.

And thirty light-years closer to Sian. Thirty light-years closer to Romano Liao.

Chung turned in his chair but could barely make out his passenger in the shadows. "Are you certain you want to continue this journey? You need not go, you know."

"I have no choice, Chung." A fist sheathed with a black glove emerged from the shadows. "Romano Liao killed my beloved. She all but orphaned my children. Her predations have slaughtered hundreds of millions within the Capellan Confederation." The fist vanished, to be replaced by a heavy thump of something hitting the bulkhead. "This is a journey I should have made years ago. I waited too long and it has cost me dearly. No more."

A metallic thunk echoed through the ship. "We're linked. Brace for jump."

Though he made his living piloting DropShips between JumpShips and planets, Nicholas Chung never got used to the sensation of jumping between worlds. Everything he saw blurred, then each star expanded until the brilliant rainbow of lights swirled around in a crazy mosaic of colors. He felt himself being smashed flat down into one dimension, then cycling around through a dozen other dimensions until suddenly he was back in the solid reality of the three dimensions where he spent most of his time.

He shook himself, then grabbed the command couch arms as a wave of nausea passed through him. He swallowed against the bile, then hit a switch on the panel at his right. "DropShip *Te Kuaiche* is away. Thanks for the lift, *Kensing Bay*."

Chung glanced over at his passenger. "You said you had passage for us into the Compact from Daniels?"

His guest nodded. "Bring up a system chart. The Jump-Ship is supposed to be waiting in a wide orbit around the fourth world."

Chung punched up the chart for the Daniels system and touched the icon of a JumpShip near the fourth planet. "The only thing there is the FCSS *Valiant Heart,* and it's at 2 AU from the world. Is that it?"

"Steady as she goes, Captain Chung."

Chung's jaw dropped. "You can't be serious. That's a Federated Commonwealth JumpShip. It will be heading out toward the front with the Clans, not into the Compact."

"Chung, even Hanse Davion acknowledges the serious-ness of my mission. The *Valiant Heart* is waiting for us."

Chung set a course and started his ship accelerating toward the warship. "I hope you know what you are doing."

"Rest assured, Chung, I do. 'An eye for an eye' is a con-cept simple enough for even Romano to understand on first pass." A low laugh sounded from the corner. "Too bad it will be her last!"

20

Fort Ian Training Center, Port Moseby
Virginia Shire, Federated Commonwealth
21 March 3052

Even though the shadows of the briefing room shrouded him, Shin Yodama felt conspicuous among so many Federated Commonwealth officers. Seated at Victor Davion's left hand, across the dark table from Galen Cox, he wished he were invisible. He noticed that the seat next to him remained vacant and only Galen had made an attempt to engage him in conversation before the briefing began.

The tension in the room was so thick it almost smothered him. For a half-second, he imagined it was focused upon him, then rejected the thought with a quick, involuntary shake of his head. *Not focused on me, but on this end of the table.*

Hovering directly over the center of the rectangular briefing table, holographic BattleMechs went through their paces. The exercise footage, taken from the gun-cameras mounted in *Locust*s used for observation, showed the incredible firepower of the assembled BattleMech unit. In highly coordinated assaults, they combined their fire to reduce targets to scrap in seconds.

Shin, though he had been present at the exercise, took time to review his assessment of this unit, Victor Davion's Revenants. They had been reorganized into a reinforced battalion of just over fifty 'Mechs. The unit was further divided into a fire support company, an assault company, and two fast-response "sprint" companies. Victor's command lance was made up of swift 'Mechs, making it a complement of the sprint companies.

And what 'Mechs they are! Shin knew from conversations with Victor that even the Prince had not expected his unit to be refitted so quickly and well. In the holographic battle being waged above the table, Shin saw BattleMechs that had never before appeared in the battles of the Successor States. *Axmen, Marauder II*s, and a host of other new 'Mech models populated the Revenant ranks, making the holovid of the training session look more like a commercial HV release than a record of a unit in action.

Victor's own *Daishi* OmniMech was the jewel of the lot. Shin had seen pictures of its condition after Alyina, and yet its refitting was now amazingly complete. The squat, boxy torso showed none of the damage it had taken in battle with the Clans, and the right foot had been replaced. Though the 'Mech's birdlike legs gave it an odd gait, Shin saw in Victor's steady piloting a deadly intent that the *Daishi*'s crushing firepower fulfilled. Its array of missiles, lasers, and autocannons made the OmniMech well-suited for anything from indirect fire-support missions to the fiercest infighting.

Even the normal 'Mechs that had survived Alyina, like Galen Cox's *Crusader,* had been swapped out for the new and unusual avatars of their former selves. The *Crusader* lost some firepower in the revamping of its short-range missile systems and the removal of one machine gun, but the addition of a flamer and an anti-missile system more than compensated the loss. More important, the new *Crusader* featured jump jets, which gave the huge 'Mech far more mobility. Double-strength heat sinks meant it would not overheat as quickly, increasing its ability to sustain an assault during battle.

Victor hit a switch as the holovid ended, and slowly brought up the lights. Shin noted the seriousness of Victor's expression as he gazed at the officers who commanded his lances. *If he has changed in the time since we trained on Outreach, it is only in his maturity. It is the Dragon's good fortune that the Fox's son plots with us and not against us.*

Victor pointed toward where the 'Mechs had been battling. "You've all seen the holovids before, but I wanted us to review that section together to let you know I'm very pleased with our progress. Your people are meshing well together, and everyone has come up to speed on their new 'Mechs far more quickly than I expected. This is good, and I commend you all for this level of improvement." He toyed with the zipper of his olive jumpsuit. "Letters of commendation have been entered in all your files over General Kaulkas' signature."

That brought smiles to the officers' faces, but did nothing to dispel the tension in the room. Shin felt the gathered officers waiting for the other shoe to drop, and Victor's hesitation, feigned or not, increased the suspense. Shin suddenly felt a pang of sympathy for the man.

"Rumors have begun to circulate among the Revenants concerning the nature of our training," Victor said finally. "I have been pushing you and your people hard and plenty of them have sensed a purpose in these exercises. Yes, each is different, in that we're hitting a simulated Clan force with a different approach each time, but we're always on a mission with a time limit. Our job is to land, hit the enemy hard, keep reinforcements at bay long enough to evacuate someone, then we pull out ourselves."

Victor glanced over at Shin. "Many of your people have also noted the arrival of *Sho-sa* Yodama and his people. They're uneasy about being observed by Combine officers, and everyone on this base knows I've spent a lot of time talking with *Sho-sa* Yodama. The rumor shop has been busy forging links between our training and the Draconis Combine. Rumors will really begin to fly fast and furious when Yodama and his people form yet another lance and start working with us in equipment they brought or we have lent to them."

That statement produced whispered oaths and an isolated cheer from the assembled officers. Several stared daggers at Shin, but the yakuza turned them away with a smile. One or two blushed and lowered their gazes, while the older officers stared at the Kuritan in open challenge.

Victor ignored these unspoken exchanges. "What I'm going to say goes no further than this room for the time being. What we have been doing in these training exercises is preparing for a mission that will take us a long way from here. I haven't yet received permission to launch the operation, but I will be meeting with General Kaulkas today, and then Marshal Morgan Hasek-Davion inside two weeks to discuss it. Before I do that, however, I must be certain you're all behind me."

He held up a hand to forestall any immediate affirmations of loyalty, then his eyes focused distantly as he considered his next words. "You all know I have had, in effect, two commands shot out from under me. The Twelfth Donegal Guards collapsed when the Jade Falcons hit them during the first Clan wave." A smirk flashed briefly on Victor's lips as he patted Galen's left shoulder. "I was ordered off the planet, and Hauptmann Cox here saw to it that I obeyed.

"Most of you were there at Alyina when the Falcons again hammered my command. And some are even saying that I would have lost the Tenth Lyran Guards on Twycross had Kai Allard not done the impossible in taking out a whole Clan unit by himself. Some might now see me as a Jonah, and Kai Allard as my good luck charm. With him gone, they would believe any unit I lead will falter."

Victor took in a deep breath, and Shin's heart ached for the Prince as he bared his soul. "Things will not get better, I fear, as I explain this mission to you. In short, here it is: Hohiro Kurita, heir to the Dragon Throne, has been trapped deep behind enemy lines by a superior Clan force. Last we knew, which was a status message sent three weeks ago, he was alive and in hiding with his unit. Their continued ability to fight is in serious doubt and their intelligence concerning the force we will face is spotty at best.

"The Combine cannot spare the forces necessary to mount a rescue operation. In fact, if we are not given permission to proceed with this operation, Hohiro Kurita will never leave Teniente. What we have been training for is to slip into Teniente, pull Hohiro's forces out, and escape."

Shin read surprise on the faces of most of the officers, and outright disgust on the faces of the rest. He assumed those who appeared most annoyed at the news were veterans of more than one battle with the Draconis Combine. *They cling to the old ways and still see us as more dangerous an enemy than the Clans.*

Victor leaned forward, supporting himself on his fists. "Yes, that's right, we intend to rescue a future leader of the Snakes. I don't care if you don't like that aspect of the mission—it is immaterial and unimportant. All I need from you is your confidence in my ability to lead this mission. Without that, any mission—rescue or not—would be useless."

The Prince straightened up and folded his arms defensively across his chest. "I'll leave you to discuss this among yourselves. Speak frankly. There will be no reports back to me on who said what. When you have decided whether or not you think I can command you as effectively in a hot LZ as I do here, Galen will let me know."

Victor turned crisply and stepped through the door to the outside. Shin made to follow him, but as Galen stood and came to the head of the table, he stopped the yakuza. "I'd prefer that you stayed, *Sho-sa*. Your input will be as valuable and necessary as that of anyone else here." The fair-haired MechWarrior looked out at his fellow officers. "Start jawing, folks."

A female leftenant leaned back in her chair. "Begging the Drac's pardon, Hauptmann, I don't see how mounting a rescue mission in Kurita space makes any sense. Supply lines are too long and we've no chance of logistical support if things get messy. I say the mission is a no-go."

Galen shook his head. "Wrong answer, Livinsky. You're not voting on the feasibility of the mission, but on Victor's ability to lead it."

"A good leader would have taken all that into account, Galen," she shot back. "A good leader wouldn't have hatched this fool plan."

Seeing other officers nod in agreement, Shin leaned forward to speak. "Forgive me, but those things have been discussed. My superiors have agreed to supply the force with transport and munitions. We are working to see what kind of relief force we can muster to rescue the rescuers, if that becomes necessary."

"Old Dracs in older 'Mechs," scoffed another officer.

"I'd remind you, Carson, that old warriors in old 'Mechs kept the Smoke Jaguars and the Nova Cats out of Imperial City on Luthien." Galen turned sharply to Livinsky. "There, Leftenant, you have your support. What about Victor's abilities?"

A dark-haired man at the far end of the table stretched, signalling his desire to speak. "Not wanting to be disrespectful, Galen, but the Prince said it himself: he's lost two units. I lived through the hell on Alyina and I don't mind telling you I don't relish serving under a commander who's got a Napoleon complex."

Shin frowned. "Napoleon complex?"

The officer nodded. "You Dracs may call it something else, but it boils down to this: Victor's trying too hard to prove that being small is no disadvantage."

Shin raised an eyebrow. "It strikes me as amusing that you consider physical size any special factor affecting what type of 'Mech pilot or commander a man can be."

The man waved Shin's comment away. "It goes deeper than that with Victor, *Sho-sa*. He's trying to prove himself the equal of his father and of Morgan Hasek-Davion. That's a tall order, and one he's not up to."

"You're full of it, Murphy!" A young leftenant shot to his feet. "If you think Victor's got an axe to grind, you're crazy."

"What the hell do you know, Hudson?" The scorn in Murphy's voice lashed the tall young man. "You may be a hotshot from the Skye Rangers, but you don't know what you're talking about. Hell, you've only been on the sidelines of the war so far. Wait until you start to see *your* buddies die."

Before Dan Hudson could say anything, Galen leaped into the fray. "But I haven't been on the sidelines, Murphy, and I've seen a damned sight more of this war than you have." Galen jerked a thumb back into his own chest. "I was the guy who had to slug Victor to get his butt off Trellwan. He didn't want to go even though we both knew the planet was lost. Right up until I decked him, he was thinking and planning and trying to work out a way to deal with the Clans. Even after that, all the way out to the JumpShip that would take us away, he studied all the tactical telemetry coming up from Trellwan. He studied that stuff so much that he knew the name, age, and serial number of every man and woman who died in his command."

"Great, Galen, I'm so glad I'll be remembered when I'm dead." Murphy pounded a fist onto the table. "I'd prefer being alive and forgotten."

"Murphy, you haven't got a clue, have you?" Galen shook his head. "On Twycross, yeah, Kai saved our butts, but we all know what happened in that fight, don't we? Remember how we pulled our units around so that the Clans would have to turn, too, forcing their reinforcements to fight through their own people to get at us? And if you can't remember, Victor fought until his 'Mech was clean on ammo and then some. He was one of the last guys off the battlefield, and as I recall, you retired before he did after that one."

Livinsky sat forward. "We're not arguing Murphy's strengths or weaknesses, Galen. We're talking about Victor, remember? Maybe it's all well and good that you and this Ranger rat are behind him, but Murph's protest still stands. How can we entrust command to a man who will probably kill us trying to live up to his father's legend?"

Hudson shot Galen a hopeless look and Galen rubbed his forehead with one hand. "You don't get it, do you?"

"Get what?" asked Murphy.

"You think Victor is trying to live up to the example his father set, right? You think he's trying to become the Fox, right?"

"Hard lock and fire, Galen."

"Morons." Galen's voice dropped low and dripped contempt. "Victor's already so far beyond where his father was that someday they'll remember the Fox as his predecessor, nothing more."

Murphy snorted loudly. "That's treason, Galen."

"Galen speaks the truth."

Everyone looked at Shin as he spoke. "With all due respect to Hanse Davion, the threats you people faced from the Capellan Confederation and from my own Draconis Combine are nothing compared to the Clans. When Hanse Davion battled our forces, he was fighting against similar technology and warriors with similar skills. Yes, Davion was a genius and accomplished things that no other leader in the Successor States had done, but those deeds are nothing compared to battles being fought today."

Shin's dark eyes glittered. "In the Fourth Succession War, Hanse Davion hit the Capellan world Tikonov with the eight Crucis Lancers Regimental Combat Teams. That was the greatest 'Mech engagement in the Inner Sphere since Aleksandr Kerensky sacked Terra to kill the Usurper. The military experts of the day believed Davion could never mount such an assault, but he did it. He succeeded.

"That victory, however, is nothing compared to the recent battle for Luthien. I was there. We had sixteen crack regiments, including Wolf's Dragoons and the Kell Hounds. We had well over thirteen hundred BattleMechs against the eight hundred the Clans threw at us. Even with the advanced 'Mech technology the mercenaries had and some 'Mech-

killing aircraft we put into service, the Clans almost succeeded in taking Luthien. No one from the Inner Sphere ever
dared dream of what the Clans nearly accomplished in a single day."

Galen nodded solemnly. "Times have changed. Victor
knows how to fight the Clans, and he's spent most of his
waking hours training you clowns, reviewing intelligence
from our sources and the Dracs, or planning out his assault.
There's never been a military leader who so thoroughly understands the opposition."

Another officer, an older grizzled man, rubbed his hand
over his chin. "What are you telling us, Galen?"

"What I'm telling you, Charlie, is this: Victor isn't Hanse
Davion and he isn't Jaime Wolf. He *is* the worst nightmare
the Clans have ever had. If we're with him, we'll stroll into
Teniente and come out with Hohiro Kurita, leaving only
smoking Jaguars behind."

Galen pointed straight at Murphy. "And before you get on
about how Victor is trying so hard to be his father, think on
this: Would Hanse Davion have even bothered to ask for this
vote of confidence, or would he have just told us to go?
Give Victor credit for wanting your confidence, not just assuming he's already got it as his birth-right."

Shin saw a nervous Victor Davion look up from his desk
as he and Galen entered the office. "Galen, Shin, what's the
verdict?"

Galen smiled broadly and Shin copied the expression to
his own face. "The Revenants are behind you, boss. Now it's
up to you to get permission to go."

Relief flooded Victor's face. "I'll get on that right away."

"Good, but if they say 'no,' don't sweat it."

"Excuse me?"

Galen threw him a wink. "The Revenants voted to follow
you to Teniente even if we have to do it on a two-week
pass."

Alyina
Trellshire, Jade Falcon Occupation Zone
21 March 3052

Kai felt his mouth go dry as he pressed a hand to the sharp-edged footprint. The depression went down a full two centimeters into the slightly muddy soil. "Whoever made this is *big.*"

"And the track was made recently." Deirdre, kneeling beside him in the brush, traced the print with her finger. "What do you think?"

"I think we're correct in our suspicion that we're being stalked." Kai wiped his fingers on the soiled legs of his jumpsuit. "Someone this big has to be an Elemental."

"We're lucky, then, that he left this print, unless . . ."

". . . Unless he left it here on purpose." Kai pointed off through the woods. "Best return to our camp and gather up our equipment. This zone might have been safe for a little while, but that little while is clearly over."

Deirdre nodded in agreement and started off through the undergrowth. Even in the half-light of the false dawn, she picked her way effortlessly through the brambles and ferns carpeting the forest in undergrowth. Like a wraith, she slipped between two birch trees and vanished from sight.

Kai smiled, marveling at how well Deirdre had adapted to life in the wilderness. It turned out that she, too, had spent time as a Youth Pathfinder. As she put it, living off the land was less a case of learning what she could and could not do as it was trying to remember what she had learned on Path-finder outings. While Kai had concentrated on things like electronics and athletics in his Pathfinder career, she had done more camping and herb-lore studies that, combined with her medical training, made life away from civilization much easier.

As he came through the birch stand, he saw her crouched just below the ridgeline separating them from their camp. She glanced back at him, then waved him forward. She stood and darted ahead, her head vanishing as she sank back down on the other side of the ridge. Hurrying up the hillside, Kai reached her first position and looked down at their camp.

They'd set it up in an open area in another birch copse. Deirdre said she thought it was a deerstand and Kai had started dreaming of venison, but they hadn't seen anything larger than a rabbit in the week since settling there. The birches and undergrowth grew closely enough to conceal the camp, and the trees even broke up the smoke from the small fire they allowed themselves each night.

Kai shook his head ruefully. Any number of his friends would have described the setting, including the lovely Doctor Lear, as romantic, definitely the fulfillment of a fantasy or two. But Deirdre still held herself apart from him, even though their relations were on the friendly side of cordial, and they both slept in the same petrochemtarp lean-to. Kai was fairly certain it had nothing to do with the bounty-hunter incident, which left him back guessing about her early days and his father's adventures during the war.

As she started down toward the camp, Kai eased the autorifle from his shoulder and held it by the pistol-grip. He worked toward his left, giving himself an angle on Deirdre and another perspective on the camp. He slid down the hill on dead leaves, then came to a stop behind a thick pine. Standing, he looped the sling around his left forearm to steady the rifle.

At the edge of the birch stand, Deirdre waited and watched. As the first sliver of sun came over the top of the ridge, the light ignited the green in the leaves and slowly drew a shadow-curtain back across their campsite. Deirdre gathered up a couple of pieces of wood, then stood and walked into the camp.

He had no warning of the trap waiting for her and no way

of spotting it. As she neared the ring of fire-blackened stones in front of the lean-to, her right leg sank to the knee into the ground. The sticks flew as she caught herself on her hands. Kai saw her shoulders hunch as she tried to pull her leg free, then her body jerked and her shoulders eased.

"Calm yourself, Lear," commanded a husky voice from beyond the lean-to's black tarp. "You might as well come in, Jewell. She is stuck fast and I will kill her if you do not give yourself up."

"Stay back, get away!" Deirdre turned as much as she could in Kai's direction. "Don't come in here. Just get away."

"Admirable, Lear, but foolish." Kai saw the red dot from a laser targeting-scope meander along the sand and caress her right thigh. "Her life is in your hands, Jewell. Come in now and I let her live."

Kai stood slowly and walked into the camp. "I'm here."

"Very good. Strip the clip from the autorifle, clear the chamber, and discard it. Do the same with your pistol, please."

Kai complied with the command, but purposely made no move to toss away the survival knife tucked into the top of his right boot. "I've done it. You can come out now."

Kai nearly swallowed his tongue as the Elemental made his appearance. Dropping ten meters straight down from one of the birch trees, he landed solidly on both feet, knees bending to absorb the shock of landing. He wore his long black hair brushed back from his face and the outline of black grease around his eyes made them look sunk back into his skull. His black garb clung to his body like a second skin, covering him from throat to groin. Lacking sleeves or legs, the outfit reminded Kai of the uniforms wrestlers at the New Avalon Military Academy wore in their matches.

He's every bit as big as I imagined from the footprint, and then some! Kai knew the Clanner topped him by a head and a half, and weighed at least twice as much. The man's biceps were thicker than Kai's thighs and his chest could have doubled for a DropShip landing pad. *Maybe it would have been better if Truper had shot me.*

The Elemental bowed his head in a salute. "So you are the nit causing the uproar with ComStar. How amusing. Our Star Captain warned us about approaching you, but I deduced, after watching you for several days, that luck had more to do with your eluding ComStar than did any skill. I could have bid away my eyes and still found you."

He held up a rectangular black device. "You even let me trick you into thinking I had a gun with this laser sight. We knew this was the sector where you would most likely be lurking, so I had to bid hard to get it. Another one in my unit bid a single bullet, but I beat her by bidding a sight and a knife." Reaching around behind himself, he drew forth a wicked silver dagger and flourished it. "Dig a hole with this, sharpen some sticks with it, and I have you. Hardly worth the effort."

Kai tried to keep his face impassive as his spirit imploded. He looked at the weapons he had discarded and mentally kicked himself. *If he had kept talking, I could have. . . .* Deirdre looked over at him with an apology on her face, but he shook his head. "This is my fault. I am sorry I failed you. I . . ."

"You, Jewell, are the sorriest excuse for a warrior I have seen on this world." The scorn in the Elemental's words cut at Kai. "Taman Malthus thought to make you a bondsman to our Clan, but I think I will merely summon Com Guards to take you to their reeducation camp. You are a perfect example of everything a warrior should not be."

Kai bristled at the insult. "Oh, and a soldier who disobeys his superior officer is better than I am?" Part of him knew any reply was foolish, but two and a half months on the run had worn his sense of restraint quite thin. "Our warriors, as poor as they might seem to you, at least learn how to obey!"

The Elemental's piggish eyes opened wide as Kai's remark hit home. "Our Star Captain may have won himself a Bloodname, but it is tainted. No one would fight for it because of the disgrace of its last owner on Twycross. Taman's lack of judgement in going for a Bloodname with an inferior pedigree is again evident in his caution concerning you. Were you as dangerous as he thinks, your capture would guarantee my nomination in the next Bloodname contest for House Konrad. As it is now, you will be the core of a joke I tell."

He's right, Kai, you are a joke. The voice echoing up from the darkness of Kai's soul sought to suck him down into despair. *He is bigger than you, and far deadlier. He is a real warrior. Give in to him. He can protect Deirdre, so give her to him.*

Kai's weariness with running and hiding started to con-spire with his self-doubt, but something else clicked in him. *No, dammit, I have survived too long to be dismissed as a joke.* He slid his knife from the boot-sheath. "You want something to laugh about? Perhaps you're ticklish. We can find out."

"Oh, so the slug thinks it has teeth, does it?" The Elemen-tal barked out a laugh. "Yes, you have tickled my funny-bone with that one. Now put your knife away before I am forced to hurt you."

"Do it, do it," Deirdre shouted. "It's over. Don't do any-thing stupid."

Stupid. Cowardly. You embarrass her, as you embarrass your family and your nation. Kai felt fear rise up and con-strict his throat. He shifted the knife to his left hand, then wiped the sweat from his palm on his pant leg. *It is true. He will kill me.*

"Still game?" The Elemental raised an eyebrow in sur-prise. "Perhaps this expedition will not have been a waste."

"No!" Deirdre tried to pull her leg free, but cried out in pain and stopped the attempt. "Don't fight him. Surrender. Live."

Kai shot her a brave smile to mask his true feelings. "I don't think letting me live is quite what Demi-Precentor Khalsa has in mind, Deirdre. Remember, I killed two guards, shot up his office, and kidnapped you." He looked up at the Elemental. "As soon as we are done bargaining, I am ready."

"Bargaining?" The Jade Falcon nodded sagely and cast the laser sight aside. "I am Corbin and I will grant you a Warrior's death."

"That gives me great comfort, but it is not quite what I had in mind," Kai said as he shifted the knife to his right hand. "You are much bigger than I, so I demand a conces-sion from you. If I blood you, you will let Doctor Lear go free."

Corbin's quizzical look melted into a grim grin. "Bar-gained well and done."

"Don't do this! Not for me!" Deirdre shouted.

The Elemental nodded Kai a salute. "To honor you, if you fail, I will make her a bondswoman."

"And I will do everything I can to make sure you don't have to go to that trouble." Kai realized that his bargain and Corbin's response meant his feeble attempt at misdirection had worked and reminded Kai of another battle against the Clans. Adler Malthus, the commander of the Jade Falcon unit making its way through the Great Gash on Twycross, had fallen prey to a similar deception. *How odd that history repeats itself. Here I am again facing a superior Clan force, with Dr. Lear's fate depending upon my success.*

The two men slowly began to circle the small clearing. Kai watched Corbin and began to dread the panther-like fluidity of the man's motions. The Jade Falcon stayed up on the balls of his feet and kept his left hand weaving back and forth, continually hiding and revealing the blade of the dagger in his right hand. Corbin's steps ate up more ground than Kai's, ever shrinking the circle. *Like a noose, it tightens . . .*

Kai unconsciously dropped into his own fighting stance and switched the knife to his left hand. He concentrated on watching Corbin as a whole, not any one part of him. Kai also centered himself, bringing his breathing under control. He worried less about finding an opening through which he could thrust his knife than about reading Corbin for a sign of an impending attack.

Kai worked at ridding himself of panic. *What are my goals in this fight?* Kai took a half-step backward. *I must blood him, I must!*

Corbin closed and slashed left to right at Kai's midsection. Kai leaped back, then took a tentative swipe at Corbin's arm as the Elemental recovered. The return slash missed cleanly and the Jade Falcon pulled back to laugh. "*That* was an attack? Then I suppose she has to cut your food for you lest you starve."

Kai's face burned crimson. *Blood him? The only blood on him today will be yours.*

Corbin hunkered down in an unorthodox guard position. With the dagger clutched in his right hand and his right arm curled up over his shoulder like a scorpion's tail, the Elemental withdrew his most obvious threat. He held his left arm forward to guard his body and crouched low enough that he could get good distance on a lunge.

He flipped his left hand over and waggled his fingers at Kai. "Come on, you can have a free cut."

He mocks you! Kai snarled and darted forward. He feinted with his dagger at the man's hand, then stabbed out with his right foot and drove it into the Jade Falcon's thick left thigh. This did not slow Corbin, however, who pivoted on that leg, swept his left arm wide in a parry of the feint, then thrust his dagger forward in a move meant to spit Kai on the blade.

Without thinking, Kai shifted his knife from right hand to left and grabbed Corbin's right wrist in his own right hand. Planting his right foot, he twisted his body inside the Elemental's reach. Using the larger man's momentum against him, Kai drove his right hip into Corbin's midsection and tugged on his arm as he bent over. The Elemental shot up across Kai's back and landed hard on his rump.

The MechWarrior twisted the Elemental's arm, but before Kai could lock and break the elbow across his knee, Corbin pulled free. Kai slashed at him with the knife, but holding it in his left hand made the strike weak. Kai felt it hit, but it seemed not to affect the Clansman as he spun to his feet.

Corbin began to laugh defiantly, but when he pressed his left hand to the small of his back, it came away bloody. His brown eyes sparkled. "You are almost competent, Jewell, but I would have taken your kidneys and severed your spine with such a cut. There. You have blooded me and your doctor will go free. Now it is my turn."

Moving faster than any human being Kai had ever seen, Corbin came in again. Mirroring Kai's earlier move, the Elemental flipped his dagger into his left hand, then cut cruelly at the MechWarrior. Kai tried to jump back from the slash, but the tug he felt on his jumpsuit leg told him he had failed. The hot sting of Corbin's dagger slicing the flesh over his right thigh shocked him.

Kai half expected the Clansman to back off and gloat over his handiwork, but Corbin burrowed in close. Gingerly dancing back on his cut leg, Kai avoided the brunt of the charge, but not by much. He flicked out a right jab that caromed off his head, with the only effect being Corbin turning in Kai's direction.

Returning like for like, Corbin dropped a short right jab into Kai's ribs. The fist pounded like a sledgehammer into ribs barely recovered from being broken during the escape from ComStar. Agony exploded in Kai's chest and he hunched over to protect his ribs.

An open-handed cuff to the head blasted him on his feet and sent him flying. He landed in a heap, rolling to a stop in the ruins of the lean-to he and Deirdre had constructed. Tangled in the petrochem sheet, he fought himself halfway clear. Just as he realized he had lost his knife, a booted foot lifted him from the ground with a kick to his midsection. He slammed into a tree, then dropped to the foot of it and clawed breathlessly at pine needles and roots.

Unable to breathe and with his chest on fire, Kai braced for the next assault, thinking that Corbin would kill him this time. He tried to get up, but only made it halfway before collapsing again. *You are finished.*

Corbin's shadow fell across his face. "I was wrong. You are no Warrior, for no Warrior would just lie there." The Elemental filled his voice with contempt. "I will slay you and leave you in an unmarked grave so none of your kinsmen can be embarrassed by your failure."

Corbin's words found a willing echo in the dark voice that had always haunted Kai's thoughts. *You have ever been a failure, Kai Allard-Liao. They will erase you from the roll of Liaos, and none will dare speak your cursed name.*

Kai coughed and felt his ribs creak. "It doesn't matter. I beat you."

"You what?"

Kai panted for a second, then pulled himself up on his elbows. "I blooded you. You have to let her go. I won."

Corbin's malignant laughter filled the clearing. "Oh that? I agreed only because I thought it would get more fight out of you. I never intended to honor that bargain because only bargains struck between Warriors need be honored." Corbin squatted down with his hands resting on his knees. He stuck his face into Kai's. "No freebirth is ever enough of a Warrior to bargain with me."

As the Clanner started to bounce back upright, Kai struck. Stiffening the fingers of his right hand, he speared them into the Elemental's throat. The large man gurgled an outcry and toppled back, clutching his adam's apple. Kai kicked his feet free of the tarp and unsteadily rolled to his feet. Seeing his foe sprawled on his back, Kai stomped on his groin, then turned away and started limping toward the ruins of the lean-to to find his knife.

"Kai, look out!"

At Deirdre's warning, Kai threw himself forward onto his face and rolled to right. He saw Corbin pass through where he had just stood, then heard a heavy crunch as the Elemental tackled one of the birches holding up the lean-to. Corbin sank toward the ground, but he still clung to the tree and landed on his knees.

Kai grabbed half of the lean-to's crossbar and levered himself upright. As Corbin shook his head to clear it, Kai limped forward and swung the long club at the Elemental. It shattered across the man's broad back, but drove him face-first into the tree again. Rebounding, Corbin settled back on his haunches and Kai saw blood glistening on the tree's white bark.

The MechWarrior arced punch after punch in at Corbin's head. Each blow hit solidly and snapped Corbin's head around, but the man refused to go down. Kai's knuckles became slicked with the blood from Corbin's torn scalp and mashed nose. "Go down, damn you, go down!"

Corbin grinned up through a bloody mask. "Is that the best you can do?"

His right hand caught Kai in the ribs again, but Corbin's speed had lost its edge. The blow landed heavy and hard, knocking Kai back and making him hiss with pain, but he did not fall. Gritting his teeth, Kai sprang forward through the air as Corbin regained his feet. He caught the Elemental in the face with a flying kick.

Corbin flew back in a mist of blood and a hail of tooth fragments. He hit the ground on the same shoulder that had tackled the tree, and the resulting snap told Kai something had gone. Even so, the Clanner pushed up off the ground with his left arm and got one knee under him. Coming around, right arm dangling at his side, he snarled, "Maybe there is some fight to you after all."

Corbin charged, his left hand outstretched and twitching with murderous intent. It grabbed Kai's right shoulder and started to crush it even as Kai fell back before the assault. Grabbing the slick material of Corbin's bodysuit, Kai rolled onto his back and posted his left leg up into the Elemental's belly. At the top of the arc, Kai pushed off, and with a heave sent his enemy flying through the air.

Corbin slammed into the ground on top of the cold firepit in the center of the camp. A cloud of gray ashes rose up to smother the man lying halfway in and out of the circle of stones. Rolling over onto his hands and knees, Kai crawled toward the moaning Elemental, vaguely aware that the Clansman's head was at a peculiar angle to his shoulders.

Kneeling beside Corbin's head, Kai raised a fire-blackened rock in both hands. "Bury me in an unmarked grave, will you?" Kai stared down at the blood mingling with ashes. "Not in this lifetime, you don't."

"No, Kai, stop!"

He looked up and met Deirdre's terrified stare. "He has to die," he said.

"Kai," she whispered, "he's already dead." She reached out toward him. "Please, Kai, you aren't like your father!"

He looked from the mangled Corbin to Deirdre and back again, still somewhat dazed from the adrenaline rage that had saved his life. "My father? What are you talking about?"

She covered her face in her hands and slumped forward. Kai tossed the stone aside and struggled to his feet. He dropped to his knees again and took her in his arms. "What is it about my father? Tell me."

"Your father is a murderer." She buried her head against his chest, but he sensed she would have pulled back if not for her trapped leg. "He murdered my father in the fights on Solaris."

Kai shook his head. "He never fought anyone named Lear."

"I know. My father was Peter Armstrong, the first man he killed in the games on Solaris. Your father ambushed and killed him. My father never had a chance." Her voice grew small. "For a year or two, when I was just a little girl, my father was a martyr. The evil Justin Xiang had killed my father, as loyal a son of House Davion as ever there was in the Inner Sphere. Wolfson and Capet were also heroes. When my mother remarried, I didn't want to change my name even though my stepfather was a good man—a surgeon . . . Roy Lear. At school, I had many friends and everyone liked me.

"Then your father turned out to be some agent who helped win the war. People started to refer to my father as a no-good renegade. The same kids who used to want to hear stories about my father now teased me. They said he was as bad as the Usurper, Stefan Amaris, and that they were glad Justin Allard had killed him. Some of their parents even said I was tainted by bad blood and they wouldn't let their children play with me."

Kai pulled back, spotted his knife, and picked it up again.

Slowly he began to dig at the ground surrounding her leg. "That's why you became a doctor?"

Deirdre looked down at the ground but focused on nothing. "No. I became a doctor because I had so often fantasized about being able to save my father had I been there. I joined the Armed Forces of the Federated Commonwealth as a way of proving I was not from a traitor family. I wanted to give something back to the Federated Commonwealth to atone for whatever my father had done. Whatever his crimes had been, I didn't think they deserved death."

"My father's not a murderer." Kai scooped some of the dirt from the hole around her leg and pulled free a slender wooden stake that had been pointing downward. "He didn't want your father to die."

"How can you say that? He ambushed him and killed him. It's on a holovid available almost anywhere."

"I know." Kai pulled a second stake free from the hole. "When I was a child, in school, I got into one of those 'my father is tougher than your father' arguments that ended up with another child running home in tears. I told him my father could kill his father."

Deirdre shuddered. "Other children used to tease me about Justin Allard coming after me, too."

Kai sat back on his haunches, a lump rising in his throat even as he began to speak. "My father took me home that day and showed me the holovid of the fight with your father. He turned the sound off and told me what he had been thinking instead of letting me hear the announcer describe the fight in glowing, dramatic terms. His job was to play the stereotype of a treacherous Liao fighter, both to justify his split with the Federated Suns and to attract the attention of Maximilian Liao. With the first barrage he loosed against your father, he knew he'd damaged your father's 'Mech too much to continue the fight. He wanted your father to punch out and kept hoping he would."

"He didn't. He died in that *Griffin*."

"I know. My father said he'd underestimated the strength of the training Philip Capet had given his protégés. My father then told me that killing men was nothing to be proud of. He said killing was a last resort, when nothing else would work." Kai glanced back at Corbin. "Case in point."

Deirdre reached out and brought Kai's chin up. "Exception to the rule. You did have a choice: you could have sur-

rendered to him. You didn't, but chose to fight to save me."
Her blue eyes met his. "After the way I've treated you, why
would you do that?"

Kai pulled his chin from her hand and dug at the ground
some more. "You saved my life. I owed you."

"No, Kai, not good enough." She picked up one of the
birch stakes and started helping him free her leg. "I've been
so hateful to you over the time I've known you, but I was
very attracted to you that morning on Skondia. I was thinking the New Year would be very good to me, indeed."

Kai laughed lightly, then stopped as a twinge of pain shot
from his ribs. "Yeah, I was thinking that, too."

Deirdre swallowed hard. "Then when General Redburn
introduced us, I felt I'd betrayed myself and my father. After
that, I lashed out at you, trying to drive you away and make
you hurt the way I felt your father had hurt me. I kept trying
to find a way to focus my hatred on you, but the harder I
tried, the less I found in you to hate."

As she spoke, Kai felt the distance between them melt
away. In the two years he'd known Deirdre Lear, he had always puzzled about the apparent duality of her feelings toward him. Now that he understood, her actions made sense.
The part of him that had been afraid she hated him for being
himself wanted to shout with joy. He wanted to sweep her
into his arms and never let her go.

But a cold dread twitched to life in his belly and seemed
to rise up to claw at his throat. *Now you know her secret,
Kai Allard, but that does not change the fact that you are a
killer born of a killer. You are her antithesis and she will always revile you for that fact.*

Kai's faced closed. "You just didn't look hard enough,
Doctor. There's plenty there to hate, like my penchant for
making mistakes, getting other folks killed, or forcing people to do things they don't want to do, like shooting someone. Why was I willing to sacrifice myself for you? Because
the world would be better off with you in it than with me."

He ripped the last stake from the hole. "You're free."

She slowly pulled her leg from the hole. "You're wrong,
Kai."

"Wrong?" He frowned. "Your leg is no longer trapped."

"Not about that." She shook her head, then refused to meet
his gaze. "The world wouldn't be better off without you because I, for one, would be much worse off without you here."

"You'd survive. You know enough."

"Physically, yes, perhaps." She shocked him by leaning forward and lightly brushing his lips with hers. "Inside, I'd die without you."

22

Phelan smiled to see the ilKhan had chosen to preside over the Trial of Bloodright being held in the Grand Hall of what had once been the Third Rasalhague Freeman's base. Various members of the Wolf Clan stood at the far end of the hall, but Phelan recognized none of them. He knew most of the Thirteenth Wolf Guards were resting up from the previous two days of fighting, and Phelan would have liked to be doing the same.

The ilKhan waited until an Elemental brought in one of the gravity-well devices, then he started the ceremony. "I am the Oathmaster and accept responsibility for representing House Ward here. Do you concur in this?"

"Seyla," said both Phelan and his opponent.

"Then what transpires here will bind us all until we all shall fall." Ulric, who looked a bit weary himself, nodded approval. "As this is your third battle, you know well the honor for which you fight. You, Phelan Wolf, have seen twenty years. Why are you worthy?"

"I was chosen by Cyrilla Ward to be heir to this Bloodname. I was adopted into the Warrior Caste after proving my worthiness through service as a bondsman. I trained and tested out as a Warrior. Singlehandedly I conquered Gunzburg, and on Satalice I captured Prince Ragnar of Rasalhague. On Hyperion I led the defense of the Simmons Dam

and hunted renegades in the badlands. On Diosd I participated in the coursing and killing of the Third Freeman's
Command Lance. Prior to the battle today, I defeated an Elemental, Dean, and a flyer, Glynis, for the right to participate here."

"And you, Lajos, have seen twenty-eight years. Why are
you worthy?"

Phelan's opponent in the Bloodright contest began to re-
cite his accomplishments. A MechWarrior, like Phelan, he
moved stiffly on the left side of his body. White gauze totally covered his left arm and hand, making it look as if he
were wearing a mitten. The flesh around his left eye was
badly burned and glistened with clear unguents.

He should be in a hospital, not getting ready to fight,
Phelan thought as Lajos finished his recitation.

The ilKhan clasped his hands together solemnly. "The
heroism and courage displayed by both of you have been established and verified. Your claims are not without substance. No matter what fate you meet in this battle, the
brightness of your light will not be diminished." Ulric
waved both men forward. "Present the tokens of your legitimate right to participate here."

Phelan held his coin up to the ilKhan. Ulric took it, then
crouched to pluck Lajos' coin from his left hand. He placed
both coins in their respective slots. "The horrible chaos of
war is reflected in this Trial of Bloodright. When one coin
has successfully stalked the other and they complete their
transit through this cone, the hunting coin will be superior.
That Warrior is given the choice of style for the fight. The
owner of the inferior coin then decides the venue for the
fight. In this way, each will fight on a battlefield not wholly
of his choosing. Do you understand this?"

"Seyla."

As the ilKhan sent the coins on their spiral courses down
through the gravity well, Phelan looked at Lajos. *If I were
him, I would choose to fight augmented. Burned that badly,
fighting from a 'Mech is the only way he can defeat me.
Hell, he can barely stand up now. I would slaughter him in
a fistfight.* He looked up and watched the coins sink below
the lip of the funnel. No matter how battered Lajos looked,
Phelan knew the man was here because of his prowess as a
Warrior and deserved respect for that.

The two coins clattered down into the decision post. The

ilKhan slid the clear pipe from the center of the post and held it up. He freed the top coin from its transparent prison, then read the name on it. "Phelan, you are the hunter."

Phelan saw Lajos wince as the decision was announced. *He knows he does not stand a chance. It's over before it begins.*

"Phelan, how do you choose to fight?"

The MechWarrior gave the ilKhan a grim smile. "Augmented, my Khan."

Phelan worked his right arm around in a circle and heard the joint pop as it loosened up. "You would think they would let us rest before sending us out for this Bloodname fight, *quiaff*?"

The other MechWarrior in the elevator nodded. "You came out of the fighting a bit better than I did, I think. You Wolf Guards are an odd lot, but you fight well."

Phelan leaned back and hooked his thumbs through his gunbelt. "You are with the Eighth Dragoons, *quiaff*? You were fighting over at the oil refinery in the Oljen Valley. Are you the Lajos who took his *Adder* into the refinery to torch it and drive the militia out?"

The dark-haired man carefully raised his gauze-swathed left arm and pointed to the left side of his face. "Might have reconsidered if I had known the breach in my cockpit canopy and neurohelmet would leave me open to a toasting."

Phelan noted Lajos wore long pants, and could easily imagine gauze covering his leg from top to bottom. "You do look a bit raw there. I hate burns."

"No one likes burns, Phelan." Lajos smiled sheepishly. "When your coin came out on top, I assumed you would opt to fight unaugmented. That you chose a 'Mech allows me to acquit myself admirably. My thanks."

Phelan nodded as the elevator came to a halt on the 'Mech-bay level of the captured Rasalhague facility. Before the door opened, the ilKhan's voice crackled over the speaker built into the ceiling. "Lajos and Phelan, this is your third Bloodright contest. You both have progressed to a point that other Warriors only dream about. Take pride in this. When these doors open, the battle will be joined.

To the victor goes great glory, and to the subdued great honor."

"Seyla," the two Warriors breathed as one.

The doors slowly opened, giving both men a breathtaking view of the 'Mech bay. Rank upon rank of battle-scarred war machines stood like some terrifying legion waiting to be magically activated. Though Phelan had been witness to such scenes on a dozen different worlds, the silent assemblage of so many devastating machines never failed to impress him.

On the right stood Lajos' *Adder*. New armor plating stood out in patchy relief against the fire-blackened hull of the short, squat BattleMech. From the configuration Lajos had chosen, Phelan knew the 'Mech was armed exclusively with a dozen extended-range medium lasers. The weapons were mounted on the 'Mech's arms, but given Lajos' injuries, only half of them would be useful. Likewise, his leg injury would make using the *Adder*'s jump jets nearly suicidal.

Opposite the *Adder* stood Phelan's *Wolfhound*. The tall, sleek BattleMech looked less like a war machine than the avatar of some war god. Black by design, except where the red of the unit designators marked its shoulders, the Mech's lupine cockpit assembly gave it an animation the *Adder* lacked. The *Wolfhound*'s weaponry amounted to only a third of the lasers on Lajos' 'Mech, but the *Wolfhound*'s speed and agility and its built-in electronic counter-measures equipment made it an even opponent for the larger 'Mech.

"Skill, Phelan."

Phelan stepped from the elevator. "And you, Lajos."

Lajos never saw Phelan's left hand as he exited the elevator. The roundhouse left caught Lajos by surprise when it crashed into the unburned part of his face. The punch snapped his head around and dropped him to the hangar's ferrocrete floor.

Phelan stood over him and sucked at his bruised knuckles. "Sorry, Lajos, but the ilKhan did say the battle was joined when we left the elevators. I would fight you straight up, but not with the way you are hurting. Bloodright contest or not, I do not have to baptize it with blood every step of the way."

* * *

Phelan shuddered as he studied the datascreen again. Pale lines of green scrolled up over his face as his eyes darted from line to line in a vain search for anything that would prove him wrong. *This cannot be. It is impossible.*

Phelan had set out carefully to pierce the mystery of the Precentor Martial's identity. He wrote out all he knew for certain about the man, then ranked the information according to its veritableness and the strength of the sources. Anything he knew from the Precentor Martial himself, Phelan rated highly, though he reserved final judgment until he knew whether the man might have been lying for his own purposes.

He resolved to apply Occam's Razor: the simplest solution to the problem would most likely be correct. Phelan discovered quickly, however, that the problem had no simple solution or, at least, no simple solution he could accept and turn over to the ilKhan. The easiest answer was, of course, that Focht had been raised and educated by ComStar for his position, and that anything he had said about his past was a cover story to hide the fact that ComStar had been training warriors for a long time.

The door to Phelan's chamber opened and Ulric entered, appearing ghostlike in the circle of light cast by Phelan's desk lamp. "I have just come from the infirmary," the ilKhan said. "Lajos is chagrined at his defeat, but I think he is pleased to still be alive. I also spoke with the doctors about Glynis, who they say may have turned the corner. She is still in a coma, but her body is healing."

Phelan smiled. "I am pleased they will live. My thanks for the news."

The ilKhan smiled politely. "I am glad if it eases your mind. Of course, Conal Ward accuses you of treachery in winning the last fight the way you did. He wanted me to bring it to the adjudication of the Clan Council, but I overruled him. I pointed out that you had the choice of style in the decision, and that you acted within the letter of the law surrounding Bloodright contests."

The younger MechWarrior sighed. "So Conal has branded me a cheat as well as a freebirth? I suppose he wanted me killed and Lajos placed in the contest in my stead? Is he so worried that Vlad may not be able to beat me?"

The ilKhan suppressed a grin. "Conal has been most vocal about your perfidy, but Lajos is in no condition to fight. I told Conal that someone from House Ward would certainly nominate Lajos in the next Bloodright for a Ward Bloodname, so he has not been damaged.

"As for Conal being worried about Vlad, I would not place too much stock in that idea." Ulric stoked his goatee. "The two people fighting for the chance to oppose Vlad in the next round have managed to kill each other, so he has a bye. As of now, Vlad is in the final battle, barring death or injury on the battlefield."

"That will never happen." Phelan shook his head. "My luck is not that good."

"No, indeed." The ilKhan pointed at the computer on Phelan's desk. "Now, what is this about a possible solution to the mystery of Anastasius Focht? Tell me everything so I can follow your reasoning."

The young MechWarrior glanced down at his notes, taking a moment to mentally compose what he was going to say. "The way I began was with the base Gus Michaels created before you sent him off to Alyina. From that, Focht would be, at most, one hundred years old. He seems obviously male, but the possibility of a sex-change was not discounted. The lost eye is a possible battle injury. Though it would have ended his career as a fighting soldier, he could still continue in a command capacity. We also know that he first surfaced in ComStar a dozen years ago, speaks German like a native of the Lyran Commonwealth, and that he may have spent some time at the Nagelring. Focht also told me he met my father once."

"Not much to go on," Ulric said quietly.

"True, but it was enough to get started. Knowing Focht is an alias, or at least operating from that assumption, I ran the records for every cadet and graduate of the Nagelring from the last eighty years. Screening them for height and other Bertillon measurements, that brought me down to just over a thousand candidates."

The ilKhan leaned forward with interest, clasping his hands around one knee. "You cross-referenced those individuals with their careers to see who had lived or died in combat, *quiaff*?"

"Aff, my Khan. We included those listed as missing in action, even if they were lost in skirmishes well before the Fourth Succession War. The Fourth War cost us all but a few candidates, and follow-up on those individuals led to a dead end. Nothing."

Phelan tapped the computer screen with a knuckle. "That made me wonder about the search parameters we'd put into the program-sifting data. I ran up another set of search parameters to check for a known quantity: me. I had the computer search for me in the same way it looked for whoever Focht might be."

"And?"

"It came up blank!" Phelan's smile broadened. "I enlarged the search parameters by deleting the Bertillon stuff and adding the Kell surname. It came up with my father, but ignored me and my uncle Patrick. That was because, according to the ComStar and Lyrcom data sets we're using, Patrick and I are dead."

"But you are alive. So, it would appear, is the Precentor Martial." Ulric tugged reflectively on his goatee. "You changed the search parameters, *quiaff*?"

"Aff. I stayed with our core of a thousand candidates and started filtering for wild cards. Focht once mentioned staying at the Lestrade estate on Summer, so I sorted for individuals who had served in units stationed on Summer or folks connected in some way with Aldo Lestrade. That cut our pool by half."

Phelan counted down on his fingers. "A comment Focht once made led me to believe he'd lost his eye in the Fourth Succession War. As I'd already checked all the people who had survived the war, I concentrated on the dead and missing from that war. I also tried to cross-correlate into the equation any contacts with my father or joint service with him. By mistake, I also included social contacts in that latter line of code—I'd copied it from the Lestrade parameters and just changed the name—and got a most interesting narrowing of candidates.

"Significantly, all were listed as either dead or missing in action."

The ilKhan leaned forward as Phelan's story unfolded. "You worked to verify the deaths of those on the list, *quiaff*?"

The MechWarrior nodded. "Death certificates, autopsy reports, gravestones, whatever. The genealogical data base we picked up from Domain helped enormously. While looking through it, I found a nice little memorial marker for myself on Arc-Royal."

Though Phelan tried to make the comment come off irreverently, the words caught in his throat. It wasn't being thought dead that bothered him so much as the thought of the grief it must be causing his family. The Wolf Clan had very much become his new family, but he still loved his blood relations and regretted any pain they suffered on his account.

"I cannot imagine that was a pleasant experience, Phelan."

"It was not, ilKhan, but fortunately, it sparked a memory." Phelan punched a request for data into the computer and the image of a great marble and granite mausoleum appeared on the screen. Carved into the black marble and outlined with gold leaf was the word "Steiner."

"After Archon Katrina Steiner died, I was present at her funeral. She was interred in the family crypt along with other Steiners of note. I recall hearing, at the time, that one of the memorial plaques in the tomb marked an empty casket. If not for that bit of family gossip, I think I would have dismissed my best candidate."

Phelan punched up another data request and a picture appeared on the screen. "This is the man I believe to be the Precentor Martial. He studied for three years at the Nagelring, but transferred to and graduated from Sanglamore on Skye. It was during his time in Skye that he first came to the attention of the Lestrade family and they cultivated his friendship. He commanded both the Seventh Lyran Guards and the Tenth Lyran Guards, which rumor says may be Victor Davion's current unit. The next Archon often emerges from the Tenth Guards, and our man was a likely candidate at that time.

"His claim to the title had to be put on hold, however, when Katrina Steiner successfully rebelled against Alessandro Steiner, putting her on the throne. It was at that point in Focht's life that Aldo Lestrade became a major influence. Aldo was adept at political intrigues, including the planning and execution of several assassination attempts against Archon Katrina. The last of these came in the middle of the Fourth Succession War."

The ilKhan nodded. "What of his military career? What sort of commander was he?"

Phelan punched another key. "He was a fine leader. His men called him 'the Hammer' because of his predilection for concentrating firepower on specific targets. He was particularly effective against the Kuritans, whose old strategy used to involve numerous single, small-unit actions. In his one or two engagements against the Free Worlds League, he showed an understanding of the tactics of highly mobile forces, but he still strove to get his foes into a position where he could pound them into submission."

"It is a rare commander who will alter his tactics to suit his foes," said Ulric. "His ability to do so—and what he observed of our tactics—make him very dangerous."

"I concur, ilKhan." Phelan chewed on his lower lip. "The one anomaly here is that this man was considered incapable of subtlety, but that does not seem to be true of Focht. He seems to have learned some new tricks in this new incarnation."

"Do you believe him capable of treachery?"

Phelan frowned. *Well, he did ask me to spy on the Clans for him, but accepted my refusal after I became a member of the Warrior Caste.* "I think he is a warrior first and foremost, ilKhan. Because of Lestrade's political meddling, he and his unit were assigned to a suicide mission during the Fourth Succession War. He acquitted himself well, in the end surrendering to Theodore Kurita to save the lives of his men. His assault broke the Combine's planned counterstrike into the Isle of Skye. It is believed that Theodore executed him."

The ilKhan stood, his face a study in thought. "Age and coloration are correct. Training is correct and his military background is suitable for the position he now occupies. What I have seen of his ability at tactical and strategic analysis certainly matches his background. Have you anything that casts doubt on your conclusion?"

Phelan shrugged. "Well, he *could* be mouldering in a grave on Dromini VI for all I know, but he is the best candidate we have. Except for the fact that he is supposed to be dead, he fits perfectly with Anastasius Focht."

Ulric nodded. "Very well. We will operate on the assumption you are correct. Prepare me a full briefing file on him and the other four top candidates. I need it tonight. You will brief the other analysts tomorrow."

Phelan raised an eyebrow. "I have more checks to run. Why so quickly?"

"Because, Phelan," the ilKhan said with a smile, "I want everyone briefed before the Precentor Martial joins up with us in three days to bargain away the future of ComStar."

23

The Precentor Martial held his head high as the bridge doors slid back into the walls. The two armored Elementals standing beside the hatchway came to attention, as did the lines of Clan officers running all the way from where the ilKhan waited. Hanging down from the top of the bridge, Focht saw a Wolf Clan banner side by side with a ComStar pennant. From the speakers on the bridge came the strains of a martial tune popular back in the days of the Star League.

Focht adjusted his eye patch, then marched in time with the music across the deck to where Ulric waited for him beside the holotank. Making his passage through the gauntlet of Clan warriors, he gave them the same respectful nods due his own men when he reviewed them. *These are warriors whom I cannot but respect.* His jaw clamped down hard. *Anything less could be suicidal.*

He stopped in front of the ilKhan and gave Ulric a solemn salute. The Clan leader returned it, then offered the Precentor Martial his hand. "The Peace of Blake be with you, ilKhan Ulric."

The ilKhan nodded his head. "And with you, Precentor Martial. I welcome your company again, even if it is only for a short time."

"As I welcome yours, ilKhan." He shook Ulric's hand, then took his place beside the younger man. The Precentor

Martial searched the faces of the gathered soldiers, thinking he might have missed someone who passed on his blind side. Not seeing Phelan, he looked up at the viewing area above the bridge, but the familiar silhouette was not there, either. *Does Phelan's absence from here have some significance?*

Ulric waited for his troops to salute, then returned it and dismissed them. "If you will, Precentor Martial, I think we will find the holotank best suited to our discussions."

Focht thought he heard something more than business in Ulric's statement, but could not puzzle it out on such skimpy evidence. He bowed his head and followed the ilKhan into the holotank.

Entering the machine was to step into a world where one could truly feel godlike. Within the lozenge of black panels, Focht discovered he walked through a projected map of the Inner Sphere. At head-height, he saw the Periphery border—where the Clans had entered the Inner Sphere—and down near the floor his beloved Terra. Focht did not think it a co-incidence that ComStar's home appeared low enough for Ulric to crush it with a casual misstep.

The Precentor Martial did not even attempt to suppress a smile as he entered the virtual reality produced by the holotank. Like a child marveling at his first planetarium show, he admired the view of the myriad stars, each appropriately labeled. Focht's own computer-generated realities required datasuits and ICR helmets, which made his equipment a mere toy compared to this device.

Focht looked around the bridge one final time, then gave the ilKhan a polite smile. "I had hoped to see Phelan again. It was a surprise when Elementals met me in the shuttle bay."

Ulric shrugged slightly. He reached up and touched a label hanging in mid-air beside a star. A glowing green window opened below the world and data—mirror-written from Focht's point of view—scrolled down through the air. "Phelan would have liked to have seen you as well, but his unit is on Diosd in case another of their militia units comes out of hiding. We believe all are accounted for, but zealots destroyed the central computers on the planet, throwing all intelligence-gathering and record-combing into chaos."

As Ulric pushed up on the lower border of the window, the scroll retracted into the small label again. "Your concern for Phelan does bring up a point I wish to discuss before we start our bargaining. It is in the nature of a personal favor, for which I will be grateful."

A personal favor? "Yes, ilKhan?"

The Wolf Clan leader clasped his hands behind his back and did not meet Focht's eyes directly. "I have recorded a holodisk that I wish transmitted to Colonel Morgan Kell of the Kell Hounds unit. I wish to tell him his son lives and is one of my most valued warriors." Ulric's blue eyes flicked up to make contact with Focht. "Does that surprise you, Precentor Martial?"

Focht allowed his surprise to show. "It does, ilKhan, and it pleases me as well. It will bring great joy to the Kells."

"Yes, I imagine it would. You know families far better than I, the petty rivalries and deep feelings that run between members." The ilKhan crossed his arms over his chest. "Our culture, as you know, stresses strong Clan and House ties at the expense of family units. If this is a weakness on our part, it matters little at this point. I do not wish to cause suffering to the Kells because of our need for Phelan. Is it not what they say in the Inner Sphere: blood is thicker than water, *quiaff*?"

"Yes, ilKhan, but we generally add the caveat, 'but not as thick as duty.' " Focht studied his foe carefully. *This is not the Ulric I have known. Is he sincere, or is this a ploy to unsettle me?* "As for my understanding of family, I fear it is not as strong as you might imagine. My family thrived on misunderstandings, but you have a correct impression of the Kell household, I think."

"Good. I have not informed Phelan that this message is to be sent, but I will allow him to receive any reply. If you wish to include a message of your own to Colonel Kell expressing this, or including your own impression of Phelan's life here among us, please do so." Ulric held up a hand. "And, of course, I know that the Primus may prevent the transmission of this message, given the state of our relations at this point."

"I will tell Colonel Kell how his son has thrived here." Focht allowed himself a traitorous grin. "I think I may even be able to circumvent the Primus in this matter."

"Good, then I will not be alone in treason, for I think the Grand Council would not approve my communicating with the enemy." The ilKhan's blue eyes narrowed. "These are dangerous times, Anastasius. What we do here will be wondrous and terrible, and the greatest tragedy is that politicians may render it all for naught."

"I share your fear, Ulric. Between us, there can be trust. I will not betray you."

"Nor I you."

Focht smiled. "What our diplomats cannot divide, we must battle over. For the record, I would not have chosen to go to war with you, ilKhan. I have watched you enough to know better than to relish battling a foe of your abilities."

The ilKhan laughed lightly. "I am not immune to flattery, Anastasius. In our bargaining that may earn you a Cluster."

"Just so long as it is in the Thirteenth Wolf Guards."

"Interesting choice, my friend, but do you wish to be the one to tell Natasha Kerensky or Phelan Wolf they cannot fight against you?"

"Touché, my Khan. There are some missions not meant for mere warriors." Focht glanced back at one of the Clan computer consoles where an aide was working with a Clanner. "I have brought with me data that will help us bargain out this battle properly."

The starfield in the holotank flickered for a second, then re-drew itself. "I believe your data has been incorporated into my database here. Shall we proceed?"

"Yes." Focht pulled himself up to his full height. "I am Anastasius Focht, Precentor Martial of ComStar and Supreme Commander of all Com Guard troops. Myndo Waterly, Primus of ComStar and Keeper of Blake's Sacred Word has assigned me the duty of negotiating this battle. What I offer, I warrant is true and free of deception."

Ulric nodded, then also straightened to attention. "I am Ulric Kerensky, ilKhan of the Clans and Khan of the Wolf Clan. It is by my own authority, in action for the Grand Council of Khans, that I enter negotiations with you. What I offer I warrant is true and free of deception."

He waved a hand through a thousand stars. "As you are the defender, I ask if you have chosen a venue for our confrontation."

"I have, ilKhan." Focht reached out and touched the label attached to the planet Tukayyid. "In the fourth planet, I believe I have found us a battlefield."

The window opened and the ilKhan's left hand strayed to his goatee as the blue and gold world rotated through space.

As they watched, the holotank brought their viewpoint down through the atmosphere and sent it skimming across vast fields of ripening wheat. They flew like eagles over the flat plains, then climbed into the dark Pozoristu Mountains. From those cloud-shrouded heights, they swooped down river valleys, through swamps and deltas, then across the dark Crucible Sea.

"Hardly an exhaustive survey, but the geography appears well-suited to any number of battles." The ilKhan frowned. "The population is small and centered in very specific areas?"

"Most of those people will be evacuated from the world," Focht said. "As we bring our troops onto the world, the DropShips will take people away. The only civilian personnel left on the planet will be those essential to running factories that cannot be shut down. We will take all potentially hazardous industries offline, and we are prepared to designate some religious communities as non-combat zones, if you agree. In addition, ComStar accepts half the costs of damage repair if the Clans will agree to cover the other half."

"ComStar bears the cost of evacuation and repatriation?"

Focht nodded. "If you take the world, we will repatriate the population back onto Tukayyid, or onto any other world you or they choose. We will consider the people your subjects for this purpose, so you have first choice on where they end up."

"Acceptable," Ulric said, but his smile made Focht's hackles rise. "No reason to clutter the chessboard with impotent pieces, *quiaff,* Anastasius?"

In an instant Focht's mind flashed to the image of a chessboard. He saw the Primus as his queen and Natasha Kerensky taking up her position beside Ulric. It was not a comforting thought. Strangely, what worried him was not what Natasha would do to oppose him, but what the Primus would do to aid him.

"I would liken it to clearing a sports field of fans before a match. You know as well as I that characterizing our battle as a chess game devalues the lives of the men and women who will die on Tukayyid."

Ulric held up his hands. "Far be it from me to do that, Anastasius. But you must admit that our preparations resemble those that precede a chess match. I have conceded to you the choice of battlefield, allowing you the choice of color, as it were. Now we both must decide who should spot whom pieces, what are their value, and how we can exploit that advantage over our enemy."

Ulric's expression deadened. "I, after all, value a force more than some politico who might throw away a crack unit like a rook sacrificed in a gambit."

Focht felt suddenly as if someone were walking on his grave. *Oh, you play this game well, Ulric. Have you pierced the secret of my identity? Was it Phelan who did it for you and is that why he is not here?*

"I would expect that of you, ilKhan, because you are a military man of great insight. Still, that does not mean you would not expend a force in a suicidal maneuver if you deemed the gain worth the risk."

"The point is well-taken, Precentor Martial." Ulric again stroked his goatee, seeming more at ease than Focht would have desired. "And so, then, what force will you use to defend this planet?"

Focht touched one of the icons below the image of Tukayyid. It opened yet another window and this one remained black within the neon green border defining it. The Precentor Martial then reached up to a world firmly in the Wolf Clan Occupation Zone. "From Rasalhague I bring the 278th Division, under the command of Precentor IV Byron Koselka." As the Rasalhague window opened, Focht plucked from it the icon representing that Com Guard unit and threw it down toward Tukayyid.

It streaked like a comet through the artificial universe, then appeared in the empty window. Another icon followed it and another as Focht stripped all the troops from Com-Star's Asta Theatre. From there he worked into the Federated Commonwealth and pulled troops from the Jade Falcon Occupation Zone. Continuing counterclockwise, the Precentor Martial sent every Com Guard Division spiraling in toward Tukayyid.

When he had finished, he studied the seventy-two unit designators he had consigned to Tukayyid. "The data I have given you details the units selected, giving you a breakdown of their histories and the records of the men who make them up."

"Save your own record, Precentor Martial?"

Focht's head came up at the ilKhan's question. "The reason I provide you the records for my men is because our units have seen no real combat, yet to treat them as green troops would be a mistake. In the interest of clarity, I will provide you the record of my service since becoming the Precentor Martial. For you to infer anything from my earlier career would be a mistake."

"Would it?" Ulric turned away and slowly walked around to the other side of the Tukayyid windows. "Can an old soldier learn new strategies?"

"Is a caterpillar a butterfly? I chose the name Anastasius Focht for a most specific reason. I am not the man I once was. Deprived of an eye, I see more clearly now than ever before." Focht clasped his hands at the small of his back. "We will be defending Tukayyid with approximately fifty BattleMech regiments and appropriate air, artillery, armor, and infantry support. We have chosen not to use naval units because Tukayyid's surface water is limited and naval engagements would unnecessarily endanger the underwater city in the Crucible Sea."

Ulric appeared momentarily stunned by the declaration of ComStar's strength. "Fifty regiments?"

Focht nodded solemnly. "That is everything ComStar has, save the two 'Mech divisions on Terra itself. The Primus was disinclined to have her bodyguard units sent away."

"Then we are not fighting only for Tukayyid. Tukayyid is your proxy world for the Terran battle."

Did you expect some preliminary conflict for me to test you first? "Yes, ilKhan, it is our proxy battle. We have no more desire to fight on Terra than you do.

"If you take Tukayyid, in addition to caring for the population of the planet, we will cede to you Terra and all our facilities in your Occupation Zones. We will continue to administer your worlds for you and our revenues will become yours. If so ordered, we will cease all services for the Successor States. We will order our staffs to become integrated with your forces and, in effect, we will become part of the Clans—if you will have us."

Ulric began to pace and Focht was not sure how to read the man. Ulric had tightened down from his normally imperturbable self into an introspective cocoon. Focht almost heard the synapses going off in the ilKhan's brain, but he held no illusions about the ilKhan cracking under the pressure of the ComStar bid to defend Terra.

It was obvious, though, that making Tukayyid a proxy surprised and now troubled the ilKhan. Focht would not have thought it possible to take the man unaware. *Perhaps his knowledge of my background led him to expect something else from me.* The Precentor Martial watched the ilKhan closely, but Ulric's face gave no clue to his thoughts.

Then Ulric stopped his pacing and stared at Focht through the Tukayyid combat window. "If you win, you will want something in return."

Focht nodded slowly. "The Primus has instructed me to demand that your Clans withdraw from the Inner Sphere when we defeat you."

He expected a harsh bark of laughter in response to that demand, but instead Ulric paused to consider it seriously. "That, I am afraid, is impossible, Anastasius, as you well know. Were I to agree to that condition, the Grand Council would impeach me and repudiate the agreement. We will not withdraw."

The Precentor Martial accepted the answer without protest. "As I expected." With one finger, he drew a pulsing red line paralleling the floor that went through Tukayyid. "If you will not withdraw, grant me that you and your forces will never pass this line. Let Tukayyid forever mark the closest point the Clans ever came to Terra."

Ulric pressed his hands together in an attitude of prayer. "Forever is a very long time, my friend. It is far longer than I or anyone I know will be able to make the Clans respect this bargain. Still, I can accept drawing a line of truce at Tukayyid, and I can grant you a year's armistice, as when we broke off our advance to elect a new ilKhan."

The Precentor Martial shook his head. "A year you no doubt see as generous."

"It has allowed your forces to equip and train themselves to better oppose us. Imagine the strides you would make with another year's worth of breathing room."

"Imagine the strides we would make given a century of peace."

"A century? I could sell the Grand Council the idea of forever sooner than I could a century. Five years."

"An eyeblink, Ulric. Five years is nothing to us. Sixty years—the career-span of our finest military leaders. Give me sixty years."

The ilKhan smiled in spite of himself. "Sixty years? We

are mayflies compared to you. Sixty years is twelve generations of our warriors. I will be long dead and forgotten by the time war is again joined. Ten years at the most."

"To us tortoises, ten years is nothing. Ten years is not enough time to season a good warrior, much less train cadres to oppose you. Thirty years, then. Let the warriors who have fought you return to their homes to raise a new generation of warriors to meet the finest you have to offer."

Ulric hesitated as if reluctant to counter-bid. "I am afraid, my friend, thirty years is too much. I can grant you fifteen, and make that a solid bid. Unless you kill me on Tukayyid, I believe I can remain ilKhan long enough to guarantee that bargain. Beyond fifteen years, I will not be able to exert the influence necessary to bind the Clans by this agreement."

Focht adjusted the patch over his right eye. *I have pushed you to the wall, haven't I?* "Fifteen years I can accept. You have, after all, ceded the choice of battlefield to me."

"That is true." The Wolf Clan Khan scanned the Tukayyid data again. "What is the time-frame for this fight?"

"The start of May?"

"That is within operational possibilities. When the Clans have chosen the units that will assault Tukayyid, I will relay that information to you."

Focht extended his hand through the image of Tukayyid. "Bargained well and done, ilKhan."

Ulric smiled at his statement. "You have learned much during your time with us. Do you think you have learned enough?"

"Enough to know the answer to that question lies on Tukayyid."

24

Primus Myndo Waterly glanced over at the slender form of the Precentor from Dieron as the computer-projection of the Precentor Martial's report dissolved. "So, Sharilar Mori, what do you think?"

"I am pleased and honored that you show me this briefing before presenting it to the First Circuit," Sharilar said, but her face betrayed no emotion. "But I am a bit puzzled about why you have singled me out for this honor."

"Why puzzled?" Myndo smiled beatifically, seeking to project an image of serenity and wisdom. "Have you forgotten that I was your predecessor as Precentor Dieron and that I personally chose you as my replacement when I became Primus?"

"No, Primus, I have not forgotten, but I would not be human if I did not wonder at my good fortune." Sharilar looked down at the inlaid wooden floor of the Primus' private chambers. "I would like to think I have been of use during my time as Precentor Dieron."

"That you have, Sharilar, and you shall be of more service in the future." The Primus sat down in a chair and patted the arm of the one next to her. "Please, sit. I have something of great importance to share with you."

Sharilar moved with her usual grace, but Myndo sensed her nervousness. *Good. Were she not excited by my ap-*

proach to this situation, she would be utterly unsuited to doing what I need. "Precentor Dieron, what do you think of the bargain the Precentor Martial has struck with the Clans?"

Sharilar sucked on her lower lip for a moment before answering. "I would have wished for a longer cessation of hostilities, but I believe him when he says fifteen years is the best he could work out. In that time, I imagine the Federated Suns and the Combine will have stockpiled sufficient forces to maintain that line when the fighting begins again."

Myndo rested a hand on Sharilar's forearm and gave it a gentle squeeze. "I concur fully with your thoughts. Now, if you were to project your thoughts fifteen years in the future—say you were the Primus—what would you imagine is ComStar's chance of survival?"

Myndo took secret pleasure in Sharilar's twitch when she suggested the younger woman might become the Primus.

"Primus, that is a difficult task. If we defeat the Clans, they will surely order us off their worlds. All that we have accomplished over the last two years will be wasted. If the Draconis Combine and Federated Commonwealth are unable to stop the Clans, Terra will fall to them. I would guess our chances of survival are bleak if we cannot unite the Successor States to help us hold off the Clans."

The Primus leaned back in her chair. "And given the current attitude of Hanse Davion, what think you of our chances of uniting the Inner Sphere?"

"Very slender, Primus."

"Correct. In short, the Precentor Martial has bought us fifteen years at the best. If the Clans defeat him on Tukayyid, ComStar and Blessed Blake's dream die immediately."

Sharilar frowned heavily. "But the Precentor Martial sounded so confident. He said he had the key to defeating the Clans. Can he lose?"

Myndo snorted derisively. "Sharilar, you must learn to see the reality of the world. The Precentor Martial sees conflicts in the terms of a big wargame—a game of chess. To him, all can be decided on that game board, and nothing in the outside universe will affect that outcome. As far as he is concerned, the battle for Tukayyid will decide everything, then he and ilKhan Ulric will walk away friends."

"Are you not being a bit harsh with him?"

The Primus flicked her long white hair back with a casual gesture. "Not so, Precentor Dieron. Think of it this way: the

Precentor Martial is an old soldier and this will be the greatest battle of his career. Win or lose, his usefulness is at an end. He will never again know the challenge or glory of any war to surpass this one. His dreams will have been fulfilled, while ours must continue. He seeks to protect ComStar while we—you and I—must remain true to Blake's dream of reforming mankind."

Leaning forward in her chair, the older woman dropped her voice into a low, conspiratorial whisper. "A warrant for ComStar's death has been signed. We cannot allow this to happen."

Sharilar nodded woodenly as if the serious import of the Primus' words were slowly overwhelming her. "Jerome Blake's dream must not perish. That would be a betrayal of mankind."

"Exactly. While the Precentor Martial is putting forth his most valiant effort to shatter the Clans, we must look beyond his actions and ensure the ultimate victory of ComStar and Blake."

Sharilar stared at the Primus. "But how can we accomplish this? What can we do?"

The Primus smiled. "Computer, display the objective's list from Operation Scorpion."

The computer complied instantly. Where the Precentor Martial's face had formerly hung in the air, a list of glowing words came to life. Myndo scanned the list again, reveling in narcissistic glory, then smiled as Sharilar stared at the list with her mouth agape.

"Yes, Sharilar, it is a plan audacious in its concept, yet simple in execution. Phase one: stage revolts on all the Clan worlds we hold, trapping the garrisons and liberating the worlds in the name of ComStar. That will bring ComStar the glory of being mankind's savior."

"I see the wisdom of that, Primus, but phase two? Will not shutting down all our facilities in the Successor States sow panic and confusion among those we need as our allies?"

The Primus narrowed her dark eyes. "I want panic in the Successor States. It is the incredible arrogance of Hanse Davion, Theodore Kurita, and Thomas Marik that allows them to believe they can ignore us. Each was asked for support in our defense of Terra, but all we got were empty promises. They believed us useless and I mean to prove we can still hurt them. An interdiction that extends to the whole of the Successor States will yank their choke-chains and remind them how truly vital we are if they ever hope to oppose the Clans.

"Then, as we did with the Federated Suns twenty-three years ago, we will lift the sanctions in return for concessions. We will force them to use us as the Clans have on their occupied worlds. In fact, when communications are opened between capitals and outlying worlds, they will find that situation already exists, de facto, so they will have no choice but to accept."

Sharilar shuddered slightly at the words. "The Precentor Martial and the First Circuit will object to this plan."

"Which is why they will not know of it." Myndo saw realization dawn on Sharilar's face. "That is correct, Precentor Dieron. I have come to you with this plan because you successfully negotiated my short-lived alliance with Theodore Kurita. I know you are subtle and able to work outside normal channels. I need to cut the First Circuit out of our planning here, and I know I can trust you. You must get the messages out quickly to all of our Precentors and demi-Precentors so they can prepare. Operation Scorpion will go off at the same time as the Precentor Martial's battle with the Clans."

Myndo smiled like a conqueror. "When the Precentor Martial defeats the Clans, ilKhan Ulric will learn his troops are trapped deep behind enemy lines. The Clans will be forced to retreat and leave us alone forever."

The Primus saw an unholy gleam in Sharilar Mori's eyes. "It shall be as you say, Primus. I am curious, though, about your choice of name for this plan. Why scorpion?"

"It is because of an old folk tale, Sharilar." Myndo smiled coldly. "The story of an old blind dog and the arachnid that enlightened him about reality."

25

Victor Davion felt a leaden net tighten around his heart and start to drag it down. "Morgan, you must be joking!"

The tall Marshal of the Federated Commonwealth shot his cousin a surprised glance. "As you must be joking about this proposed plan, I suppose? You asked me to come here to evaluate *this*?" Morgan held up a holodisk as if it were a piece of trash. "I've seen more intelligent plans suggested as wargame scenarios among the criminally insane."

Victor's face flushed. "Morgan, we worked hard on that plan. My people have trained hard on this. Our morale is higher than it's ever been and we're getting full cooperation from the Combine. General Kaulkas even approved the plan."

Morgan Hasek-Davion contemptuously flipped the holodisk onto his desk. "Just because you fooled her, do not expect to fool me. Were this a script from an *Immortal Warrior* holovid, I might just *barely* begin to see how it made sense. In those potboilers, the hero can wipe out whole units on his own. But since when have you or your troops been taking super-warrior lessons? The only thing this will get us is *two* Princes trapped on Teniente."

"No, Morgan, you're wrong." Victor's hands knotted into fists. "This plan can work, and it *will*. Just give us the chance to pull it off."

"War is not about chances, Victor. War is about dead certainties, and the certainty that people will end up dead because of the war." Morgan's eyes spat fire. "You're sending a reinforced battalion into a world that, at best, has incomplete intelligence concerning the enemy. You do not know the location of your objective, but you've narrowed his possible location to a dozen different sites on the north continent. You're hoping that Hohiro will be able to direct your troops to the landing zone closest to his position as you come inbound. But you haven't a clue as to whether or not security on the planet has been breached or whether Hohiro has been captured and broken—or if he's even alive. You could be dropping straight into an ambush."

"That would be true, cousin, if we were going in hostile. You read the plan. They won't know we're an enemy force coming in."

"Oh, yes," Morgan scoffed, "coming into the system in disguised DropShips. What a brilliant, foolproof plan that is."

"It worked for you on Sian," Victor shot back.

"True, but the differences between Sian and Teniente are legion." Morgan started to tick them off on his fingers. "Maximilian Liao was both stupid and desperate; the Clans are neither. We came in using Liao's own DropShips; you are using DropShips with new paint jobs. We owned two of the top three individuals on Liao's intelligence staff; you have no such inside support. Need I go on?"

Victor felt hot and wanted to punch the bulkhead. In frustration, he tore at the collar of his shirt, accidentally touching the Stone Monkey pendant he wore under it. Kai Allard had given him the pendant, and Victor remembered with an electric jolt Kai telling him that Sun Hou-Tzu would keep him safe. *This totem is meant to remind you to be yourself, no matter what," Kai told me. What I am being now, what Morgan is driving me to be, is a petulant child. No more.*

The Prince forced his hands to unknot. "Your points are well taken, but I have Shin Yodama's solemn assurances that the deception will work perfectly. I have to assume that Theodore Kurita himself has approved the information we're working with."

Morgan looked hard at Victor. "That does not mean it is not in error."

"But it does mean that the Kanrei is willing to stake his

son's life on it being correct." Victor injected a calmer tone into his voice and willfully sought to slow his breathing and heartbeat. "Morgan, you can see as clearly as I can that this plan is very important. You yourself told me there would be other Alyinas and other lives to avenge besides that of Kai Allard."

Victor again caressed the jade pendant. "This is a chance to do more than avenge Kai's death. After Kai died, Galen reminded me that his death would only be a waste if the Clans destroyed us. To do that, the Clans have to destroy our way of life and our governments. Until then, we will always oppose them.

"You've seen the reports concerning the Free Rasalhague Republic." Victor pointed at the holovid viewer on the corner of Morgan's desk. "The loss of Prince Ragnar has hurt their morale. The people had believed, up until that point, that they were fighting to preserve their dream of self-determination. Now, with Ragnar captured by the Clans and his father's heart nearly broken, the Free Rasalhague forces just go through the motions of fighting. Even that bastard Tor Miraborg has become one of the Wolves' lap dogs, and there was never even a fight for Gunzburg."

Morgan leaned back against the edge of his desk. "What are you telling me, Victor?"

The Prince knew from his cousin's tone that he'd better make his next shot his best. "I'm telling you nothing, Morgan. I'm asking you to look at the greater importance of this mission to the Successor States. When we bring Hohiro back, the people can rejoice in our having whisked him out from under the noses of the Nova Cats. The people will also see how important it is for us to work with the Draconis Combine. It will let them know that Hohiro and I are capable of coexisting without killing each other, and that will give them hope for the future beyond the Clans. For our military personnel, it will prove the Clans can be had. It will show that the military doctrines we've been preaching do work. It will prove we can beat the Clans."

"And if it fails, Victor? What then?"

The small man shrugged. "For the Combine, it will make little difference in the short term. They still face vastly superior Clan forces. While the victory might boost their morale, Hohiro's death, if it becomes known at all, will only make them more determined to defend their holdings against the

Clans. As for what the rule of Minoru Kurita might bring, quite frankly, I don't think he'll ever take the throne and I certainly will not be around to worry about it."

Morgan nodded. "And what will your death mean to the Federated Commonwealth?"

"Little or nothing." Victor met Morgan's surprised look calmly. "Face it, Morgan. Everyone has been doubting my ability to sustain the Davion legend you and my father have created. I've always been seen as the Little-Prince-Who-Tried, not the Little-Prince-Who-Could. Besides, more than one government official would welcome my sister Katherine or my brother Peter as my replacement on the throne."

The Marshal walked around his desk and dropped into the chair behind it. "So, then, you want to do this mission to prove all the naysayers wrong?"

"No, Morgan, that game won't work anymore." Victor pulled himself up to his full height. "You won't get me to rant and rave because that will only prove I don't have the objectivity to make this operation a go. Yes, I still have my temper, but I also have a brake on it. I've worked out every angle on this mission, but I'm prepared to scrap it if the situation changes or you order me to abandon it. Still, I know this plan is solid and I suspect you do, too."

Morgan Hasek-Davion steepled his fingers. His long copper hair obscured the Marshal's epaulets on his black uniform jacket. "You have come a long way, Victor. I can still recall your objection to being assigned to Trellwan. You appealed to me to sympathize with you then, and you have done the same thing several times since. Always I opposed you or made you accept full responsibility for your actions."

He spread his hands apart. "Now you come to me with a plan for which you accept the responsibility. I sense this is in part because Kai Allard used to shoulder it for you. I regret his passing, but I am pleased that it has forced you to mature.

"You are very special, Victor. You are one of those people who burns very, very bright, determined to live up to your name. I have always known you were destined for greatness."

The Prince's eyes narrowed. "If that is true, why have you made things so difficult for me?"

"Because, my Prince, those who burn so very bright tend to burn out just as fast. I will never risk the lives of men and women in my command on a feeling. War is a crucible in which men discover their true mettle. I did not want others to suffer if you proved lacking."

Victor glanced down and swallowed hard. "I understand. Have you reached a verdict on me?"

Morgan paused before answering. "I am forwarding a copy of your briefing, along with my comments, to your father. Pending his approval or disapproval of the plan, I am authorizing the Tenth Lyran Guards' First Reinforced Battalion to head out for link with the Combine JumpShips waiting insystem. I expect full reports sent from each jump point and updates on intelligence estimates. You father has final approval, of course, but I think this is a mission that must become a reality."

Victor's heart buoyed up again in his breast. "Thank you, Morgan."

"Don't thank me, Victor. Save that energy for making sure this plan will work." The Marshal's eyes narrowed. "Be yourself and be honest with yourself. You don't have Kai Allard there to help you out in that department. If this mission can't fly, kill it. Kill it before it kills you."

26

Alyina
Jade Falcon Occupation Zone
12 April 3052

Kai traced his finger along the map he'd spread out on the ground. "It looks, by this, that we won't come any closer than two hundred kilometers to the Mahler farm."

Deirdre squatted on his left, hugging her knees to her chest with both arms. "I suppose that is just as well. Any closer and I'd be tempted to visit, and that would surely bring the Clans down on them." She reached out a finger and tapped at the map. "You said our destination has a radio-telescope facility on it, but I don't see any notation for an observatory on Mount Sera."

"It's a secret facility, more or less." He gave her hand a squeeze. "The Intelligence Secretariat maintains any number of research projects throughout the Federated Commonwealth. They all differ in the level of security and knowledge about them. For example, weapons-research project facilities run by the NAIS on New Avalon are considered top-secret, but folks know they exist and where they are. It's more that getting to them is inconvenient and very little is known about any particular project they might be working on."

Kai rocked back on his heels and stood, brushing twigs and leaves from the knees of his jumpsuit. "Remember all the UAP sightings on New Avalon ten years ago?"

"Unexplained Aerial Phenomena?" Her blue eyes nearly

shut as she concentrated. "I never went in for much of that outer-space alien stuff, but I think I remember hearing something about it. What of the sightings?"

"Well, the Federated Commonwealth, at the Hudson Gulf Aerospace Center, was testing Hammerhead prototypes built from plans recovered in a Star League-era computer memory core. The project was very secret, so the flights were made only at night and UAP buffs kept calling in sightings of aircraft doing impossible things. The AFFC refused to comment on the sightings and stonewalled the whole thing. That, of course, just made it worse and UAP 'investigators' said the government's silence proved the existence of aliens and that the government was in secret negotiations with them."

Deirdre folded up the map. "I think I saw a holovid about that. I thought it was a real laugher. It said that a crashed ship and alien bodies were on the Hudson Gulf base, in area 51, hangar 18b."

"I remember that, and I remember the crash." Kai shrugged his bullet-proof vest on, being careful not to crunch his ribs. "One of the prototype Hammerheads went down on a farm just outside Moore's Folly in the Roswell district. The AFFC folks quarantined the place and picked up every bit of material that had been on the plane, including ferro-fibrous armor.

"It turned out they missed a scrap or two, a piece of which was turned over to UAPologists, who immediately proclaimed it something mankind was incapable of producing. They claimed the government had bodies of aliens stashed away. Mostly the UAP folks were paranoid conspiracy-theorists running amok and all they did was cause trouble for clerks having to process requests for information."

"So you don't believe in 'flying saucers,' Kai Allard?"

The MechWarrior shrugged. "It's not to believe or disbelieve. I don't know if they are out there, and I really don't care. If one of them wanted to come along and give us a ride home, I'd accept it."

"And that's why we're going to the radio telescope facility, is it?"

Kai said nothing as he zipped up his jumpsuit. He had told Deirdre he hoped the radio telescope could be used to send a coded message out into space. He knew, and was pretty sure she knew, any message sent in that fashion would take centuries to reach New Avalon, and at least two decades to hit the nearest Federated Commonwealth world. They both knew it would be a long shot to hope some JumpShip was still lurking in the system and capable of carrying their message away, but they deemed it worth a chance.

What Kai had not told her was that he knew of the secret communication devices the Federated Commonwealth had developed to supplant ComStar's monopoly on interstellar communication. The black boxes sent messages at a rate much slower than ComStar's hyperpulse generators, but it would get a message to the Federated Commonwealth before either one of them had grown too old to appreciate being rescued.

He did not know if that facility had one of the fax machines or not, but the possibility was one he could not pass up investigating. Kai regretted withholding that information from her, but he only knew about it himself because of his father and things he had picked up as a child. To share that information, even with the woman he loved, would violate his father's trust and put her in needless jeopardy.

"Best bet for getting us a galactic-taxi off this rock, I think." Kai shouldered his pack. "I think it will take us another couple of weeks to get up into the mountains. We zip through Tedesco Pass and we're at Mount Sera. We send the message and wait."

Despite his seeming casualness, Kai knew it would not be that simple. The hike would take them through the Vorrei National Forest, around a city and two villages, and up into the foothills. The old-growth forest would be picturesque, with its tall pines and golden meadows, but it still meant a lot of wear and tear on their bodies. When they reached their goal, they would be ragged and tired.

Deirdre stuffed the map into her pack. "And you're sure the facility is there?"

"Very sure, in fact." Kai scattered the ashes from their little fire with his right foot. "At the New Avalon Military Academy, I attended a talk by Professor Todor Meir. He talked about research he had been doing, scrupulously avoiding any mention of where he had been. Later, at a reception, he noticed I was wearing a diver's watch and we started to talk scuba diving. He mentioned the Mar Negro on Alyina. A minimal amount of detective work put the puzzle together for me, and my father confirmed the accuracy of my deductions."

Deirdre smiled as she fell into step beside him. "Like father, like son, I guess."

Kai glanced at her, looking for any hint of her old hatred, but her beautiful face showed none. "I'd like to think so."

She stepped over a fallen tree. "Oh, I think you do well in that regard. I know your parents are very proud of you."

"Really?" The jolt of pride shooting through his chest surprised Kai. "What makes you say that?"

Deirdre silently paced a few steps further through the shadow-laced forest before answering. "When I had to testify on Outreach about your actions on Twycross, I could read it in their eyes. Though I wanted to hurt your father, I could only tell the truth. I don't think they could be more proud of you, Kai. Your background has made you the kind of person I'd like to be."

"Don't say that. You've done wonderful things, and you'll do more."

She shrugged. "I'm trying to atone for the things my father did. My background hasn't been much of a help in anything I've tried to do."

Kai shook his head and worked his way up a hill using a lattice of roots as steps. "You dwell too much on what you think are the sins of your father. Peter Armstrong might not have been the greatest father in the universe, but I don't think you're his daughter, really."

"What?"

"Look, you say you wanted to make up for your father and what he did to the Federated Commonwealth. You could have chosen a million different ways to do it." Kai reached back and helped her top the little hill. "You chose medicine as the avenue through which you contribute to the Federated Commonwealth. I think that's because your real father, Roy Lear, was a doctor. I think, in choosing what you would do with the rest of your life, you built from your real background."

Kai shrugged. "Of course, what do I know? I should leave all this psychology to the professionals."

Deirdre tucked strands of dark hair behind her left ear. "I never looked at it that way. I always thought of my stepfather as a mentor, not a father. I loved him, but not in the normal way."

"But who is to say what is normal?" Kai chuckled lightly as he thought about his family. "My parents were forever heading off for this or that reason. State dinners, meetings on other worlds, wars to plan and fight—the list had no end. Even so, they made sure we each knew we were loved. They had confidence in us and wanted us to become whatever we desired. Despite not seeing them for months at a time, it may have been better than having a parent who was always around but never loved you enough. The way I grew up might not be classed as normal by an outsider, but it was normal for me."

She slipped her left hand into his right. "You're pretty smart for a soldier, you know."

Kai smiled. "Think so?"

"Well, except for two things that I wonder about."

"Yes?"

"Isn't our projected path to Mount Sera going to bring us awfully close to Dove Costoso?" She wrinkled her nose. "I don't really want to be on the same continent with that ComStar demi-Precentor."

"There go our plans for visiting him for tea, I guess." Kai gave her hand a reassuring squeeze. "We'll skirt the city by a wide enough margin to avoid detection and capture. We'll be close, but not that close. Next?"

"Tell me again why we didn't keep the hovertruck."

The MechWarrior grimaced. "The truck wouldn't have been suited to the trip we're making. We'd have been forced to stick to the roads or less broken terrain.

"Besides, by programming the hovertruck to run all over the search sectors, we should have confused anyone following us. They won't know when or where we got off the hovertruck, and sending them their Elemental back in it is bound to cause them some problems. It nothing else, we bought time by forcing them to bid out a new hunter to send after us."

"Somehow, Kai, that is not a fact in which I would care to delight."

Kai nodded and felt the hairs at the back of his neck begin to rise. He looked over at Deirdre and let her smile infect him.

He even let himself believe the sense of dread festering in his mind was nothing more than a cold breeze playing over the jumpsuit's collar.

* * *

"And I bid no rocket pack for my armor!" roared one Elemental.

"I will not use my laser!" shouted another.

Taman Malthus vaulted the railing surrounding the small amphitheater in which the members of his command bid for the right to pursue Dave Jewell. He landed solidly, planting both feet on the ground as if driving pilings down to the bedrock below. Clad in nothing more than a pair of shorts and sandals, he balled his fists and stared hard at the last two men in the arena.

"You are pathetic. You are all pathetic." Malthus let his harsh gaze sweep over the men and women of his entire Star. "This is a man you hunt, not a BattleMech."

"But Star Captain, you saw what he did to Corbin."

"I saw. He cut him, beat him, and broke his back, then trussed him up like an animal bound for market. He tied him to that hovertruck and sent it on a crazy chase through the search sectors. That complicates things, but does not tell us if Jewell is good or Corbin was just stupid."

Malthus pointed back toward the Star's administration building. "The labs analyzed Corbin's dagger and have found blood reside on it. Jewell has been cut and could be in bad shape. Sending the truck out may have been a desperate move to utterly throw us off the track."

"I bid," began one woman.

Malthus waved her bid off. "Your bid is worth nothing because my own bid *is* nothing." He raised clenched fists to shoulder height. "I will get him with my bare hands."

"How?" shouted another Elemental. "We have not a clue as to where he is."

"Yes we do. He is hurt and must realize he cannot hope to elude us in the wilderness for much longer. That means he has to head back to a place large enough for him to lose himself and, quite possibly, make contact with partisans."

The Elemental leader folded his arms across his heavily muscled chest. "We will concentrate our search in and around Dove Costoso. We will cut across his trail and find him. He has killed a man in my command, which makes him more than a nuisance for Demi-Precentor Khalsa. Yes, we will find this Dave Jewell and then, when he thinks himself most safe, his life will be mine."

27

Phelan snarled as yet another glowing mark on the outline of his 'Mech showed him where the Elemental had nibbled away another bit of armor. "You little bastard. If you came out where I could see you, I'd kill you, but I can't find you."

Edick's actions surprised Phelan. During the ritual, the Clansman had boasted proudly of his previous victories in the Bloodright contest, giving a long account of all his deeds. Cowering and sniping were not what Phelan would have expected in this fight.

He had been happy when Natasha pulled the top coin from the cup, saying, "You, Phelan are the hunter. How will you hunt?"

He turned to Edick and smiled broadly. "I will hunt augmented."

He had expected that to give the Elemental trouble, but the huge man shrugged it off as if Phelan had demanded water-pistols at twenty paces. Phelan knew Edick had won all his previous Bloodrights and had opted to fight bare-handed against his foes. He'd killed an aerospace pilot in his first fight, and put the two MechWarriors he faced since then in the hospital. Instead of becoming nervous about the first fight where he would be at a severe disadvantage, Edick smiled calmly. "We will fight in the Camelot Industrial Park on Lothan."

The instant Phelan saw the site Edick had selected for the battle, he knew the man had some good advisors. Buildings both large and small made up the modern industrial center, all fabricated from similar building materials that turned the park into a glittering world of steel and mirrors. At the ilKhan's command, the whole facility was evacuated in preparation for the battle. Somewhere inside that looking-glass labyrinth an Elemental waited for Phelan.

The dying sun filled all the mirror faces with blood.

Phelan switched his scanner from vislight to infrared, then immediately popped it back before it burned his eyes out. The heat reflected by the mirrors made using IR useless. As nearly as Phelan could figure, Edick had taken up residence in the big building to his left. By running from floor to floor, or possibly just bashing his way through interior walls, the Elemental was managing to shoot his small laser at Phelan from the safety of cover.

Another MechWarrior might have burrowed straight into the building, but Phelan was not of a mind to do that. He knew Edick was counting on his reluctance to do wholesale property damage while defending himself. For Phelan, however, his reluctance to wade into a building came from its being the only obvious solution to the problem and because he was not entirely comfortable with the 'Mech he piloted.

Though the free selection of venue was supposed to make up for any advantage gained by the winner of the coin selection, the Clans took other steps to ensure that the Bloodright battles were approximately fair. Thus Phelan was issued a *Mercury* for his fight with Edick, rather than being able to use his *Wolfhound*. The light 'Mech was well-known for its reconnaissance ability, but its weaponry was only slightly better than what an Elemental had. None of the 'Mech's weapons could put Edick down with one shot, which was precisely why they had assigned him this BattleMech.

"All I have are lasers, which aren't useful against these damned mirrored buildings! I'd give my right arm for a simple machine gun so I could shoot out these windows." When he balled his fists reflexively, the *Mercury*'s mechanical hands aped the movement.

The buildings surrounding him rose up to a full ten stories, or three times his height. Their metal content, both in building materials and equipment, made magscan useless. Sunlight made IR scanning equally impotent. Phelan concentrated on vislight, but he knew the chances of his spotting whatever little openings Edick was using to shoot at him were impossible. As long as the man remained in the building, he had Phelan at a disadvantage.

Phelan flipped a switch on his command console to shunt his microphone to the 'Mech's external speakers. "Come out and play, Edick."

"Come in and get me, Phelan," a voice echoed back out through the glass canyon.

The gloating in Edick's voice kept Phelan from pounding a fist through the building's wall and following it with the *Mercury*'s bulk. "If I could just . . . ," he started to mumble, then stopped as he caught the echo of the words from outside. In a millisecond, fear he'd betrayed himself washed over him, then an idea hit him and he laughed.

"Yeah, might just work."

He opened his mike and flipped his external speakers on again. He increased the gain of the mike and boosted the output on the external speakers. Feedback built into a shrieking crescendo that set his teeth buzzing. He snapped his helmet's speakers off and pushed the external volume control all the way to maximum.

All around him, accompanied by the feedback's banshee wail, the buildings' mirrored walls shivered and buckled. In a diamond rain, the whole wall fragmented and fell to the ground. The deadly hail poured over his *Mercury*, but Phelan ignored it and concentrated on the building hiding Edick. What had only been a silver reflection seconds before became offices and hallways, with the telltale signs of an Elemental's haphazard progress through the building. It reminded Phelan of an exterminator's cutaway view of a house infested by rats. It was as though his surprise tactic had caught a big rat smack dab in the middle of the fifth floor.

The *Mercury*'s right arm came up and the medium laser built into its forearm flashed to life. It hit Edick dead-center while the Elemental seemed to be trying to wave him off. Phelan wondered at the man's audacity and prepared for a second shot. "It's over, Edick."

Suddenly the world exploded. A boiling, vaporous sheet of yellow flame instantly engulfed the whole building. Edick's form remained visible for a second as a black silhouette, then it vanished in the inferno. The shockwave hit the *Mercury,* knocking it back into the building behind it. The 'Mech stumbled, driving its head and shoulders down through the lower three floors of the building.

Phelan braced for the impact with the ground by pressing his neurohelmeted head back into the command couch's headrest. He hit hard, momentarily stunned, then found himself looking up the shaft of an atrium extending up the center of the building. He rotated the *Mercury*'s chin down, giving him a view back through the hole he'd made.

The burning building sagged toward him.

The *Mercury*'s heels slammed down, buckling the ferrocrete foundation. The legs extended to their full length, ramming the *Mercury*'s upper body through the other side of the building that trapped it. Its arms reached up and back in a clawing motion that dragged the BattleMech half-clear of its prison. Another powerful shove from its legs kicked it all the way clear of the building.

Flipping his 'Mech prone, Phelan gathered its hands and feet beneath it and stood. He steadied the 'Mech as another explosion shook the area. Spinning about, he saw the burning building smash down into the one that had trapped him. Heavily damaged by his coring of the lower section, that building shuddered, then slowly flopped over to bury its blazing companion.

Off in the distance Phelan saw the strobing red and blue lights of a civilian fire company coming to prevent the fire from spreading. Phelan dropped the *Mercury* to one knee and used the 'Mech's right hand to scrape away debris clogging the roadway. He stared deep into the flames of Edick's pyre and shook his head.

"You died for a Bloodname, Edick. We, the Clans, pride ourselves on being superior to the citizens of the Inner Sphere, but I wonder if a people that could cause all this destruction in the name of vanity can ever be considered civilized."

Phelan hit the freeze-frame button on the holovid viewer. "See, right there on his small laser?" The MechWarrior pointed to a blurry black cone surrounding the muzzle of Edick's small laser. "That looks like a rubber gasket of some sort. He poked a small hole in one of the windows, pressed the laser and gasket to it, and was able to shoot at me."

Natasha smiled coldly. "Edick shatters the gas main in the

building and lets it fill with natural gas. He's already cut power to the building so a random spark won't set his trap off. The gasket lets him use the laser without starting the fire."

Ranna, standing behind Phelan's position on the couch, rested her hands on his shoulders. "He expected, with the little shots, to goad you into attacking the building. You crash into it, he jumps clear, then uses his laser . . ."

". . . or his SRM launcher to start the whole thing off." Phelan shuddered, then looked up with a smile as Ranna gave his shoulders a squeeze.

"That explosion would have been more than enough to severely damage your *Mercury*," she said. "Dropping the rest of the building on top of you would have ensured your death."

"You would have been baked alive." Natasha's voice rang with horror. "Normally an Elemental would not dare even enter the melee for a Bloodright on a non-Elemental Bloodname. Still, the name for which you fight is so valued that everyone wants to try. Besides, Edick did well in the early going."

Phelan agreed. "He defeated as many as I had."

"True, Phelan, but the luck of the Bloodright had a big part in that, I think. The damnable thing is that Elementals cannot allow themselves to fight fairly. Inferno rockets and exploding buildings are hardly the way to battle for a Bloodname."

Phelan frowned. "Edick had to do something. If he had fought me out in the open, I would have splattered him."

"Agreed, which is why he should have waited for an Elemental Bloodright to become available. He gambled big and lost bigger."

The sudden opening of the door to Phelan's room brought an abrupt end to Natasha's comments. Phelan jerked to his feet as ilKhan Ulric entered. All three of the room's occupants remained at attention until Ulric closed the door behind him. "At ease," he said, giving them a smile.

Phelan and Ranna brought their hands around to the small of their backs, while Natasha dropped into a chair and reached for the beer she'd been drinking. "Forgive me for saying so, ilKhan, but you look like a man who's been through a battle."

"Battle? Try campaign." The ilKhan leaned forward, letting his hands rest on the back of the chair beside Natasha. "The Jade Falcons are doing their best to make up for Twycross, while the Nova Cats and Smoke Jaguars are trying to recoup their losses from the siege of Luthien. The Ghost Bears, Steel Vipers, and Diamond Sharks just want to reach parity with the rest of us, and everyone wants to tear their advantages out of Clan Wolf."

"Diamond Sharks? I did not know they were with the invasion force."

Ulric shrugged. "The Council decided that the battle was significant enough to warrant the activation of additional Clan forces." He waved a hand toward the couch. "Please, sit." He glanced at the bottle Natasha was holding. "Phelan, would you happen to have another of those?"

Phelan smiled and knelt beside the small refrigerator on which the holovid viewer sat. "It's Timbiqui dark. Ragnar scrounged it planetside while I was raising arson to a new height on Lothan. It is an import from over near the Free Worlds League border." He shrugged sheepishly. "It was the beer of choice at the Nagelring."

"Anything that will cut the sour taste in my mouth will be most welcome." Ulric accepted the bottle and twisted the cap off. He drank, then closed his eyes and relaxed. "This is good. Remind me to take this world."

Natasha leaned over on the right arm of her chair. The chair's white leather padding set off the black of her jumpsuit as she drew her legs up. "So did you manage to hash out the troop assignments for the battle with ComStar?"

Ulric's head came forward and his eyes opened with a flash of blue. "I told them that I believed twenty-five Galaxies would be an appropriate response to ComStar's pledge of fifty regiments. That would be three Galaxies apiece, with the extra four going to the Wolf Clan by rights."

Natasha nodded in agreement. "Of course."

"That started a firestorm. I immediately bid away two of those extra Galaxies, but the others pressed for more concessions. Quite correctly, they perceived my desire to win the battle and they moved to blunt it. I have been forced to hold all Wolf Clan troops in reserve for the first five days of battle." Ulric's grim smile sent a chill down Phelan's spine. "They wanted us out for two weeks, but I managed to whittle it down to five days."

"As if the battle for Tukayyid would last two weeks,"

Natasha scoffed. "Though I would relish the landing, I think being able to pick out fights after the battle lines have solidified is not a bad thing."

Ulric shook his head. "The problem is that those idiots then started bidding among themselves for the right to be the first to land. The Smoke Jaguars won that right, but I believe they sacrificed too much to do so. The others have nothing but contempt for ComStar because of its pacifistic message and they believe they will roll over Focht's forces with ease. They have discounted the dangers of the ComStar air, armor, and artillery assets. I am fairly certain, in fact, that Star Colonels and Star Captains will bid among themselves and further dilute their strength."

Phelan did not like the implication of the ilKhan's words or weary tone. "We will defeat ComStar, *quiaff*? I mean I have heard, all my life, strange stories about ComStar and their hidden 'Mech assets, but I have never seen anything to prove they have fifty regiments. What are the chances Focht was bluffing?"

"I have no way of knowing, which should serve as an answer to both of your questions." Ulric took another pull on the beer. "You created the briefing report on Focht and you know the way other battles have gone with the opposition we face. If Focht does have fifty regiments to oppose us, that is almost four thousand 'Mechs. If we start with the twenty-five Galaxies we are committing, less the five Galaxies of Wolves, we'll be giving them a thousand-'Mechs advantage on the first day. If we assume air, armor, and artillery units on each side balance out, our force is still only 71 percent of their force."

Planting elbows on knees, Ranna leaned forward. "Each one of our 'Mechs will have to kill 1.3 ComStar 'Mechs just to keep us even. Of course, this is predicated on full deployment, but we know the other Clans will bargain down some of their strength. The Smoke Jaguars and Nova Cats never even approached that kill ratio on Luthien."

Natasha chuckled slowly. "I don't see why you are all worried. Let the others make fools of themselves on the first day. I have hated ComStar since the first time I dealt with one of those sycophant Acolytes in negotiating a contract for the Dragoons. That is enough to sustain me and make sure the Guards destroy whatever they face."

She shot a quick glance at Ulric. "The Guards *are* going to fight, *quiaff?*"

"Aff, Natasha, aff." Ulric held his hands up in a sign of surrender. "I am not mad. I know that if I did not include the Guards, you would bargain your way into the invasion force. I would much rather have you with me than against me."

The ilKhan looked over at Phelan. "Enough of this talk, however, for I did not come here to discuss this news. I came to congratulate Phelan on winning his fourth battle to claim his Bloodright."

"Thank you, my Khan." Phelan had something even more important on his mind, however. "If we are to fight on Tukayyid in two weeks, will the final battle be held before or after the fight with ComStar?"

"After, I am afraid."

"Afraid? I do not understand."

The ilKhan's voice dropped almost to a whisper. "It is possible that you or your foe in the finals might be killed in the fighting. I urge you to be careful and watch your back."

"You are not suggesting Vlad or Conal would try anything on Tukayyid, are you?"

Ulric nodded solemnly. "After the decision on Tukayyid, you will face Vlad in the final battle for Cyrilla Ward's Bloodname. If you are in trouble and the Eleventh Wolf Guards are the force nearest you, I would not expect succor all that quickly. No one would deliberately kill you, but they just might let ComStar pick the winner in this Bloodright."

=== 28 ===

DropShip **Dao,** *Hexare*
Sian Commonality, Capellan Commonwealth
20 April 3052

House Master Ion Rush leaned back in his chair as the cloaked figure sat across from him. "You look weary."

His visitor laughed lightly. "Weary yes, but that is not so bad for someone who is dead, is it?"

Rush smiled and even managed to bring up the corner of his mouth, where a scar traced back across his cheek to his earlobe. "When I heard Romano's assassin had gotten you, I could not believe it. When I got the message you sent, I thought it was a trick. Even seeing you here and now, I have a hard time believing we have set ourselves on this course."

"Too late to turn back now, my friend." The visitor's gloved left hand slapped the arm of the chair heavily. "Even having me aboard your ship is treason. Your life is in peril and will be forfeit if even one of your men hints at my presence aboard the *Dao*."

"Waste no thought on fear of betrayal. House Imarra is fiercely loyal to me and to House Liao."

"And we agree that Romano has become a major threat to the continuance of House Liao."

"True. Were Hanse Davion not preoccupied with these invaders, he would have smashed the Chancellor for her audacity. Malignant bitch!" Rush exerted control over his emotions and forced his fists to unknot. "As for the threat to my life, when has it not been in jeopardy in the last twenty years? Because Romano had taken refuge behind a building I defended, I survived the purge after you made your escape from Sian. I luckily succeeded in some battles against the Andurien invaders and then defeated a unit of Marik Guards in later fighting. For that, Romano elevated House Imarra to her personal bodyguard unit, but we know the true duty for us is to safeguard the Liao bloodline, not the woman serving on the throne."

Rush half-hoped his devotion to his duty had not bled into his voice, but the low laugh from his guest told him he had revealed his heart. "Now I must urge you not to worry. My quarrel is with Romano and her consort. Eye for an eye, tooth for a tooth. I believe my children more than capable of taking care of themselves. I merely hope my intervention will make your mission easier."

The dark-haired man smiled solicitously. "I thank you. With that obstacle out of the way, my duty will not be in conflict."

"What is our schedule?"

"We will jump to Sian in two days; the Kearny-Fuchida drive needs that much more time to charge. When we arrive, we will head into Sian at normal speeds. I expect us to make planetfall on or about the eighth of May. I have made all the arrangements you required so you should be able to conclude your business and leave inside a week."

"Excellent, Rush, excellent." The visitor rubbed one hand over the knuckles of the other. "You get the stable government you desire and I get what I want: revenge. By the end of the first fortnight in May, the fate of the Inner Sphere will have changed forever."

29

Kai waved Deirdre forward with an over-exaggerated motion of his right hand. "C'mon gorgeous. It's not that much further."

He looked up along the grassy pathway taking them to the top of the pass. It clung to the side of the foothills like an overwide ledge. To his left, granite outcroppings played hide-and-seek amid a pine forest much like the one through which they'd been hiking for the better part of two weeks. Up this high, the trees had begun to thin, but Kai liked walking in the open and feeling the dying sun on his face.

To his left, the land dropped away as if the valley floor had been snapped off and pushed down into the ground. Though some trees did extend up to and even above the level of the pathway and the plateau toward which they headed, the geography still gave Kai an unobstructed view of the area to the north and west of the pass. Way off in the distance, he could see Dove Costoso squatting like a chalkpit in the midst of the forest. Beyond it, the mountains where they'd begun their journey slowly nibbled away at the sun's red disk.

Deirdre caught up with Kai and took his hand. "I'm exhausted, Kai. I think it's the thin air up here."

"Exhaustion just makes you prettier." Kai kissed her nose. "And the air is getting to me, too. If we make it another one hundred meters, we'll be on level ground. We can stop for the night, and then tomorrow we can descend the other side and we'll be at Mount Sera."

Deirdre blew an errant strand of hair from her forehead. "Thank God. Had I known what this hike would be like, I would have surrendered in Dove Costoso."

"You might have had a partner in that," Kai sighed. Deirdre had slowed him down in the trip, but he couldn't have made it without her. *I accepted responsibility for her, as she did for me. If we had not worked together, neither of us would have made it even this far.*

Her eyes sparkled blue. "What? You mean I could be the demi-Precentor's guest right now?"

Kai turned around and dragged her up the hill. "Sure, you could be his guest. I'm sure he'd really appreciate your bedside manner."

"In his wildest dreams."

The MechWarrior smiled. "Well, we did leave him in bad shape, and Lord knows I've healed much faster due to your ministrations."

She slipped her arm around his waist as they reached the circular plateau. "You and I have a special rapport. I sincerely doubt I could ever care as much about Khalsa's condition as I do yours."

Standing near the western edge of the plateau, Kai shucked off his pack and laid the autorifle down on top of it. He pulled Deirdre into his arms and kissed her. "Could be I have a chronic condition, Doctor. You might have to tend to me for a long time."

"I do make house calls," she whispered back and drew him closer.

"I find this touching, but I am afraid, Mr. Jewell, Doctor Lear, you will have to quench your ardor another time."

Kai turned slowly and guided Deirdre wide to his left, yet away from the plateau's sharp drop. He knew instantly from the deep timbre of the man's voice that the speaker could only be an Elemental and incredibly huge. The man he found himself facing fit that description far more perfectly than he had hoped. He wore his blond hair short and his arctic eyes seemed positively alien to the MechWarrior. His clothing consisted of only a pair of shorts and leather sandals.

Behind him, three other Elementals slipped from the trees on the plateau's south and eastern perimeter. One moved to cut off any chance of heading back down the way they had come while another blocked the trail out to the northeast. All three wore jumpsuits and carried knives, but none had their weapons drawn.

The leader pressed his right hand against his breastbone. "I am Taman Malthus, the Star Captain in charge of the Elemental Trinary Star here on Alyina. I wish to applaud your efforts at evasion. Tracking and capturing you has proved most challenging."

Kai could tell from the man's manner and tone that his words were meant as a compliment. "I appreciate that, Star Captain." Kai let his hand rest on the pistol at his right hip. "I would point out that I am armed with a pistol, so why don't you and your men leave now and things don't have to get nasty."

Malthus nodded in a matter-of-fact way that annoyed Kai. "It is a Mauser and Gray needle pistol. Given my size, it will take approximately three shots centered on my head or chest to kill me. In that time, because the projectiles do not have appreciable mass to deter me, I will cross the distance between us and carry you off the edge to your death below. At the same time, one of my aides will kill Doctor Lear."

"Your last hunter tried to use Deirdre against me."

"Did he?" Malthus straightened up. "He paid with his life for being stupid." The Elemental looked at Deirdre and indicated with a motion of his right hand that she should move away from Kai. She glanced back at him and he nodded his agreement. "I promise you, Mr. Jewell, that I will not use her against you. In fact, if you defeat me in single combat, you are both free to go on your way."

Kai snorted with derision. "That was the same deal your Corbin offered me, though he repudiated it in mid-battle. Surely you can do better."

"Can and will." Malthus dipped his head in a salute. "I will arrange for a DropShip to take you back to your people."

The MechWarrior hooked his thumbs through his gunbelt. "Dr. Lear, me, and all the prisoners of war in Firebase Tango Zephyr."

"ComStar will not like our taking their prisoners away from them, but anything that annoys Demi-Precentor Khalsa pleases me. Bargained well and done." Malthus turned toward one of his men. "You heard our agreement. You will see to it that my half of the bargain is met if Jewell defeats me."

"Aff, Star Captain."

Kai unbuckled his gunbelt and tossed it onto his pack beside the rifle. He took one step away from the edge, then stretched his right leg. "I trust you do not mind? Climbing that hill has stiffened me up somewhat."

Flexing thighs almost as thick as Kai's torso, Malthus mirrored his motion. "I would not want you at a disadvantage. As it is, waiting for you to reach this point has likewise stiffened me."

"How did you find us?"

The Clansman shrugged effortlessly. "We assumed you would be heading for Dove Costoso to lose yourself in the crowd. We cut across your trail, swinging north of the city. Consulting a map told us you had no real place to go except through this pass and out of the Costoso Valley. We have been waiting here since this morning."

As Kai shifted sides to stretch his other leg, he saw Deirdre staring at him. "You don't have to do this. You can just surrender."

The Elemental shook his head as his gaze bored into Kai's soul. "He is a warrior, woman. He is not yet captured, and freedom is within his grasp."

"Death is not freedom. Just surrender. I do not want you to die."

"In some ways, Deirdre, not fighting would be death." Kai started through some torso-twists. "Star Captain, if you kill me, make sure she does not go to Khalsa."

"Done." Malthus gave Kai an easy smile. "In honor of your having slain Corbin, I will make her a bondswoman of the Jade Falcons."

"This is stupid!" Deirdre appealed to Malthus. "Star Captain, make *him* a bondsman. Why kill him?"

"I would not dishonor him with the offer."

Kai nodded grimly at Malthus' words. "And were I to surrender, the offer would never be made."

"But if you surrendered, you would still be alive," Deirdre insisted.

Kai wanted to reach out to her, but instead he said, "Deirdre, you don't understand. As much as you are a healer, I am a warrior. You would use all your skills and abilities to keep someone alive, and here, now, I can do the same."

"But I wouldn't die to save someone!"

"With any luck, neither will I." Kai looked over at the Elemental. "If you are ready, so am I. Let us begin."

"I am ready." Malthus lowered himself into a fighting stance. "Begin."

Well aware any long fight would be one he lost, Kai glided forward. He reared back, feinting a side kick to the Elemental's head with his right foot, then lashed out at Malthus' right knee. The Elemental's left arm came up to block the head blow and his right hand partially deflected the lower kick. Still the kick hit hard and Kai danced back out of range before Malthus could come after him.

The Elemental rubbed at his leg for a moment, then nodded. "You are very good, Mr. Jewell. I see why Corbin fell to you. He would have underestimated you, but I shall not do the same." Straightening up, Malthus waved Kai forward. "Come, again!"

Kai attacked again, but as his right foot scythed through where Malthus' head should have been, the Elemental ducked and cut to the left and toward Kai's back. Something heavy and hard slammed into Kai's spine, pitching him forward. Pain shot down his back and into his legs, momentarily numbing them.

He landed on his face and instantly flipped himself prone. Lying on his back, he saw the Clanner's right foot stamp down through where he had fallen. Kai snapped his right leg up, driving his toe into the back of Malthus' right thigh, then pushed off and rolled further from the large man.

Kai regained his feet slowly and felt a pulsing of pain from the center of his back. *Blake's blood, he nearly cripples me with one punch and nothing I do fazes him.* He watched the Elemental turn in his direction and saw no weakness in the man's right leg.

Give up, Kai, hissed the small voice in his head. *Let the farce end now.*

The Elemental drove at Kai. An overhand right arced in at his head, so the MechWarrior brought his left arm up to block it while his own right hand shot straight toward Malthus' jaw. He felt his own blow connect and heard a grunt from the Elemental.

Malthus' punch drove Kai's arm back into his own head and exploded like a bomb in his brain. Sizzling rainbow balls burst before his eyes and his knees turned to water. Unable to regain his balance, he spun to the ground and tasted blood and dirt in his mouth. He pawed at his face, and his hand came away wet and red from a concussive nosebleed.

Huge hands grabbed him by the thigh and the back of his neck. Malthus shook him, then tossed him three meters. Kai crashed into the ground hard, then rolled a few times and stopped on his back. Stars still shimmered in his eyesight and the rest of the world looked as if dusk had turned to midnight.

Malthus grabbed the front of his jumpsuit and hauled him to his feet. A punch to the stomach doubled Kai over as his breath exploded from his lungs, then a knee to his ribs sent him reeling. His lungs burned and his stomach ached as he struggled to stay on his feet. He half-succeeded and held himself off the ground on a hand and one knee. He wanted to yell that he surrendered, but breathless he could not do it.

Panicked and half-blind, Kai looked up just in time for another of the Elemental's punches to hammer him into the ground. He tried to pull out of the way of the punch, but only partially succeeded, which meant he flopped onto his side instead of landing prone again. He kicked out blindly and felt his foot connect, but had no idea where he had hit Malthus.

The first bit of breath back in his lungs drove the panic from him, but did nothing to cut through the despair in him. *You have failed, Kai. Your whole life comes down to this: blind and bleeding and dying. It is a pity your parents will live with your shame and Deirdre has to witness it.* The pain in his ribs and the ache in his stomach underscored the ignominy of his defeat.

"No!" he howled in response. *I will not give up. I am not fighting for Deirdre or my parents or posterity. I am fighting for me.* "I will not be beaten!"

Kai heaved himself to his feet and concentrated on breathing his pain away. Across from him, Malthus slowly stood and massaged his right leg. Kai used his sleeve to wipe the blood from his nose, then slowly beckoned the Elemental forward. "Come on. We should end this before it is too dark to fight."

Malthus came in at him cautiously, slightly favoring his right leg. Kai knew his only chance to defeat the Elemental came in knocking him out, yet to strike such a blow would be to leave himself open to hideous punishment by the Elemental. *It doesn't matter, it has to be done!*

Kai waited until Malthus planted his right foot, then leaped forward. He led with his left foot, then snapped his right foot up and around in a kick that pinned Malthus' right ear to the side of his head. He saw the man's head twist around, but he knew from the feel of the kick that Malthus was just moving to try to lessen the effect of the blow.

Malthus' right fist swatted Kai from the air. He hit the ground solidly, crushing his right arm into his ribs and knocking the wind out of him. He bounced once and began a lazy roll through the air. Kai heard thundering in his ears and saw flickering lights high in the evening sky, but could make no sense of them or the noise.

He stabbed his right leg down to try to land on his feet, but something tangled itself around his foot, then slipped sideways. As he brought his left foot down, he saw his pack and gunbelt bind his feet together just as the plateau disappeared from beneath him.

Unable to breathe, he could not even scream as he fell into the darkness.

Khalsa saw Dave Jewell drop off the plateau as his gunner finished blowing apart one of the Elementals. Behind him, in the crew compartment, the jump master screamed, "Go, go, go!" over and over again. The jump infantry, their jump-pack exhaust burning a brilliant argent in the evening sky, made an easy descent to the plateau.

The pilot flicked on the helicopter's external spotlights and lit the plateau brighter than it would have been at high noon. He nodded to Khalsa.

The demi-Precentor adjusted his headset microphone. "This is Demi-Precentor Khalsa of ComStar. By command of Primus Myndo Waterly, our Blessed Order is taking control of Alyina. Wherever they served on our world, all of your men have been rounded up or, regrettably, killed, Star Captain Malthus. You are now our prisoner."

Malthus slowly climbed to his feet and shook his head to clear it. "*Stravag* dog! Come down here and I will pluck your heart out with my bare hands!"

"Tsk, tsk, Star Captain. Is that any way to speak to your host?" Khalsa rubbed his hands together, then scratched at where dead flesh from beneath the cast still flaked off. "I could have my men kill you where you stand, but I don't think you want that. And don't think you are alone in having been disgraced. Operation Scorpion is rounding up you invaders from all over the place."

Khalsa killed his external microphone. "Call the other helicopters to come in and get their prisoners. We will take them back to Dove Costoso until we have to send them on to the main center at Valigia." The pilot nodded and Khalsa smiled again. "Operation Scorpion, I love it." He pointed down at Malthus. "Sting, I got you!"

30

Hanse Davion kneaded the pain in his left shoulder with strong fingers as he looked up at his wife. Still the slender slip of a woman he had married a quarter century before, she wore a mask of anger he had seen only rarely in all those years. It should have made him bristle and want to fight back, but knowing the well from which her anger was drawn, he could not blame her.

"Hanse, you cannot let Victor go ahead with this plan! No matter what Morgan says, we both know it is a desperate operation with a good chance of catastrophic failure." Melissa Steiner-Davion looked at her husband with gray eyes a shade lighter than false dawn. "If you let him go through with this, you are killing him."

Hanse levered himself out of the chair and took her wrists in his hands. She tried to pull away, but he held her firm. "Melissa, please. I love Victor as much as you do. If I believed this plan was suicidal for him or his people, I would abort it immediately. You know that. You also know I cannot stop him."

"Oh, you Davion men." She turned away as he released her arms. "Hanse, here in our private chambers, I have learned of the passions that run soul-deep in you. Every time I watch you viewing battleroms from the front, I see you wanting to be out there in the thick of the fighting. Sometimes I think you Davions have been bred for the battlefield the way some dogs are bred for hunting."

Melissa crossed to a window, where the moonlight washed her pale hair with silver. "With you it is more than desire, it is a hunger."

"Then your fear is not that Victor will be killed," Hanse said, "but that he will come to glory in killing, is that it?" At her shudder, Hanse immediately regretted his words. He softened his tone. "I know you hoped to curb any Davion propensities for war by raising Victor more as a Steiner than a Davion. Yes, the Steiners have proved themselves in war, but their strength has ever been in negotiation and administration of their vast holdings. Steiners are statesmen first and warriors second."

She turned quickly and swiped a tear from her cheek. "Is that wrong? Is it a crime to hope that my children and my grandchildren would live in a time and universe where war was a secondary option? No, I was never trained as a MechWarrior so I do not fully understand the relationship between you and your machines. You speak of them like friends, like faithful companions who get ripped apart or killed and then resurrected to fight again. Sometimes it sounds as though you MechWarriors believe it is not you who do the hitting and killing, but your 'Mechs.

"That reduces war to battles of hardware versus hardware, yet we both know that is a false concept. You Davions glory in the call to war. Your brother Ian, Victor's namesake, died in a battle for a parched planet that meant nothing to him or those he fought. He should have been nowhere near Mallory's World, yet that is where he died. And you, when New Avalon was attacked twenty years ago, you immediately joined the battle and never thought of summoning aid!"

Her hands balled into fists, and Hanse felt his own heart tighten painfully. "Now my son, my Victor, has concocted a scheme that will take him deep into enemy territory on a mission that might do nothing more than collect a box containing Hohiro Kurita's remains. It is not worth the risk."

Hanse worked his left hand into a fist, then forced it open to try to ease some of the tightness in his chest. "I will not argue with you the relative merits of this mission's goals. While you point out that Hohiro may no longer be alive, the rescue effort alone will be significant to the Combine. That one act, performed by Victor at Omi Kurita's request, could seal the agreement Theodore and I made, extending it to the next generation and perhaps beyond."

He took in a deep breath and forced it out slowly. "Ian died on Mallory's World because he would not ask his soldiers to undertake any task he would not perform himself. He died defending his men. He held off the Kurita forces pursuing them, knowing he would die. He must have sensed something even before going off on that mission because he forced me to promise I would not come after him."

Hanse sat on the edge of their bed. "I often wish I had violated that promise so that perhaps Ian might have lived."

"You sent him support. It just arrived too late."

"That really does not matter, my love. What is important is that Ian, as the First Prince of the Federated Suns, had the right to place himself in jeopardy. It was his choice and he exercised it on his terms. He chose that mission because he felt it was a challenge only he could meet."

Melissa half-smiled. "You do realize that most of you Davions believe your name really means 'messiah.'"

The Prince nodded solemnly. "You are correct in more ways than you imagine. A ruler has not only the right to place himself in danger, he also has a *duty* to do so. He must show, through his example, that the causes that are important to the nation transcend the importance of his own life or death."

He slapped his hand on the bed. "I was here the night the Death Commandos landed on New Avalon. When I realized what was happening, I felt neither panic nor fear, but an outrage that they dared violate the sanctity of *my* world. I was furious that they had so little respect for me and my people that they *dared* attack us. I went to my 'Mech to defend Avalon City, but more so to show the enemy that nothing would make us cower in their presence.

"The fighting that night was horrible, but it was also necessary to preserve the Federated Suns and its future. It allowed me to prove to myself and others that I was worthy of the vast trust and power placed in my hands by the Federated Suns. Now it is Victor's turn."

Melissa shook her head. "No. Victor knows his responsibilities and duties as the heir to the throne of the Federated Commonwealth. There are times when those responsibilities—maintaining the stability of the government—must overrule his own sense of adventure."

"If you think this is about adventurism, Melissa, you grossly underestimate your son." Hanse's eyes tightened. "Victor had adventurism burned out of him on Trellwan. He learned to be a leader on Twycross, and he learned how to lose on Alyina. He knows his responsibilities far better than either you or I did at his age, and this is his way of proving he can accept them. If he cannot defeat the Clans with his strategy and planning and training of the Revenants, he will never believe himself worthy of being our heir."

"It is folly to put so much weight on one fool's errand."

"You are wrong, my wife." The Prince felt little electric tendrils of pain caress the left side of his body. "If Victor fails in this mission, he will never assume the throne. He will know he is incapable of facing the challenges the next Archon-Prince must face."

"He will die," she whispered in horror. "He will die, just like Ian."

Hanse shook his head. "No. Victor's too smart. He knows that if he cannot do the job, he still has value. This is his Steiner heritage and he will not let his Davion passions over-rule your Teutonic logic."

Melissa looked at Hanse imploringly. "You are not going to cancel Victor's mission. You never intended to, did you?"

The Prince returned her gaze. "Victor is my heir, not my puppet."

She let her head hang in a nod of resignation. "God be with you, Victor."

"Amen."

A bright flash filled the window with light, then seconds later a sharp report echoed through the night. Melissa spun and looked out through the gossamer draping. "What was that?"

The Fox smiled as his pain eased. "It sounded to me like a truck hauling toxic petrochemicals swerving to miss a small car and crashing into the wall surrounding the main ComStar facility."

She leaned forward slightly. "I see flames from near the center of the city." The wail of sirens accompanied her slow turn to face her husband. "Have you had hearing aids implanted?"

The First Prince rose from the bed and put his arms around his wife from behind. "We had a message from Theodore Kurita that ComStar might be trying to impose a general Interdiction over the whole of the Inner Sphere. Alex thought, and I agreed, that a little accident forcing the evacuation of the ComStar compound might be in order. Of course, all the clerks and Acolytes will have to be quarantined to make sure they suffer no lasting ill effects from the accident. And we'll have to decontaminate the whole area. It could be years before the ComStar facilities are safe."

"Aren't you afraid of another Interdiction?"

Hanse shook his head. "We should actually take 80 percent of the facilities we go for. We can use them and the fax machines to circumvent any Interdiction. The Primus *might* inspire rebellion on some worlds where we fail to take the hyperpulse generators, but providing food inspires more loyalty than news from abroad. Any world that wishes to join ComStar can rely on ComStar to feed it."

"So much for rebellion." Melissa smiled and laced her fingers through his hands where his arms encircled her waist. "So, 'toxic chemicals' were the best you could do?"

"The Primus provided the inspiration, really." Hanse's grin broadened appreciably. "What better than a tanker truck hauling insecticide to get rid of a load of pests? Operation Scorpion, indeed!"

31

Tukayyid
ComStar Intervention District, Free Rasalhague
  Republic
1 May 3052 (Day 1 of Operation Scorpion)

For the first time in all his years of service to ComStar, Anastasius Focht understood how the Primus could imagine herself the Mother Goddess of a humanity waiting to be born. In his headquarters hidden deep beneath the Tamo Mountains, an Interactive Construct Reality map of Tukayyid's northern continent spread out around him. A titan in his ICR helmet and body suit, he straddled the computer-created image of the mountains.

Above his head, hovering like a halo just out of sight, a circle constructed of the myriad views from his spotting stations and troops whirled in a riot of colors. Simply by reaching his right hand up and pulling down, he brought the band of information reports to eye-level. It slowed, then stopped as he selected one particular view. It expanded to enfold him, transporting him to the Przeno Plain. The other views spun up and out of sight as the radio chatter from the communications link slowly came up.

"Confirm, command. We have Jade Falcons dropping in on us."

Off in the distance, he saw four DropShips executing precision retro-burns as they disgorged their cargo. Each spherical ship hung motionless above the plain, charring the wheat fields black, as 'Mech after 'Mech of a Jade Falcon

Cluster jumped clear of its armored belly. Careful to avoid the DropShip's ion jets, but heedless of the grass fire, the Jade Falcon 'Mechs moved forward to take up defensive positions.

Focht opened a communication link. "Precentor Gesicki, you may pull your scouts back now."

Anna Gesicki's tone revealed both fear and irritation. "My people are not afraid, Precentor Martial. The White Lions will hold."

Focht smiled in spite of himself. "I do not doubt your troops' ability to fight, Precentor. You are looking at a Cluster of Jade Falcons. As you will recall, they seem susceptible to the hit-and-run tactics the Federated Commonwealth has used against them. You will recall that Prince Victor's error an Alyina was in getting bogged down before he needed to. You have a full complement of air, artillery, and armor assets. Use them as we have planned."

"Yes, sir." Gesicki hesitated. "I only meant that my scouts are willing to stay in the field until time to withdraw."

"Understood, Precentor. The time is now. We do not want them there to be spotted as the Falcons advance. When the Falcons hit your first line, I want them to be surprised."

"That they will, Precentor Martial. Pulling them out now, sir."

"Very good. Remember, the White Lions must play with the Clans the way a cat would harass a dog. Strike, hiss, appear bigger than you are, then leap away. Make them devote resources to strikes that generate no return."

Focht broke the communication by reaching up and pulling down the zoetrope. It spun around him until he selected a gray frame. With a few simple hand motions, he selected it and made it hang unsupported in the blue sky over the Przeno. The individual trapped therein looked up from a computer terminal.

"At your service, Precentor Martial."

"I need some things double-checked, Hettig." Focht opened his arms. "I have the Jade Falcons down on Przeno Plain. The Smoke Jaguars have landed in the Dinju Mountains and the Racice Delta. The Diamond Sharks are in the Kozice Valley, the Ghost Bears have hit both Spanac and

Luk while the Nova Cats are down at Joje, Tost, and Lo-sije."

"Correct, sir," replied the commtech. "The Steel Vipers are on an incoming vector that looks to put them at Hladno Springs in an hour. Our forces there have been alerted."

"Excellent. Anything from Brzo or Skupo?"

"No, sir. Looks like the Wolves have not taken the bait."

Focht frowned because he could not believe Ulric would decline his open invitation to attack at those two sites. He had placed his 66th and his 278th divisions there and let Ulric know they were two of the best the Com Guards had to offer. Focht was certain the Com Guards could hold their own against the Clan Wolf Warriors if they adhered to his strategy.

"Judge not so quickly, Hettig. Have you any indication that the Wolves have committed? Have all DropShips been successfully monitored and tagged?"

Hettig's face darkened with a scowl. "If the Clans have anything on this world that we don't know about, I'll offer to fight them with a can-opener."

"You need not take such a drastic stand, Mr. Hettig." Focht made a hand movement that put a smile on the face of his image in Hettig's visiphone. Hettig's enthusiasm mirrored that of the rest of the Com Guards. After twenty years of training, they finally had a chance to show how good they were. Whether fighting for personal pride or to save ComStar, his troops ached for battle and welcomed it here on Tukayyid.

"The answer to the question you are seeking is this, Precentor Martial: as nearly as we can determine, the Wolves have not deployed in this battle."

Hettig's analysis confirmed what Focht had guessed. *Why not? Why has Ulric been denied?* Focht chewed on his lower lip. If the ilKhan had been prevented from deploying forces, it might signal his fall from power. Were that the case, the deal struck between them might already have been repudiated. No matter the outcome, all would be lost.

Even as he considered that possibility, Focht rejected it. If the deal had been repudiated, the Clans would have renegotiated the battle. Though they did bid among themselves for the right to lead the assault on the various targets ComStar had given them, no one had offered to rebid the whole fight. *No, Ulric will be coming, but the others must have out ma-*

neuvered him. They saw it as a quick fight and they did not want him here to win it.

Focht nodded to himself. *Ulric allowed them to keep him out of the first day's battle. He'll be coming after Brzo and Skupo, but only after he sees how my troops react. He's using the others as stalking horses, and he hopes I'll have committed my reserves before he comes down.*

"Mr. Hettig, have all reserve units stand by. I want each one to trim back a battalion to form a Sixth Reserve Army."

"Noted, sir."

"Good."

Focht knew his strategy would carry the day, provided his people executed the plans they had been given. Organizationally, the Com Guards were broken down into twelve armies. On Tukayyid, one Clan landing area had been assigned to each of seven armies. The smallest and least experienced armies were being held back in reserve to reinforce their fellows when and if needed. Aside from the 66th Division, which had been transferred from a reserve unit to the Fiftieth Army to welcome the Wolves, the armies maintained the operational integrity they had known in their previous postings.

Each of the armies was broken down into its six component divisions. Unlike the forces of the rest of the Inner Sphere, the Com Guards were organized as integrated, combined-arms units. Through training, Focht had managed to erase the normal jealousies between the branches and to bind the Guards into terrifyingly efficient fighting units.

If the Inner Sphere had ever dreamed of our capabilities, they would have tried to destroy us long ago. Armor elements would attack the Clans at first, then air and artillery cover would allow them to scatter and regroup to nibble away at the Clan's flanks. The Com Guard 'Mech units would hit, then fade, keeping the Clans constantly on the move. Because each division functioned as its own unit and worked in tandem with another division, they would be able to grind the Clans down little bit by little bit.

"If everything goes as planned."

"Excuse me, Precentor Martial?" Hettig looked at his commander with a quizzical stare.

Focht shook his head. "Nothing, just thinking out loud. What are the hottest zones right now?"

"No one is shooting yet, but Dinju and Spanac look close

to—." Hettig clapped a hand to the earpiece in his left ear. "Priority 1-Alpha message coming through for you from the Primus."

Irritation burbled like acid up from his stomach. "I will take it here at Przeno." He turned as Hettig's image expanded then splashed itself across a distant thunderhead. Myndo Waterly's face replaced that of Focht's aide. "Primus, the assault has begun."

The white-haired woman nodded serenely, then her head came up abruptly. "But you are not in a 'Mech."

"Nor will I be unless things go very wrong." He tried to keep his voice even, but annoyance tinged his words.

"But it was maintaining an immobile headquarters that caused trouble for the Combine's forces on Teniente." Her stare rebuked Focht for his foolishness. "Have you learned nothing from that situation?"

"Indeed I have, Primus. From this bunker, all communications are routed to the planet's communication network. Through optical cables, they reach broadcast substations. The messages are, of course, scrambled and either broadcast directly from the substations, or sent up to satellite facilities and bounced down to our forces. It costs us perhaps a second or two of transmission time, but ultimately forces the Clans to devote forces to trying to ferret out our location."

He let the computer paint a scowl on his face. "This communication from you is tying up valuable resources."

"Then I shall not keep you over-long." Myndo let what he saw as an insincere smile twitch across her lips. "I just wanted to impress upon you how vital your success in this matter is for ComStar."

"I am well aware of how crucial is our victory, Primus."

"Good, but I want you to see you have a stake in this also." Her eyes glittered, and it was like a cold wind up Focht's spine. "If you win here, I will give you what you have always wanted."

"You need not reward me for performing my duty, Primus."

"But I shall, my friend."

Those words, coming from her, sounded more like a threat than a promise. "I am honored," Focht said.

"You shall be more than that," Myndo told him. "You shall be exalted. If you defeat the Clans, I shall return to you your birthright." The Primus of ComStar held her head up high. "I will restore you to your former glory and I will make you, Frederick Steiner, Archon of the Lyran Common- wealth."

=== 32 ===

Victor Davion looked directly into the viewscreen. He purposely set his face in the grimly satisfied smile he would have expected from Morgan Hasek-Davion addressing the troops. Clad in a cooling vest, he let Kai's pendant rest against the vest's outer kevlar surface. Punching a button with a gloved finger, he opened a line to each communications monitor in the three-ship armada racing toward the planet.

"In two days you will begin final preparations for our invasion of Teniente. We are only forty-four hours out from atmospheric entry and everything is proceeding according to plan." With those words, his grin expanded, but he trimmed it back before continuing. "This mission is a go and nothing is going to change that."

His gray eyes flicked down, then back up. "The last time a force from the Federated Commonwealth tried something like this, we were the Federated Suns and many of us could only have played at being MechWarriors. At that time, my cousin, Morgan Hasek-Davion, told his men that history would wonder at how they had accomplished so much with so little. He showed complete confidence in their ability.

"Well, I know how they managed to succeed in the face of incredible odds. I learned the solution over the last year working with all of you. We survived Alyina because of your guts and your determination to make the Clans pay for any centimeter of ground they got. We worked hard and came together as a unit because of your resiliency. We have mastered new tactics and strategies and machines because of your heart and your desire to carry the battle back to the Clans."

Victor's eyes glinted hard and cold. "This is our chance to prove to the Clans and everyone else that the Inner Sphere will not roll over and die. Our best case, our greatest victory is one in which no one fires a shot. We get in, we get our target and we get out, simple as that. If we have to fight, well, I have no doubt you'll give far better than you get. But we're not here to retake Teniente. We're on a rescue mission. We can collect scalps another time.

"This is the Revenants' first battle. It will not be our last. Take the time while we are inbound to get to your machines and strap in. Double- and triple-check everything. When we go in, we go in hot. Kid gloves are off. When we go, we go to start a legend that will haunt the Clans forever."

Victor flicked a button, closing the commlink, and looked up at Shin. "Well?"

The yakuza nodded solemnly. "Your assurances of confidence will make them do everything they can to justify that confidence. I do not envy any forces we face on the ground."

Galen gave Victor a thumb's-up. "After this, if you suggested staging a raid on Sian, they'd go for it."

Behind Galen a red light flickered atop a communications monitor. Victor and Shin both pulled out of line-of-sight of the screen. Galen slipped the cowl up on his robe, then touched a button to open communications. "This is ComStar DropShip *Serene Foresight.*"

"*Serene Foresight,* this is ComStar Ground Control, Kunkai sector."

"Go ahead, Kunkai."

The ground operator's voice lost its edge. "*Foresight,* we have no orders concerning you, *Ecstasy of Reason,* or *Valiant Wisdom.* Things are a bit screwed up here. Can you give me confirmation of your mission?"

Galen leaned back in his seat, but did not let the edge of the cowl reveal his eyes. "Kunkai sector, I have no authorization to say more than that we are on a mission with Beta

Predeir clearance. The orders were filed as Lima Zebra
0945."

"Understood, *Foresight*. Stand by."

Galen flicked the monitor into standby mode. "Shin, I
hope I got that right."

The Combine MechWarrior nodded. "Perfect, Galen. That
clearance is supposed to get us in and out with a minimum
of trouble."

Victor found himself crossing his fingers. He uncrossed
them and clutched them behind his back. As the three men
waited in the dim, narrow confines of the newly christened
Foresight's communication center, Victor wished for a place
to plug in his cooling vest. He noticed a bead of sweat roll
down Shin's face and smiled.

Galen's monitor beeped again. "Go ahead, Kunkai."

"Roger, *Foresight*. Because of Operation Scorpion, the
demi-Precentor is exercising an Alpha priority override of
your mission. Your orders say you've got troops on board
and we want them delivered at 45.33 north, 2.10 west. We
could really use the help. We have you ETA forty-eight
hours, correct?"

In the background Victor heard some muffled explosions.
He looked over at Galen and shrugged his shoulders. *I
wonder . . . ?*

Galen let his voice drop an octave into a growl. "Have
problems with Kurita insurgents, Kunkai?"

"Kurita? I wish." The man's voice became strained as an
explosion sounded louder. "Some damned Clan commander
had his people out on surprise maneuvers earlier this week.
When we went to round them up, they were gone." Another
explosion resonated through the cabin. "Now they're mad."

"Roger, Kunkai. We're on our way. Peace of Blake be
with you. *Foresight* out."

Victor's mind reeled. *ComStar is fighting the Clans? Just
our luck to be using "ComStar" ships to pull off this rescue.*

Galen draped his arms over the top of the console. "What's
the call, Victor? If we don't go to those coordinates, ground
control will know we're not ComStar."

"And if we do," Shin added, "the Clan commander will
be waiting for us."

"True. We have to assume the Clans have enough Elint
capabilities to have monitored that exchange." Victor
chewed on his lower lip for a second. "Now that we've been

identified as a target, the Clans will respond to us no matter where we go."

Shin's face closed over. "Do we scrub this mission?"

"Go home empty-handed?" Victor shook his head. "No way. I know the plan was to wait until the last moment to try to pinpoint Hohiro's position, but now we've got to go early. Find out where he is and find out what kind of fighting strength he can deliver by the time we get there."

"Hai."

Galen winced. "You gonna help ComStar?"

Victor's face showed diabolical glee. "If we were caught with our tails in a vise, what would ComStar do?"

"Charge double to send messages out?"

"You got it." Victor pointed at the monitor. "You tell Kunkai we're coming down right on top of them, so they should hold at all costs. Make sure the broadcast beam is wide enough that the Clans can pick it up, too. That will make them push harder and the both of them will grind each other down."

Galen straightened up again. "Roger. Then what will we do?"

"Hey, we're strictly here on a smash and grab," Victor said with a shrug. "We're not looking for a fight, but if someone gets in our way, well, we'll give the Clans more than they bargained for."

33

Dove Costoso, Alyina
Jade Falcon Occupation Zone
5 May 3052 (Day 5 of Operation Scorpion)

Sitting on her cot, her back jammed into the furthest corner of her cell, Deirdre Lear hugged her knees tighter against her chest. Her face buried in the protective circle of her arms, she felt where her bitter tears had soaked the legs of her jumpsuit, and her jaws ached from clenching her teeth against cries of grief.

When Kai had tried to explain what the fight with Taman Malthus meant to him, she had forced herself to suspend judgement. She knew, deep down, that it was folly for him to fight a man so much bigger than he was. Kai was already exhausted from their long hike, and though his wounds from the last fight had closed and healed, he was still not at the top of his form. The fight would be savage and brutal, and it conjured up her father's ragged ghost.

Yet even as Kai and Malthus began, she could see how suited Kai was to combat. She even took pleasure in watching him feint and strike. Knowing that Kai had to be pushing himself close to the edge, it was miraculous to see his fatigue drop away. His surprisingly fluid movements and speed made her proud to have helped care for him.

As Kai and Malthus exchanged blows, she cataloged the damage they were doing to one another. Deirdre became strangely detached, as if in a clinic watching another doctor operate. The instant Kai's foot hit the Elemental's thigh, she knew the blow had crushed tissue and ruptured blood vessels. Malthus would have a hematoma at the very least. Kai might even have bruised the large man's femur if the kick had not been so short.

Punch and counter-punch had her involuntarily swaying to avoid them. Her heart had crawled up into her throat as Kai went down, but she knew, when he came back up, that he would never surrender. Part of her wanted to scream at him to give up, but she respected too much the courage he had displayed in inviting the Elemental forward.

When Kai leaped up and kicked Malthus in the head, she had wanted to cheer. When Malthus' fist hit Kai in the ribs, she shared his pain, and when he hit the ground, she did not expect him to get up again. She knew it was over, but at least Kai lived.

Then the ComStar helicopter came with guns blazing.

Distracted by the violent death of the Elemental standing nearest her, she never even saw Kai fall from the mountain.

Feeling the sharp pain of her own fingernails digging into her palms startled her out of reliving the end of that memory. Her hands reached out to haul Kai back onto the plateau, but the helicopter's pulsed thunder stole any last words, any last sounds Kai might have made.

Kai, Kai, KAI! She wanted to shout his name aloud now, as she had not done when he fell. And she wanted to scream at the Elementals housed in the cell across from her, but she would not let them see how much they had hurt her. They might own her physically, but they would never break her. Not the Clans. Not ComStar. Not anyone.

Distantly she heard the tones as someone punched the combination code into the keypad for the door. As it creaked open, she smelled food. Her stomach rumbled out of reflex, but she was too filled with pain and grief to want to eat. She did not even look up as her anonymous jailer slid a tray beneath the iron-bar door to her cage. She knew he would come and drag it back out later.

The sound of a key rasping in the lock of her door did bring her head up. To her right, across a narrow corridor, she saw the trio of Elementals still trapped in their metal-rod walled cell. They clung to the bars with white-knuckled hands and watched their captor with a hunger that no food could assuage.

In the half-second she studied them, Deirdre took vicious

delight in noting that the bruise on the right side of Malthus' face had not yet begun to lose its color.

Her blue eyes flicked up at the rotund figure opening the door to her cell. Khalsa moved her tray forward with his foot, then slowly closed the door behind him. He smiled at her, the corners of his mouth disappearing beneath folds of chubby cheeks. In his red robe, the demi-Precentor looked like a monk bent on exchanging his contemplation of the sin of gluttony for that of lust.

"Doctor Lear, please, they tell me you are not eating." He brought his thick-fingered hands together over the ample mound of his belly. "I would have come sooner, but some Steiner partisans required suppression. Listen to me, you must not mourn that man. He was not worthy of your tears. He was a cad who only led you into trouble." His voice dropped into a whisper. "He had a wife and children back in the Federated Suns. You are too good for the likes of Dave Jewell."

Deirdre gave him the coldest stare her red-rimmed eyes could muster, but not trusting her voice, she said nothing. She took refuge in Khalsa's use of Kai's alias because it proved how much the man truly overrated himself. Keeping his identity hidden had been important to Kai and she had worked hard not to betray him. *Even as he died, I could not call out to him!* Nothing would make her betray him in death.

Khalsa got closer, inching his way across the cell, until he could ease his round buttocks onto the edge of her cot. "You must eat to keep up your strength."

She continued to regard him mutely.

A single bead of nervous sweat formed on his brow. "Well, I was going to save this as a reward, if you ate something, but I think your spirit needs some sustenance. 'Nourish the soul and you nourish the whole,' as the Primus has said more than once." He smiled like a preacher preparing to share the good word with a condemned convict. "It turns out that my superiors want the Elementals transshipped to our main compound at Valigia tomorrow. You will be able to remain here, in Dove Costoso, with me!"

Khalsa clapped his hands as if that made things right in some way. His expectant leer mixed sexual desire and child-like innocence into a volatile concoction. As the first wave of revulsion passed over her, Deirdre felt a jolt of adrenaline surge into her bloodstream. "No longer will you have to endure the sight of these outland murderers."

Khalsa's right hand pressed down on her left knee in the same motion as someone pushing down the plunger on a detonator.

Deirdre jerked her knee out from beneath his hand and stood in one pantherish motion. "Don't you dare, you worm." Her hands curled into fists. "I wouldn't stay with you even if the alternative was being dropped into the sun. The Elementals might be outlanders and murderers, but there was never any question about what they were. We knew them for enemies and they came at us with no hesitation. Even so, they acquitted themselves honorably and were interested in fair fights."

Khalsa's face changed color, almost a match for the ash-gray floor. "But ... but they murdered your paramour."

Deirdre stalked toward him. "Did they? You set them on our trail. You betrayed us. You hid in a cloak of supposed neutrality, yet you took us into custody and called them. Who is to blame, the dogs of war or their masters?"

Khalsa scrambled to his feet and half-stumbled over the food tray on his way back toward the door. "You are mad, woman! I offer you more than a lifetime spent in a prison camp." He fumbled with a key, then inserted it in the lock and cranked the door open. "You doom yourself."

She darted forward and caught the thick-set man with an open-handed slap that left a red mark and four furrows on his cheek. "Beast! You're lucky you disgust me enough that I do not take time to think things through. With my training and knowledge, I could agree to your arrangement, then make sure that however long I let you live, it would be sheer agony."

She pulled back and let him squeeze his bulk out through the door. "Run, Khalsa, run. As long as I live, you will never be safe. I will torment you in your dreams. You will taste my venom in your food and with every little ache or pain, you will wonder if I have gotten to you." Deirdre let herself laugh in the most horrid manner she could imagine. "Someday, you will be right!"

Unnerved, Khalsa locked the door behind himself, then fled from the room. Across from her, Taman Malthus slowly, stiffly stood and clutched the bars of his cell in massive hands. "What a worthy match for a warrior you are."

"Don't flatter yourself," she hissed, "I would no more be with you than I would him. You're the one with blood on his hands. You killed—no, you murdered him . . ."

The pain in Malthus' eyes shocked her enough to stop her in mid-tirade. "You are wrong, Doctor. I am no murderer. Only by going against the best can we confirm that we are the best." His hands opened, then finger by finger, slowly gripped the bars again. "Your paramour knocked me down, but I was not defeated. He knew it and he knew he would pay the price for his bold strike. To characterize what I did as murder renders my very worthy foe nothing more than a victim."

Deirdre grabbed the bars of her cell as her body began to tremble. "He *was* a victim—a victim of this stupid war!" As her adrenaline began to drain away, fatigue and weakness poured lead into her muscles.

"That, Doctor, is a foul slander. Jewell knew and accepted his part in our fight. He was more a warrior than many within the Clans." In a burst of fury, Malthus yanked at the bars but they did not give way. "Had ComStar not robbed me of my victory, I, Taman Malthus, would have made good on my promise to the both of you."

Kai died for no reason! Despite the sincerity of the Star Captain's words, she felt her spirit begin to fold in on itself. The fact that Kai had died needlessly hammered at her and slipped in to replace the trauma of her father's death. It reinforced her lifelong conviction that war and killing were moronic and a weakling's way out. She knew Kai acknowledged this, too, yet he had gone to his death like a moth drawn inexorably to a flame.

She opened her mouth to say something, but the door-lock tones stopped her. The dungeon door opened again. The fire rekindled in Deirdre's belly as she saw Khalsa's scarlet bulk, but she held her tongue as she realized he was backing into the room. The light flashed off his bald head as it tipped back in a painfully awkward position.

The reason for his deformed posture was the barrel of the autorifle stuffed up his right nostril.

"Doctor, I don't know if this is the proper time or place, but I have this pain," quipped the man with the gun as he forced Khalsa into the room. "Are you seeing patients?"

* * *

The transparent and radiant joy on Deirdre's face made Kai's heart thump faster in his chest. She retreated from the bars of her cell and pressed her hands over her open mouth. She blinked twice, then stared at him as if willing him to evaporate like a ghost.

"Is it really you?"

Kai smiled and nodded. "Either I'm here or," he jiggled the rifle, "the demi-Precentor is having a very bad nightmare."

"Urkle," commented Khalsa.

Kai guided the corpulent man by the nose over to the door. "Open it."

The demi-Precentor pulled the keys from his belt. "You'll never get away with this."

Kai refrained from jerking the trigger. "If I want your advice, I'll open your head and sift your brains for it. I'm tired and I'm angry and I bounced bough by bough down through a pine tree to a very hard landing at the base of that drop-off. Open. The. Door."

Khalsa complied, then Kai moved him aside. Deirdre flew through the open door and embraced him tightly. It didn't matter to him that her touch started bruises aching again because the feel of her body and the scent of her eased all of his pain. "I love you, Deirdre."

"It is you, it really is. I thought I'd lost you."

He felt her tears splash onto his neck and a tug at his right hip. With his left arm wrapped around her waist, he lifted her and spun to his right as Khalsa pulled the needle pistol from his holster. The autorifle came up around, clipping the demi-Precentor in the right temple as he sought to bring the gun up. Stunned, the man stumbled back across the room.

Khalsa smashed into the Elementals' cell. Malthus' hands snaked through the bars to cap and cup the man's skull. The Elemental's muscles bunched as his hands twisted. He wrenched Khalsa's head sharply to the right. The angle became extreme just before Kai heard a snap and then Khalsa slumped to the floor.

The MechWarrior clutched Deirdre even tighter to him and pressed his head against hers so she would not turn around and look. "Thank you."

Taman Malthus let his open hands dangle innocently

through the bars. "I have robbed you of a kill that was, by rights, yours."

"Saved me a bullet." Kai loosened his grip on Deirdre. "How are you, love? Are you fit to travel?"

She sniffed and swiped at tears with her hands. "I'm worlds away better now. I thought you were dead."

He smiled weakly. "Well, I feel dead, so we're close to even. Are you ready to make a run to the radio telescope? We'll use Khalsa's limo this time." He pointed with the rifle at the Elementals. "With these guys in jail here, we should be able to make it."

"Let's go."

"Wait!"

Kai looked over at Malthus. "Ah, you'll forgive me if I decline to continue our little fight. I know it's a matter of honor with you, but you had me fighting gravity and a monster tree." He opened his arms so the Elemental could get a good look at his tattered and pitch-stained jumpsuit. "Consider yourself the winner, okay?"

"I do. And I consider you as bold a warrior as the Inner Sphere has to offer."

"A bold warrior, me?"

"As brave a combatant as I have heard of during our Homecoming." The Elemental nodded toward Deirdre. "As I told her, I had won the fight. The fact that you willingly fought me marks you worthy of my respect, and has caused me to reflect upon the nature of those we oppose here. I am prepared to honor my promise to provide you transport off this world, though I ask you indulge me in one thing."

Kai's eyes narrowed. "And that is?"

"Tell me who you really are." Malthus held his hands up to forestall any protest. "I know you are not Dave Jewell. I read his dossier and I know he was left-handed. You are not. I must know who you are."

Deirdre smiled as Kai blushed. "Star Captain Taman Malthus, may I present to you Leftenant Kai Allard-Liao."

Malthus' jaw dropped open and he reeled backward to seat himself abruptly on a cot. "You are the Kai Allard-Liao who was on Twycross?"

His cheeks burning, Kai nodded.

"And you are the Kai Allard-Liao who foiled our ambush of the Davion Prince here on Alyina?"

Again Kai nodded.

Malthus stared at him, then looked at the other two Elementals sharing his cage. "Kai Allard-Liao." It started slowly, but his laughter grew both in volume and intensity. He held his stomach and rolled back, freeing his subordinates to join him. One of them was laughing so hard he dropped to the floor, while the other clung to the bars to hold himself up.

Kai, astonished, looked to Deirdre, but she shrugged, equally puzzled. "Of all the receptions my name has gotten, this is the first time for laughter."

Malthus pulled himself up to his feet and fought against the convulsions shaking him. "Forgive me, Leftenant, but we are not laughing at you. We are laughing at ourselves." Another wave of amusement swept over him. Tears streaming down from his eyes, he choked down a giggle and met Kai's quizzical gaze. "*The* Kai Allard-Liao."

"I don't understand."

"You do not? Twycross. Our Prince trap?" Malthus shook his head. "Had I known we were chasing you, I would have used a full Star in the hunt."

A full Star of Elementals? After me? That is lunacy! "I thought you Clansmen preferred evenly matched battles."

"True. Two Stars, then."

One of Malthus' men nodded enthusiastically.

"You're crazy."

"Are we?" Malthus straightened up. "On Twycross you destroyed the Falcon Guards. On Alyina you hold open the jaws of a trap that should have gobbled up the heir to the throne of the Federated Commonwealth. After that you manage to survive for four months behind enemy lines. You have eluded us while claiming the reward for our own death and you—a MechWarrior—defeated an Elemental in single combat. You fall from a plateau, get battered by a tree and hit the ground, yet you are able to hike to Dove Costoso and engineer a jail break."

Kai shook his head vehemently. "No, no, you're making it much more than it seems, really."

"Kai, stop it." Deirdre frowned sharply. "What would you say if Victor had done all those things? Would you say it was nothing?"

He looked at her as if she were mad. "Don't be silly. Of course not."

"Then why is it different for you?" She reached up and

caressed the left side of his face. "You have, for so long, held yourself to such high standards that you truly do not know how special you are. What you do is miraculous. Colonel Wolf said as much when you defeated five 'Mechs in the testing on Outreach."

"Five 'Mechs?" Malthus groaned.

"Three Stars," one of the other two mumbled.

"But, but, but . . . ," Kai sputtered until Deirdre pressed her fingers against his lips. *Is what they are saying true? Am I really that good, or are they misinterpreting what has been only a tremendous run of luck?* He smiled as he recalled one MechWarrior instructor telling him, "It's better to be lucky than good." *Have I really been too hard on myself all these years?*

He waited for that dark voice to tell him arrogance would be his downfall, but it did not come. *Maybe I am good, or maybe I am lucky. Neither of those is an excuse to be cocky or sloppy, but perhaps I'm not as bad as I imagine.* Kai smiled as he felt the weight on his shoulders lighten for the first time in active memory.

Deirdre kissed him.

"Keep up that sort of reinforcement, Doctor, and I could come to believe almost anything you tell me." He looked up at Malthus. "It seems like we're on the same side, at least for the short run. If you're serious about getting us off this rock, I'll let you out. But only on the proviso we do not have to finish our fight."

"Why would I fight with an allied warrior?" Malthus shook his head. "Before I can get you off Alyina, I must free my people and avenge the deaths that have occurred. I believe my men have been sent to the ComStar compound at Valigia."

Deirdre stiffened. "The ComStar facility at Valigia is a fortress built by the CEO of a corp who ran this world like his own personal fiefdom. Armored Elementals might do fine on the inside, but cracking open that gate would be something else."

"We have our armor cached in the mountains where we waited for you, but we have no rocket packs. We'd need something big to open that place up. ComStar has disarmed the population over the past four months, and cleaned up all the 'Mech wreckage left on the surface of the planet."

Kai let a low laugh rumble from his throat. "I know where

we can find a Gauss rifle. It'll open a hole." He plucked the keys from the lock of Deirdre's cell and tossed them to Malthus. "It's about time someone gave ComStar a message, and if you're willing to work together, I'm sure we can make it a very special delivery."

34

Strapped into the command couch of his modified *Wolf-hound*, Phelan surveyed the ocean of golden triticale stalks undulating in the wind. It extended for kilometers in all directions, with an occasional tree poking out of it like a weed in a carefully tended garden. Aside from the swaths he and his 'Mechs had cut through as they marched forward, and some small pathways shooting ahead from his position, the field lay unblemished and serene.

It gave Phelan the creeps. Not only did he not see any sign of the enemy, but the sun was slowly rising over the crest of the long, sloping hill at whose base he now stood. The grade looked steep enough to take the edge off any speed they might be able to generate and he felt dead certain the enemy waited for him just beyond the crest.

"Armorer, this is Ax Star."

"Go ahead, Ax Star."

"We are through sectors 3021 and 3022. We have met no resistance. Either the fish are not biting or we're walking into a huge trap. Request air recon of 3023 and 3024 before we proceed."

"Standby, Ax Star."

Phelan frowned. "Roger, Armorer." He flipped his radio over to his Star's command frequency. "We wait here for a second. Let's hype our sensors and see what we can find out about whatever reception ComStar has waiting for us."

At Wolf Clan Headquarters, Ulric Kerensky paced through the middle of the holotank. On his right, the OmniMechs of the Fourth Wolf Guards set themselves for a counterstrike by a ComStar force. In fierce fighting that had lasted through most of the morning, Clan Wolf had failed to close a loop around Brzo to trap ComStar's Tenth Army. The swift arrival of this new force, ComStar's Ninth Army, meant the conquest of Brzo would take far longer than expected.

He allowed himself a grim smile. *You are very good, Anastasius Focht. I had hoped that when we did not land in the first five days, you would divert your best troops to oppose some of my fellow Clans, but you did not. You've tied up the Diamond Sharks in the Kozice Valley and crushed the Forty-fourth Nova Cat Cavaliers at Joje. Now, here, at Brzo, you slow me.*

The ilKhan's head came up as an aide entered the holotank. "Yes?"

"Reports are in from the Wolf Spiders, my Khan. Ax Star is their Point Star and they want a flyover into Sectors 3023 and 3024." The aide's hand remained poised over a keypad attachment on his clipboard. Ulric nodded and the man punched a number into the device. The holotank's image shifted to a tactical map of the Skupo area. "The Eleventh Wolf Guards have just met the advanced position of the 278th Division and the rest of the Thirteenth Guards are skirmishing with the 166th Division along this broad front to the south of Skupo."

The tactical map left the whole western flank of the ComStar position open. Ulric knew it had to be defended, but by how much and what level of troops he had no way of knowing for certain. Detaching one Cluster from Alpha Galaxy to perform an end run was a tricky proposition at best. According to the map, either they were free and clear, or—if Focht had defended Skupo the way he defended everything else—they were walking into an ambush.

Ulric traced a finger along the ridgeline. "If they meet resistance, it will be this far out. They will hit them when Ax Star is halfway up the hill. Give them a flyover high, then have the wing come back and pull a strafing run along the line. While they are doing that, Ax Star will have to move fast and get up the hill. Is Hatchet Star still ahead of Ax?"

"Yes, sir."

"Good. Let Star Commander Phelan and Star Commander Fetladral both hit that line just after the strafing. Hatchet should be in first to cause confusion—hit-and-run stuff—to soften them up. Tell Star Colonel Kerensky to bring the rest of the Cluster up fast. Have this go off in ten minutes."

"Yes, sir."

As the aide left, Ulric cupped his chin in his right hand and stroked his goatee. "Make sure your first shot is the best, Anastasius. If Natasha gets through you there, Skupo is mine."

Anastasius Focht refused to surrender to fatigue. In his artificial world, he stood atop the ridgeline at Skupo and saw the Star of five 'Mechs waiting at the base of the hill. Back beyond that Star, the rest of the Cluster was slowly moving up. Even without the magnification granted him by the computer, he would have recognized the unique shape of the *Wolfhound* leading the forward element, and the night-black *Daishi* in command of the rest of them.

"This is the real stupidity of war, isn't it? I know how good you are, Phelan Wolf and Natasha Kerensky. I have read all the reports on your Wolf Spiders and I know that even though we outnumber you almost three to one, you can defeat us. Even so, even though it will cost me men and machines, I am forced to oppose you."

He opened a radio channel to Precentor IV Krag Jernberg. "Precentor Jernberg, your 138th Division is facing the Thirteenth Wolf Guards."

Jernberg's voice displayed no emotion. "Bandit's Bane will hold, Precentor Martial."

"This I trust, Precentor. Remember that surprise is your advantage. While you are dug in and shielded, they can guess where you are, but they cannot know. Be aware, however, that this unit is very good. If you must fall back, you will not dishonor yourself."

"We will hold."

"Very well." Focht found words sticking in his throat. *Yes, the stupidity of war.* "If you eliminate the *Wolfhound* and the *Daishi,* you will seriously hamper the unit's performance."

"Consider them dead," Jernberg's voice rattled.

* * *

"Switching HUD to ground mode. Quarrel Flight form up on me." Carew punched a button on his command console and shifted the combat display from air-to-air to air-to-ground mode. The 160-degree holographic display of the battlefield cycled through visible light, magnetic resonance, and infrared scanning but detected nothing on top of the ridge. *I know they're there, but where?*

"Quarrel Leader, Three and Four are negative. They must be shielded."

"Roger, Trey." Carew flicked the *Visigoth*'s joystick flight controller to the right to begin a long, looping turn. *All negative, but there has to be a way. Phelan is down there sweating LRMs and I cannot find the guys waiting for him. This place looks virgin. Wait!*

Carew punched orders into his computer. It replayed the look-down radar scan of the ridgeline, then superimposed Royal Rasalhague Geographical Society topographical data on top of it. Right along the ridgeline, he saw a moiré pattern where the current lay of the land differed from the recent RRGS survey of the planet.

Carew ordered the computer to further refine the scan discrepancy and paint it with colors, depending on the degree of difference between the two data sets. *Those people down there dug great fortifications to baffle us, but they did not have the equipment to make this a perfect replica of what it was before they did their work.*

The picture redefined itself according to his command and revealed a saw-toothed line traced with green along the top of the ridge. "Yes!" He keyed his radio to his flight and downloaded his plot of the trench. "On me. Hit them with everything you have got going in and coming out. We only get one shot at this, so let us give our mudbug buddies some help."

He punched up the ground command frequency. "Ax One, Hatchet One, this is Quarrel One. We have a target. Keep your heads down. We'll do the work, you pick up the pieces."

Phelan started his *Wolfhound* sprinting up the hill as the quartet of *Visigoth*s came in on their strafing run. Hundreds of rockets shot from the fighters, riding smoke-trails straight down to the hilltop. Like a string of firecrackers, the missiles exploded in sequence, blasting the lip of the hill away. Fireballs sprouted like great pumpkins, then collapsed into greasy black smoke-stains against the sky.

Phelan felt the ground shake with the missile barrages, but pressed on as fast as he could. From behind the smoky curtain rising above him, he saw the searing blue highlights of PPC beams stabbing down into the enemy position. Occasionally the blood-red of a laser bolt flashed through the sky, but Phelan could not see if they hit their intended targets.

He did note, with grim satisfaction, that no one from the ComStar position returned fire against the fighters. *Maybe they got them all!* Much as he wanted that to be true, he knew it was not. As his *Wolfhound* passed the halfway point going up the hill, he braced himself to face whatever ComStar was about to throw at him.

Precentor Krag Jernberg shook his head to clear it, then looked out through the cracked canopy of his *Exterminator.* He brought the massive 'Mech upright and used its hands to shred the last of the sensor canopy that had overlaid his position. Through the smoke and tattered canopy, he saw the dead and wounded left by the strafing run, but instantly put them out of his mind.

"By the Holy Word of Blake! Have at them!"

Stepping his *Exterminator* forward, Jernberg found the trench's breastwork had been torn apart. With the trench wall covering his 'Mech only from the thighs down, he felt half-naked. Still, as he brought his 'Mech's arms up and his crosshairs centered on the charging *Wolfhound*'s chest, he felt invincible.

"For Blake!" he shouted. "For the Primus! We will hold!"

As Evantha Fetladral dug her way clear of the mound of earth deposited on her by the strafing run, a status report on the Elementals of Hatchet Star scrolled down the left side of her armor's viewplate. Even though her Star had been strung out below the lip of the hill, it looked as if no one had perished because of friendly fire. *Good crew. Willing to get in close.*

"Hit them hard, Hatchets. Use your missiles on the 'Mechs, then concentrate on any missile batteries they have. Point commanders, coordinate."

A black veil of smoke curled down over her, then dissipated to reveal a ComStar 'Mech stepping up to a u-shaped divot in his rampart. The *Exterminator,* all white except for the golden star emblazoning its chest, would have looked beautiful except for where the armor had been blasted off the right side of its chest. From the way the melted armor curled up away from the endo-steel skeleton, Evantha knew a PPC had expanded on damage done by the LRM barrage that hit the ComStar position.

Evantha pointed her nose in the direction of the 'Mech as the war machine brought its arms up. She felt a sharp tug on her shoulders as she launched both of her SRMs from the backpack. As they shot forward on jets of flame, she immediately jettisoned the useless launcher.

Out the corner of her eye, she saw the missiles hit, but already her attention had shifted elsewhere. With her Point at her back, Evantha Fetladral advanced to sow yet more havoc in the trenches.

Phelan's mouth went dry as he saw the ComStar *Exterminator* rise up before him. He knew that 'Mech design had not been seen for centuries in the Inner Sphere, and for good reason. The *Exterminator* had been designed to seek out and destroy command 'Mechs. It had become so good at its task that special squads had been formed to hunt them down and destroy them.

Phelan knew the 'Mech was after him.

As the *Exterminator*'s arms came up, Phelan saw twin flashes from an Elemental crouched near the lip of the hill. Both SRMs shot straight in at the ComStar 'Mech and lanced into the gaping hole in the *Exterminator*'s chest. Phelan saw the 'Mech shudder as the shortrange missiles detonated.

The blasts provided Phelan a second or two to make an attempt to evade the *Exterminator*'s attack. Phelan cut sharply to his left, sending him in the opposite direction of the *Exterminator*'s involuntary movement. As the other 'Mech's arms began to track the *Wolfhound,* Phelan brought his own weapons to bear on his foe.

The *Exterminator* convulsed with subsidiary explosions. A muffled whump and puff of blue-white smoke announced the destruction of a jump jet. Fire wreathed the anti-missile cannon nested in its chest as a full belt of shells shot off in all directions. Armor plates shattered as the anti-missile slugs cooked off and punched their way out of the *Exterminator*'s torso.

Phelan shivered as a hail of anti-missile projectiles burst free through the *Exterminator*'s broken canopy. Smoke trailing from the hole, the 'Mech fell back as if it had been pole-axed. As Phelan shifted course again, driving in at the breach in the wall, another ComStar 'Mech stepped up to fill the hole.

Phelan let the *Sentinel* have it with all of his forward weapons. The medium pulse laser at *Grinner*'s right shoulder burned away armor on the *Sentinel*'s left arm. The pulse laser mounted in the opposite shoulder slashed at the right arm while the center pulse laser shot low and melted rampart into glass without hitting the *Sentinel*.

The *Wolfhound*'s large laser capitalized on the damage done to the *Sentinel*'s left arm and autocannon. Under the coherent light's hellish caress, the last of the armor vaporized and the autocannon flashed to a molten white heat before it melted clean away. The 'Mech, unbalanced by the loss of the limb, staggered but managed to stay upright.

The ComStar pilot proved himself game by firing back. Two SRMs corkscrewed out from the *Sentinel*'s chest and ripped armor from the right side of *Grinner*'s torso. The small laser mounted just below the missile launcher shot a beam that bubbled paint and armor on the left side of the *Wolfhound*'s broad chest, but neither attack did any real damage or anything to slow Phelan's charge.

Up into the opening he thundered. With a kick to the left side of its torso, Phelan sent the *Sentinel* stumbling through the trench. It caught its heels on the *Exterminator* and toppled backward. It hit the trench's far wall and a shower of dirt buried it in a makeshift grave.

Phelan knew better than to imagine it down, but he saw three Elementals descend on it to finish it. He turned to the left and took one step forward, clearing the breach to admit another of his Points into the ComStar position. As he did so, a ComStar *Lancelot* started to come around the corner facing him.

"Peace of Blake, indeed," he laughed to himself and dropped his crosshairs on the 'Mech's narrow silhouette. "Come on in, boys. We'll dispense all the peace you want. No waiting."

* * *

The Precentor Martial watched as Phelan's lance secured one section of the trench. While the zig-zag cut of it prevented the Clans from shooting down the trench's entire length, it made approaching the breached section of the trench extremely dangerous, especially for stiff-armed 'Mechs like the *Lancelot*. Before it finished negotiating the corner, Phelan had lased away armor from the 'Mech's chest and arms.

He opened a radio channel. "Mr. Hettig, please coordinate a withdrawal of the 138th from Skupo. Precentor Jernberg is dead or incapacitated. Use their armor to slow the Cluster following them. Remember, most of those troops are green, so pulling them out is going to be close to announcing a rout."

"Roger, Precentor Martial."

Focht again scanned the battlefield and saw the rest of the Wolf Spiders running up the hill at full speed. It had taken them just under two minutes to close the gap between Phelan's Star and the main body of the group. Already some of the fastest 'Mechs in that group had exchanged fire with the 'Mechs of Bandit's Bane. He knew the 138th's losses would be hideous.

Right place, right tactics, but the wrong people. But there was no way I could devote a more seasoned division to fight so small a unit. He stared hard at Phelan's 'Mech. *If I have to lose, better it be to warriors I can respect than those I cannot. This is not over, for one battle does not the war make. I know that and, worse yet, I know you know it.*

"Mr. Hettig, bring the reconstituted 282nd down from Brzo to take care of the Wolf Spiders."

"It will take them a day or more to get down there. The 138th won't last that long."

"I know, Mr. Hettig. I know." The Precentor Martial nodded grimly. "I don't want them to save the 138th, I just want them to slow the Wolf Spiders. If they can."

35

Victor Ian Davion looked at the chronometer on the command console of *Prometheus,* his *Daishi.* "*Kama-ichi,* where are they? They are running into our red zone."

Shin's voice crackled through the speakers in his neurohelmet. "They are coming, Highness, but they match their pace to the slowest of the 'Mechs."

"Shin, I don't know if we have time for that sort of stuff." Victor punched up a tactical map of the area. Behind where his *Daishi* and lance stood, he saw the triangle of DropShips they'd used to make planetfall. The majority of his troops were arrayed in a crescent along the northwest perimeter of the DropShips' effective gunnery range as that was the direction from which they expected the Clans to arrive. A large square represented the furthest distance they estimated the Clans could have traveled and a smaller one marked their probable last location, given speed and heading.

Both circles were far too close for Victor's ease of mind. "Shin, tell them to abandon the broken 'Mechs. We can send a chopper out from one of the ships to pick them up."

"Highness, many of these 'Mechs have been in their families for decades."

Victor cursed. "I hear you, Shin." The Prince expanded the tactical map's view to handle an area large enough to bring the Combine convoy onto the edge of it. The Clans looked to be closer and were certainly moving faster than the Combine troops. *Here we sit in the only LZ sufficient to handle DropShips. The Clans know it and we know it. Feels like having one foot nailed to the floor in a bar fight.*

Victor switched his radio over to that of the DropShip *Serene Foresight.* "Captain Coir, do you have enough fuel to take a short hop?"

"Affirmative. I'm good to go for one or two, but we'll light up the sky."

"Stand by. I may need you to recover some of us."

"Aye, sir. Standing by."

The Prince flipped the radio back to his command frequency. "Shin, pull Kama lance back and recon Hohiro's path. I want you to bring them up as fast as you can, and ready to shoot as well. Galen, you Murphy, Hudson, and Cooper form up your lances on me. We'll swing wide and try to draw the Clans off to the west. Macles, you'll take command of the rest of the unit and remain here to catch what we don't scare off. On my orders, or cessation of same, you'll pull back into the *Valiant Wisdom* and get the hell out of here. Got it?"

"Loud and clear, sir."

Victor took a deep breath. "Good, let's get to it."

The last solid sighting they'd had of the Clan unit heading their way made it a full Cluster. That put it at roughly twice the 'Mechs he was taking out after it. If the cloud had any silver lining, it was that the Clans had not left a line unit on Teniente, but had used only a garrison force. As a result, their equipment was not all OmniMechs.

Something deep down inside Victor screamed at him that he was committing suicide. He recalled at the Nagelring that certain very bad chess players were known as having mastered the "kamikaze" or "Custer" defense. That label became modified to "the Custer plan" when certain cadets proved incapable of thinking in acceptable or successful terms during tactical exercises.

Splitting one's force in the face of a superior enemy definitely had the ring of a Custer plan to it, and Victor dreaded that idea. By the same token, he knew the Clan commander could not be concentrating fully on him because of a possible ComStar offensive. *If he's distracted enough, we might be able to draw him off and get back out again.* Victor opened a line to *Foresight*. "Captain Coir, head out and pick up the Kurita stragglers."

"Aye, sir."

Back behind him, lighting the landscape with a silvery ion torch the *Foresight* burned up through the night sky. All of the Revenants' black 'Mechs cast long shadows ahead of themselves. As the DropShip climbed upward, darkness again cloaked the 'Mechs.

Victor glanced at his tactical map. "Let's pick up the pace. They can't be closer than ten kilometers by this tactical map, but I've got a bad feeling about this."

"Ditto," commented Galen. "I don't trust spy reports, especially when we get them from ComStar."

Bringing the *Daishi* up to its top speed, Victor started it on a course to the west that he intended to have loop back toward the east just before they hit the Clans. At his current pace, with their supposed distance, he had nearly ten minutes until the units should run into each other. Just six minutes out, a line of hills running north and south cut across Victor's line of march.

"Galen, just over that line of hills, we'll head north for a bit, then feint east." He glanced at his tactical map and saw the Clans still three kilometers away. "We'll surprise them."

"Roger. Heads up, boys and girls. We're in the danger zone now."

Galen's words still ringing in his ears. Victor crested the hills, then plunged down the other side. *Danger zone? No, this is hell itself.*

The relative safety of the ridgeline's western side had suggested itself to the Clan commander as well. As Victor came over the top, he saw two dozen 'Mechs running full-out through the night. His computers tagged each with an ID number and a model. In a second, he realized the Clan commander had sent his smallest and fastest 'Mechs out in a quick march to cut them off from the 'Mechs coming up to reinforce their position. The Clan commander had no way of knowing the reinforcements were a ragged group of Kurita 'Mechs that were in poor shape for any sort of serious battle.

"At them, Revenants!" Victor sent two swarms of Streak SRMs out at a Clan *Hornet* sprinting by. His *Daishi*'s hard lock on the target brought the dozen missiles in on target. The missiles repeatedly hammered the *Hornet,* stripping armor from its chest and right leg. The pilot fought against the force of the explosions, but the unbalanced 'Mech tumbled and rolled.

Victor saw a Clan *Centurion* launch a flight of LRMs at him from the center of its chest. Before he could even think about putting *Prometheus* through evasive maneuvers, he heard a piercing whine from the right breast of his *Daishi*. Of the ten missiles heading toward him, only six got a target-lock. Those missiles disappeared as the anti-missile system built into the *Daishi* spit out a hail of slugs and shredded the missiles in mid-flight.

The Prince dropped his crosshairs onto the *Centurion*'s outline. His thumb punched down, sending a silvery Gauss rifle projectile arcing out from the rifle mounted in the left arm. Victor lost sight of the ball, then saw the *Centurion* jerk as the ball all but took its left arm off. The Gauss rifle's sidecar large laser boiled away armor on the Clan 'Mech's chest, but his other two large laser beams missed the target entirely.

Held aloft by the silver jump jet spears at the back of his 'Mech, Galen's *Crusader* soared over the battlefield. He loosed flights of LRMs from the shoulder launchers to strike at distant targets, while the Streak SRMs from the *Crusader*'s legs slashed out at anyone who got too close. When he grounded himself again, a double-flight of LRMs struck down a fleeing Clan *Firestarter*.

"Victor, break left!"

Without thinking, the Prince spun his OmniMech away to the left. Out of the corner of his eye, he saw a Clan *Vulcan* shoot a large and medium pulse laser through the space he had just left. In the confusion, he almost could have sworn the voice that warned him was Kai's. *Not possible. Kai is dead. Who then?*

A barrel-chested *Hunchback* planted its feet and turned to face off with the *Vulcan*. The boxy Kali-Yama Autocannon mounted on its shoulder spit fire and thunder. The stream of depleted-uranium shells hit the *Vulcan* just to the right of its centerline, then sawed back through its torso as if the Clan 'Mech were made of soft cheese. Shards of armor mixed with fragments of endo-steel skeleton littered the ground while the *Vulcan* listed badly as if to protect its shattered side. It took one half-step forward, then the upper torso twisted and sheered off at the line the *Hunchback* had scored on it.

"Thanks for the help," Victor beamed at his savior.

Renny Sanderlin laughed easily, "Thanks for your faith, Victor."

All along the line, the Revenants poured fire and missiles into the Clan 'Mechs. Part of Victor hated watching the Clan's small 'Mechs get battered and pulverized by his own grossly superior forces. That hatred died quickly, however, when Victor remembered how the Twelfth Donegal Guards had been chopped to pieces by superior Clan forces. *They overmatched us even on Alynia when we knew what to expect. This is payback.*

The Revenants swept forward as the Clans slowed and started to turn back. As his troops pressed the Clans more, they concentrated their fire and took down 'Mech after 'Mech. Individual war machines looked, in the darkness, like the focus of a hundred lasers and missiles. Explosions would illuminate them and trip them while energy beams washed their armor away into clouds of ferro-fibrous vapor. Flayed alive, the 'Mechs kept running until more lasers and more missiles tore myomer muscles apart and crushed metallic bones.

"Revenants, pull back." Victor shook himself as he saw their line begin to drift back along the Clans' line of retreat.

"Begging your pardon, sir, but we have them on the run."

Galen's voice cut into the line. "Can it, Murphy. The Clan commander is likely to be waiting to welcome us if we get too close."

"We can take him."

In Murphy's voice, Victor heard the hopes and desires of the rest of the Revenants. He understood their desire to go after the Clans. Free of the fear of their tormentors, free of the terror that had haunted them since the first time the Clans struck into the Inner Sphere, his people wanted to make the Clans fear them.

He understood that idea because he shared it.

"Pull back. We're not retaking this rock, we're just stripping it of its valuable resources." He glanced at his tactical map, and even though he could not see the Clan's main body, he knew it had to be moving closer to the DropShips. *I had not expected Clan 'Mechs this far now. How much further along than my main body would I let scout Stars go?*

Victor keyed the radio. "Galen, use those jump jets and

pop up for a look on our back-trail. The main Clan body has to be somewhere nearby."

"Roger." Static sliced through the frequency as the *Crusader*'s ion jets lifted it high into the air. "Victor, I have a large Clan force moving toward our DropShips. They have detached 'Mechs in our direction."

As the *Crusader* descended again, Victor switched over to broadbeam frequency and addressed all his people. "Heads up. Nova Cats are between us and our ride home. Let's move."

Coming up over the hills that had hidden them from the scout Stars they ambushed, Victor saw the plains of Teniente become a circle of hell. Using spotting telemetry from two of the Revenants' smaller 'Mechs, the fire-support lances arced LRMs up over the hills and rained them down on the Nova Cats. The explosions made the ground shake and lit the night with eye-burning fireballs.

At the lead of a sprint lance, Victor's *Daishi* plunged down the hillside. He slammed into a Clan *Dasher,* dumping the smaller 'Mech on its back in a cloud of shattered armor. Half-twisting, he pumped a Gauss rifle round through its chest and left it lying on the ground with short-range missiles pouring from the hole.

A Clan *Loki,* black except for the blue blaze on the center of its torso, stepped through the missile fire and leveled its guns at *Prometheus.* The autocannon in its left arm lipped flame as it hammered the *Daishi*'s right leg with a burst of slugs. The Gauss rifle in its right arm sent a silver ball streaking straight into the right side of Victor's 'Mech, spinning it around and sending it crashing to the ground.

The Prince braced for the crash and smiled when no sparks shot through his cockpit at the impact. Pushing off with *Prometheus*' left arm, he levered himself up enough to point his 'Mech's right arm at the *Loki.* He dropped his targeting crosshairs onto the OmniMech's outline, but before he could trigger his large pulse lasers, a 'Mech moved up on his right side and engaged the *Loki.*

Renny Sanderlin's *Hunchback* let go a salvo from its Kali-Yama autocannon. The line of destruction traced from right to left, starting at one shoulder and ending at the other. Along the way, it blew through the *Loki*'s head and cockpit, decapitating the enemy war machine. Recoiling from the attack, the *Loki* pitched backward and landed in a tangled, misshapen heap.

Victor started to radio Renny another thank you, but fire blossomed on the *Hunchback*'s right flank. The FedCom reeled wildly to the left, armor shards spinning into the air. A laser cut through the resulting cloud of smoke and the *Hunchback* stumbled across the *Daishi*'s legs, slewing Victor around, as Renny crashed to the ground.

Twisted away from facing the direction of the attack, Victor still saw the *Thor* that had blown Renny's 'Mech to scrap. *Facing the wrong way!* As the *Thor* stalked forward, Victor tried to crank his 'Mech's right arm around to target it. *Out of my arc! I'm dead!*

The *Thor* pointed its left-arm autocannon at Victor. The pilot swung it into line with the back of *Prometheus'* head, as if to dispatch a wounded animal. It took one step closer, guaranteeing a kill, then jerked as if that last step had landed it on a live wire. As Victor watched, its center-torso armor went from black to red and then white. It melted over a round hole at the *Thor*'s heart, then the last vestiges of four large laser beams flashed through the opening.

"What in hell?" Victor brought his 'Mech to its feet as the *Thor* froze, then slowly toppled to the side. "Whoever got that *Thor,* thank you very much."

A distant radio call filled with static answered him. "It was my pleasure, Victor Davion."

"Hohiro, is that you?"

"It is, Revenant Leader. The 311th Pesht Regulars are joining up now." In the distance, Victor saw the Kurita 'Mechs sprinting into view. "We would hate for you to think, on your first visit to the Combine, that we would let anything untoward happen to our guests."

═══ 36 ═══

Though hardened by years of viewing the results of his mother's depravity, Sun-Tzu was shocked to see her and his father, Tsen Shang, in this way. It was not their nudity—he had seen his parents naked on various occasions—nor was it the apparent reconciliation that had placed both of them in the same bed. Tsen Shang, who had never been able to explain his attraction to Romano, had told Sun-Tzu that she would never kill him, and he would always return to her whenever she asked.

What surprised Sun-Tzu was the violence and obvious surprise that twisted their bodies. Tsen Shang had slipped out of bed, his legs apparently tangling in the sheet as he had made a dive for the bedside table. His attempt had toppled the table and spilled the laser pistol he sought onto the floor, just centimeters from his outstretched fingers. The carpeting beside his right hand had been slashed clear down to the floor by the razored fingernails on his three fingers as he clawed his way toward the pistol.

The laser wound in Tsen's back looked surprisingly bloodless. If not for the one thin ribbon running from the wound across his spine, the blackened circle could have been mistaken for an infected insect bite. It hardly looked sufficient to have stopped a man of Tsen Shang's size, but from its location, Sun-Tzu knew it had burst his father's heart.

He stood up from his examination of the body and wiped his hands on the legs of his trousers. "Given that you died trying to protect my mother, I suppose you died happily. Here, on Sian, that is unique indeed."

Looking at his mother, Sun knew the opposite had been true of her. Slumped back against the headboard, she looked as though she must have drawn herself up like a cat to hiss at her assailant. Fury still locked her face in a hideous death mask, but the position of her body made her look more piteous than frightful. Even so, Sun-Tzu could not help feeling more relief than sadness at her passing.

Sun-Tzu folded his arms across his chest to suppress a shudder. Romano's assassin had been most careful, the laser having struck his mother squarely between the eyes. Part of him recognized the wound's stigmata as being that of the Biblical mark of Cain, but he rejected that as an explanation for the shot. He knew his mother would have railed against her assassin and would have bragged that she could destroy him using the powers centered in her third eye. *What better proof that she was mad?*

Even as he became confident of his reconstruction of what had transpired in his parents' bedchamber, the allusion to the mark of Cain haunted him. *Cain was a fratricide, if I recall my mythology correctly.* He knew his mother had ordered the death of her sister and he strongly suspected her of having had her own father killed. *A symbolic gesture, then?*

Immediately he knew who had slain his mother and father. "How fitting, how appropriate." He knelt once again and scooped up his father's laser pistol. He savored the cool smoothness of its grip and reveled in its weight. He knew where he would find the murderer and he resolved to thank him before he completed the job his mother's assassin should have done on New Avalon.

As he stalked through the corridors of the palace, he felt his heart begin to pound louder and faster, though he recognized it as anticipation, not fear. Avenging his parents would be his first action as the new Chancellor of the Capellan Confederation. According to his plans, his accession to the throne was decidedly premature. Nor had he anticipated the death of his father, though he had acknowledged the possibility that he might have to destroy Tsen Shang after he had eliminated Romano.

The realization of his full responsibilities might have crippled another, but Sun-Tzu was energized by them. He knew he would have to move swiftly to consolidate power, but not with the brutal public purges his mother favored. Such measures would not inspire the people's loyalty or confidence, but bred the opposite instead. No, he would quietly repudiate his mother's actions and pay some reparations to those who had lost kin to his mother's predations.

He would show his people the velvet glove, knowing he could always wield the steel fist it sheathed. To further unite them, he would launch a preemptive strike at one of the bases his Uncle Tormana maintained within the Federated Commonwealth. *With enough evidence to prove they hoped to hit us, I will create an external threat that will bind us together.*

He shifted the gun to his left hand, wiped the sweat from his right onto his trousers, then gripped the gun firmly again. With his left hand, he twisted the knob and smiled to find the door unlocked. He opened it slowly and slipped noiselessly into the room that had become his sanctuary. Pressing the door shut behind him, he studied the second pair of tracks in the dust and traced them around to the hooded, cloaked figure sitting in the chair behind the desk.

"Reports of your death have been greatly exaggerated, I see, Justin Allard." Sun-Tzu brought the pistol up and held it unwaveringly on the seated person. "I compliment you on the accuracy of your shooting. I had heard, on Outreach, that you were good with that wrist laser of yours, but I had not imagined such exacting skill."

"There are many things you cannot imagine, Sun-Tzu Liao," Candace Liao hissed as she sat forward and let the hood slip from her head. "Justin was good, very good, and he got the assassin who would have slain the two of us, but he was not good enough to avoid dying from a mortal wound."

Sun-Tzu, his mind reeling, blinked and felt his chest tighten. "How? You are supposed to be dead!"

Candace threw her cloak back from her left shoulder with a stiff motion. "You know, of course, that I was treated for breast cancer on New Avalon six years ago. I underwent a radical mastectomy and had the muscles rebuilt with myomer fibers. Your assassin's laser had enough power to burn through flesh, but myomer is a bit tougher than that. When I fell, I hit my head and was knocked out, creating the illusion that the smoking hole in my chest had killed me."

"So now you come here, kill your sister, and think you can simply take the throne, is that it?" Sun-Tzu bared his teeth as though the display would frighten her off. Candace stood before him like a dark void that could swallow his plans and destroy his dreams. "You want to become the Chancellor of the Capellan Confederation."

"I know you are smarter than that. Your act on Outreach did not fool me. You are no more impulsive or insane than I am dead." Candace laughed derisively. "The Capellan Confederation could have been mine any time I wanted it. When I left here twenty years ago, Justin and I discussed any of a number of plots that would have given me the throne. We could have claimed a kidnapping from which I was later saved through a miraculous escape. My father would have embraced me again, as would the people. If not that time, then when the troops from the St. Ives Compact moved to fight against the Andurien invaders, or when the St. Ives Compact severed diplomatic relations with the Federated Commonwealth to prevent Hanse Davion from attacking the Capellan Confederation.

"There were plans within plans, and I always had more than enough aid available from within the Confederation itself. Romano's purges may have gotten one or two of my agents, but they created dozens more. You would not be far wrong if you imagined that I have had more palace people on my payroll than did my sister."

I relied too much on my mother's view of her sister. That mistake I will not make again. Sun-Tzu leaned back against the door and concentrated on the pain of the knob grinding into his spine. "Why did you wait this long to strike?"

Candace laced her fingers together and peered over them at him. "It is because I do not want to be Chancellor of the Capellan Confederation. While your mother painted me a whore and traitor for my alliance with Hanse Davion, I found it a way to allow my people to maintain their cultural identity without being absorbed into the Commonwealth. Though I think Hanse was far more responsible a ruler than

Romano could ever have been, I had no desire to see my people denatured through union with his empire.

"Had I been the Capellan Chancellor, I would have concluded an alliance with Hanse Davion to stop the war. That would have made me a buffer between him and the Free Worlds League. I would have been forced to strike at House Marik in the 3039 war just to keep the fighting on their worlds instead of our own. Eventually we would have been absorbed into the Federated Commonwealth."

The cold logic in Candace's words surprised Sun-Tzu because of the distance between it and the motives his mother had imparted to everything Candace had done. "If this is so, why come here now?"

Candace looked in the direction of her sister's bedchamber. "What I did to Romano was personal, not political. It was the last act in a drama that had gone on far too long."

Her nephew shook his head. "But news of her assassination will create demands for revenge."

"Even Romano knew to keep the true manner of our father's death private. Let this be your first lesson as Chancellor. Here in the Capellan Confederation, the truth is what you say it is." Candace stood slowly and let her cloak enshroud her again. "I did not murder your mother. She, in a fit of anger, shot and killed Tsen Shang, then killed herself. She left a verigraphed message to that effect, which you read and destroyed because it discussed matters that could not be made public. You will be vague in statements about their death, but you will mourn publicly and privately. Of course, you will threaten vengeance against whoever did the deed."

Not all that far removed from what I had planned to say when I killed her. Sun-Tzu felt some of his confidence returning. "And my second lesson as Chancellor?"

"Never trust your sister. Kali is as mad as her mother, if not more so." Candace held up one hand to stop him from speaking. "And your third lesson: Stay away from my children. None has any desire to sit on the Celestial Throne. Leave them alone and you never need fear them."

"By their very existence they threaten me."

"They threaten you only if you act against them." The look in Candace's gray eyes chilled Sun-Tzu to the marrow of his bones. "There are more ways into and out of the Capellan Confederation and this palace than you can ever know. If forced, I can and will return, or I will unleash any number of my agents to avenge them. I may be reluctant to accept responsibility for the Confederation, but that does not mean I am unable to do so if need be."

He motioned with the laser pistol. "What if I shoot you now?"

She shrugged. "In that event, a full briefing on the security breaches here in the Confederation—including enough information to stage a successful coup to put Kuan Yin on the throne in your place—will find its way into Hanse Davion's hands. I can assure you that he will be less reluctant to make use of it than I ever would be."

Sun-Tzu lowered the gun. "Why just my mother and father? Why did you spare me and my sister?"

Candace smiled humorlessly. "You I spared because I know you are not stupid. If the Confederation is to endure, it will do so based on your actions. I hated my sister, but that does not mean I want the Capellan people to suffer. After Maximilian and Romano, my homeland needs a shrewd ruler, and I deem you capable of being such. As for sparing your sister, I had to live with Romano. Adversity makes you stronger, and I'd rather you looked for adversaries within your own home than outside."

She crossed the room and touched a switch that opened a secret door in the far wall. "Remember, the future of the Capellan Confederation is in your hands. Consider it a sacred trust. The difference between the real world and the games you played on Outreach is this: now you get no mistakes. Remember that and live. Forget it and you will be broken."

Sun-Tzu stared at the panel after it had snapped shut, then tucked the laser pistol into the waistband of his trousers. *So, my mother's reign of terror is over, and I have survived to see it so. Very well.*

He walked around Justin's old desk and dropped into the chair. He touched one button on the computer console there and, to his surprise, the antique monitor lit up as power surged into it. *How interesting. It still works. There is yet life in the machinery that destroyed the Capellan Confederation.*

Sun-Tzu leaned back in the chair. "My mother and grandfather so hated Hanse Davion that they could not see how well his methods worked against us. I am not that blind. In me, Hanse Davion will see his own tactics and strategies come to haunt him." He smiled and steepled his fingers. "The Capellan Confederation is not dead, and what has not killed us will make us stronger."

37

Assuming the stature of Atlas in his artificial world, the Precentor Martial stood in the Dinju Mountains and watched the Smoke Jaguars retreat. As the battle evolved over the first eight days of the war, Focht realized the Smoke Jaguars had never correctly identified the Second Army as reinforcements for the Fifth Army division that had originally held the mountains. As a result, the Smoke Jaguars had expended incredible amounts of ammunition to eliminate what they believed were the last of the defenders. When the second half of the Fifth Army, fresh from killing the First Jaguar Cavaliers, came up from the Racice Delta to trap the Jaguars in the mountains, the end was in sight.

Focht smiled as he watched the Clansmen retreat and allowed himself to take some pride in the victory over the Smoke Jaguars. The invasion's original ilKhan, Leo Showers of the Smoke Jaguars, had been a particular annoyance in Focht's mission to the Clans. It had also been the Smoke Jaguars who had laid waste to the city of Edo to suppress a rebellion on Turtle Bay. That they had been crushed made him feel happy.

Be careful, Anastasius. Do not believe you or your people are invincible. Even as he cautioned himself, he did acknowledge that his analysis of the Clans and their tactics had given him an advantage. His people had exploited that advantage and turned it into a victory in the Dinju Mountains. The same outcome looked certain for the Przeno Plain, Hladno Springs, and even the Kozice Valley. If things did work out, that would give him victory over four of the Clans.

Still, that will not win you the war. Focht reached his right hand up and brought the viewing halo down. He selected the window that opened onto the Brzo theatre. As it expanded to replace the mountainscape far to the southeast, Focht opened a radio line to Hettig.

"Yes, Precentor Martial?"

"Any reports of activity by the Wolves, Mr. Hettig?"

"Checking, sir."

Brzo, a fairly large agrocomplex, looked to the Precentor Martial much like a concrete disk sitting at the hub of a golden circle. Beyond it, the Pozoristu Mountains clawed at the sky with snow-sheathed fingers. In and around Brzo, he saw evidence of a few skirmishes, but no active fighting.

"Precentor Martial, it appears the Wolves are resupplying and waiting to head into the mountains. With the exception of the Wolf Spiders, all Wolf units appear willing to accept your invitation to fight in the mountains. Our Eleventh Army has already taken up defensive positions and are reported to be in good supply. The Ninth and Tenth Army fragments are likewise pulling back, though the 282nd is continuing to be harassed by the Wolf Spiders."

Focht sighed heavily. "Have Precentor Wollam withdraw the 282nd and get them into the mountains."

"He says he is trying to do that, and will accomplish it as soon as he can figure out where the Wolf Spiders are waiting for him."

"With Natasha Kerensky leading them, that could be impossible." He shook his head. "Have our scouts pinpoint all Wolf Clan supply bases on the plains below the mountains and target them for raids. If one appears to be near the 282nd, you can send Wollam after it."

"Yes, sir."

Stroking his chin, Focht suddenly realized he'd picked up the mannerism from ilKhan Ulric. *So what are you thinking, Ulric? Why are you accepting my choice of battlefields, here in the mountains? Is it just to get my people out of the positions we have prepared and to stretch out supply lines as yours are stretched, or have you seen something I have not seen?*

Phelan dropped his *Wolfhound* into a squat as three electric-blue PPC beams shot over his head. "Ax Star, pull back. We've got armor up ahead." He flipped his radio over to ClusterTac. "Natasha, I've got armor holding the Bloody Basin Pass. Download coming."

With the push of a button, Phelan started a datafeed to Natasha Kerensky in her *Dire Wolf*. Even with the brief glimpse of the forces opposing him, the computer had sorted out all the sensor data and provided a simple breakdown of the forces it had detected. "Looks like ComStar really wants to hold this pass."

The computer reported that he faced a trio of Burke heavy tanks, two Fury heavies, and a single Rhino. The Burke sported a trio of PPCs in its turrets and an LRM launcher built into the front of the tracked vehicle. Though the Furies could kick out the most damage in one assault, they worried Phelan more because of their incredibly hard armor. Furies were known for slugging it out with 'Mechs, and Phelan's *Wolfhound* could not hold up to that kind of pounding.

The Rhino was a heavily armored rocket-launcher with a couple of medium lasers to keep 'Mechs honest if the fighting got close. It was faster than the Burke, but couldn't match the Furies' pace if the unit was forced to move quickly. This, along with the fact that they had dug in, gave Phelan some ease of mind because it meant the tanks would not be rushing out toward his Star.

"Natasha, the tanks are dug in. Is Quarrel flight still available?"

"Ax One, please be advised that we are pushing the Com Guards around to your position. I suggest you move the armor and appropriate their fortifications. This is where you earn your pay, Phelan."

"Roger, Black Widow." Phelan knew his 'Mechs should be able to dislodge the armor, but its being dug in made the nut just that much harder to crack. "Do I have air?"

Carew's voice cut in on the frequency. "ETA thirty seconds, Ax Star. Be ready to act then."

"Roger, Quarrel One. We'll take the pass." Quickly he switched back to his own tactical frequency. "Heads up. We have an airstrike coming in. Thea and Ace, you'll jump your

'Mechs in. Concentrate on the Rhino. It is a tough target, but they are known to explode if you hit them hard enough. The rest of us will hit the first Burke. The Furies have run speed and they will if we give them the chance."

"Roger, Star Commander. On the strike."

Carew keyed his radio over to his wingman. "Cover me while I run in, Virgil, then I will cover you. ComStar has some other ships up, but I have nothing on my screen."

"Roger, Carew."

The Clan pilot switched his HUD to ground mode and kicked his *Visigoth* over into a steep, wide bank. His computer showed him the location of Phelan's Star and the reported position of the ComStar armor. He set a course that connected the two lines, then dove the *Visigoth* until he screamed in at 650 knots only 500 meters above the ground.

For a millisecond, the ComStar armor flashed as viable targets on his HUD, but his finger hit the trigger buttons while they still remained on holograph. The PPC and twin medium lasers mounted in his nose backlit his canopy with a reddish-purple glow. Two flights of LRMs streaked out from the wing-mounted launchers and actually dropped his speed by 40 knots.

As the heat spiked in his cockpit, he hauled back on his stick and pointed the *Visigoth* into the sky. With a flip to the left, he spun the aerospace fighter into a barrel roll that took him out along a course at right angles to his strafing run. As he righted himself again, he switched his HUD over to air-to-air mode and saw Virgil begin his run.

Warning klaxons started going off in Carew's cockpit. Instantly he spotted the fast-approaching pair of ComStar fighters. His computer immediately identified them as *Rapiers*, which meant he and Virgil were in for a nasty dogfight. "Break off, Virgil, we have company."

Explosions still ringing in his ears, Acolyte R. G. Flute tightened the restraining strap holding him in the turret gunner's seat of the Rhino. "Dammit, that run melted armor and it's congealed in my turret drive. Anderson, get us ready to move because we're only going to be able to shoot at what you point us at."

"No can do, Acolyte. I've got a damaged track. We're not going anywhere."

"Agree, Fury One is untouched, but Fury Two has a turret lock. Burke One is in the same shape we are, Burke Two lost armor, and Burke Three lost its missiles and one of the PPCs." The radioman craned his neck back and peered up into the turret past Flute's feet. "They want to know what to do."

"Fight! What else is there to do here? Peace of Blake be with you, boys," the Acolyte intoned solemnly. "Here they come."

Phelan had his *Wolfhound* up and cruising in toward the gap as Virgil swooped in toward the pass. The second *Visigoth* let go with his PPC and lasers, but broke off in mid-run. The MechWarrior knew of only one thing that could possibly make a fighter stop a strafing run. That was the arrival of enemy fighters, and with memories of his bloodfight against Glynis flashing at the back of his mind, he did not want ComStar to return the favor of a strafing run on his 'Mechs.

Sprinting into the pass, Phelan saw how much damage Quarrel Flight had done to the tanks, and whispered a prayer to help Carew and Virgil in their battle with the ComStar fighters. Everything save one of the Furies looked as if it had been attacked with a blowtorch. Fire-blackened armor crisscrossed with laser and PPC scars covered the turrets and front ends of the vehicles. None had been destroyed by the run, but five of six had been softened up.

I hope that's enough.

Up over him soared the *Summoner* and *Viper.* Thea's *Summoner* sent two flights of LRMs streaking down at the Rhino. Over half of them impacted the ground in front of the hulking vehicle, but the remaining missiles further savaged the armor on the tank's nose.

The Rhino's gunner tracked the missile pods up and sent a full forty missiles back at the *Summoner.* His hurried aim and difficulty following the flight meant only a quarter of them hit their target. Explosions fragmented armor on the *Summoner*'s left arm and left leg. Nothing got through the armor, but any damage on 'Mechs so lightly armored hurt significantly, especially with the Furies and Burkes still operational.

Ace piloted his *Viper* with such skill that Phelan thought it could as easily have been a giant alien lifeform rather than a BattleMech. The squat juggernaut stabbed its left-arm PPC at the Rhino and sent a sizzling beam into the vehicle's front armor. The beam of a medium pulse laser, mounted on the underside of the 'Mech's right forearm joined the larger light shaft and punched through.

A single flash spit fire back out through the front of the craft, then a fireball ripped it apart from inside. Like an escape pod, the turret jetted straight up into the air. Before it reached the apex of its arc, the missiles in the starboard launcher cooked off and imparted a backward spin to the turret. It slammed into the mountainside, then tumbled back out of sight.

Somewhere beyond that something else exploded, but Phelan had no time to figure out what it was. He dodged to the left as one of the Burkes tried to impale him with a pair of azure PPC beams. They shot wide, but his evasive maneuver spoiled his aim against the damaged Fury. His large laser beam and two of the medium pulse laser beams chewed up the dirt in front of the Fury. Only one of the beams hit and it just blistered off more front armor.

Initiate Elza Speer hauled back on both drive controls for the damaged Fury. On the holographic display surrounding her, she saw the golden crosshairs hanging in the center. Letting the left control slip forward for a second, she brought the cross to bear on the *Wolfhound* leading the charge.

"I lined him up for you, Perry. Bring him down."

The Fury's Gauss rifle pulsed out a silvery ball that caught the *Wolfhound* just below its right knee. *Grinner* half-stumbled in that direction, but Phelan fought gravity and kept the machine upright. *Stravag! One more hit like that and I lose this leg.* "Let's shut these Furies down."

The Clan *Nova* looked to Phelan like nothing so much as a large, aerodynamic toad bred for combat. The cylindrical autocannon that made up its right arm sent a stream of slugs tracing a straight line through the dirt up to the undamaged Fury, but never actually hit it. The *Nova*'s LRM swarm overshot the autocannon shells and wreathed the Fury's turret with fire.

Apparently that attack did not impress the Fury's crew. The turret swung around with ease and sent a Gauss rifle ball out to shatter the armor on the *Nova*'s left leg. Though the 'Mech had more armor than Phelan's *Wolfhound,* the pilot realized that another shot in that leg from any of the weapons left operational would strip the leg down to bare bones and practically doom the *Nova.*

Dimitria's *Ice Ferret* had drifted to the far left side of the formation. Its autocannon missed the targeted Burke, and the flight of LRMs she launched went dead-in, but exploded in the dirt. Only the medium laser from the *Ice Ferret*'s chest actually struck the target, doing no more than cause some armor to ooze away.

The Burke returned better than it got. Though one of its three PPCs missed high, the other two bracketed the *Ice Ferret* with electric fire. The beams stripped armor off each arm in equal proportions, leaving the *Ice Ferret*'s head and shoulders shrouded with armor vapor. Another Burke tried to add to the *Ice Ferret*'s misery, but its attacks missed.

Phelan shivered. *This is harder going than I imagined. Please, God, let Carew keep the buzzards off us.*

Carew pulled his fighter up and over through a split-S that brought him in above and behind where the *Rapier*s were setting up on Virgil. He rejoiced in the advantage that gave him, but the fact that they had position on Virgil filled him with dread. "Virg, you have two. Break right!"

Virgil's *Visigoth* started its sharp right turn, but the lead *Rapier* hung with him and actually turned tighter than he did. With its twin, forward-jutting fangs and paired tails, the slender-winged fighter looked not nearly as menacing as Virgil's compact craft. But it sailed in with the grace of a raptor, then opened up with the autocannon mounted in its nose.

Virgil's maneuver brought his ship up into the stream of shells. They peppered the sleek craft's fuselage, stripping away sheets of armor that followed the *Visigoth* like a glittering rain. A PPC beam sliced off more armor, then LRMs arrowed out from the *Rapier* and skewered the damaged craft. With a flash and puff of black smoke, the *Visigoth* began to break apart in mid-air.

Virgil's icon vanished from Carew's holographic battlescape and the lead *Rapier* cut up and toward the sky as his outline burned white on the infrared scale. Whipping the *Visigoth* into a right spiral, the Wolf Clan pilot brought it out of its spin and watched the *Rapier*'s wingman follow the leader right into his sights.

Both medium lasers raked claws through the armor over the single aft thruster, and half the missiles Carew launched similarly blasted away shards of ferro-ceramics. Other missiles corkscrewed into the fuselage and left wing, shattering armor and denting the *Rapier*'s aerodynamic profile.

The damaged *Rapier* dropped its left wing and started to pull around in a tight circle while his wingman continued to pull up and to the right. *If I go after you, wounded duckling, your mate will pounce on me. No!* Carew refused the gambit and pulled his ship up to the right. *We play this game by my rules.*

As he expected, the wounded aerofighter leveled out when the *Visigoth* declined to chase him. Carew kept the crosshairs on target and triggered the two aft-arc medium lasers the *Visigoth* carried. One burned away more armor from the engine while the other further clipped the *Rapier*'s left wing.

Carew smiled involuntarily as the fighter in front of him pulled a tight series of twists. *Yes, you know how to fight better than your wingman. It will come down to the two of us, but I owe you for Virgil.* His teeth clenched, Carew pushed down on the thruster pedals and brought the *Visigoth* around to again join the battle.

On the ground, Phelan glanced at his auxiliary monitor, and learned that the distant explosion must have been from the crash of one of the two fighters. *I hope to God it's not Carew!* Then he noticed that two *Rapiers* and one *Visigoth* still fought in the skies above him and he truly did not know if he wished Carew already dead or about to die in the battle with two enemies overhead.

The ground war gave him no time for any thoughts beyond that. Lee's *Nova* drifted across in front of him, eclipsing his view of the Fury that had hit him before. The *Nova* poured both autocannon and LRM fire into the Fury, chipping away at yet more of the front armor. In return, the Fury backed up and jerked to the right, then delivered a shot with the Gauss rifle that opened a great rent in the *Nova*'s center torso armor.

Phelan brought *Grinner* to the right to complete a crossing pattern with the *Nova*. Sprinting forward, he flanked one of the Burkes. He opened up with all his weapons, but the large laser that replaced his 'Mech's right hand missed high. The trio of pulse lasers stitched back and forth across the Burke's left side. They reduced all its armor to molten slag that dripped thickly from the shredded tread on that side.

Because its turret was locked in the forward position, the Burke could not bring its gun to bear on *Grinner.* Unable to move and with its gun locked in one position, the Burke was as good as out of the fight. Phelan hoped its crew realized it, too, because he had no desire to kill them if it was not necessary.

Ace's *Viper* touched down in front of the Fury the strafing had left untouched. The 'Mech's PPC fused armor plates on the Fury's nose into a molten lump, then its medium laser chipped away at the armor left behind. The Fury brought its gun around and pounded a silver ball into the *Viper*'s chest, half-slewing it around to the left.

Dimitria's *Ice Ferret* brought its weapons to bear on another of the Burkes, but the tangle with the first Burke had shaken the pilot. The autocannon, medium laser, and LRMs all missed their target, while the Burke's crew brought its PPCs around. Two blue bolts of man-made lightning blazed into the *Ice Ferret.* One carved armor from the center of the 'Mech's chest. The second beam flayed the rest of the armor from the *Ice Ferret*'s left arm and started grinding away at the arm's metal bones and rubbery muscles.

The third Burke lashed out with two PPC beams at the *Summoner.* As with the *Ice Ferret,* the *Summoner* lost steaming shards of armor from its left arm and chest, but Thea weathered the storm without losing her weapons lock on the Burke. Two LRM flights shot out from the launchers and burst through the armor on the Burke's nose.

Their detonations set off a string of secondary explosions that lifted the Burke from its pit and flipped it over. Both treads whipped off like steel ribbons and started to disintegrate. The boxy tank's turret whirled off and smashed into a mountainside, then the body of the vehicle plumped in the middle and splintered into a million fragments. The nova in its heart was born of ammo and fuel explosions and managed to do with far greater effect what the Clan's attacks had not accomplished.

Locked in a cockpit he found as comfortable as a womb, Carew made two discoveries. The first was that his aerofighter could out-climb and out-dive the *Rapier*s. He found this out as his *Visigoth* swooped down on the stricken *Rapier*. The pilot tried to boost his ship forward, but Carew closed on him and pulled away from the second *Rapier*.

The *Visigoth* struck at the *Rapier* with both lasers and missiles. The rockets hammered the fuselage and left wing. Carew saw several holes open up in the cylindrical body of the fighter and knew some control computers must have taken damage because the tailfins locked in their straight-ahead position.

One of the lasers finished the armor on the *Rapier*'s engine. In a bright spark on the IR readout, the laser damaged the engine. Immediately the engine darkened, and the *Rapier* began to lose air-speed. With its control surfaces locked and sending the slowing plane forward, Carew knew one more set of shots would destroy it.

The second discovery he made was that he would die if he indulged his desire to flame the *Rapier*. Its wingman powered down into his aft arc, but bounced around enough to deny Carew a solid weapons lock. The Clansman cursed and jerked his stick to the right. His craft sideslipped nicely. Then, in response to the command he gave it as the *Rapier* juked in behind him, it pulled up hard and to the left.

The ComStar pilot brought his *Rapier* into a sharp turn that would cut inside the *Visigoth*'s turn radius, so Carew flipped the aerospace fighter over in a roll that stood the *Visigoth* on its left wing. Cutting back on his thrust, he let the *Visigoth* drop like a rock. Regaining control, he feathered it into a sideslip that brought him in behind the *Rapier* at less than a kilometer's distance.

Before he could fire on him, the *Rapier* pilot pulled his nose up in a Immelmann and shot back down at the *Visigoth*. At their speed, their flight paths intersected and passed in three seconds. In that three seconds, both fighters fired every weapon they had at each other, and did it at point-blank range.

Carew felt the *Visigoth* shake violently as the *Rapier*'s autocannon ripped a jagged scar across the armor on his left wing. Blue light filled the cockpit and static crackled in his earphones as a PPC slashed armor away from his right wing. The *Rapier*'s second PPC and its LRMs missed, but not by much, and Carew felt certain he'd used up whatever luck he'd been granted for the day.

His computer's estimate of the damage done to the *Rapier* cheered him. His own PPC had missed the target, but the LRMs more than made up for it. They hammered the *Rapier*'s fuselage and blew out chunks of aircraft in locations the computer marked as belonging to heat sinks. The missiles also blew armor from the engine, while the two forward lasers flashed into the right wing and fuselage, possibly damaging a fire-control computer.

Carew nodded and studied the *Rapier*'s nova-white IR signature. *You're running hot—as hot as the pilot you think yourself to be.* Kicking his left wing up, he swung over into a split-S and grinned as the *Rapier* came around to meet him.

The least-damaged Fury cranked its turret to the right and drilled a Gauss rifle projectile into the *Summoner*'s left arm. The silver ball punched through the fragmentary armor and crushed the LRM launcher pod nestled therein. The *Summoner* shuddered, but remained upright and blasted back at the Fury with a missile barrage that chewed up the tank's nose armor.

Ace's *Viper* oriented on the most dangerous Fury and opened up with both his PPC and medium laser. They continued the job the *Summoner* had begun and one beam even sliced through the right-side track. The ribbon of metal spun off the wheels, awkwardly freezing the Fury in mid-turn. Dirt sprayed high into the air as the Fury fought to move and escape its tormentors.

Because of the heat washing up through his 'Mech's cockpit, Phelan only used his pulse lasers on the Fury. The stuttering hail of red bolts pierced the tank's weakened nose armor as if it were not even there. An internal explosion shook the Fury, then it stopped dead while dust settled over it and oily black smoke curled up out of the hole beneath it.

Frantically working the control levers, Elza Speer fought to track the *Black Hawk* circling to the right. "I'm trying, Perry, dammit, but the 'Mech isn't helping."

Whatever reply Perry might have made was swallowed in the hideous din of metal gnawing away at metal. Elza saw the muzzle flash of the *Black Hawk*'s autocannon, then felt the Fury jerk hard to the left. The loud explosions of missiles against the hull left her ears ringing. She felt the sting of metal spalling up off the interior bulkheads and saw the flesh of her arms and hands crisscrossed with small, bloody furrows.

She redoubled her efforts to turn the Fury, but that only brought the sight of the other Fury's smoking carcass into view. "Damn." She watched the *Fenris* exchange shots with the remaining operational Burke and took some joy in the 'Mech reeling back, its chest armor in tatters. At the same time she saw the Burke's nose had been crushed and the crew already popping out to surrender.

Elza shook herself and jammed the tank into reverse. "I am but a tool of Blake's Wisdom. Dammit, Perry, shoot something!"

The *Rapier* homed in on Carew's *Visigoth* like a guided missile. Its autocannon vomited fire and metal in a storm that punched through the aerofighter's fuselage. Warning klaxons blared at Carew in the cockpit, but he forced himself to ignore them. *In atmosphere that does not matter.* The fighter bucked and the computer informed him one of his heat sinks had been destroyed. *Well, that does not matter as much in atmosphere.*

His return salvos cut into the *Rapier* as it shot over him. The one of his two medium lasers that hit the ComStar fighter claimed another heat sink from that craft in retribution for the damage he'd taken. The particle projection beam's azure scalpel followed some LRMs into the engine cowling and pierced the protective shielding guarding the fusion reactor. A heat corona surrounded the engine, and the *Rapier* shot forward as if the pilot had kicked in the overthrusters.

Carew found himself holding his breath as the pilot struggled to pull the *Rapier*'s nose up. He got it started in that direction, then the heat signature of his engine dimmed. Carew punched up another scan on the target, then he realized the ship's computers had shut the engine down to prevent an explosion.

The *Rapier* started a slow roll and, without thrust, it nosed down toward the earth. The ship's canopy fragmented as the explosive bolts holding it in place detonated. The pilot rode a rocket out of the cockpit, then the escape chair's gyrojets flamed on to stabilize its flight.

Carew keyed his radio. "If we have Elementals in Sector 4123, ComStar has a pilot down. I don't know who he is, but Clan Wolf definitely wants him as a bondsman."

Elza jerked against the restraining straps in her chair, then found the right-hand tread controls went slack. "It's done, Perry!" Try as she might, she was unable to turn fast enough to prevent the more mobile 'Mechs from zeroing in on the Fury's damaged right flank. The *Thor, Fenris,* and *Dragonfly* had all hammered it with fire while Perry had been unable to return fire at all.

She punched the engine's shutdown button, then waited a bit and popped her hatch. The cold air pouring down into the cockpit refreshed her until a breeze carried in the scent of burning tanks. She wrinkled her nose, then slowly climbed out of the tank to join the crew of the other Fury and the last two Burkes in surrender.

"I hope the Precentor Martial knows what he is doing." She jumped down from the hull and raised her hands. "Wisdom of Blake be damned. Fighting this sort of battle is stupid."

Phelan was pleased when the crews started leaving their vehicles. He flipped open his external communication channel. "You fought well and bravely." He pointed back down the direction from which the ComStar forces had originally come. "Please take cover. More of your forces are headed this way and things are not likely to be very hospitable here."

He tuned his radio over to the Cluster's tactical frequency. "Black Widow, this is Ax One. We have the pass. We are operational, but will not last long. Quarrel lost one of the planes, but I have no ComStar air elements present. Please advise concerning our disposition."

He heard the disgust in Natasha's voice as she answered him. "Report back to Cluster HQ for refit and resupply."

Phelan frowned. "What happened? ComStar run away too fast?"

"Not so fast we could not have caught them. We have been ordered back and when the pressure dropped off him, Wollam and his troops pulled back to the northeast."

"What?" The MechWarrior surveyed the burning armor and the damage to his Star. *We could have been killed here.* "We took the objective, Colonel."

"I know that, but who can puzzle out the ilKhan's mind?"
So, Ulric is the one who has pulled us back. Something
big *must be going on.* "Orders understood. We will be bringing in some prisoners."

"Noted, Ax Star. You did good work out there."

"Roger that, Black Widow. We are coming in."

Ulric pulled his head up as Conal Ward's face appeared on
the monitor in his office. Sweat had pasted the warrior's
dark hair to his forehead, and the padding of his neurohelmet had crushed it into place. "Thank you for finally reporting to me, Galaxy Commander Ward. I would have preferred
more immediate communication to your waiting until it was
safe to leave your 'Mech."

Conal stared out of the screen with nothing of his intensity lost by transmission. "Forgive me, ilKhan, but my Red
Wolves have been fighting hard and ComStar jammed our
communications. It took a runner from my HQ to bring me
your message."

The ilKhan frowned. "Do not lie to me, Conal. You remained engaged with the 278th Division of the Com Guards
long after I ordered you to break off."

"We are beating them, Ulric. You cannot take that away
from us."

"Yes, you are beating them, but you are using up your
supplies at nearly double the allowable rate."

"What matter that we run out of missiles and autocannon
ammo after we have destroyed them?" Conal let his anger
color his words. "You seek to disgrace me and my men."

"Nonsense," Ulric snorted. "I have noted with great pleasure how well you have done. I have made sure that all the
Clans know that Vlad and your Eleventh Wolf Guards have
outmaneuvered one of the most elite Com Guard units on
Tukayyid."

"If what you say is true, why are we reined back to go
into the mountains while the Wolf Spiders are allowed to
continue their fighting? It is disgusting for you to let that ancient witch continue her career beyond her years."

"She gets results, and her troops are not using up their
supplies more swiftly than ordered." Ulric narrowed his blue
eyes. "Besides, you are not Natasha Kerensky. Her name
alone, from her years with Wolf's Dragoons, strikes fear into
the hearts of the Com Guards. The man commanding the

282nd Division formerly fought in the Marik civil war and she beat him. She owns him, and his distress must be demoralizing to his compatriots. Furthermore, she has been called back as well."

"It is still unnatural, as is this whole battle. The Com Guards run and duck and hide instead of fighting us."

Ulric nodded in agreement. "Unnatural it is. The Precentor Martial has seen our weakness and he has already used it to break the Smoke Jaguars. We are used to quick and decisive battles. Throughout this invasion, we have been plagued by partisan battles that do not allow us to concentrate our strength. Now we face that on a grander scale on a world where we do not have the resources for a long battle."

Conal shook his head. "Bah. It could be won tomorrow, as well you would see if you were here."

"You are wrong, Conal, and if you persist in your belief, you will not survive the fighting." Ulric let himself smile slyly. "As for your suggestion that I come to see for myself, you are right. I have remained too long away from battle. When we engage the Com Guards in the mountains, I will lead our troops into battle. There, once and for all time, we shall decide the fate of the Inner Sphere."

38

From the cliff top, Kai saw the two Elemental divers surface amid a boiling circle of bubbles. They gave him a thumbs-up, which he relayed to the people behind him. Someone threw a switch and the winch started. The steel cable on which he rested his right hand grew taut and *Yen-lo-Wang*'s Gauss rifle began its ascent to dry land.

Kai could scarcely believe all that had happened in the previous five days. The actual escape had gone perfectly. Kai and Deirdre had taken the demi-Precentor's limo and headed south by a roundabout route to the Mahler farm. The Elementals had appropriated a heavy hovertruck and returned to the mountains to recollect their armor, then they joined up with the other two at the Mahler farm.

Kai turned and smiled as Erik Mahler locked the winch's drive handle down, then showed Malthus how to undo it when the time came. Erik had reacted coldly to the arrival of Elementals, but Hilda had treated them with the same courtesy she had showed Kai when he arrived. Kai's truce with the Elementals helped win Erik over, and when he learned they had joined forces to oppose ComStar, the elder MechWarrior insisted on helping them organize their rescue mission and monitor the Steiner resistance.

Erik had been able to tell about the salvage operations ComStar had performed on the peninsula as he had been dragooned into a workforce. As nearly as he knew, all the 'Mechs had been taken offworld, but he could recall no undersea salvage operation. That news made Kai more confident that *Yen-lo-wang* and its Gauss rifle might be salvageable.

The morning after the Elementals' arrival, they all headed out to where the *Centurion* had gone into the water. They were very careful about their route, scouting continually for any ComStar patrols, but they saw no opposition. They were not alone at the site, however, and that surprised them.

Gus Michaels walked over and rested his right hand on Kai's left shoulder. "Sorry we couldn't get more of *Yen-lo-wang,* kid. The *Centurion* can be salvaged, but not with a winch. The Omni has it pinned to the shelf, which is the only reason it didn't drop for a full kilometer."

"I know." Looking down into the dark water, Kai began to see a white cylinder waver beneath the waves. "If it had gone down all the way, the cockpit would have been crushed and I would have died."

"Better to be lucky than good, kid."

Kai found he liked the solidly built little man. Malthus had been suspicious about Michaels, but the MechWarrior put that down to Gus' identifying himself as being on a mission for the ilKhan. The battle reports of Kai's action on Alyina had hinted at a 'Mech with superior myomer technology, so Gus had been dispatched to check further into the story. He'd just located the site of the battle when they arrived, and they found his winch and cable equipment very helpful.

The Gauss rifle broke the surface and water poured from the bore. Aside from a few tendrils of seaweed and dangling wires where it had been freed from the *Centurion,* it looked in fine shape. The Elementals helped guide it toward the shore, then flopped padding and old tires over it to prevent it from being injured by bumps and scrapes against the cliffside.

Malthus walked over and draped his arm across Gus' shoulders. "Be sure to remember all of this for the ilKhan, little man. Now begins the liberation of Alyina."

With the Gauss rifle loaded in the heavy hovertruck's bed and well-hidden within its canvas-covered body, a heated discussion about the nature of the liberation started. "It does not matter to me, Michaels, that you are an envoy from the ilKhan." Malthus planted his fists on his hips. "You are going to stay behind at the Mahler farm."

The historian's green eyes blazed. "Now wait just one minute. I got you the plans to the Valigia facility ComStar is using."

The Elemental shook his head. "You redrew them from memory from a hurried tour two weeks ago, and you've been on the run since."

"I'm trained to remember details. I got you a map. You owe me."

Malthus drew himself up to his full height. "I owe you nothing. You are a recorder of events."

"Damned straight. Now how am I to write a report on all this if I don't go along?"

Malthus gave him a predatory grin. "You will be allowed to view our battleroms after the fight. Our armor will record everything."

Gus matched the man's grin tooth for tooth. "Fine, then give me a suit of the armor so I can record my own chronicle of the attack."

The Elemental leader chopped that suggestion down with his right hand. "But you are not of the Warrior Caste."

Kai frowned. "Begging your pardon, Taman, but you have four sets and there are only three of you."

"True," Malthus said. "One is for you if you would like to use it."

Kai looked at him, then slowly closed his mouth. "Me? In Elemental armor?"

"You are a warrior, Kai Allard-Liao. Our armor is not the same as having a 'Mech, but in it a warrior becomes the ultimate possible for a living creature. You have the heart and mind and soul of a warrior, now you can have the flesh and muscle of a warrior as well." Malthus looked down. "We will understand if you refuse."

Kai glanced at Locke and Slane. The two Elementals nodded and silently echoed Malthus' words. *They offer me the highest honor they can imagine.* Excitement filled Kai's chest. "Though I am not worthy, I accept your invitation and will do my best to honor the memory of the warrior who wore this armor before me."

All three Elementals smiled and congratulated him with fierce pats on the back. Kai laughed. "Provided, of course, that you can size the armor to fit me, and I get some time to practice in it."

"Agreed." Malthus gave Kai a wry grin. "We will all want time to drill again."

Gus, standing across from him, nodded his acknowledgement. "So, Malthus, you're going to stuff Kai and your men into your armor, head into Valigia in the truck, muzzle-load the cannon, and blow open the ComStar fortress, right?"

"Correct."

"Bingo!" Gus folded his arms across his chest. "I'm coming with you because you won't have time to change into your armor in the war zone."

Malthus frowned. "We prepare before we go into battle."

"Right, so unless you can figure out how to fit in the driver's seat after you pull on your tin-skin, you need a driver—and I'm him."

Kai looked from the little man's bearded face to the larger man and back. Malthus shrugged his shoulders and Gus' grin pulled the corners of his mouth halfway back toward his ears. "Never argue with a historian, Kai. The victors might write the histories, but we're the ones who do the actual work. Unless you want to be remembered as nothing more than a footnote, let the historian win."

Alone in the woods back behind the Mahler farm, Deirdre let Kai enfold her in a tight embrace. "I don't want to lose you either, Deirdre." His mind raced as he searched for the words to explain things to her. "I've seen the plans for the ComStar fortress. If I don't go in with them, they stand little or no chance of succeeding in their attempt to liberate their friends. But if they succeed, then Malthus will honor his oath to let us and the Federated Commonwealth prisoners of war go free."

"I know, I know, but I still hate the idea of being separated from you. When I thought I would never see you again . . ."

Kai felt her tremble and held her more closely. "Don't worry. You will not lose me. I'm not going to die."

"Don't tease me, Kai." She pulled back from him and wiped away her tears. "You cannot tell me you are not going to die."

How do I explain? Kai took a deep breath, then sighed

heavily. "I don't expect you to understand because I cannot say that I truly do. It's just that the confidence that you and they have in me has opened my eyes. I can see, now, that I have abilities and skills that let me be very good at what I do. No more than you could stop tending to the sick could I . . ."

"Stop killing?" She looked away disconsolately. "I think I have already lost you."

He grabbed her shoulders and shook her lightly. "No, you know that's not true. I am not a killing machine. I am not!"

"Who are you trying to convince, Kai? Me or yourself?"

Kai smiled and glanced down. "Deirdre, being a warrior is different from being a killer. What I do is to prepare for conflicts to safeguard the freedoms we, as civilized people, have agreed we possess. The Clans want to dominate us and take away our freedoms, so I oppose them. ComStar has similar yet more virulent aims, and I must oppose them, too. I do not do this as an instrument of state policy, but as one human fighting to preserve what all humanity should hold sacred."

He swallowed hard. "Some might argue that by using drugs or antibiotics you wage war on a cellular level where what I do is on a multicellular level. I think that is fallacious because I realize another living creature is more valuable than some virus or bacillus. Still, in some ways the idea of combating disease does hold and I have to hope that by acting to minimize problems early, I can help prevent the spread of something that would destroy humanity.

"Can you understand that?"

Deirdre nodded. "All too well." She smiled and cupped his face in her hands. "It is just that I understand what it is and how it feels to save a life and to take one. I would not wish for you a lifetime of taking lives."

"Nor would I wish that for anyone." Kai's eyes grew distant as they focused well beyond their surroundings. "I am willing to accept that responsibility. It is my choice and my duty. I do not revel in it, but I bear it so others will not have to."

"I know, and I love you for that." She kissed him lightly on the lips. "We have a week before you go?"

"Yes. Mahler, Michaels, and Malthus plan, Slane and Locke train. Sun-up to sundown, I am theirs."

She took his hand and led him back toward the house.

"Then you will be mine for the rest of the time, Kai Allard-Liao. As your days will be filled with death and horror, let us fill the nights with life and love."

39

**DropShip Serene Foresight, *Teniente Transfer Orbit
Smoke Jaguar Occupation Zone*
14 May 3052 (Day 14 of Operation Scorpion)**

Victor Ian Davion left the airlock and crossed to the side of
the needle-nosed shuttlecraft. Seeing the Federated Commonwealth's crest emblazoned above the legend *Arcturus*
made him smile. He patted the ship's hull as the hatchway
opened and an emerging soldier saluted him. He returned the
salute, then saw Galen struggle through the airlock doorway
with both of their kits.

Behind him the Prince saw Shin Yodama and Hohiro slip
into the shuttle bay. Hohiro leaned on his cane far more
heavily than Victor thought right in the light gravity provided by the ship's acceleration. *Months on the run really
hurt him. Still, he and his people put up one hell of a fight.*
He left the ship and crossed to where his two hosts stood.

"I'll be leaving soon. My gratitude and best wishes to you
and your people. If not for your intelligence services and the
spirits of your men, we'd never have gotten off Teniente."
Victor shook his head. "In many ways, I cannot believe we
made it."

Hohiro smiled, but the smile died quickly from lack of energy to sustain it. "When I sent Shin off to get help, I never
imagined he would find it in the Federated Commonwealth."

"Good help is hard to find," Shin offered.

"And we come cheaper than most," Victor finished with a
laugh. "When I was asked, I felt certain you would have

done the same for me had our situations been reversed. I would hope that my father would have been wise enough to accept your help."

Hohiro looked down, then glanced over at Shin. "My friend has told me how you came to be called to this task. I know what it cost and I regret causing you and my sister pain."

Victor leaned back against the cool bulkhead. "You and I did not originally see eye to eye about much of anything on Outreach. There we learned to respect each other. We learned that we would accept what we had to do to successfully fulfill our duties. Personal pain falls into that category. I know that your safe return will lessen any pain your sister might feel because of the bargain she struck with your father. As I would feel her pain more sharply than my own. By saving you, I save myself."

"You continue to amaze me, Victor." Hohiro looked to Shin for confirmation. "You do not come from our samurai tradition, but you understand *giri* and *ninjo*—duty and compassion—as well as any of us."

The Prince of the Federated Commonwealth forced a shrug. "I had a good teacher. Moreover, the conflict between duty and feelings is not unique to samurai or the yakuza. Those of us born to the throne understand it quite keenly. Your father and my father were lucky that their marriages did not conflict with feelings for another. I fear that I will not have the same good fortune when I choose to wed. Perhaps, however, I will be the last Prince to be skewered by that particular dilemma."

Hohiro leaned with both hands on his aluminum cane, then nodded slowly. "I hope reality exceeds your imagination. You do not have to leave, you know. You could travel with us to Luthien, then continue your trip from there."

"Me, at Luthien? Do you wish my father's heart to explode in his chest?" The image of Omi danced tantalizingly before his mind's-eye and he almost agreed. Then he realized that Omi would not be allowed to see him. *Do you wish my heart crushed?*

Galen arrived and filled the awkward silence. "Worse than that, do you want the Archon to have my head? The Davion and Steiner heir on Black Luthien? That would be enough to bring Amaris the Usurper back from the dead."

All four men shared a laugh over that and the tension of

the moment passed. "Hohiro, I appreciate the offer. I would, at some time, like to see Luthien, but I think the masters of protocol in both our realms would scream if I were just to drop in."

"Understood," Hohiro said, then added softly, "my friend."

Victor chuckled silently. "I never thought to hear those words from a Kurita."

"And I never thought to say them to a Davion." The heir to the Dragon shook his head. "Imagine that. The Clans come to destroy us, but they only succeed in uniting us."

"I'm afraid it will take more than one joint operation to unite us, Hohiro. Centuries of distrust and blood will not evaporate so easily. Who knows what the fear and suspicion that has existed between our Houses may one day force us to do?"

Hohiro reached out and took Victor's right hand. He sandwiched it between his own hands on top of the cane. "You saved my life, which means, in our tradition, that you are now responsible for it."

Victor recalled the Clan *Thor* coming at him in the battle. "And you saved my life, so you are responsible for it."

"Yes." Hohiro squeezed the other man's hand. "Let us both remember, come what may, this burden we bear. It may not stop us from being forced to strike at one another, but it will cause us to seek more rational solutions first. I do not want to face you in battle, Victor Davion."

"Nor I you, Hohiro Kurita."

"Then we can learn not to fear one another. In that way, we cannot be warped. We cannot be poisoned against each other."

Victor capped Hohiro's hand. "For at least one generation, we can learn not to fear each other."

The two men stared into each other's eyes and Victor read no treachery in Hohiro's steady gaze. Their grips remained strong, then broke apart as Galen and Shin shook hands. Victor turned and offered his hand to Shin. "Though your Prince credits me with the success of the rescue, without you, there would have been nothing. It has been my distinct pleasure and honor to work with you."

Shin bowed his head. "And I have been most honored by the faith you have shown in me. Someday I hope to be truly worthy of it."

Victor smiled and turned quickly to Hohiro. "Keep him by

your side because he'll be more valuable than any courtier. And if you manage to clone him, send one to me."

Hohiro laughed. "Only if you will send me a copy of your Galen Cox and Kai Allard."

Victor stiffened. "I am afraid Kai never left Alyina."

"Then the crimes committed by the Clans are compounded beyond redemption. I am truly sorry, Victor. I will offer prayers in his name."

"Thank you, I will tell his sisters and brother." Victor looked back as the Techs disconnected the fueling hoses from the shuttle and closed the cargo bay doors. "I must go."

Hohiro began his unsteady walk toward the airlock. "Travel well and safely, my friend."

"Have a swift journey home, my friend," Victor shot back. "Tell your sister . . ."

"Yes?"

"Tell her . . ." Words failed him. He shrugged and shook his head.

"I will tell her." Hohiro waved from the airlock doorway. "From me she shall learn all the things she would want to know about the man who terrorized the Nova Cats. I will tell her about the man who saved my life. The man who is my friend."

═══ 40 ═══

Pozoristu Mountains, Tukayyid
ComStar Intervention Zone, Free Rasalhague
Republic
16 May 3052 (Day 16 of Operation Scorpion)

Sheet after wind-driven sheet of rain lashed Phelan's *Wolfhound*. The computer-projected holographic display wavered and blurred as the torrential downpour washed over the sensors built into the *Wolfhound's* upstanding ears. Viewed from the infrared mode, the surrounding mountainous landscape looked as dark and bleak as it did under visible light.

Inside the cockpit, working in the harsh rainbow backlight of a half-dozen monitors and weapon-condition displays, Phelan punched new commands into his computer to get it to define the incoming data in slimmer and slimmer slices of temperature. The projection melted, then reformed itself with little change in the dark blue and black representation of it.

"Damn! This cursed rain is soaking everything to a universally wretched temp." The whole assault on Tukayyid had begun to get to Phelan. He and the Wolf Spiders had spent days cooling their heels and occasionally going after ComStar raiders. Then, all of a sudden, they had been rushed into the mountains just in time for a hideous weather front to move in. *Hurry up and wait, hurry up and wait!*

He knew that Ulric was, in fact, working from a plan, but it bothered Phelan to have to hear reports of the other Clans in combat while the Guards were stuck in place. They had successfully fended off two ComStar attempts to overrun their supply depot, and Phelan knew their efforts had pleased the ilKhan. Still, it made Phelan feel like a storekeeper chasing off shoplifters, not a warrior fighting for the ownership of Terra.

Frustrated with the weather, he flipped the sensor over to visible light and shifted the *Wolfhound* up so the tips of its ears could rise above the solid granite boulder that hid it. He rose slowly, annoyed that his holographic display revealed a jagged, rocky landscape while his viewports only allowed him to see granite.

A forked bolt of lightning arced up from the valley beyond his position to tickle the belly of the black thunderclouds overhead. Phelan winced and ducked away from the brutally bright light. With afterimages slashing lines through his vision, he forced himself to look at the holographic display. He shuddered, then punched up a replay of the one instant the lightning froze with its stroboscopic explosion.

"One, two, three . . ." Phelan continued counting silently to himself as he used the targeting joystick to tag each 'Mech image on the display. After finding a full company of them, he started in on armor and infantry squads. Very quickly his mouth went dry. "Dammit all to hell, this is a ComStar thrust that'll split the Guards from the 341st Assault. Not at all what Ulric thought the Precentor Martial would do."

Phelan hit two buttons on his command console. Because of the storm raging outside and the countless valleys in the mountains, using the radio was impractical. Avoiding its use also prevented the possibility of ComStar locating him by triangulation. Only the fact that the storm made all kinds of sensors useless had prevented him from being discovered so far, and with a company of 'Mechs inserting itself between his Star and his Cluster, he wanted to remain hidden.

Using his left hand, he manipulated the crosshairs for his rear-firing laser. The buttons had downgraded its power to a fraction of what it used in combat and extended its focal length. He punched in a set of coordinates, waited for the weapon to acquire its target, then patched his communication system into the beam generator.

"This is Ax One. I have forty, four-zero, 'Mechs inbound to Sector 4134. They have armor and infantry support. Stand by for data download." He sent out a check-signal, and something back along the line of relay stations sent a go-ahead to his onboard computer. In 2.3 seconds, the scan and the analysis of it shot off at the speed of light to the Guards' headquarters.

Phelan watched his computer put a roster for the ComStar unit up on his secondary monitor. *Hmmm. The computer says they're designated the Thirteenth Army, which means they are brand-new. The individual 'Mechs date from the Star League era, as is to be expected, and they're all virgin. Definitely a new reserve unit.*

"Black Widow to Ax One. Hit them from the flank or rear."

Phelan blinked his eyes with disbelief. "I have a Star here, Colonel. Even if we *are* the Clans, those are mighty long odds."

"The rest of the Cluster is coming up fast, Ax One. We need you to stop them. Khan Garth Radick is bringing up the 341st Assault to finish them. Go, now!"

Phelan snapped off the laser and returned its power output to martial specifications. He flipped his communications over to the radio and boosted its power output. "Ax Star, we are to go up and into the ComStar company in the next valley. Move fast and worry less about being accurate than causing a commotion. Do not worry about aim. They are packed cheek to jowl. You cannot miss."

Ace came back at him. "We getting help, Commander?"

Phelan recognized the question as a request for information, not the voicing of an opinion about the intelligence of the order. *That's the Clans. Do or die without a worry.*

"That is the rumor, Trey. Give them everything. They are new, and if we are lucky, they are green. They will break." He cut his radio link with the rest of his Star. *If they are not, they will kill us.*

Initiate Horagi Kano hunched his shoulders against the rain and pushed on forward. He watched the back of the man in front of him, and did his best to keep his balance on the narrow ledge. Down below, rolling its way through the canyon, a Rhino just waited to grind a clumsy foot soldier into protoplasm beneath its treads.

Kano tightened his grip on the disposable Inferno rocket launcher. *The Precentor Martial has put us here to stop the Clans. The weight of humanity is upon our shoulders.* He fought to keep his thoughts pure and away from the clammy squishing of soaked socks inside his boots. *Be alert and ready. ComStar is depending upon us.*

Above, twenty meters upslope on the canyon wall, he saw some rocks shift and a little slide of pebbles cascaded down to bounce off his helmet. He cursed, then followed the line of their fall with his gaze. As he looked up, lightning flashed and burned stark white highlights into the avatar of a war god.

"Waaahhh!" he screamed and unlimbered the Inferno launcher. The man behind him fell off the ledge in the excitement. Kano extended the launch tube and flipped the sights up into place. *ComStar is depending upon us.*

As the 'Mech swung its large laser into line with his troop, Kano hit the firing button. "I give my life for the glory of the Primus!"

The Inferno rocket exploded as it pulled up to the middle of the *Wolfhound*'s chest. A clinging cloud of jellied petrochem covered the 'Mech with a burning coat. The rain diluted it somewhat, but that just caused it to turn the 'Mech into a living torch as the liquid covered all of it.

Phelan heard warning klaxons go off and saw the heat in his 'Mech spike from cool green to blue and almost up into the yellow zone, but the rain had so cooled everything that it minimized the chances of his overheating. Hitting the thumb button on his right joystick, he swept a line of laser fire above infantrymen who had fired the missile and into the side of a Rhino.

Even as the tank started to rotate its turret toward him, Phelan stepped the *Wolfhound* off into space and let it drop toward the valley floor. He bent the legs to cushion the shock of hitting the slope, then kicked off and landed solidly on the ground, crushing a hoverjeep beneath his 'Mech's right foot.

For a split-second, everything froze. The *Wolfhound* stood like a fire elemental mocking the puny mortal force gathered in the valley. The light from his fire splashed gold over the rainslicked stone and sent the shadows of terrified soldiers wavering like black flags over the canyon walls. Towering over the equipment nearest him, Phelan felt alien and immortal. He reveled in the terror he saw on faces.

Then, just as quickly, his own companions stalked into the valley. The ComStar armor began to swing its turrets around to blast the impudent intruders. When one whole company of ComStar 'Mechs turned back to engage Ax Star, Phelan knew he was in trouble.

Jerking to the left as a PPC fired at him, Phelan smiled and whispered to himself. "Phelan, Phelan, burning bright, can you survive this fight tonight?"

The Precentor Martial, standing unseen at the other end of the valley in his virtual world, shuddered as he saw the fiery 'Mech descend like an avenging angel. *How could they find us here? If they blunt this thrust at splitting them . . .*

In a second, a computer command readjusted the construct's scale so Focht became a titan huge enough to be able to see the curvature of the world. Instead of seeing the whole length of the Pozoristu Mountains, he saw pockets of clarity in a sea of cloudy gray floating around his feet. The storm made it impossible for him to have information on anything except the areas his troops or scouts inhabited.

We grapple blindly in a minefield. If I cannot see them, they cannot see me, but having both of us at a mutual disadvantage does nothing to reassure me.

He shrank himself back down to the size of a 'Mech and opened a direct communications line to the troops beset by the Clan Star. "Acolyte Durkovic, turn Gamma Company and destroy the Star behind you. Precentor Leboeuf, your Alpha Battalion is under attack. Move now to reinforce it."

His troops moved to comply, but he saw it would not be easy. The Clan 'Mechs moved as swiftly as they could to present difficult targets for Alpha Battalion. Though they could duck and dodge at will, scattering troops and destroying vehicles, his own troops had to wade back through their comrades. This slowed their counterstrike and allowed the 'Mechs to terrorize the infantry enough that it broke.

Angry and heartsick, Focht watched Phelan Kell's *Wolfhound* drop down on its haunches to take cover behind a ComStar Rhino. He locked his left hand over the turret and twisted it back so the missiles, if launched, would pepper ComStar troops. Laser beams swept out at him, but the heavy tank shielded him. When a *Black Knight* missed with a PPC shot and two large laser beams, the *Wolfhound* popped up like a jack in the box and blasted back at it. Two of the medium pulse lasers and the large laser stripped the armor from the *Black Knight*'s right arm. The third pulse laser ripped a nasty scar in its chest armor.

The other 'Mechs in the Clan Star proved equally effective. Their fire hit a multitude of targets. The *Thor* and *Fenris* sprayed their missiles over the narrow canyon in a haphazard pattern that maximized panic. Giving much better than he got, the *Dragonfly* traded shots with a *Lancelot,* while the *Black Hawk* made an apelike *Kintaro* pay a dear price for trying to close to its weapons' optimum range.

Phelan Kell is not stupid. This attack would be suicide unless . . . "Hettig, ETA for Beta and Gamma Battalions to reinforce Alpha?"

"Ten minutes, Precentor Martial."

Focht clenched his fists. "Hurry, Durkovic. Scatter them now, or Alpha Battalion will be a memory by the time your reinforcements arrive."

Compared with his feelings at the beginning of his assault, Phelan was overjoyed with having survived more than one exchange with the battalion he had been asked to ambush. Another shot with his large laser took the *Black Knight*'s right arm off at the shoulder. The others in his Star had inflicted more damage and the infantry had been completely routed, but the 'Mechs being sent after them were closing fast.

The brilliant blue of a PPC bolt lit the valley for a second, then darkness closed in again. Red and green light stabbed from one end of the valley to the other. The stuttering flame of an autocannon burst and the torchlight of rockets being sent skyward contributed to the hellishness of the landscape. Real lightning mocked all the artificial illumination while smoke and fog mixed into impenetrable curtains that hid the combatants from each other.

Phelan sighted back along the lines of laser beams, shot, then ducked and dodged. Slowly but inexorably he gave ground before the company bearing down on his people. From what little he could see of them in the inky blackness, they had avoided taking major damage, but even he knew that was a slim source of hope. After days and days of battling, his Star's 'Mechs were not running at the top of form. The armor he'd lost in the fight for the pass still had not been completely replaced, so his right leg remained vulnerable.

A thick, searing bolt of lightning hit high on the ridgeline at the far end of the valley. Its light burned tall shadows on the smoke and fog, then sank the valley into even greater darkness when it vanished. Phelan squeezed his eyes shut against the afterimage, but when he opened them again, he saw spots of light dotting the ridge. He blinked his eyes and wished his neurohelmet would allow him to rub them, then he kicked magnification into his vislight display.

Natasha and the rest of the Cluster had arrived.

Leaving their identification lights on, the Wolves poured a withering volley of fire down into the valley. Natasha's *Dire Wolf* let fly with everything it had, and beside her, Ranna's *Warhawk* blasted ComStar troops with twin PPC bolts. LRM impacts and explosions ripped through the valley like a string of volcanic eruptions. Red beams and blue lightning raked back and forth through the ComStar forces. Phelan saw fire sputter from the muzzles of autocannons, then seconds later, the cacophony of reports and explosions reached him.

Phelan punched up his tactical channel. "Get set, Ax Star. We've got the back door here. Either they come through us to escape, or they drive deeper into our territory. Either way, it won't be pretty."

The Precentor Martial watched as the Thirteenth Wolf Guards fell on the 282nd Division's Alpha Battalion. Gamma Company, caught between Phelan's Star and the newly arrived reinforcements, faced a choice of running through a gauntlet to rejoin the rest of Alpha Battalion as it pushed on through where the canyon started running west or else finding another way out. He smiled as Acolyte Durkovic started his people heading up through the gap Phelan had used to ambush the troops.

"Good, Durkovic, good. You will force them to hunt you down." Focht keyed his line to Hettig. "How far out is the rest of the 2/82nd?"

"ETA one minute, but outriders are picking up Clan activity."

From his vantage point, the Precentor Martial looked up the slope at Natasha Kerensky and her Cluster. His image of her 'Mech vanished in a microsecond of static, then reformed, shifting slightly to the left as the computer shifted to the datafeed from a 'Mech that still existed. On his right, he saw the smoking ruin of a *Thug*.

All around him Alpha Battalion broke and started to run. Though a veteran of a hundred battles, Focht still felt his stomach twist into knots as the Clan forces descended into the valley. He knew retreat was the only possible way to survive, and he hoped the retreat would drag Natasha's troops blindly on to where the rest of the 2/82nd could turn the tables back on them. Still, given that the 2/82nd was composed totally of green troops, he expected the Thirteenth Wolf Guards to smash through them.

"Damn the storm, I can't put air up! Hettig, can we shift the 9/247th artillery assets to this fight?"

"Yes, sir. The range is at the edge of their capabilities, but they can drop something in."

"Excellent. Sow the 2/82nd Alpha Batt's line of retreat with clusters. Do it now."

"Artillery allocated."

Precentor Susan Litto accepted the printout, then punched the open-channel button on her intercom system. "Sector 91534, four volleys of clusters, all batteries. Make the trajectory high because we have a mountain to go over."

"Got it," she heard Gunner Bob Rule drawl. "We have friendlies in that sector?"

"These will take thirty seconds to get there. My guess is, one way or another, by the time they get there, the answer will be no."

When the artillery barrage hit, the Precentor Martial saw that all but one lance of the 2/82nd Alpha had cleared Sector 91534. The artillery shells opened above the valley and distributed a liberal supply of fist-sized submunitions. As the little bomblets tumbled through the air, a plastic casing kept the titanium ball bearings studding the high-explosive in place. Already primed, the bomblets exploded on impact.

Most went off when they hit the ground.

Many went off when they hit a charging Clan *Mad Cat* dead on its nose. For one second, it looked as if the Omni-Mech had run full force into a wall of fire. Smoking, armor scales dropping like feathers from a wounded bird, the 'Mech stumbled forward, then pitched over onto its face. The second volley shrouded the 'Mech with a blazing cloak and lifted it into the air. When the smoke cleared, the Precentor Martial saw a twisted, glowing hulk where he last had seen the *Mad Cat.*

The next two volleys failed to catch anyone, but did force the Wolf Guards to pull back. Quickly typing on a phantom keyboard, Focht shifted his view from Alpha Battalion's rear guard to its lead element. "We should be linking up with the rest of the division just about now . . ."

As the *Wyvern* supplying the Precentor Martial with videofeed came around the canyon turn, he saw Clan 'Mechs pouring through a gap and blasting straight through the rest of the 2/82nd Division. Like knights of ages past, the sheer weight of the Clan charge bore it into and beyond the ComStar lines. 'Mechs went down, bowled over, to be crushed beneath the feet of enemy and comrades alike.

Silhouetted higher up on the canyon wall, other Clan 'Mechs supported the charge with murderous laser and LRM fire. One OmniMech, a monstrously huge *Gladiator,* attracted Focht's immediate attention. Typing furiously, he made the computer magnify it and clarify the image. In the backlight of a ruby energy burst, he saw the Clan's wolf-head crest and five stars emblazoned below it.

Five stars! That 'Mech belongs to a Khan. Natasha is behind them. Is this Ulric?

Before he could paint the *Gladiator* with a computer tag and relay it out to the troops, a ComStar *Highlander* trotted up beside the *Wyvern* and thrust its right arm at the *Gladiator.* The Clan 'Mech began a slow turn toward the new arrivals. In a burst of argent energy, the *Highlander*'s underslung Gauss rifle sent a silver ball sizzling out.

The *Gladiator*'s head came around just as the ball hit it in the right cheek. Fractured armor cascaded down from the 'Mech's face, reducing it to a skeletal death's-head. The cockpit viewports shattered and blew out, then the ball tore an exit wound out through the back of the head.

The *Gladiator* waved for a second, then toppled forward. It slowly rotated as it fell and landed on its head. The 'Mech's heavy bulk crushed the head and shoulders when it slammed into the ground. Even if the pilot had miraculously survived the Gauss rifle shot, the fall would have killed him.

Somehow the Precentor Martial knew the troops under his command understood the significance of that one 'Mech's death. With a soulless abandon he would have expected from

Clan troops, the remnants of Alpha Battalion charged forward and hit the Clan flank. Their attack clearly shocked the Clans and began to throw them into disarray.

Yet as quickly as his emotions spiked to a high, they shot back down again as he saw the silhouettes of the Wolf Spiders coming through the valley. Just as he began to designate the Black Widow's 'Mech with a computer label, his video feed went to static and continued to fill his world with gray as the computer sought, in vain, to cure his blindness.

=== 41 ===

Kai, clad only in MechWarrior shorts like the other Elementals wore, stood very still as Slane eyeballed him and made a minor adjustment to the armored suit. Taman and Locke grinned at him. Erik and Hilda watched the whole proceeding with keen interest, while Michaels appeared to be bored with the whole ritual. Deirdre stood behind the Mahlers and used them as a shield.

Part of Kai wanted to reassure her as he had done the night before. Somehow, though, vanquishing phantoms was not so simple in the harsh glare of reality as it was in the afterglow of intimacy. He gave her a smile, which she forced herself to mirror bravely.

Taman dragged the lower half of the Elemental armor over to him as Kai pulled himself up on the side of the hovertruck. He scraped the grass and dirt from his feet, then pointed his toes and lowered himself into the armored trousers. The lining, a shiny black fabric, felt warm against his legs. His feet pressed down into the split-toed boots and encountered a bit stiffer resistance there.

"All in?"

Kai nodded at Taman. "The leg adjustments are perfect. I don't have that binding feeling at my left knee like yesterday. Waist pressure collar, clear." While making this announcement, he pressed down on a latch that loosened a band of metal running around the rim of the suit.

"Correct."

Locke and Slane next slotted the armor suit's arms through either half of the chest piece. Locke approached first and let Kai slip his left arm into its metal sleeve. At the end, Kai felt a glove with a thumb and two finger slots. Slipping two fingers each into their parts, he felt a tightness at the first joint around all three glove parts. By moving his fingers and thumb, he saw the triple claw on the end of that arm move.

That brought a grin to his face. "Claw operational."

"Check." Taman looked up from where he was inspecting the fit of the left chestpiece into the waist collar. "Kai, review firing procedure for the machine gun."

The MechWarrior nodded. "When the weapon has been armed, I point at the target with my index and middle fingers. Once I have a target lock or when I want to fire, I make a fist with my thumb hooked under my last two fingers. Same thing goes for the laser in my right arm."

Kai worked through the instructions as he spoke them. The obvious wisdom of the system made him smile. Simply pointing at the target automatically swung the weapons into line, and point-shooting was a technique that had been used for eons to teach infantrymen how to aim without thinking. The unnatural hand position made accidental discharges extremely rare.

Slane let Kai put his arm down into the right sleeve, then worked to hook the two halves of the torso armor together at the overlapping seam in the back. The metal halves of the torso armor rose up to cover his shoulders and even gave him a high collar that protected everything up to the tips of his ears. The same black fabric pressed in on his chest, and the suit reminded him of the various diving outfits he'd worn from time to time.

Kai looked up at Taman. "I'm glad to have you here to help me put this armor on. It must be difficult to get equipped during an emergency or if you are alone."

Malthus shook his head. "Normally the chest assembly is already together and just lowered onto the waist. If really pressed and very tired, an Elemental can lay the whole thing out on the ground and wriggle down into it. We are only helping to ensure a good fit. How does it feel?"

Kai thought for a second, then nodded. "Great. Best fit yet. It doesn't feel as bulky as earlier in the week."

Locke approached with the head and chest piece, but Deirdre split the Mahlers and laid her hand on Locke's forearm. "Give me just a minute?"

Malthus nodded and Kai stiff-legged a half-turn away from the others. "What do you think?"

Her blue eyes flicked down. "I think you have the flesh to match your heart of steel."

Her somber tone caught him by surprise. "Deirdre, I have no heart of steel when it comes to you. I love you."

She nodded, then reached out and ran her hand over the part of his chest the armor left exposed. "I know you do, and I love you. I also know . . ." Her voice failed her.

"What?" He started to take her in his arms, but his metal limbs moved with a mechanical blockiness that frightened them both. "What?"

Deirdre forced a smile onto her lips and wiped away the lone tear from her cheek. "I know you are the finest warrior on this planet. I know you will not die." She stood on her tiptoes and gave him a kiss, then turned and walked away.

Kai reached out after her, then shuddered as the metal claws on his left arm ripped through his image of her. Hilda Mahler put her arm around Deirdre's shoulders and led her away into the house. Meanwhile, Erik approached bearing the headpiece for Kai's armor.

"Women never like to see their men go off to war, *ja*?"

Kai nodded. "Any suggestions for me in that department?"

"Understand it. Expect anger mixed with joy and relief when you return." Erik lifted the head and chest assembly and Kai bowed forward. "She is a strong woman, Herr Allard, and you need each other. Be careful that your strengths do not destroy one another."

"Thank you."

As the last piece of armor fitted down into place, the waist collar snapped back into position, tightening down to seal the suit. Kai heard a low hum as the black fabric slowly pressed itself solidly against his body. While the interior of the suit molded into a warm, snug fit, the underside of the boots became more solid and resized themselves to accommodate his smaller feet.

Then a holographic display materialized between Kai's

face and the V-shaped viewport. Besides the normal 360-degree view of the world truncated into 160 degrees, he saw twin lines of boxes running above and below the display. As he glanced at the one labeled IR, it flashed for a second, then the holographic display shifted to infrared mode. He looked at vislight to bring it back to normal, then glanced at the box labeled Taccom.

"Suit checks, all systems go," he reported. "This voice-operated radio is good, but don't you have trouble with folks chattering nervously?"

Malthus frowned at him. "If a warrior were given to such a habit, he would be removed from the unit. Elementals are not given to idle chatter."

"Right. Sorry about that." Kai smiled and saw Malthus' expression ease.

The suit, Kai knew, was a marvel of technology the like of which the Inner Sphere had never seen. In the suit he could lift approximately 500 kilograms on a normal one-gravity world. The claw could generate 30 ksc of pressure, more than enough to strip armor off a 'Mech and a good ten times that required to shatter bone. His running speed increased marginally despite the added weight, and his ability to jump was doubled in terms of distance. He knew the suit also had jump jets, but Malthus had disabled them because Kai had not had time to train in their use.

Locke snapped his own helmet on. "Kai, remember that once your arm your weapons, you may fire them at will using the hand position you mentioned earlier. You can disarm your weapons through the glance system, but the machine gun is always live while you remain in a suit whose weapons are armed."

"Just in case I run into something I did not expect?"

"Correct. If your armor is breached or if you are injured, the suit will initiate drug therapy to combat shock and to kill the pain. The suit itself will seal the wound and start a distress signal that will enable us to home in on you. That homing signal is different than the one keyed by the Initiate Alert box on your display. The latter is only for use in emergencies."

Kai smiled and started moving the limbs around to reacquaint himself with their feel. With power to the suit, they moved smoothly and fluidly. He started walking toward where the other Elementals camouflaged in green and gray were climbing into the back of the hovercraft. He drew close enough to see Malthus' eyes sparkling through his viewport.

"Thank you, Taman, for this honor."

The Elemental rested his claw on Kai's shoulder. "Now you know what it feels like to be a real warrior. Let us go rescue our friends and give our enemies no quarter."

The joy of driving a hovertruck, Gus Michaels maintained, was that its being an air-cushion vehicle meant they did not have to travel over conventional roads. Almost from the start, Kai noticed that their chauffeur seemed to take perverse delight in sailing the hovertruck over the most rutty terrain, but he marveled at the suit's ability to absorb the shocks that rattled the truck and sent the cable coils resting on the Gauss rifle flying.

Whereas Dove Costoso was north and inland from Mar Negro and the Mahler homestead, Valigia lay along the coast 400 kilometers to the west. Had Taman not forbidden it, Kai believed Michaels would have opted for a skate across the Mar Negro and entry into the city through the port sector. Though the hovertruck could easily have skimmed the waves, the possible loss of the Gauss rifle in case of a fan failure forced them to travel overland.

Conventional wisdom had put Valigia four hours distant, but their truck made it in just over three. They cruised into the city unchallenged and unchecked. Michaels, paying strict attention to the traffic laws, drove the hovertruck through the whitewashed brick city with a minimum of delay.

He nosed the truck into an alley across from the front gate of the ComStar fortress. "ComStar central, as ordered." Michaels looked back through the open window into the cargo area. "Shall I leave the meter running?"

"You stay put!" Malthus commanded him. "Team, arm your weapons."

Kai glanced at the Arm Weapons box. The holographic display melted down into an outline of his armor suit. He glanced at the left arm and brought the machine gun online. As he activated the small laser that capped the right arm, he thought about his father and the weapon built into his left arm. *I hope I do as well with this as you did with yours, Father.*

He smiled as that old feeling of self-doubt failed to materialize. "Armed and ready, Star Captain."

"Deploy."

Kai hopped out of the truck and took up a position at its aft end. He scanned the top of the ComStar fortress walls, but saw no one atop the massively thick pile of stone blocks. The guardhouses at the corners of the walls looked idle. Overhead, thick power cables ran from the street over the wall and into the compound just above the eight-meter-high iron doors blocking the arched gateway. A huge broadcasting tower stood in the middle of the compound, and a red light slowly blinked on and off at its apex.

Locke left the truck, playing out the two cables as he went, working his way out toward the street and the massive power poles running its entire length. Slane lowered the hovertruck's back gate, then helped Taman slide a steel I-beam out from beside the Gauss rifle. Kai didn't like to think of the damage being done to the Gauss rifle's bore as the I-beam was muzzle-loaded.

"Weapon ready."

Taman laid his laser on top of the Gauss rifle and used the armor's weapon to paint the target for him. Using his claw, he shoved it a bit to the right. "Target aligned. Status?"

Kai checked the walls again. "Clear."

Locke unlimbered the grappling hook connected to the first cable. Holding it in his claw, he sent it sailing upward to where it hooked over the top cable. As with most cables running high above the ground, that one was uninsulated. Picking up the second grappling hook, Locke sent it flying upward, too.

Accelerated to a blurring speed an instant before the cables connecting the gun to the powerline melted away, the steel shaft slammed into the iron doors. It hit the tall doors just above their middle, ripping them from their hinges. The larger pieces cartwheeled through the courtyard and embedded themselves in the main building, while the smaller bits of shrapnel ricocheted around and shredded the half-dozen Acolytes caught in the open.

Kai and Locke sprinted across the street, hurdling skidding cars. As they burst into the courtyard, Kai saw some Com Guards pouring out of a building to his left. He brought the machine gun up, then pointed and triggered a line of fire running from left to right. Bodies flew back in a bloody haze, but Kai did not pause to consider the ease with which those men had died.

I have a mission and I am not going to sabotage it!

As they had discussed on the way in, Locke hit the doorway to the holding cell area first. Kai saw his machine gun flash, then Locke pulled back and let Kai go forward. Ignoring the red droplets streaming down the wall, he kicked in the door to the gallery of cells. When his holographic display showed Locke turn to hold the doorway, he strode into the fortress's dungeon.

A Com Guard popped around a corner and blazed away at him with an autorifle. Kai felt the impacts as the bullets washed over his armor like a gentle mist. Without conscious thought, Kai pointed at his enemy and the machine gun blew the man's heart out through his spine.

Reaching the first of several steel doors, Kai reached out and fitted his claws around the lock. Punching his thumb up between his middle and ring fingers as they curled down, he scythed the claw through the lock mechanism and tore it from the door. A solid kick from his right foot sent the door in to crash against the wall. The six Elementals in the room stood abruptly.

Activating his external speaker with a glance, he said, "Let's go. You're free."

One of them, a dark-haired Elemental with blackened eyes, hesitated. "Who are you?"

"Does it matter? Star Captain Malthus sent me." Kai pulled back out of that cell, then proceeded to kick in the other doors. "Go, go!"

Reaching the end of the line of cells, he sprinted up the stone steps at the far end and burst through the doorway into the main building itself. As he had expected, he found himself across the hall from the Com Guards' armory. One trooper turned and tried to fire his SRM launcher, but a stream of slugs from the machine gun ended that threat.

Kai pointed the freed Elementals to the armory. "Arm yourselves. We have to pacify this facility."

Seeing the flash of explosions in the courtyard, Kai sprinted forward and smashed his way into a room looking out. A Rotunda armored car had arrived at the fortress from somewhere in the city and stood in the shadow of the entryway. The SRM launchers, set just below the vehicle's headlights, sent two missiles spiraling into the place where Locke had been standing. Their resulting explosions scattered mortar and stone over the courtyard, but Kai heard nothing over the radio from Locke to indicate his condition.

The Rotunda started forward, intent on trapping Malthus and Slane at their positions deeper in the courtyard. Just as it began to make its turn to bring its weapons to bear, the hovertruck shot through the gateway and tagged it in the left hindquarter. The Rotunda slewed around as the hovertruck tipped up on its side and began a tumbling roll.

Kai vaulted himself through the window and dashed into the courtyard. The Rotunda began moving forward again, so Kai leaped at it. He landed belly-first on the roof and began to slide over the top, but his claw caught and held. Pulling himself back around to the right, he punched his laser down through the windscreen. Tightening his hand into a fist, he filled the cockpit with fire.

From the top of the main building, an SRM lanced down and hit the hovertruck's exposed belly. It exploded and tore the vehicle in half. Kai spun off the burning Rotunda and started to track the Com Guard, but the lasers from Slane and Malthus met at the target and turned the man into a torch.

Two of the freed Elementals ran out along the top of the fortress wall. One pointed toward the street. "More vehicles and troops, Star Captain!"

"Star Captain, clear the wall!" Kai shouted. He hunched down at the back of the Rotunda and started to push the wheeled vehicle forward. As it picked up speed and headed back toward the gateway, Kai gave it a final shove, then stood to the right and lased a chunk out of the right front tire. The vehicle swerved into the gateway, then began to bump its way out into the street.

The lead ComStar vehicle hit the sloped nose on the Rotunda and vaulted up into the air. The light Gabriel hovercraft soared high enough that the rear air rudders clipped the top of the gateway and imparted a slow backward spin to the hovercraft. It came down just on the other side of the burning hovertruck, landing on its tail, then flopped back on its turret and spun into the compound garage.

The hovertruck following the Gabriel likewise hit the Rotunda moving fast, but failed to clear it. Fans screamed and disintegrated as the truck came down on top of the armored car. Then the short-range missiles still remaining in the Rotunda's magazines exploded in a staccato series of flashes.

Bodies of the troops in the truck flew everywhere, then the top of the gate collapsed and buried the burning mess.

An unarmored Elemental appeared in the doorway of the compound's main building. "Facility secure, Star Captain. We have their hyperpulse generator and it is still in operational condition. We are also getting local radio that indicates an armored infantry battalion is on its way. ETA one-half hour. We also have reports that their garage has six full suits of our armor and a *Daishi*."

Malthus pointed toward the garage. "Get another Star suited up and have someone join my Star. I would have liked to have bid more than two Elemental Stars against a battalion of armored infantry, but this will have to do."

Kai turned to face him. "Did your man say they'd found a *Daishi* in the garage?"

The man in the doorway nodded. "Operational and fully armed, but stripped of code modules. We're lucky no one got to it and brought it into this fight."

"Star Captain, how would you feel about adding a *Daishi* to your bid of two Elemental Stars?"

Malthus' armor bowed to him. "Somehow I am not surprised you know how to use one of our OmniMechs."

Kai smiled. "I used a *Daishi* to kill those five 'Mechs during my testing."

The Elemental pointed toward the garage. "Go, then, and claim your 'Mech. It is time ComStar learns how truly bad an idea it was for them to launch Operation Scorpion."

=== 42 ===

"**I**f this was done in accordance with Blake's Will, then Jerome Blake is as much of a monster as Amaris the Usurper." Striding like a titan through the mountain passes of the Pozoristu Range, Focht's invisible feet could not land without falling upon a burned-out tank or shattered 'Mech. Some fires still guttered in the blackened bodies of broken war machines. In other places live munitions still exploded without warning even though the battling had ended.

All around, Clan footsoldiers helped to herd the scattered Com Guards toward the exchange center. Wounded soldiers helped yet more grievously wounded men and women limp or drag themselves across the uneven terrain. The Elementals who had been so fierce in battle now stooped to help their wounded enemies, silently acknowledging their fellow warriors valiant even in defeat.

Also silent were the bodies lying everywhere, rain-soaked, partially clothed, stiff in death. Everywhere he looked, the Precentor Martial saw the dead. He desperately wanted the computer to make him too tall to see the pale, bloated corpses or the pools of blood, but somehow he knew he could not escape them.

They are here, they are all over this planet. How different we are from the Clans in customs and manners, yet how alike in death and injury. He relived the pain of losing his right eye to a gunshot decades before. *As much as these Clansmen hold themselves apart from us, and as much as we do not want to claim them, we are all of us so pitifully human.*

He rubbed at one temple to ease away the pain. *I should have seen this coming. I should have known better—about this and about Scorpion.*

A window opened on the face of a mountain and Focht saw Hettig's haggard face. "The ilKhan has established communication. He is waiting to be linked in."

The Precentor Martial had the computer swath him in rough, undyed woolen clothing and black leather boots. A black eye patch covered his missing right eye. He let the computer etch the fatigue lines on his face, then sighed at the realization that he *did* feel as exhausted as his image showed him to be.

"I believe, Mr. Hettig, that I am ready for you to patch the ilKhan through to me." He paused for a second, then added, "Once you have done this, you are relieved of duty. Get some sleep."

Ulric materialized across from him, still clad in cooling vest and MechWarrior shorts. A bloodied rag hung from his right bicep and his legs looked badly sunburned. Ulric, projected into the Precentor Martial's virtual world from his holotank, looked just as tired.

"Hail to you, ilKhan of the Clans. Your people fought valiantly." Focht hoped the sincerity in his voice came through despite the computer processing. "I appreciate your willingness to meet with me in this way."

"And hail to you, victor of Tukayyid." Ulric bowed his head solemnly. "I would have hoped to meet with you face to face, but I agree that this method is more suitable for what we have to accomplish."

Focht smiled wryly and shook his head. "How strange it is that you call me the victor when, in fact, all that has happened here was your doing. You knew exactly what would happen, when and probably where. The Clans lost because you wanted them to lose."

The ilKhan stiffened, then clasped his hands at the small of his back. He slowly began to pace, moving to avoid the fallen hulk of a *Mad Cat.* "There are two errors in what you have said. The first is that I would be guilty of treason had

I done what you accuse, and treason is punishable by death. As I do not desire death, I would not do that. What happened is that you discovered a way to defeat us. You found our weakness, and you exploited it. You knew our war doctrine was not suited to long battles, and saw our supply problems would doom us."

"No, Ulric, I did not discover that strategy." Focht opened his hand and took in the war-torn landscape with the gesture. "Victor Davion and Theodore Kurita both saw that the Clans were geared toward swift and decisive warfare. They knew that forcing you into an extended campaign would give you trouble."

Ulric let a low chuckle rumble from his throat. "You're not half as blind as you would make me think. You saw the greatest flaw in the Clans. Our bidding does promote brilliance and audacity, but it also *minimizes* losses. We cauterize our wounds before they happen. If a commander is defeated, it is because he failed in his strategy or failed in his bidding. The troops who lose are not shamed, but rehabilitated so they can be used again. We reward victory with genetic longevity, but insulate ourselves from the sheer, grinding brutality of war."

He stabbed a finger at the hideous tableau surrounding them. "Never, since the time Nicholas Kerensky formed the Clans, have we faced such a crushing defeat. Your troops forced half of the Smoke Jaguars from the field in three days! The rest of them were forced off the planet by the tenth day, but only because their leaders were too stupid to know they were beaten. Not only are they not accustomed to fighting that long, but they never lose that quickly. The Sixth Jaguar Dragoons have been shattered and the Jaguar Grenadiers have more ghosts in the ranks than living warriors."

"Yet I note, ilKhan, that the Smoke Jaguars and the Wolves are political enemies. I know well there is no love lost between the two Clans, and I cannot but wonder if you did not force a Smoke Jaguar Khan to woefully underbid by challenging him to do so."

Ulric's blue eyes glittered like chips of ice. "That is a question that cannot be answered, as both Smoke Jaguar Khans died in the Dinju Mountains."

"Or is it a question you will not answer?" Focht slowly

circled the ilKhan. "I watched the fighting in the Pozoristu Mountains closely."

"Then you saw Khan Garth Radick fall."

"Yes, and I saw Khan Natasha Kerensky and ilKhan Ulric Kerensky have their way with all that I threw at them. You knew I had prepared for long battles, so you, too, created stockpiles of munitions and supplies. You put your troops on a strict ration of ammunition and had the majority of your OmniMechs configured with energy weapons. You crushed the units I sent to destroy your supply centers, then hunted down and exterminated the units I had in the mountains.

"In this one battle that was directly between you and me, you beat me."

Ulric scratched at his goatee. "Perhaps that is so, Precentor Martial, but the Pozoristu Mountains were not the world. On the Przeno Plain, the Jade Falcons moved twenty kilometers from their landing sites—and that only because of the Falcon Guards—then became bogged down in a stalemate. They went no further, and had you committed a reserve unit to them, you would have driven them back. By the second week, the Diamond Sharks were ousted from the Kozice Valley. The Ghost Bears held Spanac at the end, but had lost Luk and most of the Seventh Bear Guards. The Nova Cats held the Losije district for all of five days, but lost at Joje and Tost, and eventually were dislodged by your Com Guards. You forced the Steel Vipers from Hladno Springs on day thirteen.

"Even if we count the Ghost Bears' victory at Spanac and consider Przeno a draw, you have won the battle for Tukayyid. You have won our bargain. The Clans will press no further toward Terra than this world for the next fifteen years."

Focht shook his head. "Would I sound like a hopeless romantic if I said I did not think even fifteen hundred years would be worth this cost?"

"You would sound to me like a general who has accurately assessed the consequences of war, and one who greatly values his troops." Ulric wiped sweat from his forehead with his hand. "I have seen the casualty reports for my troops. My deaths are running at 20 percent, with an overall casualty rate of 35 percent and equipment damage of 62.3 percent—half of that being suitable for salvage. And I know my people got off lightly."

Focht turned on him. "Your people got off lightly? Are you not the ilKhan? Do you not lead *all* the Clans?"

The ilKhan slowly shook his head. "As this battle would prematurely decide the end of our quest, our crusade, it was determined that control of the individual operations would fall to the Clan Khans. Though I was permitted to review all data coming up from the planet, I was not obliged to distribute it unless asked. As no one saw fit to request my thoughts, I was free to act to the benefit of my Clan."

So, they forced you to act on your own and you let them twist in the wind. "Had you led them, coordinated them, you would have defeated me."

"You are the victor, Anastasius. You need not flatter the vanquished. Through what you have done, through the death and the misery, you have shown my fellow Khans what I could not. Had I led them and been defeated, I would have been taken down—I might yet be—because the failure would have been mine." Ulric again looked around the valley at the grayish bodies covering the hillsides. "Now they must understand what their crusade has caused and they must accept responsibility for it."

"Yours is not an easy lot, Ulric. You lead a people who are bred for war. They will not take defeat lightly."

"I think my lot is easier than yours, Anastasius. At least the attacks on me will come in the open. We may play at politics in the Clans, but we resolve the conflicts like warriors." Ulric looked straight into Focht's good eye. "Do not second-guess your victory, Precentor Martial. Operation Scorpion, while an annoyance, did not detract from our operations here."

Focht sighed heavily. "I give you my word, had I known, I would have warned you."

"I know that." Ulric let a tired smile expose his teeth. "I have one more request of you, *quiaff?*"

"Aff," the Precentor Martial nodded. "Ask."

"In three days there is to be a Bloodname battle for the right to claim Cyrilla Ward's name. I would like to hold it here, on Tukayyid. Phelan Wolf will fight with Vlad for that honor. Allowing them to stay on the planet will let them rest up for the final fight."

"By all means. Is there anything you need to prepare for it?"

Ulric shook his head. "I think not. However, Phelan has

petitioned the ilKhan for permission to invite you." He smiled more broadly. "The ilKhan has graciously consented."

Focht bowed his head to the ilKhan. "Please tell Phelan I am honored by his invitation, but I will be unable to attend. Within the hour, I leave Tukayyid."

"Within the hour?" Ulric's eyes sparkled. "The Primus is obviously very pleased with your performance here."

"I fear this is so, my friend." Focht folded his arms across his chest. "Primus Myndo Waterly has summoned me home. For me, she says, she has a reward."

=== 43 ===

The terrible calm settling over him intrigued and frightened Phelan Kell Wolf. Clad in a gray jumpsuit showing a red dagger-star patch on his right shoulder and the Thirteenth Wolf Guards red and black spider patch on his left, he held his head high, as any warrior had the right to do. Almost arrogantly, he hooked his left thumb through the gunbelt looped over his left shoulder and refused to care that others thought his wearing a gun in the cockpit was stupid. He was a Wolf and their Clan had not tasted defeat at the hands of the Com Guards. His unit, in particular, with Natasha Kerensky at its head, had purposely destroyed every Com Guard unit thrown at it.

The weight of the silver coin in his right hand marked the importance of what it represented. When his opponent arrived, he and Vlad would both place their coins in the gravity funnel device standing at his right hand. The coins would spin and spin around, racing each other down to the clear collection tube. The coin on top would determine who had the choice of weaponry, and to the loser would go the choice of venue.

Phelan had already engaged in this ritual four times. He had met and defeated four other warriors from the House of Ward. He had killed only one, and he regretted that the Elemental had given him no other choice. Though part of him was weary of fighting after the war with ComStar, he held himself proudly. *I will not be defeated.*

Standing there in the middle of a show ring in an agrocomplex whose owner bred and trained horses as a hobby, Phelan could feel the tension in the crowd slowly filling the building to the edge of the central circle of light. They had come to see the final battle in the Bloodname contest for the name of Cyrilla Ward. That name had a nearly sacred reputation, and the finalists were known to hate each other. If the crowd was lucky, the two MechWarriors would decide to fight it out with bare hands, right there in the center of the ring.

Above him circular screens filled with an image of the center ring. The camera slowly zoomed in on him, then the image cut to two men approaching from the north end of the building. As they broke through the crowd, Phelan instantly recognized them both and a spark of anxiety flashed in his chest. Vlad *had* to be present for the Decision of the coins, but the other man was not the individual he had hoped to have overseeing it.

Conal Ward removed his arm from around Vlad's shoulders and mounted the wooden dais before the two MechWarriors. Tall, dark-haired, and handsome, he exuded confidence and majesty. "I am the Oathmaster and accept responsibility for representing House Ward here. Do you concur in this?"

So this is the reason for Conal's presence here. For the final test, he, the Clan Loremaster, will represent his own house. "Seyla." Out of respect for the office, Phelan bowed appropriately, then straightened and watched his enemy.

The bright spotlight burned silver highlights into Vlad's slicked-back hair. The MechWarrior, as he bowed his head to Conal, adjusted his belt and let Phelan see the buckle. A black hound's-head, its eyes were filled with malachite. "Seyla," Vlad breathed solemnly.

Phelan forced down his anger. He had become a bondsman in the Wolf Clan when Vlad defeated and captured him. Vlad had taken that belt buckle from him and used it as a symbol to remind Phelan of his inferiority. As much as Phelan wanted it back—because of what it represented and because it had been made for him by a lover who had died fighting the Clans—Phelan refused to let Vlad know he had gotten to him.

He saw Vlad studying him for a reaction. *You want to play little games, Vlad. Here, interpret this.* Phelan kept his face blank, but raised his left hand, and as if scratching an itch, traced a line from above his left eye down to his jaw.

Vlad jolted as if hit with lighting. The line Phelan had drawn mirrored the scar on Vlad's face. Seeing Vlad's cheeks flush, Phelan knew the man was dying inside because the scar reminded him that he owed his life to Phelan. He had been weak and Phelan had saved him. *It is a shame he believes can only be expunged by killing me.*

Conal looked from one man to the other. "What transpires here will bind us all until we all shall fall. You are the best the House of Ward has to offer. This is impressive because, unlike other Houses and other Clans, House Ward lost no Bloodnamed warriors in the fighting here on Tukayyid, and covered itself with glory instead. That you have come this far means you will forever be remembered, but only one of you will win a Bloodname here today.

"In accepting your part in this battle, do you understand that you sanctify, with your blood, Nicholas Kerensky's determination to forge the Clans into the pinnacle of human development? Do you understand that being chosen to participate marks you as elite, but victory here will rightly place you among the few who have existed at the zenith of all the Clans hold sacred?"

"Seyla."

The Loremaster smiled easily. "You are Vlad and you have seen twenty-four years. Why are you worthy?"

Vlad's head came up and he played to the crowd through the viewscreens. "I have consistently tested out in the top 2 percent of my sibko. As a result of my actions against the Nova Cats, I was chosen as a Star Commander for the scouting expedition that brought us again into the Inner Sphere. In my first engagement, I killed a number of pirates and mercenaries. Without appreciable effort on my part, I likewise captured this Warrior standing before me."

Vlad paused to let that comment sink in, then continued. "In the invasion of the Inner Sphere, I have participated in every assault mounted by the Wolves. On Rasalhague, I personally killed four of their feared Drakøns. In the most recent fighting on Tukayyid, my Star did not give back one millimeter of the terrain we took. Prior to the battle today, I killed two MechWarriors and an Elemental for the right to participate here."

Conal turned to Phelan. "You are Phelan Wolf and have seen twenty-one years. Why are you worthy?"

Phelan swallowed to clear his throat, then began reciting his history. "I was chosen by Cyrilla Ward to be heir to this Bloodname. I was adopted into the Warrior Caste after proving my worthiness through service as a bondsman. I trained and tested out as a Warrior. Singlehandedly I conquered Gunzburg, and on Satalice I captured Prince Ragnar of Rasalhague. On Hyperion I led the defense of the Simmons Dam and hunted renegades in the badlands. On Diosd I participated in the coursing and the killing of the Third Freeman's Command Lance. Prior to the battle today, I defeated two Elementals, a flyer, and a MechWarrior for the right to participate here."

The Loremaster started to speak, but Phelan cut him off. "And, as a bondsman, I rescued my opponent from certain death at the battle of Radstadt."

Faux pas it might have been to make that statement, but the flush of crimson on Vlad's face made it worth risking censure. Conal looked at Phelan as if he wished to strike him dead with a word, and Vlad's nostrils flared with fury. Vlad hooked his thumbs in his belt again, but Phelan refused to take the bait and never broke off his stare into the other man's eyes.

Conal Ward extended his hands toward both men. "The heroism and courage you both have displayed has been established and verified. Your claims are not without substance. No matter what ensues and what fate you meet in this battle, the brightness of your light will not be diminished. Present the tokens of your legitimate right to participate here."

Phelan snapped his medallion between thumb and forefinger, then held it out to Conal. The Loremaster accepted it and placed it in a slot within the gravity funnel. He did the same with Vlad's coin. "When one coin has successfully stalked the other and they complete their transit through this cone, the hunting coin will be superior. That Warrior will be given the choice of style for the fight. The owner of the inferior coin will then decide the venue for the fight. In this way each will fight on a battlefield not wholly of his choosing. Let the coins choose among equals."

"Seyla," Vlad and Phelan intoned as one.

Conal pressed the release button and the gold coins started their spiral downward. Phelan watched his coin like an eagle. He felt fairly certain, before sight of them slipped below the lip of the funnel, that his coin was lagging behind. *Yes, I will win the decision!*

Phelan had considered over and over what his choice would be if he won. He knew Vlad would choose to fight augmented because that gave him the best chance of killing Phelan. In their two previous 'Mech fights, Vlad had won the first by pitting an OmniMech against Phelan's *Wolfhound.* That granted Vlad a gross advantage in that fight, and Phelan admitted that, in the second, having Natasha Kerensky on his side had given him a gross advantage.

While content to fight in 'Mechs, and expecting it if Vlad won, Phelan wanted to fight his rival bare-handed. *No good getting rid of a hate in an impersonal manner.* Moreover Phelan knew a fist-fight would be less likely to result in death. Though he was willing to kill to win this Bloodname, he took no small pride in having killed only once during the whole contest.

Phelan's confidence spiked as the only clink of metal on metal he heard came when the coins landed in the clear cup at the bottom of the funnel tube. Conal slid the collection cup from the stand and held it in his left hand. Instead of plucking the top coin from the stack, Conal flipped the cup over and dumped both coins into his right palm. Vlad, meanwhile, doubled over with a hideous cough. Conal's thumb pushed the top coin up against his forefinger, while the coin that had lost the race remained hidden in his palm.

Phelan's jaw dropped open. *He cheated. He flipped the coins to reverse the results!* Outrage filled him, but as he started to protest, something deep down stopped him. *Why protest? Fair or unfair, you can beat Vlad. You can beat all of them. They are* just *of the Clans, but you are the best of two peoples.*

"Vlad, you are the hunter."

Vlad casually reached up and unzipped his jumpsuit to reveal the cooling vest he wore beneath it. "Phelan Kell has claimed, since the first, to be a MechWarrior. Though he has shown some facility in this area, his greatest victories have come outside a 'Mech. Now I will give him the chance to prove his prowess against a *real* MechWarrior. I will hunt augmented."

Phelan wanted to laugh at Vlad's attempt to intimidate him. He aped Vlad's action and showed the cooling vest he had also worn beneath his jumpsuit. "Not desired, but not unanticipated or dreaded." He let his confidence bring a smile to his face.

Conal's brown eyes narrowed to hide his surprise. "Phelan, the style has been decided. Where will you be hunted?"

"The fields here are flat, so the terrain allows for no tricks, no illusions." Phelan looked toward the east. "Five minutes should be long enough for them to set up the cameras. Here, now."

"Here, now." Vlad smiled cruelly. "You are too weak to defeat me, Phelan. I have killed *all* my foes in the Bloodright and I will kill you, too."

"Do the best you can, Vlad. I might not have killed any of the others on purpose, but in your case it is a job I will savor."

Conal raised his hands. "To your machines, then. Let the true Warrior win!"

Phelan turned on his heel and stalked away toward the south. As he walked into the crowd, he saw the twin doors at the far end of the hall opening. As they slid back slowly, shafts of sunlight shot into the show barn like laser bolts. Phelan squinted at first against the sun, but when the opening door revealed the silhouette of his *Wolfhound,* he grinned in delight.

Natasha appeared at his left shoulder and accepted his gunbelt. "You saw what happened?"

Phelan shrugged. "Does it matter? A fistfight, a 'Mech battle, it's all the same." He glanced back over his shoulder. "Vlad is mine. Cyrilla's name is mine."

The Black Widow smiled happily and slapped him on the back. "Spoken like the Wolf Cyrilla knew you would become."

"No, Natasha, not that." He turned and met her gaze. "Spoken like the Wolf that you and Cyrilla and Ulric wanted me to become. Tukayyid has shown the Clans that the warriors of the Inner Sphere can defeat them. Now it is up to me to show them that despite their exile, despite their training and their breeding programs, the Inner Sphere is not so far distant that one of us cannot become one of the best of them."

He paused at the foot of his *Wolfhound* and stripped off his jumpsuit. He took the gunbelt back from Natasha and fastened it around his waist. He bent over to tie the holster to his right thigh, and when he straightened up, saw Ranna had replaced her grandmother by his side.

Ranna reached out and hugged him tightly. "You are the best of the House of Ward. When you come back, we will celebrate your victory."

Phelan held her close and covered her mouth with his. He clung to her for what seemed like forever as their bodies pressed one to another, then broke off the embrace. "Ranna, I know you and Vlad were in the same sibko. I cannot promise you he will live through this fight."

"He knows the danger he faces." Ranna's head rose to a regal height and her blue eyes flashed. "You, Phelan Wolf, are the man I love. You will do what must be done. If he dies, I will mourn because of the loss to the Clan. If you die, I will mourn because of the loss to me. You are the rightful heir to Cyrilla Ward's name. Go, answer to your heritage and reap your legacy."

Phelan gave her one last kiss, then climbed up the *Wolfhound*'s leg, stepped onto the left arm, and up to the 'Mech's left shoulder. He slipped into the cockpit through the hatch on the BattleMech's neck, then brought down the bar to secure it and pressurize the cabin. He pushed up on a large switch above the hatch and felt the fusion engine rumble to life in the 'Mech's heart. All around him, buttons, displays, and monitors flickered to life, filling the cabin with muted color.

Take it easy, Phelan. By the numbers. Do it right. He twisted his gunbelt around and seated it correctly. *No matter how stupid or useless, make it like every other time.*

Locking that switch into place, he turned and dropped to one knee at the cabinet behind the command couch. He opened it and pulled out four medical sensor patches. He peeled the backing from the adhesive, and stuck one each on his upper arms and thighs. He also pulled out the cables that went to them and clipped the rounded end to the sensor lead on the patches. He threaded the red cables up through the loops on his cooling vest so their plugs hung down at his throat.

Going around the far side of the cabinet, he squeezed past the command console and dropped into the command couch. He took the cable assembly from the pouch on the right hip of his cooling vest and plugged it into the command couch. Instantly the vest started circulating the coolant through the tubes trapped between the kevlar outer layer and the goretex inner layer next to his flesh. Goose bumps rose on his arms as the vest chilled him, but he knew combat would heat things up quickly enough.

"Vlad's probably packing Inferno rounds, so relish the cold while you have it."

After snapping the restraining belts across his chest and waist, and checking them twice, he reached up and behind his head. From a niche above the command couch, he pulled down his neurohelmet. He settled it over his head and onto the vest's padded shoulders. He twisted it a bit to center the wedge-shaped viewport and to get the neurosensors pressed against the right areas of his skull, then used velcro tabs to fasten it in place. He cinched the chin strap up firmly, then poked the medical sensor plugs into the sockets at the helmet's throat.

He hit a button on the right side of the command console. "Pattern check: Star Commander Phelan Kell Wolf."

The helmet's speakers faithfully reported the computer's monotone voice. "Voiceprint pattern match obtained. Proceed with initiation sequence."

Each 'Mech, to prevent unauthorized use, checked for a voiceprint match against the pilots permitted to use it. Because it was possible to counterfeit such a thing, each pilot programmed in his own check phrase. Because it had to be something he would remember, and because it would be something he would utter before going into battle, a pilot chose something meaningful to him. Impossible to guess, the code let each MechWarrior personalize his war machine and keep it safe.

Phelan slowly exhaled. "Check code: A Warrior shrinks not from duty, but neither does he revel in death."

"Authorization confirmed, Star Commander. Full control is now yours."

The holographic tactical display materialized before him and, one by one, his weapon systems came online, then went through a series of diagnostics. The trio of forward medium pulse lasers in the torso checked out with no problems. A

minor glitch seemed to exist with the recycling control on
the extended-range large laser in the right arm, but the computer smoothed things out in an instant. The extended-range
medium laser that fired into the rear arc had no problems,
and the electronic countermeasures equipment rimming the
Wolfhound's upstanding ears appeared to be in perfect working order.

Phelan knew Vlad would be given a 'Mech similar to his
in armor and weaponry, so he was not surprised when he
saw an *Adder* walking away from the north side of the building. The OmniMech had a wider assortment of weapons
available to it because of the modular system that allowed
weapons to be swapped in and out. Phelan's computer
painted a diagram of an *Adder* on his auxiliary monitor and
cycled through the standard weapon packages to pick out the
one with the highest probability for that 'Mech.

The computer determined Vlad would go with a package
that would maximize damage in close. That meant that he
would find a pair of Streak SRM launchers beneath the birdlike 'Mech's flaring shoulder shielding. The 'Mech's left
arm carried a large laser similar to the one in the *Wolfhound*'s right arm. The autocannon in the *Adder*'s left arm
was not terribly powerful, but in a battle between light
'Mechs, it could prove very effective. Similarly, its chest-
mounted flamer could also prove damaging at close range.

Conal's voice crackled through Phelan's speakers. "You
have your battlefield. Skill, Warriors. Let the battle com-
mence!"

Neither 'Mech moved for a full second after Conal gave
the signal to fight. Then Phelan dropped his crosshairs on
the *Adder*'s compact outline and triggered his weapons. His
large laser slashed armor on the Omni's left leg into steaming ribbons of ferroceramics. His pulse lasers punctured armor on the *Adder*'s left arm, right flank, and the center of
his chest.

As Phelan hit a button on his command console, the holographic display switched over to infrared and painted a
white-hot dot in the center of the Omni's chest. *Yes, that got
through and hit some engine shielding! He'll be running hot.*

Vlad's return shots at the longer range betrayed a weakness of his 'Mech's configuration. The *Adder*'s large laser
struck back at the *Wolfhound*'s own left leg and sent armor
shards flying on vapor jets. The autocannon blasted away

sheets of armor on *Grinner*'s right leg, but Phelan successfully fought against the impact and kept his 'Mech upright.

As his computer updated a visual of his *Wolfhound* and showed him the damage to its armor, he started it off in a loping run toward the northwest. That exposed more of his right side to Vlad, but also started to close the range between them. *He won't expect this. I'm playing into his hands, and he'll get cocky.*

Vlad turned his Omni to keep Phelan square in his sights, but Phelan noticed the *Adder* moved a bit awkwardly. *Could the shot to the chest have damaged the gyro, too?* The sensors in the neurohelmet enabled the computer to use the pilot's own sense of balance to regulate the gyros, but if one of those had taken damage, the *Adder* was in serious trouble. *If I got that lucky with one shot, it must be divine retribution for Conal's cheat.*

Despite his 'Mech's movement, Phelan tracked the *Adder* with his crosshairs as if they were painted on it. His thumb pressed down and sent the large laser's scarlet beam scything through what little armor remained on the right side of the *Adder*'s chest. Another flash of heat told Phelan he'd nailed a heat sink, but more important, he saw bits and pieces of the Omni's internal structure spray out into the fields behind the 'Mech.

One of the pulse lasers mounted in the *Wolfhound*'s torso stitched a line of burning holes across the *Adder*'s head. The other two combined to complete the ravaging of the *Adder*'s left arm. Having evaporated the last of the armor, they went to work on the myomer muscles and endo-steel bones. They melted the artificial tissue away and heated the metal to the boiling point. Glowing white hot, the *Adder*'s left arm dropped to the ground.

Yet even as Phelan triggered his weapons, Vlad fired his. The large laser mounted in the left arm fused the armor on the *Wolfhound*'s right arm before the weapon melted away. The little that remained smoked as the rest ran off like water to drip onto the ground. The right-arm autocannon peppered holes in the *Wolfhound*'s left-flank armor, and the one of two SRM flights that hit shattered the armor around the central chest-mounted pulse laser.

The missile impacts and the autocannon shells shook the *Wolfhound* and rattled Phelan's teeth. He wrestled the light 'Mech upright and kept it closing as the *Adder* stumbled.

Unbalanced by the loss of its arm, the other 'Mech tipped to the left and started to go down. Vlad wrenched the torso up and to the right in an attempt to keep the machine on its feet, but the weakened structure in its chest screamed and started to warp.

The *Adder* sprawled forward and hit hard on its chin. The 'Mech bounced once and the viewport blew out to litter the ground with glittering glass fragments. Its feet clawed futilely at the ground, but only managed to gouge up great clods of dirt and grain as the soft earth refused to hold. Cranked straight back by the fall, the 'Mech's right arm could not get enough play to come forward and help lever the machine up, though Phelan doubted the *Adder*'s torso could have supported the effort anyway.

He stopped his *Wolfhound* twenty meters off and watched as Vlad's feet sought the edge of the *Adder*'s viewport. Like a drunk stumbling from a bar after some hard drinking, Vlad stepped from the cockpit, then started to fall back and caught himself on the viewport frame. He took one step forward, then tumbled down the dirt pile and sprawled prone on the ground.

Phelan flipped open his external speakers. "It is over, Vlad."

Vlad pushed himself into a sitting position and pulled off his neurohelmet. "Freebirth!"

With deliberate precision, Phelan slid the *Wolfhound*'s right arm over and pointed the laser's muzzle at Vlad. "Freebirth?" He shivered. "I have just blown you out of your OmniMech. You cannot believe that curse hurts me, *quineg*?"

Vlad stood and threw his helmet at Phelan. It glanced off the *Wolfhound*'s muzzle and made a mild thump in the cockpit. "You are a freebirth, Phelan. Foundling. You will never be my equal."

"That does it." Phelan hit his restraining belt release switch. He brought the *Wolfhound* down on one knee and planted its left hand on the ground. "I'm coming out there to settle this once and for all. We have fought in 'Mechs three times and I have won twice. We have split the two fistfights we have had. Time to decide that, too."

He removed his neurohelmet and dropped it on the command couch. He reopened the hatch and started to walk down *Grinner*'s left arm. At the elbow, he paused and shook his head. "You are a fool, Vlad."

The other MechWarrior shucked off his cooling vest. "And you are a brave man because you have a gun."

Phelan smiled. "Couldn't expect you to forget about that, could I?" He untied the holster, unbuckled the belt, and tossed the whole thing to the ground. He leaped from the 'Mech and pulled off his own vest. "This has been a long time coming."

Though he knew better than to underestimate Vlad, Phelan could not help but smile as they closed. Vlad hooked a right into Phelan's stomach, but that left Vlad open to a roundhouse left that snapped his head back. Phelan moved in quickly and drove a murderous jab into Vlad's midsection. That doubled the scarred man over, and another left to the side of his head dropped him to the ground.

Phelan danced back. "Freebirth, eh? You had it right when you said I would never be your equal. I would never stoop so low!"

A feral scream of rage burst from Vlad's throat as he scrambled up and rushed at Phelan. The younger Mech-Warrior drifted right as Vlad came in, and smiled as Vlad's blind charge took no notice of his shift. *A jab and it's all over.*

Phelan cocked his right hand, then dropped his jaw with surprise as Vlad veered away from him. He thought Vlad had gone utterly insane, when his foe tucked his arms in and sprinted back toward the *Wolfhound*. *He's going for the gun.*

Vlad launched himself through the air and pounced on the gunbelt. Rolling through the dust, he clutched it to his dust-caked chest. He fumbled with the holster flap for a second, then drew the pistol and eared back the hammer. Brandishing it triumphantly, he stood slowly.

"Yes, Phelan, freebirth!" Vlad laughed mockingly. "I told you, Phelan, you were too *weak* to win this contest. You were a bondsman, made so when I captured you. I took this belt buckle as a trophy because the ilKhan robbed me of you! You have never been my equal, and here and now it has been proven!"

"Only one thing has been proven here, Vlad," Phelan spat out, "and that is how unbelievably stupid you really are." Shaking his head, he started walking toward Vlad.

Homicidal fire in his eyes, Vlad's finger tightened down on the trigger.

The pistol went click.

Phelan smiled. "Remember how supplies got a bit shy here on Tukayyid, Vlad? I gave all my side-arm ammo to Evantha."

"No!" Vlad shrieked. He ran at Phelan, brandishing the pistol like a club.

Phelan ducked the ill-aimed swipe, then brought his right first up and through the point of Vlad's jaw. The punch lifted the scarfaced man from his feet and his eyes rolled up into his head. When he hit the ground again, he collapsed like all his bones had been removed.

Phelan knelt beside his foe and pried the pistol from his fingers. "Just as well I am out of bullets. I might be tempted to waste one." Reaching over, he undid Vlad's belt and slid it off. He slung it over his right shoulder and stood. As he started to back away, Vlad's groggy voice stopped him.

"You are a Warrior. Kill me."

"You do not get it, *quiaff*?" Phelan looked down at him and shook his head. "I am more than a Warrior. Maybe you will understand what that means by the time you win your Bloodname."

= 44 =

Unity Palace, Imperial City, Luthien
Pesht Military District, Draconis Combine
30 May 3052

The brand-new silken robe Shin Yodama had been given made him uncomfortable. He knew it was not really the fault of the garment, which had been faultlessly prepared by Imperial tailors at the express command of the Coordinator, Takashi Kurita. The black *hakama* felt cool and whisper-soft against his legs after the pressure suit Shin had worn for a speedy trip down to Luthien from the jump point they had used to enter the system. The green kimono with its black trim also felt good against his skin, but the crest embroidered in red silk against black on the breasts, sleeves, and back reminded him of nothing so much as a highly stylized form of the Dragon's Claws crest.

The obi sash holding the robe closed was so finely embroidered that to consider it anything less than a work of art would be blasphemy. The stitching was in gold thread and, like the tattoo on his left arm and the left side of his torso, seemed at first to be patterned after a boiling black cloud highlighted in gold. Seen up close, however, the pattern revealed trigrams and other symbols reflecting Shin's adventures in service to House Kurita.

He knelt self-consciously on a pink *tatami* mat at the left of the firepit in the center of the tea house. The location of the mat placed him far closer to the table in the middle of the tea house than he had any right to be. Though he took pride in his service to the Lords of the Draconis Combine, he had no illusions about himself. As Takashi Kurita had made quite clear during the battle for Luthien, Shin was nothing more than a yakuza. Had Theodore Kurita not enlisted the aid of bandits like him during his difficulties with his father, the chances of Shin's ever having made it to Luthien would have been nil.

Kneeling there, alone in a tea house in the center of the gardens at the center of the palace in the center of the Imperial City, Shin knew his luck had far exceeded itself. From earning a commission in the military and being able to survive the first Clan assault to being able to defend Luthien and organize a rescue for Hohiro, Shin had gone places and done things that he had never dared even dream. Yet, for all that, he recalled the oyabun of the *Kuroi Kiri* assuring him that his fate was unbound by normal convention.

To Shin's right, the western *shoji* panel slid back. Theodore Kurita bowed toward the table in the center of the room, then again to Shin. Shin returned the bow, letting his forehead press against the edge of his mat. Straightening up, he saw Omi follow her father into the small building, then Hohiro came last. Both of the younger Kuritas exchanged bows with Shin and their father, then took their places in the room. Theodore and Hohiro, as was correct, occupied the red mats yet closer to the table than Shin's mat. Omi took up a position behind the three of them on a white mat.

Hohiro looked as ragged as Shin felt. The dark circles under Hohiro's eyes marked his lack of sleep, but Shin noticed more color in his skin and the flash of a blue drug patch on the inside of his left wrist. Clothed in a kimono identical to Shin's, Hohiro managed to kneel correctly despite his fatigue and weakness.

Being trapped on Teniente had not been good for Hohiro, but he *had* survived, and had *made* most of his people survive. Shin had no doubt that the songs and poems and paintings depicting what was already becoming known as the Covert Exile would stress the endurance and bravery of the Prince over any other details. Shin had no quarrel with that, but having so close a vantage point to the creation of a legend awed him somewhat.

By slightly turning his head to the left, Shin saw Omi, resplendent in a robe of white silk with red trim and crimson and gold embroidery. It took him a moment, but he recognized the robe as the one she had worn in the last holodisk recorded for Victor Davion—the one that had brought the Revenants to save her bother. Observing the way she had correctly arranged her robe against the mat, he knew that the symbolism inherent in her choice of attire, as with everything else in the tea house, had been engineered to produce a certain effect.

What that effect was, he could not guess, and he was beginning to dread discovering what it was.

Shin saw a shadow kneel at the *shoji* panel to the north, across the table. The panel slid back like a whisper. On his knees, Takashi Kurita entered the room. He bowed to those assembled and they returned the courtesy. Wordlessly, the old man closed the panel behind himself, then moved to the red *tatami* mat set only twenty centimeters from the northern edge of the table.

Takashi's *kimono* of black silk with green trim instantly struck Shin as being the opposite of the garment he and Hohiro wore. The yakuza looked more closely and saw that the crests embroidered in black silk thread on red background *appeared* to be the same as the ones on his own robe, except in reverse colors. Even so, the design, when done in black on red, looked like the Dragon crest of the Draconis Combine.

From just out of sight at the far edge of the table, Takashi produced five matching cerulean bowls. He set them in a line on the table, but Shin noticed it did not parallel the edge of the table. Furthermore, the third was placed a hair closer to the edge than its fellows, breaking the flow of the line.

From the steady, purposeful nature of the Coordinator's motions, Shin realized this seeming esthetic error was deliberate. Aware only that a *cha-no-yu* was a ceremony with strict formalities to be observed, he realized that rigid adherence to formality could drain the ritual of individual significance. By breaking an esthetic pattern, the Coordinator called attention to esthetics and formality, reinforcing the importance of the ritual.

The Coordinator sank an ancient bamboo ladle into a water urn hidden within the tea house's firepit. He let it sit in the urn for a moment or two longer than necessary, then pulled it out. Producing a water bowl, he slowly dribbled the water down into it, turning the bowl so the water could wash away any dirt clinging to the sides.

As Takashi dumped the water out into the firepit and re-filled it with five full ladles, Shin took a good look at the vessel. Old and battered, it looked to have been pounded out of BattleMech armor. *Wasn't there a legend about Takashi making a water urn from the armor of his first 'Mech? Is this the urn?*

Takashi set the water to boil on the charcoal urn nestled down in the firepit. As if by magic, a puff of smoke rose toward the hole in the roof and the scent of fir trees filled the small room. That familiar and pleasing aroma brought a smile to Shin's face, and he saw his happiness reflected in the Coordinator's blue eyes.

"Komban wa," the Coordinator greeted them.

"Komban wa," his visitors replied.

"You honor me with your presence here this night." The old man's eyes tightened around the corners. "Sixty-four years ago today, I first laid eyes on my beloved Jasmine." He lifted a tea chest from his side of the table and placed it to complete the line of the bowls. "This is the very tea chest from which I was served that night, and it is the chest from which I will serve you this night."

Takashi glanced at the water, then back at his audience. "It is well that I serve you for it is the least I can do to repay what all of you have done for the Combine. More important, though, it reminds an old man that only through serving can one become worthy of being served."

The trail of steam rising from the water thickened enough to satisfy Takashi. He dipped the ladle into the boiling water and let a ribbon of steam trail out as he brought it to the first bowl. He filled that bowl to the brim, then dipped a small portion of the water from it and let that splash into the other bowls in succession. The ladle then returned four more times to the urn and each of the bowls was filled. The last of the water in the ladle went into the first bowl, completing the circuit.

Opening the tea chest with his left hand, Takashi drew some tea leaves from it with a bamboo spoon and sprinkled them into the second bowl. With the bamboo whisk in his right hand, he deftly stirred the leaves into the darkening water. Withdrawing the whisk, he gave the bowl a quarter-turn to the right and set it in front of his son.

"Theodore, you have persevered where others would have given up or revolted. You fought against me because your eyes could see through the fog shrouding the future of the Combine. Your vision preserved us and it preserved our home here. It also forced you to make a decision concerning the safety of your son that the gods should not demand of anyone."

Takashi prepared the third cup of tea in a similar manner and placed it before his grandson. "Hohiro, you accepted the mantle of leadership and endured great hardships for the sake of your nation. You have not shrunk from your duty, nor have you lacked for compassion. The survival of so many of your people on Teniente is because you took the time to care for and about them. You have earned what your blood will thrust upon you in time."

Shin heard the rasp and crackle of the spoon digging into the tea as Takashi scooped up the leaves for the fourth bowl. This one he worked over as diligently as the first two, then placed it between the others and a bit forward of them for Omi. "You, granddaughter, have shown a resourcefulness and clarity of purpose at which I both marvel and envy. In a House that has known internal strife in the past, your devotion to your brother promises a solid foundation for the future. Your willingness to sacrifice to rescue Hohiro is an example that I would use to chasten anyone who cries out at the hardships the war has thrust upon them, if I felt those persons were worthy of such noble direction."

As the Coordinator swirled the whisk through the fifth cup, Shin felt his own innards begin to whirl. He bowed his head as Takashi placed the cup before him and then kept his eyes lowered so he would not stare like an ill-mannered lout.

"And you, Shin Yodama, what am I to say about you? You are a bandit, a yakuza who has dared become a Mech-Warrior—a role reserved for those steeped in the ways of *bushido*. There are those who still maintain my son's recruitment of your people is an offense to the Dragon and that I should have slain you all to purify our forces.

"And yet again and again you have risked your life for my grandson, my son, and even myself. You, who claim no noble blood, no formal education, have proven more worthy to be entrusted with the fate of the Combine than any ten nobles or twenty courtiers. Were you not a criminal, I would induct you into the Order of the Dragon for all you have done."

The Order of the Dragon! I would be a Knight of the

Realm. Shin almost looked up to see if Takashi were sincere, but the phrase *were you not a criminal* stopped him. *He is correct. Tradition would never allow a* yakuza *to be given so high an honor. Just being served tea by the Coordinator is great enough reward for me.*

"No, Shin Yodama, it is not possible. Yet I *will* reward you. This is why you and my grandson wear the same robes, for you are to assume the leadership of my personal bodyguard unit, the Dragon's Claws. In honor of your exploits, however, we will rename them the Izanagi Warriors."

Shin stared blankly at the steaming bowl of green tea. Izanagi, he knew, was a legendary warrior who traveled to Hell, then fought his way back out again. *It cannot be denied that Hohiro and I have faced many foes and have returned from a living hell time and again.* He glanced at Hohiro and was pleased to see his friend grinning.

Takashi tugged his kimono straight at the waist and stirred his own bowl of tea. "I know that each of you would like to protest that what you have done would not have been possible without the help of this Victor Davion and his people. My tailors have prepared for each one a similar set of robes and I will endow a fund providing educational grants for all their children, to be administered by the Davion court and overseen from Luthien by a member of our family. I would think it an excellent experience for one who will someday become the Keeper of the House Honor."

Behind him Omi bowed in acceptance.

"I salute you, for you are heroes all." Takashi lifted his bowl and the others followed his lead. "Let us five who have done all we could to hold the Combine together drink as one. Let this ceremony mark our resolve to meld our efforts and rededicate ourselves to serving and preserving our nation for all time."

45

Anastasius Focht, Precentor Martial and Victor of Tukay-yid, stood in the central courtyard of the First Circuit Compound and stared at the monument raised to his victory. The black marble obelisk towered over him and the sunlight glittered from the gold leaf that had been applied to the words carved into its base. Choking down the lump in his throat, he spoke the words to see if they sounded better than they read.

"Aware of the threat the Clans presented to the dreams of our Blessed Order, Anastasius Focht and his Com Guards—by order of Primus Myndo Waterly—met and defeated the invaders in the first three weeks of May 3052. In stopping the Clans, he facilitated the rebirth of our Blessed Order and its acceptance of the role Jerome Blake envisioned when he founded ComStar."

Focht studied the words again in silence, then shook his head. Despite his dispatches to the Primus, she obviously had no concept of the death and destruction Tukayyid saw. To her, the battle with the Clans was a tree from which monuments could be plucked. She saw it as a beginning for ComStar, not as the end of so many lives. *She must be made to see reality!*

The Precentor Martial tugged at the clasp of his white cloak and let it fall from his shoulders. Beneath it he wore the olive jumpsuit he had been given six months earlier by the 82nd Division of the Second Army when he inducted a new group of MechWarriors into their organization. In the heavy pouch on his left hip was a book with the names of each of the 82nd Division's warriors who died fighting Natasha Kerensky's Wolf Spiders. As he pressed his hand against the book, he also felt the pistol hidden in the pouch. *She must be made to see!*

Following the pointing shadow of the obelisk, he walked across the granite-paved courtyard to the Hall of History for his appointed meeting with the Primus. Waiting for him in the rotunda were she and her aide, Sharilar Mori, clad in robes of gold and red, respectively. He stopped and saluted smartly, only continuing forward as the Primus clapped her hands appreciatively.

"You have, of course, seen the monument?"

"Yes, Primus. It is impressive."

"I am glad it pleases you." Myndo smiled and brushed her long white hair back from one shoulder. "In the twenty years since we formed the Com Guards, we have never had to fight a battle of any seriousness or importance. I cannot tell you that my confidence in you was 100 percent. There were members of the First Circuit who believed sending untried troops against the Clans was sheer folly." She glanced at Sharilar. "Fortunately, we were able to prevail to give you that opportunity."

"Your support was most encouraging, Primus." Focht frowned. "I thought you indicated this meeting was for me to debrief the First Circuit? Where are the others?"

Myndo opened her hands in a gesture of dismissal. "They are really redundant now that a new age for ComStar has dawned. You should be happy, for you are our Light-bringer."

Light-bringer! "Are you saying I am your Lucifer?"

"Prometheus is more appropriate, I believe, Anastasius. You have empowered our enlightening of humanity." She took his right hand in her left and guided him deeper into the building. "You must see this. Our artisans have been working day and night since the victory. This is much better than your computer reality."

She led him through a doorway and he stopped short. The massive gallery that had been devoted to displaying all the relics of Jerome Blake and the early days of ComStar had been stripped to the walls. In their place, countless tables had been erected. Drifting in toward the nearest, he saw mountains and trees in miniature that matched perfectly with the images of battlefields burned into his brain.

Burned-out swaths of ripe wheat and aching holes dotted the tiny landscape. 'Mechs, scaled down to match the area of the world where they stood or had fallen, were twisted and broken, yet each was exact down to the details of paint scheme and pilot's name emblazoned on his 'Mech. Little human figures lay strewn around the miniaturized battlefields as they had on Tukayyid. The artisans had somehow even mixed a paint to match the gray pallor of their flesh.

My God in heaven! "This is Luk." He moved to the table next to it and saw more destruction. "These are the Dinju Mountains, and there, that is the Przeno Plain."

Inexorably, like a moth drawn to a flame, Anastasius Focht moved through the models with the same ease he had crisscrossed the planet in his virtual reality, always working in toward the massive gray display in the center. With each tableau, he recalled hideous details the model-makers could in no way match. Their little worlds did not ring with the moans and screams of the wounded and dying. Their work lacked the cloying stench of rotting corpses or the snarling voices of scavengers coming to feed on the dead. Their artificial worlds did not have the same cold chill that had marked Tukayyid after all the guns had stopped.

At the very center of the room, Focht found the Pozoristu Mountains. Slowly orbiting the table, he followed the line of destruction that marked the Wolf Clans' methodical campaign. He saw the valley where Khan Garth Radick had fallen, but the number of lost Clan 'Mechs looked insignificant compared to the number of Com Guard bodies, tanks, and 'Mechs littering the terrain.

"It's all here, Anastasius, and this is just the beginning." Myndo's dark eyes flashed with an infernal light. "These models only show the aftermath of the battling, but we will recreate each of the fights, second by second. Each battlefield will have its own building, and people will be able to watch the battle unfold as it did on Tukayyid."

Focht could not believe his ears. "Why do that when you have our own and Clan battlerooms to piece together an accurate history?"

She smiled patronizingly and looked at Sharilar. The Kurita woman returned the smile, but Focht saw her shudder as Myndo turned back to him. "Anastasius, the victors write the history. The reality of what happened on Tukayyid is not nearly as important as the symbolic nature of your victory. You have proved ComStar to be the savior of all mankind. We have stopped the barbaric hordes from overrunning the Inner Sphere and extinguishing the light of knowledge. Now the people will look to us for leadership."

Before he could question her interpretation of what had happened, the Primus again took his hand. "Now, you must come see this. Around us is history, but I will show you the future!"

She dragged him to the next gallery and his heart rose into his throat. "Yes, Anastasius, this is the future of ComStar! You are its father and I am its mother."

They studied the room's sunken floor from a catwalk encircling it. The whole room remained dark except for the glowing pinpoints of light Focht recognized as a three-dimensional display of the Inner Sphere's many worlds. The largest light sat in the center and as it pulsed gold, a cone of worlds reaching up and out toward the roof flashed in answer to it. A gold light marked every world the Clans had taken and ComStar had administered.

The worlds of the Draconis Combine were shown in red, but as he watched, a central world in that mix went gold, and with it the rest of them began to change. "Luthien," he breathed quietly. Again, below that, one of the worlds in the blue swath that cut across the sphere went gold. "New Avalon, then Sian and Atreus." Another blue world changed colors and Focht felt his chest tighten. "Tharkad, my Tharkad."

Myndo nodded, the thousands of gold pinpricks reflected in her eyes. "You thought I had forgotten?" She turned and touched one of the darkened panels behind them. "This will be Tharkad under you, Archon Frederick Steiner."

Another miniaturized model appeared, this one protectively warded by a lexan barrier. He had a nagging feeling that he recognized the city represented as the capital, Tharkad City, but strange elements confused him. He allowed himself to be mistaken because it had been more than two decades since he had seen the city, but then he realized it had been warped to conform with the Primus' insane vision of the future.

A colossal statue rose from the center of the Triad,

dwarfing the trio of buildings that marked the center of the city and its government. Clutching an upraised sword, he saw himself clad in the manner of classical Roman statues. His left hand carried a book, and on it he could make out the ComStar insignia and the legend, "The Word of Blake."

Like the rays of the sun, twelve roadways soared over or through the buildings as they focused down to the Triad. On the dozen flagpoles standing over the Triad, he saw fluttering the flag with ComStar's twelve-pointed star. The buildings were painted in the white and gold favored by ComStar officials. The whole city had been made over in ComStar's image.

Suddenly the back wall of the display case opened and the cityscape withdrew as another model descended to replace it. Of a much larger scale, it showed a place he knew well. Two *Griffin* BattleMechs stood in the dark hall. They flanked a throne that sat beneath a ComStar banner with the Steiner armored fist beneath the gold starburst. The 'Mechs were no longer painted the blue and white that would have proclaimed them part of the Tenth Lyran Guards, but had been repainted with the colors of the Com Guards.

Focht stiffened as he saw the figure seated in the throne. Long, lean, with a shock of white hair and a black eye patch over his right eye, it was he who occupied a throne he had not desired since losing his eye. *The only time I have sat in that throne was in a bad dream. Has life become a nightmare from which there is no waking?*

"Yes, Anastasius, as I promised, the throne of the Lyran Commonwealth will be yours. As a ComStar protectorate, it will enjoy all we have to offer." Myndo pressed her hand against the glass. "I reward those in whom I can place my trust."

Focht brought his head up. "I must ask, Primus, how we are to take Tharkad? Your Com Guards are not in any shape for a campaign at this moment."

Myndo clapped her hands. "That is just it, Anastasius. We will not have to fight them. While you dealt with the Clans, we have brought the rest of the Inner Sphere to its knees. I ordered a total Interdiction of all communications and shipping. Though we lost control of some facilities, we will regain it again. The worlds we now administer are loyal to us and others will follow, including Tharkad. Our interdiction is crushing them."

"This is your Operation Scorpion." Focht narrowed his good eye. "I thought you trusted me."

"I did." She thrust a finger back toward the battlefields. "I trusted you to distract and hurt the Clans, but this, this was much too big to place on your shoulders. The Clans have shattered the Inner Sphere and we will rebuild it. You see, I know you very well and I know your desires. Fear not, Tharkad *will be yours.*"

Focht began to laugh then, a low sound that began to build as bewilderment spread over Myndo's face. "You don't know me at all. You judge me by the man I once was. Yes, Frederick Steiner would have welcomed being rewarded with the Steiner throne, but even he would not have stooped so low as to conspire with ComStar to get it. But I am not Frederick Steiner, and I have not been Frederick Steiner for over twenty years."

He smashed his right fist into the lexan between him and his simulacrum. "Anastasius Focht is a name I chose so that it would remind me every day that I am just a warrior. I am not suited to dabbling in politics. I paid a dear price for having done that once and, worse yet, I nearly made my nation pay, too. If you thought you could buy me with a tarnished dream, you never understood me at all."

The Primus started to speak, but he cut her off by stabbing a finger at her. "You had no need to bribe me. I was, body and soul, a creature of ComStar. I fought on Tukayyid because I believed ComStar should devote its resources to stopping the Clans. I did not bargain with the ilKhan just to have my word undermined by *you!*"

"That may well be," the Primus spat back, "but the reality is that my Operation Scorpion has crippled the Successor States. The Inner Sphere has been broken and only we can mend it. It is a pity that you do not want to be part of the solution to this situation because I *could have* used you." She folded her arms across her chest. "I hereby accept your resignation and will see to it that you are turned over to the Clans for whatever justice they care to administer to you for stabbing them in the back!"

Focht laughed again and his lack of fear clearly shocked her. "That will not work, Primus. IlKhan Ulric knows very well that I had nothing to do with Operation Scorpion. Furthermore, that operation has been a joke. It did nothing to the Clans but cause them to put down a few revolts. Retaking those worlds we did succeed in liberating will be a minor diversion of their might, and will likely be left to the forces they have coming in to the Inner Sphere to settle here.

"As for having crippled the Inner Sphere, I think you are mistaken. I was easily able to send an Alpha Priority message to my cousin, Melissa, on New Avalon, and she replied within the hour. It seems that in the Federated Commonwealth our facilities are functioning normally under their control."

"That is not possible!" Myndo leaned against the balcony railing and stared out at her empire of lights. "They are infidels. They cannot know the secrets of hyperpulse generators!"

"Science is not a god. Technology requires neither belief nor ritual, Primus. They discovered how to make them work." Focht drew his needle pistol and pointed it at her. "I am afraid your resignation is, in fact, in order. It is true that someone needs to pick up and mend the pieces of the Inner Sphere, but you are not the one to do it."

She looked from the gun to his face and back again, then turned and faced away from him. "You underestimate me and how much I *do* know about you, Anastasius." Her left hand playing along the railing, she slowly began to walk past Sharilar and away from him. "You are a warrior. You have a code of ethics that binds you and blinds you. It would never permit you to shoot me in the back, which means I can walk away from here and find other warriors with a code of ethics that demands they obey their *superiors.* Your little revolt will end now because the dream must live!"

Focht shook his head. "Lunatic dreams become nightmare reality for the sane." His finger stroked the trigger twice and the Primus sprawled forward.

He swung the gun into line with Sharilar Mori. "And what am I to do with you?"

The oriental woman opened her hands. "I have done nothing that could be considered a capital crime."

"Really? And I had always remembered treason carried with it the supreme penalty." He raised his left eyebrow. "After all, isn't spying for the Draconis Combine treason against ComStar?"

"What? How could you know?"

"I am the Precentor Martial. Security is very much a part of my job and discovering the leaks in ComStar's First Cir-

cuit is an important facet of maintaining my security. I had
to be suspicious of a Combine agent being inside the First
Circuit because of the way my presentation to the Primus by
Theodore Kurita so many years ago pleased her. I was the
answer to her prayers and Theodore certainly got everything
he desired in return for my service to ComStar. The leaking
of information to the Combine concerning the Clans and
their activity, then of Operation Scorpion, said the spy was
highly placed. Melissa confirmed a Combine connection
with the warning about the Clans' return and Scorpion. The
latter pointed to you, for the Primus would have sent the order out through you so she could repudiate the plan if it
failed. You also had to be the one insulating her from full
knowledge of its dismal failure."

Sharilar smiled respectfully. "Your analysis is flawless. I
knew there was a risk, but I had to take it even if it put my
cover in jeopardy."

"As spies have ever done."

"Indeed." She looked down at Myndo's body. "So, will
you shoot me because I have betrayed a dead organization?"

Focht shook his head. "I, too, have a dream for ComStar.
The war with the Clans has convinced me that we must not
waste the resources we have, and the internecine battling between the Successor States has given me some ideas for a
new direction for ComStar. I have a problem, however."

"You are not a politician, nor do you have any desire to
become one."

"I do not have enough *time* left to become one. You, on
the other hand, have negotiated the labyrinth of ComStar
with enough skill to become a member of the First Circuit in
a fairly short time." The Precentor Martial raked the fingers
of his left hand back through his hair. "Have you the skill
necessary to make a dream come true?"

"Would you trust me if I said yes?"

Focht chewed his lower lip for a second, then nodded.
"The fact that you came into ComStar because you or your
masters saw the order as an evil that had to be stopped tells
me you are not married to the pseudo-sacred mythological
foundation for all of this. That you risked your life to actually subvert the perversity the Primus wished to work on the
Successor States indicates you can take action when war-
ranted. If you tell me you want to use all we have to repair
the evil we have wrought, I will trust you."

"Where do we start?"

Focht put the pistol back in the pouch and slipped his arm around Sharilar's shoulders. "The first thing we do, my child, is drive a stake through *her* heart, then bury her in the same grave where we inter the Word of Blake."

46

Valigia
Alyina, Jade Falcon Occupation Zone
10 June 3052

Kai Allard looked up and waved as Erik Mahler honked the horn on the aircar. He handed the metal brush and actuator fitting to the Tech beside him, then wiped his hands on a rag. "I'll be with you in a minute," he shouted through the 'Mech bay's open door as he crossed to the wash basin. He scrubbed off most of the grime, rolled his sleeves down, then donned his jacket.

Heading out, he paused and looked back. Five months of sitting beneath Mar Negro had taken its toll on *Yen-lo-wang,* but it had been cleaning up nicely since they'd salvaged it. Malthus had suggested that its refurbishment become something of a project for the Techs and MechWarriors who had been released from Firebase Tango Zephyr. Those who were able quickly agreed to work on it and the prospect of taking part in the rebuilding had prompted a number of warriors to press their doctors for early release dates from the hospital.

The BattleMech stood tall and proud despite the places where it had lost paint to the scraping off of barnacles. Wires and actuators dangled from the right-arm stump, but the Gauss rifle waiting to replace the one lost when Michaels' hovertruck exploded sat below on a pallet. The viewport canopy likewise lay at the *Centurion*'s feet, and men wandered in and out of the cockpit through it.

"For obvious reasons, I think that is one of the most beautiful sights I have ever seen. It brings back many memories of my service. I can well understand your love for that machine." Mahler stood beside the driver's door. "I have no doubt that Clan children will be frightened into correct behavior with tales of *Yen-lo-wang*."

Kai gave Mahler a smile, then climbed into the passenger seat. As Mahler climbed back in behind the wheel and started the fans going, he handed Kai a slip of paper. "The people manning the ComStar facility got a reply to the message you sent out. A ship coming from Yeguas will arrive at Morges to pick you up in two weeks. The Clans will ship you out in twenty-four hours so you can make the rendezvous."

"What about the people too sick to make jumps?"

Mahler gave him an easy smile. "We will send them out later. Malthus has chosen to expand your arrangement concerning the Firebase Tango Zephyr prisoners to include all Federated Commonwealth military in thanks for your help in pacifying the ComStar units here. They will make regular relays to Morges for as long as it takes to repatriate all of them."

"Twenty-four hours, eh?" Kai glanced down at his hands as Malthus guided the aircar into traffic. "That's not much time."

Mahler kept his eyes on the road. "You have yet to decide what to do about her?"

"No." The MechWarrior sighed heavily. "I love her, but I fear our natures are so contrary that we will rip each other apart."

The older man laughed lightly. "Isn't that the reason they say opposites attract? Is one not drawn to that which is different? Hilda and I fought like cats and dogs when we first met."

Kai shook his head glumly. "There is one thing I have learned in my time on Alyina. It is something I suspected before, and it is something my parents and Victor and others had told me: I am a good warrior."

"You are a *superior* warrior—Star Commander Malthus continually assures me of that."

"I . . ."

Before Kai could contradict him, Mahler fixed him with a steady stare. "He says that had you been made a captive of the Jade Falcons, he would have made you his bondsman only so he could immediately petition for your adoption as a Warrior into the Jade Falcon Clan. The Wolves did that with someone they captured and it is believed to be their intention for Prince Ragnar of Rasalhague. In you, he said, the Jade Falcons would have had a Warrior to put the Wolves' adoptees to shame."

"Malthus is given to exaggeration." Kai felt the heat of a blush on his cheeks. "I know what you are saying has its basis in fact, and that's a lot more than you would ever have heard me admit not too long ago. Deirdre is right in reminding me that I would consider remarkable in another what I consider barely adequate in myself. I am a warrior—therein lie my skills and my drive and my desire. Therein lies my problem."

"What's the problem?" Mahler made a left turn in the aircar and Kai saw the Valigia General Hospital swing into view further down the road. "In my time I saw plenty of troopies fall in love with anyone who was close during a leave. You and Deirdre are different. If there is a problem, I don't see it."

"The problem is that we *do* love each other, but that love was born here on Alyina. Living on the run is a totally artificial situation. How can we know if our love is genuine?"

"It strikes me, Kai, you've shifted the focus of your inquiry. By stating your question in that manner, you have already begun to take refuge in the perception that it isn't genuine." Mahler's voice dropped in tone. "Furthermore that has nothing to do with your being a warrior, does it?"

Kai winced. "You're right. I know what I have to do and I'm going to do it. If we stay together, having to live with what I do and what I am will tear her apart."

"Are you underestimating her emotional strength, my friend?"

"It is possible, but if I am not, I could destroy her." He looked over at Mahler. "I cannot take that risk, for her sake and for mine."

Mahler steered the aircar into the hospital's parking garage. "So what will you do?"

What I've done before. "I will tell her that all of this was a mistake."

The older man laughed. "She is quite strong-willed. She will ignore you."

"I know that." Kai nervously picked at his left thumbnail. "I will take on the tone of a noble talking to a commoner. Lord knows I've been accused of being a snob at times because I tend to be fairly private. Well I can turn around and use that. I'll tell her that I only stayed with her because it wouldn't be proper to leave one of *our* women alone with the Clansfolk around. Now that I can return home, however, this ridiculous liaison will have to end."

Sympathetic pain tightened the flesh at the corners of Mahler's eyes. "You are setting yourself up to be hated."

"It'll give her a focus for her anger and make her think she is better off without me." *Which she probably is.*

"Oh, then be sure to offer her money, too, so she can buy herself something to remember you by."

"In for a bullet, in for a barrage." Kai gave Mahler a sidelong glance. "For someone who is happily married, you seem knowledgeable about how I should do this."

Pulling the aircar into a parking place, the retired MechWarrior shrugged. "As I said, I have had many kids in my commands who got 'engaged' on a Friday night, then looked at being shipped out on a Monday. I learned how to deal with it, *ja?*"

"Yeah." Kai pulled back on the handle and opened the door. "I don't know how long this will take."

Mahler patted him on the shoulder. "I'll wait for you."

Kai nodded and left the vehicle. He walked across a bridge to the hospital proper and entered on the fourth floor. He asked after Deirdre at a nurse's station and was told she was up in pediatrics. Using the stairway to which he had been directed, he took the steps one at a time to delay his confrontation.

Dread welling up in his stomach, he opened the door to the pediatrics floor and immediately saw her down the hallway with her back to him. She had a young child in her arms and rocked it back and forth. He could not hear the words she sang, but the lullaby's melody fell softly on his ears.

Kai, you are mad if you send this woman away. You do *love her, and she loves you. The reconciliation of your differences will make for a very strong partnership. Hell, if your parents could love each other despite being from different backgrounds and from nations at war with each other, how can you fail in a much easier situation?*

As that thought occurred to him, the anxiety building in him drained away. He smiled and started to feel very good. A nurse came from the room near Deirdre and pointed Kai out to her, then accepted the child from her arms. Deirdre brushed the child's dark hair away from its face, then turned and smiled at him.

"The Clans have . . ."

She held up a hand and pointed to another open doorway. "Let's not talk in the hallway. In here."

Kai nodded, a bit puzzled, but entered the room ahead of her. He realized that discussing their departure from the world might be confusing to some folks and he imagined she wanted to avoid upsetting children within earshot. As he turned around, she closed the door, then pointed him toward a chair.

"Kai, we have to talk."

He nodded. "I know. Erik Mahler says we have a ship leaving tomorrow. I can make arrangements for both of us so our gear will get on board without you having to cut back any of your hours here." He pulled up the chair and sat. "When we get to the Commonwealth, I'll get us passage back to New Avalon as fast as possible."

Still standing, she glanced down at the plastityle floor. "Kai, I'm not going with you."

"What?" A fist tightened around his heart. "Not going?"

"I am going to stay here. There is a lot of work to be done. There are a lot of people who can use my help."

"Fine, then I'll stay, too."

"No, Kai, you're leaving!" Her hands balled into fists. "You have to go."

"I don't understand, Deirdre." He started to stand again, but she slid by him and pressed him back down into the chair. He half-turned to watch her. "What's going on here?"

She stared out the window. "It will never work, Kai. We come from different worlds and have different goals."

He stood and slipped up behind her. "It will work, because we will make it work." He started to put his arms around her, but she pushed them away and whirled on him.

"Enough games, Kai. I didn't want to hurt you, but you leave me no choice." She folded her arms across her chest and met his stare unflinchingly. "You're a nice guy and it was wonderful to be with you on the run behind the lines. The Mahlers certainly couldn't defend me, and I wouldn't have wanted them to be hurt for harboring me. Just my luck that you had to be the first soldier to come along. You're not half bad as a lover, either, but you were just a diversion for me."

Kai felt as if his heart had collapsed into a black hole. *A diversion? Sex for protection? All the things she said were lies?* He staggered back and dropped into his chair. *How could I have been so stupid?*

"You see, Kai, you have a military mindset. You could never begin to understand the sort of complex individual I am. Your occupation would keep you tied down, and I cannot allow myself to be anchored to someone like you. Besides that, I really want someone with more maturity." She shrugged with only a hint of stiffness. "Someday, perhaps, you'll understand."

Stunned, Kai closed his eyes as blood rushed to his face. A lump thickened his throat, but somehow he was devoid of anything but mortification. He felt totally empty. *I must have been insane to think . . .*

He hesitated, then hung his head in resignation. It finally occurred to him that he was hearing her version of the "I will make her hate me" talk he had prepared to deliver. *That means she, too, thinks my being a warrior will tear us to pieces. I've gone and shirked my duty, forcing her to bear the responsibility for this. How could I do that to her?*

Kai opened his eyes and nodded his head. "I hear what you are saying, Doctor, and I understand it all too well." He looked over at her as he slowly regained his feet. "Whatever your motives, I appreciate all you did for me during our time together. You healed me and made me understand many things about myself and the world. For that I will never forget you, and I will labor all my life to make your sacrifices on my behalf worth it."

Deirdre Lear, silhouetted against the window, said nothing, but Kai saw a slight tremble in her shoulders.

"I will inflict myself no longer on you, Doctor." He turned toward the door so he would not have to look at her. "We will never again see each other but I hope, once in a while, you will think of me kindly." He pulled the door open and stepped through it. "For I will certainly think that way of you."

With all the softness and finality of a coffin lid closing, the door slid shut behind him.

47

Clad in gray ceremonial leathers and pinned in place by an overhead spotlight, Phelan held his head high. Standing before him, on a raised dais and similarly lit from above, Ulric wore a black cloak with a mantle of gray wolf fur and a black-enameled wolf mask. On a raised stand between them stood a golden lamp in the shape of a wolf, the wick rising from the middle of its back guttering gently. Phelan knew other members of the Wolf Clan had gathered outside the intersecting light circles, but he could neither see nor hear them.

"Trothkin, seen and unseen, near and far, living and dead, be of brave heart. Another of your number has been blooded." Ulric's hollow voice filled the room, yet failed to echo back from the walls. "Five battles he has fought, defeating a Star of his peers, and he is victorious. We have all witnessed his contest and none may deny the rede of it."

"Seyla," whispered the invisible Warriors surrounding them.

The wolf's head tipped down toward him. "Phelan, you came to us a bondsman but proved your worth in a way that only a Warrior could. We adopted you, a foundling, into the Warrior Caste and you trained hard to pass your Trial of Position. Given combat duty, you succeeded beyond all expectation, capturing the world of Gunzburg by yourself, and bringing to us the Prince of Rasalhague. Even in this last battle, the losing effort on Tukayyid, you and your people won out where so many other Clans failed."

Phelan smiled at the last comment and he heard a nearly imperceptible rustling among the others in the room. Ulric paused long enough to let the image of the other Clans' failure sink in for his audience. *This may be a most solemn ritual, but the ilKhan is not adverse to using it to remind us of the superior things we have done.*

"While all those deeds mark you as special, your taking of a Bloodname exalts you above the mere Warriors with and against whom you have fought. Ten and ten and five are the number who bear the same surname as you do. With it, you become a member of the Clan Council and are eligible for election to even greater office and responsibility.

"Your Bloodname has a particularly proud pedigree. Of the fifteen who have worn it before you, ten became Khans. All were known for their skill and bravery in combat. You, winning the Bloodname just after your twenty-first birthday, have already added to its legend by being the youngest Warrior ever to win a Bloodname."

Phelan glanced down as the image of Cyrilla's face floated before his mind's eye. *"Do not mourn me, Phelan Wolf. Make me proud of you."* *Those were her final words to me. I hope I have succeeded.*

Ulric took one step forward and his right hand came out from beneath his cloak. "Give me your dagger."

Phelan's right hand fell on the ceremonial silver dagger he had been given when adopted into the Warrior Caste. As he drew the knife and presented the wolf's-head pommel to the ilKhan, his left hand rested over the hound's-head belt buckle he had rescued from Vlad.

Ulric accepted the dagger in his right hand, then took hold of Phelan's wrist with his own left hand. He gently caressed the blade across the palm and bore down only slightly at the edge of his hand. The resulting cut stung and immediately welled up with blood.

Phelan closed his hand into a fist and squeezed hard. A drop of blood fell into the lamp's fire and immediately climbed upward as a puff of smoke. The flame flickered and sizzled for a second, then continued burning brightly.

The ilKhan reversed the knife and returned it to Phelan. "You are now and for all time known among the Clans as

Phelan Ward. All are to abide by the rede given here. Thus it shall stand until we all shall fall."

"Thus it shall stand until we all shall fall," echoed the crowd.

The light above Ulric faded to black, leaving Phelan alone in the light. He had expected the room to be empty, as it had been during his adoption ceremony, but as the lights came up, he saw many people seated in the semi-circle of chairs. Immediately he recognized Natasha and Evantha, then saw Conal Ward make his way toward the front of the room. Natasha reluctantly got up and followed him, so Phelan headed back and took up the chair she had abandoned.

Evantha smiled at him. "Welcome, Phelan Ward."

"Thank you, Evantha Fetladral." He jerked his head toward the front of the room where Conal was seated in a chair on the level floor while Ulric—now unmasked—and Natasha both occupied chairs on the dais. "Is this a Clan Council meeting?"

The Elemental nodded solemnly, her red queue rising and falling at the back of her head. "It is indeed. Despite the losses we have taken in the battling, we have a quorum present in the room and"—she pointed at a camera in the corner—"within communication range."

"Why a meeting so fast?"

She smiled. "It may seem swift to you, Phelan, but the meeting has actually been long delayed. We have lost a Khan and we must replace him."

Phelan nodded and looked over at Conal. *That man almost became a Khan during the last election, and he is Loremaster now. He's also the bastard who cheated to give Vlad an advantage in our last fight.* Almost instantly Phelan found himself thinking as Cyrilla would have. "Evantha, what are the chances Conal will win?"

"He has his supporters."

The MechWarrior's green eyes burned with a mischievous light. "How would it affect his candidacy if it were revealed he cheated during my Bloodname contest?"

Evantha's smile broadened. "Natasha said you'd ask that question."

"And?"

"She said to tell you the matter has already been discussed and the punishment more than fits the crime."

Conal Ward stood. "I, the Loremaster of this Conclave, do call it to order."

Natasha uncoiled from her chair and stared Conal back down into his. "As you all know, Garth Radick died in the fighting on Tukayyid. This means we must elect a new Khan because there will be a Grand Council immediately following our election today. This will be a very important meeting because of the bargain the ilKhan struck concerning Tukayyid, so we want to choose one who understands what really happened there. I throw the floor open to nominations."

Phelan leaned over to Evantha. "Look, you did great things on Tukayyid. I'll nominate you, okay?"

She frowned. "You must learn to speak properly, Phelan, if you expect to get anywhere in the Clan Council."

"Does that mean no?"

"That means wait and see what we are up against."

Conal pointed slowly to a man in the back. "I recognize you, Kevin Carson."

A youngish man rose and clasped his hands behind his back. "Fellow Wolves, there is only one obvious choice for Khan. He is a man who, leading the Red Wolves, managed to inflict incredible damage on the Com Guards. His unit proved crucial in the final push that drove the Com Guards from the Pozoristu Mountains. Furthermore, he should already have been made a Khan when Ulric was rightfully elevated to the role of ilKhan. I speak, of course, of our Loremaster, Conal Ward. I hereby place his name in nomination."

As Carson seated himself, he noticed Conal had lost some of the color in his face. *What is going on?*

Natasha leaned forward. "Would you not like to speak to that nomination, Conal?" she asked, her voice rimed with irony.

Conal cleared his throat. "Yes, Khan Natasha, I would." The Mechwarrior stood and nervously folded his hands together. "I am honored by the nomination, but I must decline that honor. I feel it is not my time."

He smiled weakly and glanced at Natasha.

The Black Widow smiled coldly. "And?"

Conal looked stricken. "And while I realize this is a very difficult and critical time for the Wolf Clan, I do not feel I am able to continue in my role as Loremaster. I, ah, hereby tender my resignation, effective immediately."

Natasha's smile grew wider. "And?"

Conal winced. "And I have decided to ask the ilKhan to excuse me from my position in the Red Wolves so I may go out and hunt down bandits."

Natasha nodded slowly. "Is there anything else?"

"Yes, Khan Natasha." Pain writhed across his face like a sidewinder. "I would like to take this opportunity to place in nomination the name of the candidate I, ah, personally believe should be elected as Khan. I throw my full support behind his candidacy. I, ah, nominate Phelan Ward."

Phelan rocked back in his chair as Conal all but collapsed into his seat. *My God, they did make the punishment fit the crime.*

Evantha stood and Conal recognized her. "I would second the nomination of Phelan Ward. How could we deny this honor to the youngest individual ever to win a Bloodname? Who among us, for all of our glorious actions in battle, has taken a world without a single weapon being fired?" She rubbed at her jaw. "And what MechWarrior among you has defeated a single Elemental in hand-to-hand combat?"

Light laughter greeted her question. "As well, who among us knows so intimately the people we have conquered and will yet have to fight? There is no question as to his qualification for this honor, the question is: are we wise enough to see that?"

Evantha sat back down and slapped Phelan's leg with an open hand. "See? Now you have no need to nominate me."

"What Ulric did to Natasha, you have done to me." Phelan shuddered. "And I thought you were a friend."

"I am, Phelan. I am a friend of yours and a friend of Clan Wolf." She looked over at the ilKhan. "I am his instrument, as are you. Ulric has been grooming you for this since you first showed more intelligence than any other captive. He knew, as did many of the rest of us, that having leadership who could understand the Inner Sphere was vital. Natasha returned to us after half a century of living within the Inner Sphere. You, having been born and trained there, bring a different perspective to things. This knowledge, this enlightenment, must be brought to the Grand Council.

"Besides," she smirked, "watching Conal squirm was fun, *quiaff*?"

"Aff." Little by little, bits and pieces of things were beginning to fit together. Ulric had constantly probed and tested him, but Phelan had never been able to see the reason behind it before. He had assumed much of what Ulric put him through was to gain information on the Inner Sphere, but he had also known there had to be something else. If not, why would Phelan's understanding of and acceptance into the Clans have been so important? Even more so, Phelan's adoption into the Warrior Caste and his gaining the respect of the others was a goal that Ulric pushed him toward.

I had assumed that Ulric might have seen me as a younger version of himself. That may have been true, but he wanted me to succeed because he wanted a bridge between the Clans and the Inner Sphere. Prince Ragnar is on a similar track. Ulric, perhaps alone among the Khans, realized that if we did conquer the Inner Sphere, we would then have to rule it.

Natasha pointed to a woman standing over on the right. "Conal, before you go, I believe you should recognize Katya Kerensky."

Conal grimaced and Katya spoke. "I move we close nominations."

"Seconded," announced Natasha. She smiled again at Conal.

The Loremaster stood wearily. "In light of the motion on the floor, we would be electing Phelan Ward to replace Garth Radick. Given the gravity of the meeting he will attend, I, ah, believe, ah, fervently that we should elect him by acclamation."

"I see no objection to that." Natasha stood and started to clap. Conal joined her half-heartedly, then the others in the Clan Council started in. Evantha grabbed Phelan's shoulder and half-hurled him to his feet, then he walked up the aisle and stood beside Natasha. As the applause died, she sat and winked at him. "Say something."

Phelan took a deep breath and willed his heart to stop pounding so loudly. "Words are insufficient to express what I feel at this moment of great honor. As we all know, words are valueless when compared to actions, so I will let my actions in acquitting this vast responsibility show you how grateful I am." He let a wry smile onto his lips and looked out at everyone assembled in the room. "Let me just add that finally I feel as though I am where, freebirth or not, I was born to be. Thank you."

Applause washed over him again and Phelan could not

help smiling broadly. Conal stood and dismissed the meeting with the words, "Thus shall it stand until we all shall fall," and Phelan repeated the words with conviction. *I am really home.*

He turned to Natasha. "Now that you and Ulric have gotten me into this, what am I supposed to do?"

She looked over at Ulric and the ilKhan smiled. "Be yourself."

The Wolf Clan Council filed out of the room and the room underwent a slow transformation. Panels slid up on the bulkheads to reveal monitors evenly spaced around the room. One by one, they flickered to life. In them Phelan saw the head and shoulders of various Clan Khans. The masks they wore—similar to Ulric's during the ceremony, but appropriate to their Clans—obscured their identities.

The doors at the far end of the room opened and twelve individuals marched in. The Khans of the Clans who had participated in the attack on Tukayyid filed into the rows and sat down in silence. Because they also wore masks, Phelan could recognize none of them, but two—one from the Smoke Jaguars and one from the Steel Vipers—walked with limps he put down to injuries from the recent fighting.

Phelan glanced at Natasha and whispered, "Shouldn't we be wearing our masks?"

The Black Widow shook her head. "Slavish adherence to formal ritual is a sign that one has nothing . . ."

" '. . . better to think about.' I know. I remember."

The ilKhan stood. "I convene this Grand Council and I note to you that we are still under the Martial Code handed down by Nicholas Kerensky. We are at war, and we shall conduct our business as befits that circumstance."

A Smoke Jaguar stood. "I would challenge that assertion, ilKhan. Your agreement with Anastasius Focht prevents us from continuing our invasion. Yet, while it prevents us from pressing forward, his ComStar forces strike behind our lines. You have not bargained well for us, and we must remove you from office so your agreement with him can be repudiated."

The ilKhan's smile sent a chill through Phelan. "You claim we are no longer at war, then use the fact that we are under attack as justification for what you demand. You have failed to convince me we are at peace."

The Smoke Jaguar nodded slowly. "I accept that judgement reluctantly, but I will not contest it. The matter at hand is most grave, ilKhan. I place before the Grand Council a motion that you have failed to carry out our wishes in striking your deal with Anastasius Focht. You bargained in good faith with a man who is treacherous—as the aforementioned attacks on us show. I say you should be stripped of your office and the agreement with Focht destroyed."

A Nova Cat rose to second the motion and Ulric accepted it with an expressionless face. "The motion is then for my removal and the repudiation of the agreement with Anastasius Focht? Very well, this is what shall be debated. Because we are under the Martial Code, we shall only allow one speaker for and one speaker against the motion."

With his right hand, he motioned toward the standing Smoke Jaguar. "You, Lincoln Osis, will speak for your motion." His left hand swung wide and pointed at Phelan. "And you, Phelan Ward, will speak against it."

The ilKhan half-turned back toward his seat, then straightened around again. "By the way, Lincoln, it may interest you to know that Focht has reported that the Primus who initiated the strikes behind our lines has been retired. As I am certain you know from the few worlds your Clan has occupied, all ComStar resistance has stopped."

What am I going to say? He looked at Natasha, but she just shook her head.

"Be yourself, Phelan. Listen to what Osis offers, then destroy it."

Be myself. He nodded and watched Osis move to the center of the room.

The Elemental opened his arms to encompass all but Clan Wolf members. "Trothkin, we have seen that this agreement only benefits the Wolf Clan. Because ilKhan Ulric has carefully engineered a line across which we will not go for three generations, he will remain IlKhan until he dies, resigns, or is forced out. In this manner, he has assured his dominance over us in a way that Nicholas Kerensky never intended when he created the office of ilKhan."

Osis balled his left hand into a fist and brought it back in toward his shoulder. "Ulric and the Wolf Clan have consistently violated the spirit of our agreement concerning the conquest of the Inner Sphere. In accepting the right to negotiate a battle with Focht, he prevented any of the rest of us from consulting with him or offering advice on the agreement. We are now all bound by a pact that we had no part in creating. Furthermore, Ulric did not act as ilKhan in the assault on Tukayyid. He failed to coordinate our actions, and because of that, our effort to conquer the world was for naught."

The Elemental turned to face Ulric. "Your distaste for this invasion is well known. Your negotiation of this deal with Focht served your goal of stopping the invasion, not our goal of reestablishing the Star League. As war leader, you have brought us peace, and that peace is useless to us. I should not have to call for a vote to remove you, I should only have to listen to you tender your resignation. As you will not do so, I do call for a vote.

"We must strip you of command and press forward to our original goal. That is the will of the Clans. That is the destiny we must fulfill and we shall not let you or your agreement stand in our way."

Osis returned to his seat and Ulric looked at Phelan. The young MechWarrior wished he could read the man's face to learn what he was thinking, know how he would handle things, but he could not. Phelan tugged at his belt and touched the cool metal of the buckle. *Be yourself.*

"Trothkin," he said almost skittishly as the word nearly stuck in his throat, "I do not have the benefit of knowing what arguments and discussions were offered when the Clans began to move into the Inner Sphere. I was, as you know, captured in one of the first engagements in the Periphery. Because of that, I can only speak to what I have seen of the Clans and what I know of the ilKhan."

Phelan saw a smile slowly spread across Natasha's face and he took heart in it. "You, Lincoln Osis, accused the ilKhan of doing all this for the benefit of his Clan, and you said his reluctance to engage in this crusade was well known. How is it then that the Wolf Clan, whose invasion corridor contained more worlds than any other, has progressed so far and so fast? Are ilKhan Ulric's actions those of a timid, avaricious, or reluctant leader? Clearly they are not."

Phelan narrowed his eyes as he studied the Clan totems placed before him. "The ilKhan has seen what you have not. You all dreamed of an Inner Sphere torn by war and utterly unable to withstand your onslaught. True, their level of technology is not as high as yours, but it approaches it swiftly.

At the end of the first year of your invasions, you had made great headway, but the Inner Sphere had already learned tactics that put you at a disadvantage. At Wolcott, the Draconis Combine beat you at your own bidding game. One member of your own Bloodname House died because he so poorly negotiated that battle. And again at Twycross we tasted defeat."

He clasped his hands at the small of his back. "In the time it took us to elect Ulric ilKhan, the Inner Sphere came together. They trained together and exchanged information. They learned from each other and new technology began to be shared between their ruling Houses. We managed, with a few exceptions, to unite people who had not worked together since before our ancestors left the Inner Sphere. And, yes, we learned, too, during our time away and shifted our tactics, but they beat us."

He pointed at Osis and the other Smoke Jaguar Khan. "You lost a battle for Luthien. The Jade Falcons failed in their attempt to capture Victor Davion. We did take worlds, but these crucial victories eluded us.

"We have dismissed these losses and have blamed them on circumstance. At Twycross, for example, Kai Allard-Liao tricked the Jade Falcons into a trap. On Luthien you met the Wolf Dragoons and the Kell Hounds, in addition to the best the Draconis Combine had to offer. Again on Alyina, Kai Allard spoiled the trap we laid for Victor Davion. Then Allard eluded us for four months and finally ended up freeing *our* people so that they could liberate the planet from ComStar. And Victor Davion led an elite unit to Teniente to free Hohiro Kurita—who we did not even know we had trapped!"

Phelan felt his heart begin to pound again, but it was no longer from nervousness. Suddenly he saw what Ulric had always wanted from him. *I am a fusion between the Clans and the Inner Sphere. I know, I understand, what Ulric could only ever hope was true.* He nodded his head, then slammed his fist into his left palm.

"Special people, you say. Special circumstances, you sputter. I disagree with every cell in my body! Yes, Kai is special, and so is Victor and so are the Dragoons and the Hounds and the Genyosha, but they are *not* unique. There are countless special people in the Successor States. The Com Guards, before they fought us at Tukayyid, were untried forces. The Wolf Dragoons you faced are all orphans adopted at the end of the last war or freeborn offspring of those Wolf Clan members who originally ventured out into the Successor States.

"Look at me. In the Successor States, the only thing remarkable about me was my family and my hardheadedness. Granted the latter has been of help in the Clans, but had I completed the course of study at the Nagelring, I would have been just another MechWarrior—probably not even a Leftenant. Yet here I stand among you, the leaders of the Clans, having commanded a Star and having won a Bloodname."

He pointed back at the ilKhan. "This is the truth the ilKhan has seen. Three hundred years of breeding has not made us all that different from each other. Were we to proceed, it would be the battle of a knife against a grindstone. Yes, we would get sharper, we would win great victories, but in the end, we would be ground away to nothing.

"The ilKhan's agreement with Focht buys us the time we need to prepare ourselves for the future. This invasion will never again know the lightning victories it did at the start. As ComStar showed us, our tactics are not suited to a long, drawn-out conflict. You did not prepare for that and you lost. The Wolf Clan did prepare for that and we won."

Phelan pulled his head up. "The world-by-world conquest and administration of the Successor States will be nothing if not long and drawn-out. In the fifteen short years the ilKhan has bought us, we can prepare the bases we need to continue our conquest. He has been true to his role as war leader because in seeing defeat on the horizon, he has stopped us from rushing headlong into it.

"Remove him, repudiate the deal, and the Clans will be a memory long before the agreement has run its course."

Phelan returned to his seat and Natasha gave him a wink. Ulric graced him with the barest of nods, then turned to the assembled Khans. "You have heard the arguments. Weigh them, then make your decision. Shall the ilKhan be removed and his deal with ComStar rescinded? How say you, children of Kerensky?"

"Nay," he and Natasha cried as one. They smiled at each other because their voices were not in the minority.

As the monitors winked out and the other Khans left the room, Ulric approached him and Natasha. "You were able to point out that of which I could never convince them."

"Thank you, IlKhan." Phelan shrugged. "Of course, the vote was not unanimous, so the losers could have demanded a combat to contest the outcome. Why did they not?"

"Because, Phelan," the ilKhan said, "they knew I would have asked you and Natasha to defend the decision and that would have decided things more than quickly enough." As Phelan and the Black Widow laughed, Ulric pulled a holo-disk from inside his cloak. "This is for you."

Phelan hesitated, remembering that the last holodisk he had received was from Cyrilla. "Do I want it?"

Ulric nodded. "I think so. Anastasius Focht had it relayed here to us. You were effective just now because you are part Clan and part Inner Sphere. I never want you to lose that." He pressed the disk into Phelan's right hand. "It is from your father and, among other things, it includes his acceptance of my invitation to visit us here."

═══ **48** ═══

ComStar First Circuit Compound, Hilton Head
  Island
North America, Terra
16 June 3052

The Precentor Martial watched the members of the First
Circuit resume their places behind the crystal podia from
which they had often interrogated him. Both Ulthan Everson
and Huthrin Vandel rubbed at their wrists and looked thinner
than he'd last seen them. Gardner Riis seemed to be his sul-
len self; weeks spent in a holding cell had done nothing to
improve his disposition or mushroomlike complexion. Precentor Sian, Jen Li, and Precentor Atreus, Demona Aziz,
seemed to have weathered their confinement more comfort-
ably, but they did seem tentative as they took up their old
positions.

"Welcome back to the First Circuit." Standing where the
Primus normally did, Focht greeted them with open arms. "I
am pleased to see you all so healthy."

"What is the meaning of this outrage, Focht?" Everson
pointed back toward the doors leading into the chamber and
the two Com Guards with rifles standing there. "Why have
we been held captive and why are guards posted in this
chamber? Why is not the Primus here to answer for impris-
oning us? Blake's Blood, I never would have expected you,
of all people, to cover for her."

Focht held up his hands. "Calm yourself, Precentor
Tharkad. You have been inconvenienced but not hurt. Your

robe no longer strains against your belly, so I might even suggest you have benefited from your detention."

"Detention. Ha!" Huthrin Vandel braced himself against his podium. "You make it sound as if solitary confinement were a mere annoyance. The Primus will pay for this affront. Given barely enough to eat until I felt I was dead."

"How appropriate, because that's just what 40 percent of my Com Guards are." He let that sink in for a moment, then frowned heavily. "Because of you, because of actions you took or did not take, many more people lie dead right now than need be. We are going to make some changes, *fundamental* changes, in ComStar to be sure this never happens again."

Gardner Riis' head came up. "What are you talking about? What things? I did nothing."

"Precisely, Precentor Rasalhague, you did *nothing*. You did nothing to tell the Primus her ideas for dealing with the Inner Sphere and the Clans were lunacy. She had ComStar aiding the Clans because she wanted the Clans to destroy the people Jerome Blake wanted us to protect. In the name of rebuilding humanity, she tried to tear it down even further than it has done by its own hand." Pointing, Focht moved his finger from one member of the First Circuit to another, but stopped before coming to Sharilar Mori. "Though you did not protest her actions here, did any of you work against her outside?"

Everson folded his arms across his chest. "We did what we could."

"Did you? Why did people in your area place Davion stragglers in ComStar-run prison camps when they could just as easily have taken them off-world? What was in your mind when you failed to send messages telling families their warriors were alive or, worse yet, when you sent fraudulent messages saying they were dead?" He shook his head. "At times I have wondered whether you, the people who wanted to protect humanity, have forgotten what it is to be human."

Precentor Sian draped her black hair over the scarlet shoulders of her Precentor's robe. "We did as the Primus directed."

"Really?" Focht skewered her with a steely stare. "And in your case, that meant allowing a message to go out that activated an assassin to kill Justin Allard. You let Romano Liao kill a man whose skills were vital to defending the Inner Sphere from the Clans. For you, for the whole lot of you, I had boys giving their lives?"

"Why attack us? The Primus is the key to this. It is her fault." Riis looked at his fellow Precentors. "Let us strip her of her rank, get rid of her. She's been mad for years."

He glanced up at Focht. "Isn't that a step in the right direction?"

"It's a step." Focht pulled his needle pistol from the pocket on his fatigues. "A bit late, but a step nonetheless."

Everson blanched. "She's dead?"

"Yes. I did your dirty work for you." He displayed the pistol, then put it back in his pocket. "Now you will do a few things for me. It is time to change ComStar."

Vandel hunched his shoulders. "If we are going to talk about substantive matters, I demand you send your gunsels out of here. Our councils are private affairs."

Focht shook his head. "They will hear only what I want them to hear."

The blond-haired Precentor Atreus shook with rage. "This is unbelievable. This man tells us the Primus is dead—murdered—and now he will dictate to us changes in the Blessed Order while his gunmen hold us hostage! We cannot condone this."

"Save your righteous indignation for later. You've condoned worse crimes in the last three years than you will condone today." Focht nodded toward Sharilar Mori. "Over the past eight days, Precentor Dieron and I have worked out a plan that will let us repair the damage done and permit us to return to our mission of playing Prometheus to a mankind who has lost technology.

"Computer, project Com Guard Abstract 1."

In response to his command, the computer materialized a table of organization and equipment for the Com Guards in the middle of the room. It spun slowly, then fragmented into smaller identical charts in front of each podium. "As you can see, the Com Guards are going to be reorganized into a highly mobile, ready-response group. Eventually we will build back up to the strength we had at Tukayyid, but for now, each of our armies will have four divisions. In the short term, we will deploy forces on Free Rasalhague Republic worlds to discourage adventurism by the Combine or Federated Commonwealth."

Demona Aziz narrowed her green eyes. "If you do this,

and these forces are stationed in the places you have indicated, you will leave most of our stations unprotected."

"They won't need protection under the second half of our plan." Focht looked around the room, then smiled ironically. "When I helped clean up the horror the Primus had created in the Hall of History, I was able to sort through some of the items that had been in the Jerome Blake displays. That is how I discovered a copy of the first book Jerome Blake ever wrote. The content will probably surprise you as much as it did me. This book by Blake dealt with a highly technical subject in a way that made it comprehensible to anyone."

Vandel's fist slammed into his podium. "You lie, Focht! I am a scholar of Jerome Blake and I say no such book exists."

The guards at the door cocked their autorifles.

"To my knowledge, that is," Precentor New Avalon quickly added.

"It is true, Huthrin. This is no lie like so many others propagated under the guise of the 'discovery' of new Blake diaries. Given his obvious gift for sharing the complex with those who could barely comprehend it, we have to look at Blake's plans and intentions in a different light. No longer should we see him as a man who believed ComStar should wait until mankind had clubbed itself back into the Stone Age before we could return technology to them. Instead he was merely insisting that, if that were to happen, ComStar *had* to step in to share information and technology with them."

"Heresy!" Demona stared at Focht with wild eyes. "You are a viper we have clutched to our bosom. We defied the Word of Blake when we formed the Com Guards and we doomed ourselves when we placed you at their head. This is heresy and I will not stand for it."

Focht smiled at her. "If you think that is heresy, let me tell you the whole of it. Adopting a role similar to the one we played with the Clans, we will begin to instruct people throughout the Successor States in the ways of technology. We will share with them the knowledge that will help make their lives better."

Precentor Atreus turned purple.

Riis pursed his lips as he considered what he heard. "In essence, you want us to secularize all of ComStar?"

"Hardly. We will secularize the Com Guards, but that

should not be difficult because most are recent recruits or MechWarriors who already have a certain disdain for the magical trappings of ComStar. Unlike the majority of the populace on non-metropolitan worlds, they've seen technology work up close and they know a kick is just as likely as a prayer to get something to work. We would only teach basic, low-level information that enhances the quality of life, but absolutely nothing that would have military applications. Our Techs will still be needed to keep HPGs running, but the nation-states will administer the facilities and finance the building of new stations."

Everson chewed on his lower lip for a moment. "It would still increase our effect on society without making us a threat. It could also create some good will between us and the heads of the Successor States."

Jen Li nodded in agreement. "It is not that radical a departure from what we were doing under the Clans, but instead of propagandizing, we will actually be doing something positive. The only difficulty is that we have told our people for so long that sharing even the most trivial of technological information with outsiders is cause to excommunicate them and declare them apostate. We need to deal with that."

Demona finally found her tongue again. "I cannot believe you are talking like this! We have been entrusted with a sacred duty and you are discussing it as if ComStar were nothing but a corporation positioning itself to take better advantage in a marketplace. I pray the ghost of Jerome Blake will come to haunt you in your dreams."

Focht caught Sharilar's eye and smiled. "In fact, Precentor Atreus, I have been visited in my dreams by Jerome Blake. He said that we had gotten it all wrong. 'Technology is not to be regarded as mystical. What is mystical is that which technology enables man to accomplish. We must not be misers nor spendthrifts, but teachers.' "

"Blasphemy, but what could I expect from the man who has murdered the Primus?" Demona looked around the room at all the others. "You are in a league with him and you have Myndo Waterly's blood on your hands. I will not be a party to this."

She turned and stalked, head held high, toward the doors. The Com Guards moved to bar her, then stood aside as Focht gestured to them to let her go. The door closed behind her and Focht realized the others were straining to hear the sound of gunshots from outside.

"She will not be harmed. A squad of Com Guards will escort her to a waiting DropShip. It will take her to a Jump-Ship that should have her back in the Free Worlds League in a week or so."

Sharilar Mori nodded. "We assumed there would be some hardliners who would not brook this opening up of ComStar. We fully expect Demona to declare Thomas Marik 'Primus in exile.' Given that she will have to rely on us for spare parts for hyperpulse generators, at least in the short term, she will not break relations with us. However, she will probably provide a haven in the Free Worlds League for anyone else unable to reconcile the new ComStar with the old. Their orthodoxy will, in time, mellow if the Free Worlds League is to compete with the advances we give to the other states."

Focht adjusted his eye patch. "Does anyone else dispute the veracity of my dream?"

Everson shook his head. "It might require some expansion to fit the format of similar revelations in the past, but it will do."

"Excellent." Focht signaled the guards and they opened the doors. "It is now up to you to present our new ComStar to the leaders of your nation-states. That done, we can start to repair the damage done to mankind by our neglect."

=== 49 ===

New Avalon
Crucis March, Federated Commonwealth
17 June 3052

Victor Davion's stomach lurched up into his throat as the Ferret light scout helicopter pitched forward and out of the DropShip's starboard 'Mech bay. It fell 200 meters toward the dark, sleeping Avalon City before the pilot kicked power to the auto-rotating propeller. In doing so, he brought the nose up and jammed Victor down into his seat in the crew compartment.

Victor looked over at Galen. "See, I told you it would work."

Galen Cox, who looked paler than Victor had ever seen him in their years together, nodded weakly. "Couldn't land at the Royal Brigade Base like everyone else, could you? Just have to get chauffeured to the palace right off."

Victor shrugged. "Look, we're not even supposed to be arriving for another month. We got lucky that some of those ships were waiting around when we arrived in-system."

"I fail to see how sending a message ahead ordering them to wait can be considered luck." Galen smiled and a little color came back to his face. "Actually, I'm anxious to see Avalon City—during the day, that is. An air tour at three in the morning is fine, but it lacks the color promised in all the travel brochures."

Victor nodded sharply. "And you shall have that tour, my friend. Tomorrow night we go out and celebrate. We celebrate our being alive, and if the message from the Jade Falcons is correct, we celebrate Kai's return from the dead!"

"Only Kai." The blond Hauptmann shook his head. "He probably *was* killed on Alyina—several times over in fact, but he came back because you had a deal to meet in twenty years and he didn't want to disappoint you."

Victor remembered Kai's smiling face and the suicidal charge *Yen-lo-wang* made to save his life on Alyina. *Somehow I would not put it past him to return from the dead.* He sobered up for a moment. "I wonder if Kai knows his parents are dead?"

Galen shrugged. "I don't think he could get all the way to New Avalon without someone expressing their regrets to him along the way."

"Tomorrow I'll record a holovid and send it out Alpha Priority. My father had wanted me to break the news to him. If I can't do that, I can express my sympathy."

"I think Kai would like that."

Victor saw the palace swing into view through the porthole on the starboard side. "We're over the Peace Park right now. See, that's the palace. The front remains lit up at night for insomniac tourists, which is why private quarters are around back in the dark. Only offices occupy the front quarter."

Galen pointed to one set of three windows lit from inside. "Fancy that, the government has night owls."

Victor squinted and used his left hand to form a viewfinder. "Not surprising. That's my father's office. He probably fell asleep at his desk again."

The two men laughed as the helicopter swooped over the palace, then settled down in the middle of a ring of lights out by the back lawn. Victor thanked the pilot, and the two of them disembarked. Running hunched over, they cleared the circle and clutched their caps against the air blast as the helicopter climbed into the air again.

As they straightened up, a man in the uniform of the Intelligence Ministry's Bodyguard service saluted. "Welcome home, Prince Victor. Per your radio instructions, no one has been notified of your arrival. The household is asleep."

Victor nodded. "My father is still in his office?"

"Yes, sir, at least he was five minutes ago. Minister Mallory brought him a priority holodisk about an hour ago, but your father viewed it in private."

"As you said, the household is asleep."

The bodyguard smiled. "I believe so, sir." He looked over at Galen. "We have Hauptmann Cox billeted in the suite down the hall from your rooms. Just use your service number as your lock code, Hauptmann."

"Thank you, Leftenant."

Victor started walking toward the Palace's rear entrance, and the security man fell into step on his left while Galen secured his right. "I think we will slip in and surprise my father, then retire for the night."

"Perhaps you will be more successful at persuading him to get some proper rest, Highness. He spends so much time in his office that the men guarding him must have sunk roots into the hall by now."

Victor smiled as he heard the concern in the man's words. "I appreciate your frankness, Leftenant. I will see what I can do."

The Leftenant returned to his own office on the ground floor while Victor and Galen climbed a broad marble staircase to the third floor. Turning right at a massive bronze statue of Ares, they entered a long corridor lined with white marble pillars. The walls were decorated with an elaborate mural depicting the history of House Davion. Victor slowed so Galen could study the painting.

"This is it, Galen, the history of humanity according to the Davions."

His companion grinned. "A tad solipsistic, but I don't have to mind it now because we're all one big happy family, right?"

"Well, it does help that the Federated Suns and the Lyran Commonwealth never really got a chance to go at each other." Victor sniffed the air in an exaggerated way. "Hmmm, no new paint. I guess they haven't immortalized the Revenants yet."

"Damn, ignored by history again!" Galen grumbled lightly.

The two guards at the door to Hanse Davion's office snapped to attention and saluted when Victor approached. Both MechWarriors returned the salutes, then one of the guards quietly opened the heavy bronze door. Victor and Galen slipped into the room noiselessly and shared a smile.

Hanse Davion sat in a big, wingback chair behind his desk. The chair had been turned so they could glimpse only a bit of his profile. The Prince faced the holodisk viewer built into the oaken cabinets on the far side of the room, but his chin had dropped to his chest, and he looked to be sleeping.

As Victor approached his father's desk, the holovid viewer speakers suddenly began to play muted strains of the Capellan anthem. Victor turned to look at the screen, which showed the Capellan crest dissolving into the image of Sun-Tzu Liao. He stopped short and Galen stopped behind him.

Sun-Tzu smiled slowly. "Prince Davion, in attending to the affairs of state subsequent to the deaths of my parents, I came across the holodisk your agent, Justin Allard, had left for my grandfather. I believe you are aware that this holodisk was the straw that broke my grandfather's last feeble grasp on reality. I also believe it unbalanced—or further unbalanced—my mother's mental state. In light of the effect it had on them, I thought I would return the courtesy and record this for you.

"Of course, I know you are too strong for the recording to affect you the way it did them." The new Chancellor of the Capellan Confederation seated himself on the edge of a stone desk. "Still, if this provides for an hour or two of sleeplessness on your part, I will consider the expense more than worth it."

Victor glanced over at his sleeping father and grinned. "Wrong again, Sun-Tzu."

"As you know, Prince Davion, my realm is small and not that powerful. The St. Ives Compact is poised at our belly like a knife. My uncle, Tormana, is active in the occupation zone you call your Sarna March. He agitates against us, infiltrates agents into the Confederation, and constantly bellows about invading and liberating the rest of the Confederation. Of course, acting as your agent in a war of conquest is hardly what I would call an act of liberation.

"I realize the utter folly of attacking him or the St. Ives Compact, for you would immediately crush my tiny nation-state. However, even pledging never to attack you cannot relieve me of the threat you pose to my realm. For this reason, I have taken steps to ensure our survival."

The camera slowly zoomed in toward Sun-Tzu. "Again, in a tradition you started with my grandfather, I wanted to convey to you personally my marriage plans. I have asked for and been granted the hand of Isis Marik in marriage. The ceremony will take place on Atreus later this year. I would give you exact details or even an invitation, but having heard of your conduct at the last wedding between two realms, I thought it wiser to leave you at home."

Victor stared at the screen, unbelieving. *Sun-Tzu marrying a Marik? That backs up the Confederation with the might of the Free Worlds League, who are now producing new 'Mechs and equipment designed to fight the Clans. How much of that will be diverted to shore up the Confederation's defense?*

"I bid you a fond adieu, Prince Davion. Do devote all your resources to fighting the Clans. You do *not* want to go to war with me."

The image faded, then the Capellan crest came up and the anthem started again. Disgust on his face, Victor pointed at the machine. "It's on an endless loop. Shut it off." He turned toward his father. "It's a wonder he could sleep through that."

"Bored him after the first time, I think."

Victor again headed toward the desk, then saw his father's head lying at an odd angle to the side. Instantly, he knew something was dreadfully wrong. He sprinted forward, and posting off the corner of the desk, vaulted to his father's feet. "Oh my God, Galen, something's happened!"

Hanse Davion did not move even though Victor's shout came right beside him. His face looked gray and his eyelids were shut. Victor grabbed him under the armpits and knew from the blue of his father's lips that he was dying.

"Father, father!" Victor hauled him up and kicked the chair out from behind him. "Galen, he's having a heart attack! He's barely breathing."

As Victor laid his father down on the floor, he saw gravity flood color back into his face. Hanse's eyes snapped open and he looked right through his son. The elder Prince's eyes focused down and the hint of a smile parted his lips. He reached up to grab Victor's shoulder. "Victor?"

"I'm here, Father. Help is on the way. Take it easy."

"Victor." Hanse Davion smiled proudly at his son, then closed his eyes forever.

Epilogue

Unity Palace
Luthien
20 June 3052

Dear Victor,
   It is with great sadness that word of your father's passing reached Luthien. He was a remarkable man. Upon learning of his death, my grandfather commented that now, even with the Clans, there are no longer any opponents worthy of the Combine.
   I have been informed that your father will lie in state for the month, then be interred in a family crypt in a private ceremony. I am directed to inquire if we may be permitted to send a delegation to represent the Combine at the ceremony. It is not from lack of respect that my father or grandfather are not able to attend, but they cannot leave Luthien, given the nature of the war with the Clans. With humble apologies, we ask permission for attendance by lesser members of the family, if our participation is appropriate and desired.

Indebted to you yet,

Omi

Glossary

AUTOCANNON

This is a rapid-firing, auto-loading weapon. Light autocannon range from 30 to 90mm caliber, and heavy autocannon may be 80 to 120mm or more. The weapon fires high-speed streams of high-explosive, armor-piercing shells.

BATTLEMECHS

BattleMechs are the most powerful war machines ever built. First developed by Terran scientists and engineers, these huge, man-shaped vehicles are faster, more mobile, better-armored, and more heavily armed than any 20th-century tank. Ten to twelve meters tall and equipped with particle projection cannons, lasers, rapid-fire autocannon, and missiles, they pack enough firepower to flatten anything but another BattleMech. A small fusion reactor provides virtually unlimited power, and BattleMechs can be adapted to fight in environments ranging from sun-baked deserts to subzero arctic icefields.

BLOODHERITAGE

The history of the Bloodnamed warriors of a particular Bloodright is called the Bloodheritage.

BLOODING

This is another name for the Trial of Position that determines if a candidate will qualify as a Clan warrior. To qualify, he must defeat at least one of three successive opponents. If he defeats two, or all three, he is immediately ranked as an officer in his Clan. If he fails to defeat any of his opponents, he is relegated to a lower caste.

BLOODNAME

Bloodname refers to the surname of each of the eight hundred warriors who stood with Nicholas Kerensky during the Exodus Civil War. These eight hundred are the foundation of the Clans' elaborate breeding program. The right to use one of these surnames has been the ambition of every Clan warrior since the system was established. Only twenty-five warriors, which corresponds to twenty-five Bloodrights, are allowed to use any one surname at one time. When one of the twenty-five Bloodnamed warriors dies, a trial is held to determine who will assume that Bloodname. A contender must prove his Bloodname lineage, then win a series of duels with other competitors. Only Bloodnamed warriors are allowed to sit on the Clan Councils or are eligible to become a Khan or ilKhan. Most Bloodnames have gradually been confined to one or two warrior classes. However, certain prestigious names, such as Kerensky, have shown their genetic value by producing excellent warriors in all three classes (MechWarriors, Fighter pilots, and Elementals).

Bloodnames are determined matrilineally, at least after the original generation. Because a warrior can only inherit from his or her female parent, he or she can only have a claim to one Bloodname.

BLOODRIGHT

A specific Bloodname lineage is called a Bloodright. Twenty-five Bloodrights are attached to each Bloodname. A Bloodright is not a lineage as we define the term, because the warriors who successively hold a Bloodright might be related only through their original ancestor. As with Bloodnames, certain Bloodrights are considered more prestigious than others, depending largely on the Bloodright's Bloodheritage.

BONDSMAN

A captured warrior, called a bondsman, is considered a member of the Laborer Caste unless and until the capturing Clan releases him or promotes him back to Warrior status. A bondsman is bound by honor, not by shackles. Custom dictates that even Bloodnamed Warriors captured in combat be held for a time as bondsmen. All bondsmen wear a bondcord, which is a woven bracelet. The base color of the bondcord indicates to which Clan he belongs and the striping indicates which unit captured him.

CLAN OMNIMECH NAMES

During the course of the Clan invasion, the Inner Sphere assigned code names to the various types of Clan Omni-Mechs they encountered. The list below provides the Clan names for their own equipment.

Inner Sphere Name	Clan Name
Black Hawk	Nova
Daishi	Dire Wolf
Dasher	Fire Moth
Dragonfly	Viper
Fenris	Ice Ferret
Gladiator	Executioner
Koshi	Mist Lynx
Loki	Hellbringer
Mad Cat	Timber Wolf
Man O'War	Gargoyle
Masakari	Warhawk
Puma	Adder
Ryoken	Stormcrow
Thor	Summoner
Uller	Kit Fox
Vulture	Mad Dog

CLANS

During the fall of the Star League, General Nicholas Kerensky, commander of the Regular Star League Army, led his forces out of the Inner Sphere in what is known as the Exodus. After settling beyond the Periphery, the Star League Army itself collapsed. Out of the ashes of the civilization Kerensky's forces tried to create rose the Clans.

DROPSHIPS

Because JumpShips must generally avoid entering the heart of a solar system, they lie at a considerable distance from the system's inhabited worlds. DropShips were developed for interplanetary travel. As the name implies, a DropShip is attached to hardpoints on the JumpShip's drive core, later to be dropped from the parent vessel after in-system entry. Though incapable of FTL travel, DropShips are highly maneuverable, well-armed, and sufficiently aero-dynamic to take off from and land on a planetary surface. The journey from the jump point to the inhabited worlds of a system usually requires a normal-space journey of several days or weeks, depending on the type of star.

ELEMENTALS
The elite battlesuited infantry of the Clans. These men and women are giants, bred specifically to handle Clan-developed battle armor.

FREEBIRTH
This epithet, used by trueborn members of the Warrior Caste, is a mortal insult to another trueborn warrior. It generally expresses disgust or frustration.

FREEBORN
An individual conceived and born by natural means is freeborn. Because the Clans value their eugenics program so highly, a freebirth is automatically assumed to have little potential.

JUMPSHIPS
Interstellar travel is accomplished via JumpShips, first developed in the 22nd century. These somewhat ungainly vessels are made up of a long, thin drive core and a sail resembling an enormous parasol, which can be up to a kilometer wide. The ship is named for its ability to "jump" instantaneously from one point to another. After making its jump, the ship cannot travel until it has recharged by gathering up more solar energy.

The JumpShip's enormous sail is constructed from a special metal that absorbs vast quantities of electromagnetic energy from the nearest star. When it has soaked up enough energy, the sail transfers it to the drive core, which converts it into a space-twisting field. An instant later, the ship arrives at the next jump point, a distance of up to 30 light years. This field is known as hyperspace, and its discovery opened to mankind the gateway to the stars.

JumpShips never land on planets, and only rarely travel into the inner areas of a star system. Interplanetary travel is carried out by DropShips, vessels that attach themselves to the JumpShip until arrival at the jump point.

LASER

An acronym for "Light Amplification through Stimulated Emission of Radiation." When used as a weapon, it damages the target by concentrating extreme heat on a small area. BattleMech lasers are designated as small, medium, and large. Lasers are also available as shoulder-fired weapons operating from a portable backpack power unit. Certain range-finders and targeting equipment employ low-level lasers also.

LRM

This is an abbreviation for Long-Range Missile, an indirect-fire missile with a high-explosive warhead.

PERIPHERY

Beyond the borders of the Inner Sphere lies the Periphery, the vast domain of known and unknown worlds stretching endlessly into interstellar night. Once populated by colonies from Terra, these were devastated technologically, politically, and economically by the fall of the Star League. At present, the Periphery is the refuge of piratical Bandit Kings, privateers, and outcasts from the Inner Sphere.

PPC

This abbreviation stands for Particle Projection Cannon, a magnetic accelerator firing high-energy proton or ion bolts, causing damage both through impact and high temperature. PPCs are among the most effective weapons available to BattleMechs.

QUIAFF/QUINEG

This Clan expression is placed at the end of rhetorical questions. If an affirmative answer is expected, *quiaff* is used. If the answer is expected to be negative, *quineg* is the proper closure.

REMEMBRANCE, THE

The Remembrance is an ongoing heroic saga detailing Clan history beginning with the Exodus from the Inner Sphere to current time. *The Remembrance* is continually expanded to include contemporary events. Each Clan has a slightly different version reflecting their own opinions and experiences. All Clan warriors can quote whole verses of this marvelous epic from memory, and it is common to see passages from the book lovingly painted on the sides of OmniMechs, fighters, and even battle armor.

SEYLA

This word roughly means "unity." It is a ritual response voiced in unison by those witnessing certain ceremonies. The origin and exact meaning of the word is unknown, but it is uttered only with the greatest reverence and awe.

SIBKO

A group of children of the warrior caste eugenics program who probably have the same male and female parents and are raised together is known as a sibko. As they mature, they are constantly tested. Additional members of the sibko fail at each testing, and are transferred to the lower castes. A sibko is made up of approximately twenty members, but usually only four or five remain when they are given their final test, the Trial of Position. These tests and other adversities bind the surviving "sibkin" together as closely that they form bonds of mutual trust and understanding that often last for life.

SRM

This is the abbreviation for Short-Range Missiles, direct trajectory missiles with high-explosive or armor-piercing explosive warheads. They have a range of less than one kilometer, and are accurate only at ranges of less than 300 meters. They are more powerful, however, than LRMs.

STAR LEAGUE

The Star League was formed in 2571 in an attempt to peacefully ally the major star systems inhabited by the human race after it had taken to the stars. The League prospered for almost 200 years, until civil war broke out in 2751. The League was eventually destroyed when the ruling body, known as the High Council, disbanded in the midst of a struggle for power. Each of the royal House rulers then declared himself First Lord of the Star League, and within months, war engulfed the Inner Sphere. This conflict continues to the present day, almost three centuries later. These centuries of continuous war are now known simply as the Succession Wars.

SUCCESSOR LORDS

Each of the five Successor States is ruled by a family descended from one of the original Council Lords of the old Star League. All five royal House Lords claim the title of First Lord, and they have been at each others' throats since the beginning of the Succession Wars in 2786. Their battleground is the vast Inner Sphere, which is composed of all the star systems once occupied by Star League's member-states.

TRUEBORN/TRUEBIRTH

A Trueborn or Truebirth is born as a result of the Warrior Caste's eugenics program.

Author's Bio

MICHAEL A. STACKPOLE, who has written over 14 novels and numerous short stories and articles, is one of Roc Books' best-selling authors. Among his BattleTech® books are THE BLOOD OF KERENSKY TRILOGY and THE WARRIOR TRILOGY. Due to popular demand BLOOD OF KERENSKY is now being re-published. This trilogy has also been adapted for television, and is currently one of the highest-rated animated series on Saturday morning, featuring state-of-the-art computer animation. Three other Stackpole novels, also set in the BattleTech® universe, continue his chronicles of the turmoil in the Inner Sphere. A fourth, MALICIOUS INTENT, due out in March of 1996, promises to turn the universe upside-down once again.

Stackpole is also the author of DEMENTIA, the third volume in Roc's Mutant Chronicles series. In 1994 Bantam Books published ONCE A HERO, an epic fantasy. He is also currently writing the first four Star Wars® X-wing® novels. The first, ROGUE SQUADRON, will appear in February of 1996.

In addition to writing, Mike is an innovative game designer. A number of his designs have won awards and in 1994 he was inducted into the Academy of Gaming Arts and Design's Hall of Fame.

COMING IN MARCH 1996

MALICIOUS INTENT

Another epoch-making novel by Michael A. Stackpole

Katrina Steiner wises up

Blood threatens to flow like water as internal strife and external enemies continue to put pressure on the Inner Sphere. Katrina Steiner decides it's time to dispossess her brother Victor of his half of the Federated Commonwealth. But when Clan Jade Falcon launches a new offensive heading straight for Tharkad, and even the regiments of Wolf's Dragoons are unable to stop them, Katrina is forced to turn to Victor for help. But his intervention won't interrupt her plan: to see that he does not survive what he thinks will be his greatest victory.

1

*N*ow *the Wolves belong to me.*

As he regained consciousness, this was the first thought that came to him. It worked its way past the fiery ache in his left forearm and the scattering of stinging annoyances on his arms and legs. He clung to that thought and made it the core of his life and universe. *All the others are dead, now the Wolves belong to me.*

Vlad of the Wards slowly turned his head, alert for any pain in his neck that might indicate a spinal injury. He thought this unlikely since his arms and legs were faithfully relaying their discomfort to his brain, but with his responsibilities, he could take no chances. As he moved his head to the left, the dust and gravel on the faceplate of his NeuroHelmet rattled off, pouring more grit down into the collar of his cooling vest.

Through the dust he thought he could see his left forearm, but it seemed distorted and odd. He brushed the viewplate clean with his right hand and was able to correlate the bump on the top of his arm, and the bruise surrounding it, with the lightning-like shooters of pain emanating from that spot. Glancing up he saw the hole in the viewport of his *Timberwolf* through which some of the bricks and mortar that had once been Wotan's Ministry of Budgets and Taxation building had fallen.

One of those bricks had fallen against his arm and had broken the radius—the forearm bone that ran thumbside. The bump meant the break was dislocated. As such it was a crippling injury because, unset and unhealed, it rendered that arm all but useless. As he was a warrior buried beneath a building in an enemy zone, the injury could easily turn out to be fatal.

For most warriors it would have been a cause of panic.

Vlad smothered the first spark of panic rising in his breast. *I am a Wolf.* This thought was sufficient to forever hold panic at bay. Unlike the *freebirth* warriors of the Inner Sphere, or even those of the Jade Falcon and other Clans, Vlad would not allow himself to worry. Worry and anxiety, in his mind, were for those who abandoned all claim on the future—they chose to exist in a state of fear instead of pressing on to a point where fear was banished.

He had no fear because he knew his present situation was but one datapoint in the legend that was his life. It could not end so ignominiously, with him dying of exposure or starvation or suffocation in the cockpit of an entombed Battle-Mech. He did not allow that possibility to exist in his universe. *The Wolves belong to me.*

That fact alone was vindication and confirmation of his destiny. Six centuries earlier the BattleMech—ten meter tall, humanoid engines of destruction—had been created and had dominated battle just so he would be able to pilot one. Three hundred years ago Stephan Amaris had attempted to take over the Inner Sphere and Aleksandr Kerensky had taken the majority of the Star League's Armed Forces away specifically so Vlad would be born into the greatest of military traditions. The Clans had been created by Nicholas Kerensky to further his father's dream, and Vlad had been given life so he could guide the Clans into the ultimate realization of that dream.

Such thoughts allowed him to soar beyond the pain in his body. He knew that seeing himself as the end-product of six hundred years of human endeavor might seem ridiculous to another, but he saw no other way to interpret his life. He shied from the mysticism for which the Nova Cat Clan was famous and examined the events with cold logic. Occam's Razor sliced his conclusion from events cleanly—his explanation, as extraordinary as it might seem, clearly had to be true because it was the most simple explanation that wove everything together.

If his view were wrong, the Clans would have returned to the Inner Sphere a century before or after his lifetime. It it were not true, he ever would have suffered humiliation at the hands of Phelan Kell—a humiliation that allowed him to see the true evil Phelan represented while others like ilKhan Ulric Kerensky and Khan Natasha had not. The emotional and psychic trauma visited upon him by Phelan had made him immune to the man's charm and had made Vlad the last true Wolf in the Clan.

Ulric knew that, which is why he entrusted the Wolves to me.

A cold chill sank into Vlad. He had come to Wotan with ilKhan Ulric and had led him to a battlefield chosen by Jade Falcon Khan Vandervahn Chistu. Ulric and Chistu were to fight a battle between them and Ulric would have prevailed had Chistu not cheated. The last Vlad had seen of his Clan's leader was the fire-wreathed silhouette of a _Gargoyle_ pressing one step closer to the enemy despite being engulfed in a withering firestorm.

Lying on his back, Vlad glanced up at the dead instruments in his cockpit and smiled. He had watched and recorded the Falcon Khan's treacherous murder of Ulric. Chistu had to know that incriminating evidence existed in the cockpit recorder. Vlad would have recognized the threat immediately and would have poured fire into the midden in which he had gone down until there was no trace of him or his _Timberwolf_ or the building left behind, save perhaps a huge crater. That Chistu not done that marked him as even more of a fool than Vlad had thought before.

This means they will be coming for me. Chistu would not order the destruction of the building now—_though he should._ Vlad decided Chistu would send people to look for the 'Mech and recover the recorder—under the pretense that the medical data recorded there would provide information on how Vlad of the Wolves had died. It would also allow Chistu to view for himself Ulric's destruction from another angle, and to see how handily his marksmanship had blown Vlad back into the building heaped above him.

They will be coming and I will need to be ready.

With his right hand he unbuckled his belt and pulled it free from around his waist. Inserting the end back through the buckle, he slipped the loop around his left wrist. He slid the buckle down until it snugged against his flesh. Pain shot up and down his arm, leaving him weak for a moment and nauseous.

He waited for his stomach to subside, then he pushed on with his plan. He pulled his right knee up to his chest and hooked the heel of his MechBoot on the edge of his command couch's seat. He fumbled with the buckle at the top of his calf and undid it. He slipped the end of his belt through backwards, stabbing the tongue through one of the holes at the very end. He thrust the tip of the boot's belt back over his other belt and fastened it in place. He tugged on the waist-belt to make sure it would remain in place and was satisfied it would not pull free.

He lowered his leg again and his foot hit the pedal at the bottom of the command couch without using up all the slack in the belt. He took a deep breath, then gently pulled his left leg up and hooked the heel of that boot over the belt. He eased his left forearm into his lap and let the intact bone rest on his thigh. With his right hand he took up all the slack in the restraining straps that crossed his chest and lap to keep him in the command couch.

Sweat began to burn into his eyes. He pulled the medpatch wires from the throat of his NeuroHelmet, then unbuckled it and tossed it off back over his head. He heard it clatter onto debris, but he didn't care. He shook his head violently, spraying around into a vapor that drifted back down like cold fog over his face.

He knew what he had to do, and he knew it would hurt incredibly—worse than any physical problem he had endured before. He imagined that the blow that had laid the left side of his face open, accounting for the scar that ran from eyebrow to jaw, must have been equally painful, but medics from the Clan's Scientist Caste had dosed him with enough painkillers that he wouldn't have felt a 'Mech tapdancing on him. Those same drugs all existed in the medkit located in one of the command couch's storage areas, but if he were to use them, he'd be unable to set his arm.

Pain is the only true sign you are alive.

The light brush of his fingertips over the break felt as heavy as stone and started agony rippling out in waves that seemed to liquify his body. His breath caught in his throat and a sinking sensation threatened to suck his guts down into his loins. Icy slush filled his intestines and his scrotum shrank as his body shied from the pain.

Vlad smashed his right fist against the command couch's right arm. "I am *not* a Jade Falcon. This pain means *nothing!*" His nostrils flared as he sucked in a lungful of chill air. "I am a Wolf. I will prevail."

He slowly straightened his left leg. His vision blurred as the belt tightened on his wrist. He tried to lean forward to give the belt slack, but the restraining straps held him in place. His left arm extended and the elbow locked. Shimmering balls of pink and green exploded before his eyes, and blackness crept in at the edge of his vision.

He continued pushing and dropped his right hand over the break. The fiery agonies consuming his left arm magnified what his right hand felt in incredibly fine detail. Millimeter by millimeter bone slid against bone as the belt tightened and the break began to slide into place. Each little bit of motion would send seismic tremors through Vlad's body, wrapping him in pain that seemed to have existed his entire life and promised to engulf his future. Yet despite that, he knew from the sensations in his right hand that ends of the bones were still kilometers apart and would never slide into place despite eons of torture.

The squeak of teeth grinding together echoed through his brain and almost drowned out the first faint click of bones beginning to slide into place. He almost let the tension on the belt go, convincing himself that everything was repaired and that what his right hand felt could not be right. A firestorm of pain flared up and through him. He felt his resolve begin to melt in its inferno and that translated into weakness tremors playing through his muscles.

Then he remembered the image of Ulric's 'Mech taking just one more step.

I will not *surrender.*

Screaming incoherently, Vlad straightened his left leg. Bone grated on bone, the lower half pulling even with the break, then slipping past it. The gulf between ends of the break seemed to stretch on forever, but he knew that was an illusion. He clenched his right hand over the break, clamping it down. Bones snapped into place.

The argent lightningstorm that played out from the break bowed his spine and jammed him hard against the couch's restraining straps. He hung there forever, his lungs afire with oxygen deprivation. He wanted to scream and his throat hurt as if he was, but he could only hear the wheezing hiss of the last of his breath being squeezed from his chest.

His muscles slackened and the restraining straps slammed him back down into the couch. He felt more pain, but his nervous system had not recovered from being overwhelmed and could only report faint echoes of it to his brain. He took a shallow breath, then another and another. Each one came deeper and as his body learned that breathing wo uld not hurt him, it allowed itself to return to normal functioning.

The break throbbed, but the bones had been slid back into place. Vlad knew he would find a splint in the command couch's medkit, but he didn't have the strength to free himself from the restraining belts and go digging around for it. He let his head loll to one side and then the other to drain sweat from his eyes. It was not much, but along with breathing it was enough.

Little by little strength built up in him and Vlad wasted a bit of it in a smile. He had passed the first test in his ordeal, but he knew there would be many more. There would be enemies to be destroyed and allies to be used. The war—technically a Trial of Refusal—between the Jade Falcons and Wolves would have left both sides devastated. Vlad knew, based on the fact that he had not been rescued immediately, that the Jade Falcons had won. This meant he would have to appeal to the Falcons who shared his disgust with the Inner Sphere if he were to hav e any help from them. *Better I seek aid from the Ghost Bears, as they have long been allies to the Wolves.*

Vlad nodded slowly. *There are many considerations with which I will have to deal. I can use the time here, in my cockpit, to consider them all. Those who come for me will think themselves scavengers, and then will find themselves rescuers. Little do they know they will be midwives for the future of the Clans.*

THE CLAN SIDE OF THE STORY

Legend of the Jade Phoenix
A Trilogy by Robert Thurston

In 2786 the elite Star League Army fled the Inner
Sphere, abandoning the senseless bloodshed ordered
by the Lords of the Successor States. Three hundred
years later, their descendants are ready to return.
They will stop at nothing until the Star League Banner is raised over Terra once again.

DEEP SPACE INTRIGUE AND ACTION FROM
BATTLETECH®

☐ **LETHAL HERITAGE by Michael A. Stackpole.** Who are the Clans? One Inner Sphere warrior, Phelan Kell of the mercenary group Kell Hounds, finds out the hard way—as their prisoner and protegé.

(0-451-453832—$6.99)

☐ **BLOOD LEGACY by Michael A. Stackpole.** Jaime Wolf brought all the key leaders of the Inner Sphere together at his base on Outreach in an attempt to put to rest old blood feuds and power struggles. For only if all the Successor States unite their forces do they have any hope of defeating this invasion by warriors equipped with BattleMechs far superior to their own.

(0-451-453840—$6.99)

☐ **LOST DESTINY by Michael A. Stackpole.** As the Clans' BattleMech warriors continue their inward drive, with Terra itself as their true goal, can Comstar mobilize the Inner Sphere's last defenses—or will their own internal political warfare provide the final death blow to the empire they are sworn to protect?

(0-451-453859—$6.99)

Prices slightly higher in Canada

BATTLETECH®
Loren L. Coleman

□ **DOUBLE-BLIND** The Magistracy of Canopus has been the target of aggression by the Marian Hegemony, and in hiring Marcus and his gutsy band of can-do commandos, it hopes to retaliate. But the fact that the Canopians are armed with technology that is considered rare in the Periphery is the least of Marcus's problems. Marcus and his "Angels" will have to face the real force behind the hostilities—the religious cult known as Word of Blake. This fanatical group has a scheme deadly enough to trap even the amazing Avanti's Angels....

(0-451-45597-5—$5.99)

□ **BINDING FORCE** Aris Sung is a rising young star in House Hiritsu, noblest of the Warrior Houses that have sworn allegiance to the Capellan Confederation. The Sarna Supremacy, a newly formed power in the Chaos March, is giving the Confederation some trouble— and Aris and his Hiritsu comrades are chosen to give the Sarnans a harsh lesson in Capellan resolve. But there is far more to the mission than meets the eye—and unless Aris beats the odds in a race against time and treachery, all the ferro-fibrous armor in the galaxy won't be enough to save House Hiritsu from the high-explosive cross fire of intrigue and shifting loyalties....

(0-451-45604-1/$5.99)